# THE

## BOOKS BY SALLY GREEN

*The Smoke Thieves*
*The Demon World*
*The Burning Kingdoms*

*Half Bad*
*Half Wild*
*Half Lost*

Short stories (ebook only)
*Half Lies*
*Half Truths*

# THE BURNING KINGDOMS

## SALLY GREEN

VIKING

VIKING

An imprint of Penguin Random House LLC, New York

First published in the United States of America by Viking,
an imprint of Penguin Random House LLC, 2020
Published simultaneously in the UK by Penguin Books Ltd

Visit us online at penguinrandomhouse.com.

LIBRARY OF CONGRESS CATALOGING-IN-PUBLICATION DATA IS AVAILABLE.
ISBN 9780425290279

Printed in the United States of America

1 3 5 7 9 10 8 6 4 2

Text set in Fournier MT

*For Anna, Hannah, Indy, Jack, Joy,*
*Lily, Lucy, William, and Zoe*

War is not a poor man's game.

War: The Art of Winning, *M. Tatcher*

The art of war? Nonsense. War is not art but a series of blunders.

*Queen Valeria of Illast*

# HAROLD
## HAWKS FIELD, NORTHERN PITORIA

A girl sits, still and silent,
Waiting for the prince's bidding,
She's pretty, poised, and pliant.

*Traditional Brigantine song*

IT WAS a gloriously warm and sunny afternoon, and young Prince Harold wandered along the edge of the woodland humming to himself, trying to devise more verses to an old song.

"The princess waits, cunning and silent,
Ready to do her killing,
She's pretty, murderous, and defiant.

Prince Boris rides up, strong and fast,
He's speared through the heart,
Dead at last.

Harold steps forward his future to meet,
Royal and brave,
The world at his feet."

Harold stopped and put his right fist to his heart, just as he would do at court when they acknowledged his new position as heir to the throne of Brigant.

*The world at his feet . . .*

The old song was about a pure girl yearning for a boy to give her life purpose. Boris had often sang it when he was drunk.

"Well, brother, our sister has certainly given *my* life more purpose."

The bright red of a tiny wild strawberry growing low to the ground caught Harold's eye and he plucked the delicate fruit. It was deliciously sweet, and he scanned for more, picking the ripest and trampling the rest. He moved into the full sunshine, out of the woods, and sucked the juice from his stained fingers. Before him, gray smoke still clung to the battlefield, not quite concealing the detritus of war—bodies, wounded horses, and weapons; spears stood at odd angles, piercing the burned earth. Harold let his head fall back as he closed his eyes, feeling the sun on his face and feeling truly blessed.

"What! A! Day!"

The words he shouted seemed to hang and vibrate in the still air.

"What a glorious day," he called out again. He was in awe of it all—of his position and of how it had come about and of just how good he felt.

But no one replied. It was silent apart from some distant squeals—perhaps a wounded man or horse, though it didn't sound like a noise either should make.

In the middle of the battlefield were two burned-out

carts—one that had carried Harold's sister, Princess Catherine, and the other, Prince Tzsayn. The mules that had pulled the carts were there too, lying in contorted positions, still harnessed to the wreckage; one with its head back and its mane flickering with small flames, another with a leg pointing skyward. Harold had inspected the carts with his father and Boris when they'd been made. They'd looked impressive enough then, but now, like everything else, they looked small and insignificant.

Across the field, some Pitorian soldiers appeared through the smoke, walking slowly, heads down, probably looking for wounded. One of them glanced over to Harold.

Harold gazed back. Would this man challenge him?

No. Already the Pitorian's attention had returned to the ground as he and the other soldiers continued their slow progress. Perhaps they thought Harold was one of them, or perhaps they'd had enough fighting. But there was still that niggle in Harold's mind that perhaps they saw him only as a fourteen-year-old boy—not a soldier, not a threat.

They'd learn. They'd all soon learn.

Harold was surprised how good the Pitorians were in a fight; they'd won this battle easily and with few losses. Harold had listened while his father and brother had planned the Brigantine attack. He'd tried to ask a question, and Boris had told him, as usual, to "stop interrupting," so Harold had sat quietly and worked out how he'd counter his father's simple tactics of full-on force.

Lord Farrow, the Pitorian general, had obviously considered his options too. And Harold's father had completely misjudged his enemy, assuming that because Farrow was inexperienced in war, he would be easy to defeat. Harold had seen a little of Farrow in the negotiations over the ransom of Prince Tzsayn. The Pitorian lord was vain and greedy, but it had been obvious to Harold that he was neither stupid nor lazy. Farrow had prepared the battlefield by crisscrossing it with pitch-filled ditches. Setting fire to them—and their enemy—had been a simple way for the Pitorians to see off their opponents. Admittedly it wasn't really a true victory, as the Brigantines had managed a retreat, but the point was that the Pitorians had controlled the situation. Yet again, King Aloysius had underestimated his opponent, just as he'd underestimated his brother, Prince Thelonius, in the last war, and he risked making a fool of himself again. And Boris was no better.

*Had been* no better.

A smile played at the corner of Harold's lips.

"Father underestimated the Pitorians and you, dearest brother, underestimated our rather marvelous sister."

Harold had watched Boris and Lang talk to Catherine when she was chained to the cart during the botched exchange of prisoners. Even in chains Catherine had looked stunning in white silk beneath shining armor. Boris had undoubtedly insulted her, but Lang had touched Catherine's breastplate, right over her breast. Boris shouldn't have allowed that; Lang was an oaf and a nobody, and Catherine was a princess. But Lang was dead now. And Boris too. Harold had had a perfect view of Boris's final moments: the spear flying low from Catherine's hand, the brief look of surprise and confusion on their brother's face. Harold had almost laughed out loud at that look. And then there was the delight in seeing Boris falling back, mortally wounded.

And that was all it had taken to elevate Harold to heir apparent.

"Thank you, sister." Harold smiled as he looked toward the Pitorian camp, where Catherine had escaped afterward. Harold had always liked her more than their brother. She was clever and crafty. But she must have taken some smoke to throw like that.

Harold had tried the purple demon smoke himself for the first time only a few days earlier. He'd been rather nervous. His father despised anything that "perverted" nature, even wine and beer, and Boris had warned Harold against it, saying, "It'll addle your mind—and, let's face it, your mind is not normal at the best of times." Harold was very much aware that his mind wasn't like those of ordinary people. But who wanted a normal mind, and who wanted to do as Boris ordered? And in the Brigantine camp there were a number of boys with smoke who were more than happy to share what they had with a son of the king.

Harold had inhaled only the smallest amount but immediately knew his old life was over. The smoke transformed him. Harold was small and slight—unfortunately more his mother's build than his father's—but with the smoke he was faster and stronger than even the best men in the army. That was why Boris hadn't wanted Harold to have any—he'd been afraid that Harold would be stronger than him. But now it didn't matter. Boris was dead, and Harold could do whatever he liked.

"And I'll do it better than you ever did, brother," he muttered. "I'll have my own troop while I'm still fourteen."

Boris hadn't got his until fifteen.

Harold knew exactly which troop he wanted—and it certainly wasn't Boris's oafs. Harold wanted the boys' brigades. He'd seen them training, seen how the demon smoke had transformed them from children into—

"Hey, you."

It was one of the blue-haired Pitorian soldiers who had been looking for the wounded. He wasn't alone, but the others were farther back.

Harold smiled and waved. "Hello."

"What are you doing?"

Harold replied in his best Pitorian: "I'm admiring the view." The man came closer, and Harold could see the face below the blue hair was unusually ugly, with fat lips and a broad, shallow forehead. "And you're ruining it."

"You're Brigantine, aren't you, boy? You shouldn't be here. You should go."

"I most certainly am Brigantine. I'm Harold Godolphin Reid Marcus Melsor, second son of Aloysius of Brigant and the future king of Brigant, Pitoria, Calidor, and any other place I fancy, and I'm in an exceptionally good mood, despite looking at the ugliest man in Pitoria. And I'll go when I jolly well like. And this"—Harold drew his sword—"is why."

With that, he ran at the Pitorian. He performed a low somersault, swinging his sword as he turned in the air, feeling the strength of the smoke, his blade as light and easy to control as a feather. It felt like a dance, and Harold wanted to laugh again as his sword severed the soldier's leg cleanly, just above the knee. Harold landed firmly on both feet as the man toppled to the ground and lay on his back, staring at the sky, his fat-lipped mouth opening and closing soundlessly like a blue-finned fish gasping for air. The other two Pitorians shouted in alarm and ran toward their comrade, drawing their swords. Everything seemed to be moving slowly to Harold, and he grinned at them and held his arms out, wondering if they'd attack, but they came to a halt, glancing around nervously.

Harold shouted, "You were looking for wounded men, weren't you? Well, now you've found one. You should help this fellow. He'll bleed to death if you're not quick."

One of the men edged forward and knelt by the fish-mouthed man.

"Why did you do that when the battle is over?" the other asked.

Such dull questions! Harold could hardly be bothered to reply.

"To show you what I'm capable of. And, now that I have your attention, take this message to my sister, Princess Catherine: tell her that Tzsayn and Farrow have won this day, but they won't win again. Next time, my boy army will cut you all off at the knees."

With that, Harold turned and ran back to the trees, as fast as the wind. The soldiers didn't even attempt to give chase but knelt by their wounded friend. And above the smoldering fields, above the river and the opposing army camps, above them all, the clouds began to gather. And late that afternoon, the first of the summer rains began to fall.

# CATHERINE
ARMY CAMP, NORTHERN PITORIA

War never ends for the living; only for the dead
is it ever over.

*Pitorian saying*

A SHORT cry broke the silence of the night. The queen
turned over in her bed, still half-asleep. Every night was full
of strange sounds and screams from the gaping mouths of
men and demons.

*It was just a dream . . .*

She could deal with her dreams, since they dissolved
away harmlessly with the day, but her dreams rarely woke
her, and she was half-awake now.

*Perhaps it was a fox's bark . . .*

Though there were no foxes in the camp.

*Or a soldier shouting to a comrade . . .*

Perhaps that's exactly what it was.

Catherine opened her eyes.

The fabric of her tent hung limp in the gloom above her.
The rains that had fallen for over a week had finally stopped,
leaving puddles at the corners of the royal marquees and a
dampness lingering in the air. Splotches of black mold had

appeared and quickly bloomed across everything in her tent; wool partitions, silk hangings, even the bedsheets were turning into black shrouds.

Outside, the light from a lantern moved closer, casting wavering, stooped shadows with hushed voices.

*Savage and his assistants.*

Another pained cry and Catherine was up and out of her bed, pulling on her cloak as Tanya ran in. Though Catherine's maid spoke no words, her face said it all—Tzsayn was getting worse.

Catherine pushed through the double-curtain partitions that divided the royal tent, separating her "chambers" from the king's. General Davyon was there already, straddling the bed, holding down Tzsayn, who was struggling against him and flailing his arms. Tzsayn's eyes now fixed on Catherine and he shouted out her name. Catherine ran to him, knowing a moment's delay would send him further into panic. She grabbed Tzsayn's hand and held it tight.

"Hush," she said softly. "It's me."

"You're real? You're here?" He stared at her, as if still unsure who she was.

"Yes, I'm real. I'm here."

"But they took you. The Brigantines. I thought I'd lost you."

"No. I escaped from them . . . on the battlefield. You remember that, don't you?"

Tzsayn stared and stared at her, tears filling his eyes, and he shook his head and tried to stop them from falling.

"I thought they'd taken you. I thought . . . that man."

*That man*, every time. It was Noyes he meant, Catherine was certain, though Tzsayn had never said his name. But he was the one who had tortured Tzsayn and his men, the one who now haunted the king's mind.

"It was a dream, a bad dream. You have a fever, my darling. Please lie back. I'm safe. But I want you to be safe too."

Catherine sat beside the bed holding Tzsayn's hand while Doctor Savage poured a cup of milky medicine, but, as he held it out toward his patient's lips, Tzsayn knocked the cup away.

"No more of that stuff. Let me go, dammit."

But Davyon just shook his head, and the doctor's assistants held Tzsayn's shoulders while Savage poured the medicine down his throat. Tzsayn spat and swore but eventually fell back into his pillows, still clutching Catherine's hand.

When the king was still again, Savage pulled back the sheets to check Tzsayn's wounded leg. Whenever he did this, Catherine usually focused on the good side of Tzsayn's face—his smooth cheekbone and arching eyebrow—but this time she made herself glance down as Savage unwound the bandages.

A glimpse was all she could stand. Below the knee, Tzsayn's leg was a raw length of bloody meat and pus, his foot swollen like a pumpkin.

She turned to Savage and Davyon.

"What's happening to him? It's getting worse!"

Savage shook his head. "The childhood burns mean the new burns take longer to heal."

Immediately after the battle of Hawks Field, Tzsayn had

seemed to recover, but after only two days, an infection had swollen his leg and delirium swamped his mind. Catherine had recovered quickly from her own ordeals before and during the battle. She had a deep scar on her hand from the metal skewer that had held her in chains, but the demon smoke she'd inhaled had healed her instantly.

*If only it worked for Tzsayn*, she thought. But he was too old for the purple smoke to have any useful effect.

Catherine had physical scars but few mental ones. She had come to terms with her actions—she had killed her own brother. She wasn't proud of it, but neither was she ashamed. It was a fact, a necessity. Men killed all the time, with little thought, but she had examined her actions with all the logic of a judge and had no doubt that what she had done was right.

Boris was evil, and their father had made him that way. Aloysius himself had probably been made that way by his own father, and no doubt his father could also be blamed in turn, and on back through the royal line. But the rot had to stop. And if the men couldn't, or wouldn't, do it themselves, Catherine would do it. She had begun by killing Boris, but she had to do more. This was now her certainty. She would do all she could to stop her father from causing more death, destruction, and misery. That was her grand ambition, and it didn't weigh her down but carried her on.

And "on" meant acting—no, *being*—a queen: Queen Catherine of Pitoria. She'd lied about being married to Tzsayn while he was a prisoner of Aloysius, but he'd gone along with the lie upon his release. So had Davyon, Tanya, and even Ambrose, so now, for all intents and purposes, she *was* queen—with all the responsibilities that brought.

Thankfully everyone who had been involved in the treacherous plan to hand Catherine over to her father in exchange for Tzsayn had been swiftly dealt with. Lord Farrow, along with his generals and supporters, had been arrested and imprisoned immediately after the battle. In the few days that Tzsayn was lucid, he had made it clear that Lord Farrow would be tried for his treason, and few doubted he would be found guilty and executed.

But then Tzsayn's fever had taken hold and the responsibility for running the army, and indeed, the country, had fallen to his queen. These responsibilities—some small, some huge—filled Catherine's mind. Decisions needed to be made over the army, the navy, the food, the horses, the weapons, and the money.

*The money . . .*

Most of Pitoria's wealth had gone to paying Tzsayn's ransom, which was now in the hands of the Brigantines. The people had already been taxed to the hilt. Money—or lack of it—was a serious threat; money and war.

*Not enough of one and far too much of the other.*

Catherine stroked Tzsayn's forehead. He was sleeping now, and looked peaceful, but Catherine knew she wouldn't be able to sleep again. She could take some demon smoke, which had the wonderful ability to make her both more relaxed and stronger, but Tanya was awake too, and would make her displeasure felt if she saw her mistress taking smoke. Being a queen, Catherine had discovered, meant even less privacy than being a princess. The idea of time to herself, unobserved, seemed an unimaginable luxury. She went outside, shadowed by Tanya. Davyon, grim-faced as ever, was there, staring into the distance. The sky was clear and beginning to lighten in the east.

"At least the rain has stopped," Catherine said.

"Yes, we have that," Davyon replied.

Catherine thought of the piles of papers she had on her desk. But she couldn't quite face them yet.

"I want to go for a walk."

"Of course, Your Majesty. Within the royal compound? Or—"

"No, a real walk—in the fresh air, among trees."

In the past, Catherine would have happily ridden out with only Ambrose as her guard, and she'd have loved to do that now. But what she wanted to do and what she was able to do were very different things. The last thing she needed was to rekindle the rumors about her relationship with her body-guard, and besides that, Ambrose was still recovering from wounds received in the battle. At the thought of that, she felt guilty. Many of her soldiers had been wounded; she should support them. "I'll go through the camp; I'd like to see my soldiers."

Davyon frowned. "You'll need some of the Royal Guard to accompany you."

"In my own army's camp?"

"You're the queen. There might be assassins," Tanya

muttered loudly, as only Tanya could. "And in case you've forgotten, there is *definitely* a hostile army just over that hill-side."

"Very well," Catherine said. "Summon the Royal Guard."

Davyon bowed. "I too will accompany you, Your Majesty."

"Will you require your armor, Your Majesty?" asked Tanya.

"Why not?" Catherine sighed. "I'm sure the extra protection will please Davyon. Let's dazzle."

Though she felt not at all dazzling.

As the sun rose over the camp, Catherine, in a white dress under her shining armor, part of her hair plaited round her crown and the rest loose down her back, set out with Davyon (a fixed smile on his face), Tanya (dark-eyed, wearing a blue dress with a white fitted jacket that Catherine hadn't seen before), and ten of the Royal Guard, all with dyed white hair.

Catherine felt her mood brighten as she greeted the guards by name and stopped to ask one, "How's your brother, Gaspar?"

"Improving, Your Majesty. Thank you for sending the doctor to him."

"I'm glad he was of help."

Catherine hadn't set foot outside the protected enclosure since the battle of Hawks Field. She'd been in meetings, nursing Tzsayn, or sleeping. Now, as she stepped out past the high wall of royal tents, she saw the Pitorian army. Her army.

The camp stretched as far as she could see, and although it hadn't moved since the battle, it was completely unrecognizable. It had always been slightly haphazard, full of tents, horses, and people, even chickens and goats, but it had been set in pleasant, open fields of grass. Seven days of rain and thousands of pounding boots had changed all that. There was no grass to be seen, only thick mud interspersed with pools of brown water, above which clouds of tiny flies hung like smoke in the morning light.

"Midges," Tanya complained, slapping her neck. "I got bitten all over my arm yesterday."

Davyon picked a route through the camp that was as dry as possible, but as they moved among the tents, there was something else hanging in the air besides the midges: a smell—no, a *stench*—of human and animal waste.

Catherine put her hand over her face. "This aroma is rather overpowering."

"I've been in farmyards that smell sweeter," Tanya said.

Farther down the field, some of the tents were entirely waterlogged. Soldiers were walking ankle-deep in mud, clouds of midges around them.

"Why haven't they moved their tents?" Catherine asked Davyon.

"They're the king's men. They need to be near the king."

"They need to be dry."

"We didn't expect the rains to last so long, but the men are hardy. It's only water, Your Majesty, and as you said yourself, the rains seem to have passed."

Catherine splashed over to a group of soldiers standing

on a small island of relatively dry ground, their boots thick with mud. The men saluted and smiled.

"How are you handling the rain?" she asked.

"We can handle anything, Your Majesty."

"Well, I can feel the water soaking through my boots, and I've only been out here a short time. Aren't your feet wet through?"

"Just a bit, Your Majesty," one admitted.

But another, braver man added, "Sodden and have been for days. My boots are rotting, Josh's feet have turned black, and Aryn's got the red fever, so we might not see him again."

Catherine turned to Davyon. "The red fever?"

Davyon grimaced. "It's a sickness. The doctors are doing what they can."

Catherine thanked the men for their honesty and set off again. When they were out of earshot of the soldiers, she hissed at Davyon.

"Men dying of fever? General, this isn't what I expected from you. How many are sick?"

Davyon rarely showed emotion and his voice now was more tired than angry. "One man in ten is showing some signs. I didn't want to trouble you with it."

Catherine almost swore. "These are my men, my soldiers. I want to know how they are. You should have informed me. You should have moved the camp. Do it today, General. We can't assume the rains won't return. And even if they don't, this place is already a wasteland of flies and filth."

Davyon bowed. "As soon as you're safely back in the royal compound, I will begin the process—"

"You'll begin the process *now*. I've got ten guards with me, Davyon; I don't need you too. And it seems to me I'm more likely to die of drowning or fever than an assassin's arrow."

Davyon's lips were tight as he bowed again and left without another word. Catherine continued her tour, making a point of stopping and talking to both her white-hairs and Tzsayn's blue-hairs. Most of the men seemed happy to see her, and all of them asked after their king.

"We knew he'd escape the Brigantines. If anyone could, he could."

Catherine smiled and said how proud Tzsayn was of his men for their loyalty and courage. It was clear that none knew Tzsayn was ill, and it was probably best to keep it that way.

She came to a halt at the northerly end of the camp that overlooked Hawks Field. It too was unrecognizable as the place where the Pitorians had fought and beaten the Brigantines. The river had burst its banks and flooded everything. The only feature that remained was a crooked wooden pole poking up at an angle from the brown water—the remains of the cart Catherine had been chained to, which had somehow survived both fire and flood. On the far bank, where her father's troops had gathered, there was nothing but grass. In the days since the battle, the Brigantines had fallen back to the outskirts of Rossarb, half a day's ride north. No one knew when, or if, they would attack again, but while her father made up his mind, it seemed he had more sense than to stay put in a swamp.

As Catherine surveyed the ground, she felt her stomach

tighten. On the maps in the war meetings, it had all seemed somehow remote, but here the true extent of their plight felt uncomfortably real.

Even if Catherine had escaped his clutches, Aloysius had got almost everything else he wanted from his invasion— gold from Tzsayn's ransom to finance his army and access to the demon smoke on the Northern Plateau. His army had retreated, but he wasn't beaten, while her own men were knee-deep in mud and riddled with fever.

Catherine set her jaw. She wished Tzsayn was able to help her, but for now she'd have to work alone.

# AMBROSE
## ARMY CAMP, NORTHERN PITORIA

THE INFIRMARY was cool in the morning light. The dawn chorus of groans, coughs, and snores had given way to quiet talk peppered with curses and weak cries for help. Ambrose lay on his side in his rickety camp bed looking to the door, willing the next person to enter to be Catherine. She would smile at him as she approached, walking quickly, leaving her maids well behind, as she used to do when she saw him in the stable yard at Brigant Castle. She'd take his hand, and he'd bend and kiss hers. He'd touch her skin with his lips, breathe on her skin, and breathe in her smell.

The man behind Ambrose coughed wheezily, then spat.

Ambrose had been here a week, sure at first that Catherine would visit him, now not so sure. He'd filled each day with thoughts of her, remembering the days he'd spent with her, from the early days in Brigant, when he rode with her along the beach, to the glorious days in Donnafon, where he'd held her in his arms, caressed her smooth skin, kissed her hand, her fingers, her lips.

A cry of pain came from a man at the far end of the room.

*What are you thinking?* Catherine shouldn't come here. The place was full of misery and disease. He had to get out and go to her. But for that, he'd have to walk. He'd been injured in the shoulder and leg in the battle of Hawks Field. He'd seen soldiers heal from worse injuries than his, and he'd seen men give up and die from less serious wounds. There had been a moment, after the battle, when he thought he couldn't go on, but that feeling of despair had left him, and he knew now he would never give up. He'd fight on for himself and for Catherine.

Ambrose sat up in his bed and began his exercises, slowly bending and straightening his right arm as the doctor had instructed. He moved on to the next exercise: rotating his bandaged shoulder. This was more painful, and he had to do it slowly.

The battle of Hawks Field was won, but the war was far from over. And as for Ambrose's part in the battle . . . well, he'd tried to save Catherine, but killing Lang was all he had managed. He'd wanted to fight Boris, but the Brigantines had overpowered Ambrose, and it was Catherine, fueled by demon smoke, who had sent a spear into Boris's chest. She'd saved Ambrose and killed her own brother. *How must it feel? To kill your own brother?* It was impossible for Ambrose to imagine; his own brother, Tarquin, had been the complete opposite of Boris. Though now they were both dead. And Ambrose had no idea how Catherine felt about anything. *Why hadn't she come? Was she herself ill?* So many questions and no answers at all.

"Shits!" He cried out at a sharp pain as he swung his arm too fast.

He had to get out of this bed. He had to get out of this infirmary! The place was miserable. Every bed had a man in it, but few were casualties from the fighting; most had the fever that had swept through the camp. The red fever, they called it, for the color your face turned as you coughed up your guts. Several more had died in the night, their beds lying empty, though Ambrose knew it would only be a short time before another shivering body was laid in the grubby sheets. It was a miracle he hadn't caught the fever already.

Ambrose swiveled round until both feet were planted firmly on the floor. With the help of a chair back, he could just stand, wincing and wobbling slightly as he put more weight on his left leg. It was weak, but the pain was bearable; he *could* walk out of here if he tried. The doctors had removed the arrow from his calf and had sewn him up neatly. Most doctors would have amputated for such an injury, but the doctors had operated carefully, given him herbal treatments, liquors, and compresses.

Ambrose had the best doctors—sent by Tzsayn.

He had the best medicine—sent by Tzsayn.

The best food—sent by Tzsayn.

The best clothes and bedding and . . . everything.

Everything except any word from or about Catherine. Was Tzsayn keeping her from him? That had to be the explanation.

"You're looking well, Sir Ambrose."

Ambrose had been so caught up in his thoughts that he'd

missed seeing Tanya enter the room. He looked to the door, hoping Catherine would appear.

"One of the doctors asked me to give you this. For strength or something." Tanya held out a bowl of porridge and saw the direction of his gaze. "It's all I bring. There's no one else with me."

Ambrose nodded, trying to hide his disappointment. "It's good to see you, Tanya." He reached for the bowl but lost his balance and grabbed the back of the chair to hold himself upright. But this shocked his arm, and he grunted in surprise at the pain. He lowered himself to the side of the bed as casually as he could manage.

Tanya stifled a laugh.

Ambrose glared up at her. "Do you always laugh at the injured?"

She shook her head. "Not always, just when their hair is a strange green color."

"Oh that. We were infiltrating Farrow's men," he started to explain, reaching for his unfamiliarly short locks, but Tanya was merely grinning more. "Anyway, it won't wash out."

"You'll have to dye it a different color; that's the only way." She sat next to him on the bed and leaned toward him, her voice lower, "But which will you choose? White for the queen? Or blue for the king?"

"Blue? The old king had purple as his color. Won't Tzsayn have to change all his blasted clothes and body paint now his father is dead?"

"No, the royal colors alternate with each king. So Tzsayn's

color will remain blue. When he has a son, that son will have purple as his color, just as Tzsayn's father did. Anyway, I expect you'll go with white. Or will you go with nothing at all?"

"Can we discuss something other than hair?"

"I wasn't discussing hair, Sir Ambrose."

Ambrose eyed Tanya closely. "Did she send you? Why hasn't she come herself?"

"The queen knows that to be seen with you would be . . . disadvantageous to her position. But she consults with the doctors daily."

"She sent the doctors? Not Tzsayn?"

"She sends doctors to many of her men—her white-hairs."

"You sound like a politician."

"Good. You have to be one round here."

"And is my mistress a politician too?"

Tanya pursed her lips. "She is. But politics alone won't win this war. She needs men who can show loyalty and take the fight to the Brigantines—even though they've lost much and may lose even more. She needs your support, Sir Ambrose."

"She will always have it, Tanya. You know that."

Tanya nodded but didn't reply.

"Can you tell me more?" asked Ambrose finally. "Is she well? Last time I saw her she was chained to a cart. Actually, last time I saw her she was throwing a spear at me . . . Well, not at me—at Boris. So let me rephrase that. Is the queen well? Last time I saw her she was in the act of killing her brother."

Tanya looked away for a moment. "She's recovered from the wounds she received from being chained to the cart. Thank you for your concern about that. Her brother was a monster. I don't think I'm speaking out of place to say so. And his death doesn't weigh heavily on my mistress's heart."

Thinking of Catherine's heart, Ambrose wanted to know more and found himself asking, "And Tzsayn? How is he?"

"Recovering from his injuries."

Ambrose raised an eyebrow. "Injuries?"

Tanya almost looked flustered as she replied, "Minor wounds from his imprisonment. But I don't see him much; he's a busy man. Being king is . . . a full-time job."

But did Catherine see Tzsayn? How often? Daily?

Tanya seemed to have recovered as she said, "We're still at war, Sir Ambrose. The king has many responsibilities, as does the queen. Catherine's position depends on many things, including you. She needs your help. She needs people around her who can fight and lead and inspire."

"So I'm allowed to be around her, then? Can I meet with her?"

Tanya shook her head. "She can't be seen with you, Ambrose, and you know why. If you try to see her, you risk ruining her reputation—ruining her. If you care for her— and I know you do—she needs your support as a fighter, not a lover."

"Before, when we were fleeing across the Northern

Plateau, she wanted me to be both." Ambrose spoke quietly, uncertain if he should say this, even to Tanya.

"Yes, she told me. And in Donnafon you both used every little trick to spend time together. And for that she nearly paid with her life. But the stakes are even higher now, Ambrose. It's not just Catherine's life in the balance but all our lives. She is our queen. Her honor has to be above reproach and her loyalty to Pitoria unquestionable."

"And I'm questionable?"

"You're a good man and a good soldier, Ambrose. And you need to prove it."

"Haven't I done that already?"

Tanya smiled. "We must all prove it again and again. Now eat your porridge before it gets cold."

# EDYON

## CALIA, CALIDOR

"HERE ARE the procedures for the day of your investiture." Prince Thelonius handed a scroll to Edyon. "All is organized. There will be celebrations throughout Calidor. I couldn't be happier. You're the future of this country."

Edyon was already recognized as Thelonius's son, but the investiture was a formal procedure to confirm his positions and titles: he was now a prince, the Prince of Abask, and, most importantly, heir to the throne of Calidor. Edyon glanced down the events listed on the scroll, but considering he was the country's future, he wasn't mentioned all that much.

"Thank you, Father. I'll ensure I follow it all to the letter. But, speaking of letters, may I raise an issue with you? When I arrived from Pitoria I carried with me an important message from King Tzsayn and Queen Catherine. That was a week ago. The letter was an urgent request for your assistance. I feel that we must reply, and soon."

It took all of Edyon's willpower not to shout *"Now!"* but he didn't think it likely that his father, whom he had met for the first time just last week, would take that well. However, *now* was what was needed. When Edyon left Pitoria, they had learned that Aloysius was farming demon smoke. Once he had enough smoke to power his boy army, there would be no stopping him. They had no time to waste. Thelonius had defeated his brother, Aloysius, in the last war, and everyone was counting on him to do it again.

"You're right, Edyon. And I've decided that we will send a delegation to Pitoria to ensure we're fully aware of the situation there."

*A delegation!* It didn't seem like much; Edyon had been imagining that his father would send in the entire army once he understood the threat. But a delegation had to be better than nothing, and at least it was a first step. Perhaps then the two countries could work closely together, sharing information, men, supplies . . .

The Lord Chancellor, Lord Bruntwood, took a step forward and addressed Thelonius: "Your Highness, I feel it is my duty to remind you of the old issues relating to dealings with foreign lands, and also to raise your awareness of another, small problem."

The chancellor's face never seemed to show any true emotion; his smile was obsequious, his frown aloof, his sorrow humdrum. And he always seemed to Edyon like he desperately needed to break wind but was holding it in.

*Perhaps that's his small problem.*

"What problem?" Thelonius frowned.

"Talk, Your Highness. Rumors. Tittle-tattle. Relating to

Edyon." The chancellor winced as if the wind was causing much internal discomfort.

"Not more objections to Edyon being legitimized, I hope." This came from Lord Regan, Thelonius's dearest friend, the one man he'd entrusted to track down his son and deliver him safely to Calidor. Of course, that hadn't gone according to plan, thanks to March . . .

But Edyon wouldn't think of March now.

The chancellor turned to Regan and corrected him. "Actually, there were no objections to the legitimization, only concerns about a precedent being set."

Regan nodded. "Of course, yes, *concerns*, not objections."

"And we've resolved these already. We've set no precedent," Thelonius interrupted.

"Quite so, Your Highness," the chancellor agreed.

The first obstacle to Edyon's legitimization was that Thelonius hadn't been married to Edyon's mother. A number of lords were concerned that putting Edyon next in line to the throne would allow all bastard sons to come forward, claiming lands and titles off the lords or off the lords' sons. No one was safe. The system would crumble. Chaos would reign where there was now order.

Edyon had wondered how his father would deal with this difficult situation and assumed it would take weeks or months to consider and argue the legal points, but his father had swept the issue aside with ease. Thelonius had claimed that he'd married Edyon's mother in a ceremony in Pitoria when they'd met. He said that they'd married and quickly divorced. The papers had been lost, but Thelonius had a diary of the events. Lord Regan, who'd traveled with him in Pitoria those eighteen years ago, had been called upon to confirm it all. And, as easily and quickly as that, the lie had become truth.

Edyon, however, found it less easy to confirm. He was surprised to discover that, although he could lie about most things, he couldn't lie about his mother or his own birth. He *was* Thelonius's illegitimate son. His parents had not been married, and his whole life had been shaped by that fact. It had made him who he was, and Edyon had always been determined not to be ashamed of it. When the chancellor had pressed him to confirm Thelonius's lie, Edyon found that the most he could do was to not deny it. He'd argued, "I wasn't there. I was in my mother's womb. And she never spoke to me of it." Edyon felt he could say only that, as none of it was an actual lie, but none of it was the whole truth either.

Edyon's father had no such qualms and even embellished the lie one evening, admittedly after a few glasses of wine, talking of the wedding as if it had happened: "a simple affair, promises made, a beach, the sea, young lovers, but we *were* married." He had looked into Edyon's eyes with a smile. "And everyone agrees that you are my image. Your face, your stature—you are just as I was twenty years ago. It's obvious that you are my son." And that was true. At least there were no arguments, concerns, or objections about that.

"However, there are still apprehensions among the lords." The chancellor's voice interrupted Edyon's thoughts.

"Ah, so it's *apprehensions* now," Regan murmured.

"The lords are always apprehensive." Thelonius sighed and looked to Edyon, adding, "About money, about power, about the future."

*And now about me.*

"And we must always be careful to soothe their concerns," the chancellor continued. "The letter that Edyon brought from Pitoria, the request to join forces with Pitoria, again raises the fear that Calidor may lose its independence to a stronger neighbor. It's an old fear but no less compelling for its age, Your Highness. There are concerns that any partnership with Pitoria would be unequal, as Pitoria, a far bigger and more populous country than Calidor, will dominate. What may start as aid may end with us being infiltrated and overpowered."

"An argument we had in the last war many times," Thelonius said.

"When we fought alone, stood firm alone, and were victorious alone," Lord Regan added.

"And these concerns have returned, stronger than ever. The lords need to know that Calidor will remain independent. They need to know their future is in safe hands." The chancellor looked to Edyon and pulled a strange face; his trapped wind appeared to have returned. "There's talk that Edyon has been sent by King Tzsayn of Pitoria, concern that Edyon's Pitorian heritage may sway his allegiance."

"That Edyon is an infiltrator? A spy?" Thelonius looked appalled.

"No one would go that far, Your Highness," the chancellor replied. "But we must tread carefully. We need the lords to support Edyon. Fortunately, I believe a few simple steps will ensure this."

"And what are these simple steps, Lord Bruntwood?" Thelonius asked.

"A clear declaration in Edyon's investiture swearing to ensure Calidor retains its independence."

Thelonius nodded. "I don't have a problem with that. It seems reasonable, and a neat solution. Please arrange it, Lord Bruntwood."

"Gladly, Your Highness."

"Is that it?"

The chancellor's wind appeared to get worse. "Alas, no. I believe as well as a declaration, we must ensure we're not seen to be working with Pitoria. While your idea to send a delegation—a *small* delegation—would be understandable, no forces, no arms, no men, no equipment must be exchanged."

"But what about the demon smoke?" Edyon asked. "The boy army?" The chancellor did not seem to be taking this seriously.

"With all due respect, Your Highness, for us to agree to send even a small delegation seems like a strong overreaction to an untrained pack of boys calling themselves an 'army.' "

"But the smoke works," Edyon insisted. He needed to make them understand the severity of the threat, the pressing need for action. "I brought a bottle with me from Pitoria. May I demonstrate its power? Perhaps if the lords see how it works, they would better understand what we're up against."

Thelonius nodded. "A good suggestion, Edyon. I agree a demonstration to the lords would be helpful. Lord Regan will assist you in setting it up."

Regan did not look happy about this assignment, but he nodded his assent.

"It all seems unnecessary," the chancellor said. "They are attacking Pitoria. They are not attacking *us*."

"Not *yet*," Edyon said. "But the Brigantines are our enemy. Surely the lords agree on that!"

"They most certainly do, Your Highness," the chancellor replied. "But our enemy's enemy is not necessarily our friend."

"Nor is he necessarily our enemy!" Edyon shot back. "Tzsayn is a good man; he wouldn't betray us, infiltrate us, or overpower us. He's not like Aloysius. And he's asked for help. He's offered us help in return. Together we can fight Aloysius and win."

Thelonius put a hand on Edyon's arm. "I must balance your perspective with the views of the lords, Edyon. We must be seen to act carefully with and independent of Tzsayn."

"Exactly," concurred the chancellor. "We must be seen to act purely for the good of Calidor. Pitorian troops on Calidorian lands, for example, would be seen as dangerous. The lords know what happened when just forty or fifty Brigantine soldiers were allowed into Tornia—many nobles were killed."

"Those were Brigantine soldiers, not Pitorian. Tzsayn

doesn't want to kill our nobles. This is nonsense!" Edyon exclaimed.

"Tzsayn is married to Aloysius's daughter. A marriage arranged by Aloysius," Regan interjected. "I wouldn't trust her as far as . . . well, as far as any woman. She's a puppet, for certain. And we've received news that Tzsayn was freed by Aloysius. Surely Tzsayn offered Aloysius something more than gold in exchange for his release. Perhaps he also promised to betray us."

"No." Edyon shook his head. "No. Tzsayn's not like that. And Catherine hates her father."

"Catherine is immoral," Regan said dismissively. "Rumor also has it that she killed her brother, Prince Boris."

"Then she's hardly a puppet of Aloysius, is she?" Edyon replied.

"Well, I'm not sure what to believe of that rumor, but if it's true, it doesn't make me trust her more," Thelonius commented.

"She's as ruthless as her father," Regan added with a sneer.

"So you'll do nothing?" Edyon looked from his father to the chancellor to Regan. "You'll let the Pitorians fight and die, and you'll let Aloysius continue to farm demon smoke until no army on this earth could overpower him, and you'll sit and wait for him to attack us. That is how you want the future to go, that is how you'll defend your country?"

Thelonius turned to Edyon, stony-faced. "Do not accuse me of failing in my duty, Edyon. I fought with my countrymen against Aloysius in the last war. Many men perished. I won't risk losing our country to Aloysius, but neither will I risk losing it to anyone else."

Edyon's face flushed, and he looked down. This wasn't how he'd imagined one of his first political meetings with his father would go.

Thelonius turned from Edyon and addressed the chancellor, his voice still stiff with anger. "We will accept a small delegation of nonfighting men from Pitoria, and we'll send our own small delegation to them. We will share information. You are correct that we must be sure of our friends. We must never be too trusting. I was hoping that that was a lesson my son had recently learned, but it appears he has already forgotten it."

Edyon knew his father was referring to March. March, who had been involved in the attempted murder of Lord Regan. March, who would have sold out Edyon to the Brigantines. March, who was now banished. Edyon had loved, trusted, and respected March, only to find that he had been lying all along. "No, Father, I haven't forgotten it. Nor will I ever," he replied sincerely.

Thelonius turned back to Edyon. "Then trust me, and trust the lords for their support." He added more quietly, so that only Edyon could hear, "Our lords are more vital to you than Tzsayn or Catherine or any other foreign power. You must be seen to be loyal to Calidor above all else."

Edyon nodded and bowed his head. "Of course, Father."

# MARCH
## CALIDOR-BRIGANT BORDER

"KEEP GOING. Your new home is straight ahead."

March barely had the energy to take another step. It had taken three days to walk from Calia to the border of Calidor, and the only food he'd had were scraps the guards had thrown on the ground. Ahead, all he could see was an impossibly high wall of stone with a lookout tower on it. The guard put the butt of his spear into March's back and shoved him forward. As March got nearer to the wall, he saw there were stone steps built into it. Toward the top was a narrow ledge that led to the lookout tower where four soldiers stood, staring down at him.

The wall had been built by Thelonius after the last war. It was made of solid stone, with forts and lookout points to keep watch and protect Calidor. There were gates too, one in the east and one in the west, though clearly March wasn't going to be allowed to use either. He was a traitor. He'd been part of a plot to kill Regan and then Edyon. The gates were not for him.

He started to climb. The stone steps were narrow, and he was dizzy with hunger and thirst.

"Get a move on, shithead," the guard below shouted.

The wonderful thing about being this exhausted was that March really didn't care about the guards. He didn't care about much anymore. He almost didn't care about falling; he just kept putting one foot in front of the other.

And then he was there, at the top of the wall and looking over to the other side, to Brigant. It didn't seem too bad— green with lush grass, bushes, and trees. Though getting there was not going to be straightforward. There were no steps on that side of the wall. Looking directly down, March saw the long drop ended in a tangle of brambles. On the far side of that was another, smaller wall that he'd have to scale to enter Brigant. He would have to try to find a way to climb down this large wall first, or he could just throw himself off and put an end to the torment. But for the moment, he didn't go with either option; he looked back to Calidor . . . to Edyon.

He'd traveled a huge distance over the last few months— across Pitoria to Dornan to find Edyon, then fleeing with Edyon to Rossarb across the Northern Plateau, and then back again, pursued by Brigantine soldiers. And now he realized how much Edyon's company, Edyon's soul and spirit, had kept him going. He missed Edyon's presence more than he'd ever imagined possible. He was leaving Calidor and would never return. He'd never see Edyon again. If only he'd told Edyon the truth earlier, perhaps things would have been different. Perhaps Edyon would have listened; perhaps he'd have understood.

"Are you having a final tearful good-bye, White Eyes?"

a guard hollered. "Well, your time's up. You're on our wall, and if you don't get off it yourself, we'll throw you off." The guard began to climb.

March had a feeling the guard's words weren't an empty threat. He took a final look to Calidor—Edyon's country, Edyon's home now. Then, as the first guard was reaching the top of the wall, he swung his leg over the parapet and lowered himself down. He felt for footholds in the stone and found small gaps that could just hold the toes of his boots. He grabbed at the rough stone, scraping his knees but somehow clinging on, and moved down. But then his hand slipped and he had no energy left, and so he half jumped and half fell the final stretch, landing on the branches and brambles. Above him the guards hooted with laughter. March shouted in pain and despair but discovered he hadn't broken any bones, and, though the brambles tangled him, ripped his shirt, and scratched his arms, he was intact. He struggled across a pile of broken branches and realized the ditch below him was deep, and he could smell pitch. The wood had been put there for a reason. This whole area between Calidor's outer wall and Brigant's wall, this no-man's-land, was a huge fire pit waiting to be lit.

He scrambled to the next wall, again finding steps built into it, and again knowing there'd be none on the other side. He made it to the top, lowered himself over the parapet, and clambered down as best he could to stand on Brigantine land, though thankfully there were no Brigantines around. He wasn't sure how he'd be treated by Brigantines, but they didn't have a reputation for being kind and generous. Though could they be worse than the Calidorian soldiers he was leaving behind?

March set off walking, looking back only once to see the wall in the distance and the soldiers silhouetted on the top. He followed a gradual slope down, reasoning that'd be the most likely way to find a road and possibly people and hopefully food. He was relieved when he found a stream. He drank and washed, cleaning his dusty skin and hair, and cooling his feet. After he'd rested, he followed the stream down, eventually coming to a stony road. He had nothing to carry water in, so he took a last drink and followed the road east.

March plodded on. He saw no sign of human life, apart from the road. When evening came, he couldn't manage to start a fire. He had nothing, not even a blanket to keep him warm. He lay down to sleep. At least he could rest whenever he wanted now. At least he wasn't being cursed or kicked. But he woke during the night, alert and fearful—this was Brigant after all, enemy territory. March crouched close to the ground, listening to the noises of the night, but there were no human sounds here. And it was at this point the tears came. He was truly alone, without friends, family, a home, or even a country.

He remembered being in the cell with Edyon that last time. Edyon had said that March had been "a true friend. And a true love," but March had betrayed him. And, even when Edyon had confronted him, March hadn't been able to tell Edyon how he really felt. He had never been sure, until it was too late, that he loved Edyon enough. The tears rolled down March's cheeks, and he closed his eyes and imagined Edyon standing before him, imagined telling Edyon he loved him, imagined kissing him and begging his forgiveness. And in his dreams, Edyon kissed March's tears away.

The next morning March trudged on until he spotted a small farmhouse not far from the road. He staggered toward it to beg for food. There were chickens in the yard, as well as goats and a pig. It was a small, poor place, and yet it seemed like heaven. March banged on the farmhouse door, but there was no answer. He had to eat, had to have something. An egg and some milk from the goats would keep him going for the rest of the day. Surely the farmer could spare him that.

March went to the henhouse and slipped inside. He ran his hands over the shelves, finding two eggs, which he gently placed into his pocket. He left feeling guilty, but he still needed to take more. To survive, he needed a blanket and a skin for water. The house was standing quiet and empty— dare he go in?

"It's that or die," he muttered to himself as he opened the door and stepped inside.

The house was tiny and almost bare of possessions. There was one room with a single bed to the side and a rough wooden box containing a few clothes and a blanket. March took the blanket. Then he went to the kitchen—the other side of the room—which had a fireplace, table, and two small cupboards. There was a small pitcher full of milk in one. March licked his lips and his stomach growled. The milk hardly touched the sides of his mouth, yet its flavor was fatty and full. The cupboard also contained some cheese and apples. March grabbed a sack to put the food in, and then found some cabbages and rutabagas. He took one of each and put them in the sack too.

He was leaving the house, closing the door carefully behind him, when he heard a shout. "Hey there, boy. What you doing?"

March turned. An old man was approaching. March had to choose: confess and beg for forgiveness, or run.

He looked at the man, who was wiry with a short gray beard. "Well, what you after?" the man shouted, scowling and moving surprisingly fast toward March, who backed away. "Is that my sack you got there? You stealing off me?"

"I'm just hungry."

"And what's with your eyes?"

"I didn't steal *them*."

"You're Abask! I thought your kind were dead. They were all thieves and lowlifes." The man snatched at the sack, but March jerked it out of his reach, so the man grabbed at March instead.

March pushed the man away.

"That's my sack." The man snatched at it again, but March pulled it away and ran a few steps, turning to plead, "I'm just hungry. I just need some food."

The man bent down and picked up some stones from the path, throwing them with fierce accuracy, while shouting, "Thief! Abask thief!"

The stones struck March twice on the back of the head as he ran off, and the man shouted, his voice carrying surprisingly well in the still air: "I'll have your eyes out for stealing, you Abask bastard."

March slowed at the top of a rise before he looked back. The man was far behind, staring at him. March took out the eggs from his pocket, cracked them open, and sucked their contents down. He threw the shells on the ground and shouted at the man, "I should have taken a chicken too."

That night March managed to make a fire. He wrapped himself in the blanket and ate some of the food, saving what he hoped would be enough for the rest of his journey. He didn't know how long he'd be walking, and he couldn't risk stealing too often. He needed to get to a town or city. He needed money, work, something. But, as the night wore on, his thoughts fell from those things and returned, as always, to Edyon.

The next morning, he set off at first light, not sure where he was going and not sure he wanted to get there. To make things perfect, it started to rain. March put the sack over his head and trudged toward a line of small trees, away from the road, to find some shelter. As he neared, he saw that the trees were growing in a small, narrow valley. He slid down the slope of wet grass and mud, landing on his backside, which elicited a snigger above him. March looked up to see a boy leaning against a tree trunk.

The boy was smaller than March, painfully thin, with a swollen black eye, straggly red-blond hair, and boots that looked way too big for him. By way of greeting, the boy opened his tattered jacket to reveal that his trousers, which were also too big, were held up by a leather belt that was thick and worn, and into which was tucked a long knife.

The boy said, "I don't want trouble."

"Me neither," March replied. "I just want to get out of the rain."

"Same here." The boy nodded to the next tree along. "There's room there."

March went to the tree, laid his sack out, and sat on it. He looked at the boy, who was watching him intently.

"My name's Sam."

"March."

"Rain doesn't look like stopping soon."

March wasn't in the mood for a conversation about the weather, but it would do no harm to be friendly. "No, probably not."

"You got any food?"

"A bit."

Sam wrapped his jacket close to hide his knife and pulled a smile wide across his face. "What you got?"

"Cheese, an apple, rutabaga, and cabbage."

Sam licked his lips. "Nice."

"When did you last eat?"

The boy shrugged. "Yesterday . . . or the day before, maybe."

"Do you know how to set rabbit traps?"

Sam shook his head but looked hopeful.

"Lend me your knife and I'll show you."

"I'm not going to fall for that one."

March sighed. "Look, there are rabbit holes all round here. How about . . . I show you what to do, and you do it? I won't touch your knife."

Sam nodded. "Sixes."

"Sixes? What's that mean?"

Sam looked confused. "Sixes! Agreed. Deal. Six of one. Sixes."

"Oh, right."

March showed Sam how to get a length of a branch, cut it, and strip it down to make a flexible piece that could be fashioned into a loop to catch a rabbit. Sam was a quick learner and worked well with his hands, but he never let March close to the knife, always tucking it back in his trousers when he wasn't using it.

After they'd set the traps, Sam asked, "You're not Brigantine, are you? Where you from?"

"I'm Abask by birth. Traveled quite a bit, trying my luck here now." March quickly changed the subject from himself, asking, "And you, where are you from?"

"Blackton. Tiny village in the north by the sea."

"So how come you're here?"

"My master couldn't pay me, couldn't even feed me. I ran away."

"Did you steal his clothes?" March smiled, looking at the oversized trousers and boots.

Sam's face went stiff. "I'm no thief. They're mine."

March nodded. "Did your master give you the black eye then?"

"Do you ever stop asking questions?"

It was clear that Sam had been in a fight of some sort and those were not his normal clothes. But March didn't press further. They both had stories they didn't want to share. "So you've run away from the north all this way. Where are you headed? Calidor?"

"Calidor! They're our enemy. Why would I go there?"

"Work. Money. Food. It's the land of milk and honey, after all."

Sam shook his head. "Not for much longer, they say. Anyway, I'm joining the army. That's the place to be." He smiled. "Work, money, food to be had there."

"And war and fighting." March thought back to Rossarb. "And death and destruction."

"Not for the winners. The winners aren't destroyed."

March looked Sam up and down. He was a child. He shouldn't be in the army. "You're a winner, are you?"

Sam shrugged. "I can hold my own."

March didn't mention the black eye. "How can you join the army? Don't you have to be an apprentice to a lord or something first?"

"Not for the boys' brigades. You just have to be loyal to the king, and young enough."

"Really?" March's interest piqued. Was this the boy army Edyon had to warn his father about?

"They're the best. They say that they've got special powers, special strength. They live forever."

It had to be the boy army, fueled by demon smoke. "Hmm. I'm not so sure about the living-forever bit, but I do believe they have special strength."

Sam's face lit up. "You heard that too? Some say it's the work of demons, but I don't care how it works as long as I get strong enough to fight anyone I like."

"It's true. If you inhale the purple demon smoke, you get strong for a short while. It heals wounds quickly too."

Sam laughed and slapped his thigh. "Yes! It's true. It's true. We'll be indestructible."

"You'll still have to destroy other people," March reminded him.

Sam pulled his shoulders back. "People get what they deserve. The enemies of Brigant need to be shown who's boss."

"Women and children too? Babies? Old people?"

"I'm not going to fight *them*! They're not in the army. But"—Sam shrugged—"if you're on the wrong side, you suffer."

March nodded as he thought of his family and all the Abask people. "That's certainly true."

They sat quietly for a while and then Sam said, "I've seen eyes like yours before. In the north. The Abask slaves working in the mines have silver eyes too."

"Uh-huh."

"My master dealt with the mine owners, buying and selling tin." Sam poked at the ground with his finger. "Is that where you're from? When you said you traveled around a bit, do you mean you escaped?"

March shook his head. "No. I wasn't a slave of the Brigantines. I was a servant in Calidor. But a servant is pretty much a slave."

"You don't need to tell me. So how come you left Calidor if it's the land of milk and honey?"

March shrugged. "Like you, Sam, I'd had enough of being a servant."

"So you're going to join the boy army too?"

March had no plans for what he'd do next, but it seemed that whatever he tried, and wherever he went, the war was in his path. The war was his destiny. He had not avenged the deaths of the Abask people, as he'd originally left Thelonius's castle to do, and he knew now that it wasn't possible. They were gone years ago. But Edyon was still alive, and the Brigantines were certainly going to attack Calidor. Could March help in some way? Could he somehow spy on the boy army and return with valued information to give to Edyon? Could he win back Edyon's trust?

It seemed like an absurd idea. Most likely he'd just be killed in the first battle. But he had to do something. He couldn't just pretend the war wasn't happening. He couldn't pretend that he'd never met Edyon. He didn't want to do that. He wanted to return—not to Calidor, but to Edyon.

March's stomach growled, bringing him back to the reality of sitting in a wet ditch with Sam. The simple fact was that he was starving, and at least in the army he'd get food. He said, "Yes, I'm going to join the boy army too."

# EDYON

## CALIA, CALIDOR

EDYON STOOD on the edge of the field in the hot after-noon sun, a bottle of demon smoke in his hands. With him were two young noblemen named Byron and Ellis. They would be his assistants for the demonstration. Byron was Edyon's age, handsome with a long black plait of hair draped over his shoulder, and Ellis was a couple of years younger, broad-shouldered, and blond.

Across the field, a few of Lord Regan's men laughed loudly at some joke, while another man stretched and yawned. To Edyon's right, in the shade of a long, open marquee, servants in bright white shirts stood ready to pour refreshments.

Edyon looked round toward the castle for the hundredth time, hoping to catch sight of the audience arriving for his demonstration. Lord Regan had said he'd get the other lords there after quizzing Edyon on what he'd planned to do. Regan had told him, "You can make the demonstration on the knight's practice ground. I'll have it prepared and set up." But Edyon had been waiting for what seemed like hours in the hot sun, and no lords had arrived.

Edyon paced around until finally Regan came into view, walking beside Prince Thelonius and leading a throng of well-dressed men—the lords. They strolled up and slowly gathered in the shade of the marquee, sipping cool drinks and talking to each other, ignoring Edyon. Edyon was just about to call for their attention when Regan turned to him and shouted, "Are you ready yet, Your Highness?"

*As if you've been waiting half the afternoon for me!*

Edyon smiled and said, "I hope we are all ready, Your Highness and my lords." He stepped closer to his audience. "Thank you, Father, for allowing me to make this demonstration. And thank you, my lords, for sparing your time on this glorious afternoon.

"I left Pitoria just a couple of weeks ago to come to Calidor, and I was given the responsibility of bringing two things with me. Both of these things were handed to me by Queen Catherine herself. The first item was a letter of warning. A warning that King Aloysius of Brigant is building a new army, with which he intends to take over the world. First, he intends to crush us, his neighbors—Calidor and Pitoria."

Edyon had to be careful not to mention that the Pitorians had asked to join forces with the Calidorians, but he felt he should explain that the Pitorians had warned Thelonius of the threat. And that seemed to be going fine so far. Edyon continued, "This new Brigantine army is powerful and terrifying, but also unusual, as it is made up not of men but of boys."

There were a few laughs and smiles among the lords at this. "How old are these boy soldiers?" one asked. "Out of nappies, I assume?"

Edyon was beginning to wonder if there was alcohol in the drinks being handed out. He tried to quell their mirth. "I know it doesn't sound either powerful or terrifying. It sounds absurd. But I can prove that it's quite real. And that brings me to the other item that I carried with me from Pitoria: purple demon smoke."

Edyon raised the bottle of smoke for his audience to see. But in the heat, sweat had run down his arm, and as he raised his hand—possibly with a little more enthusiasm than was needed—the bottle swung up and out of his slippery fingers. It tumbled through the air, falling down toward the ground. Edyon watched in horror. He couldn't let the bottle break, and so he flailed after it, tripping and stumbling and somehow managing not to catch it but to knock it sideways.

Thelonius frowned, some of the lords laughed, and Lord Regan rolled his eyes. However, Byron, the older of the two demonstrators, stepped nimbly forward and caught the bottle.

Edyon muttered thanks to Byron and cautiously took the bottle back and held it up. "This strange purple smoke escaped from a demon as it died."

"It nearly escaped from you too, Your Highness," someone called out to more laughter.

"Indeed it did, though when smoke leaves a demon, it doesn't slip from its hands but exits the mouth in a long stream." Edyon tried to look serious. "This purple smoke comes from young demons. You perhaps know that the older demons release a red smoke that is used by some in Pitoria as an illegal pleasure drug—though I'm sure none here have ever tried it."

This remark was met by laughter too, though Edyon was relieved that now it seemed to be with him rather than directed against him. "This purple smoke has much more sinister uses. If it is inhaled by young people, adolescent boys or girls, it can give them great strength and speed. It also has the power to heal quickly, almost miraculously. It sounds like a wonderful drug. But in the wrong hands—in the hands of Aloysius—it could be used for war.

"But it's better if I demonstrate the power of the smoke, and then the implications will be clear. Sir Byron and Sir Ellis have volunteered to assist me by inhaling a small amount of the smoke and then showing you how their strength and speed are altered."

Edyon was satisfied to see that his audience was now watching intently. Byron let the cork out of the bottle for just a moment so that a wisp of purple smoke could escape. Some of the lords stepped closer to see as Byron and Ellis inhaled the smoke.

"I thought they were going to turn purple," someone called out.

"The smoke doesn't affect appearance, my lord, just ability—and it is already working on Byron and Ellis, as they will now demonstrate. First of all, Ellis will show you his running speed. He will chase down Byron, who will be on horseback."

In practice both of the young men had handled the drug well, without going giddy and light-headed—the effect the smoke had on Edyon. So Edyon was confident that this simple demonstration would go smoothly. Byron mounted and set off at a gallop. Edyon shouted, "Catch him, Ellis!" And Ellis set off. However, Ellis now seemed a little distracted by the lords. He ran past them all first, as if to show off his speed, before turning to chase after Byron, who was already half-way across the field. Soon they were both disappearing into the distance.

Lord Hunt shouted, "Are they off to Brigant to fight?"

It did almost seem that way, but Edyon replied, "Ellis is now catching Byron." Thankfully, Ellis seemed to find an even faster pace, caught up with Byron's horse, and leaped high to cling to Byron's back. However, by this stage they were at the far end of the field.

"It looked like Byron slowed the horse," someone commented. "Though it's hard to tell from here."

"I can't see a thing," another lord complained.

"He slowed the horse," said another. "But even so, it's faster than I could run."

"My lords, don't worry. We'll repeat the demonstration in this direction." Edyon tried to sound like it had all been planned this way. "You'll have a perfect view." And Edyon ran across the field, waving his arms to Byron, who thankfully rode over to him before Edyon had gone far, and quickly understood the problem, saying, "We'll do it right in front of them next time. Signal when you're ready."

Edyon ran back to his position.

Lord Regan asked, "Is all well, Prince Edyon?"

"Yes, fine. Thank you, Lord Regan."

But Edyon waited. And waited. And nothing happened.

*Shits, the signal.*

Edyon waved his arm and Byron set off, galloping toward the group. Ellis waited a moment before setting off at a dramatic pace. Horse, rider, and runner came hurtling toward the group of lords. Some were already stepping to the side as Ellis leaped up onto the horse's back and grappled Byron to the ground. Both young men fell to the earth as the horse ran through the marquee, knocking a table of drinks over and sending lords and servants scrambling.

"Well, we can't say we didn't see it that time," Lord Hunt commented.

"Exactly," Edyon replied, though he felt like screaming. Why did things always go wrong for him?

Edyon's father, however, came to the rescue with a serious question. "The boy has impressive speed. How long before it wears off?"

Edyon was relieved to reply in an equally serious manner. "Ellis could run at that pace all afternoon. He could repeat what he's just done a hundred times over. He's not even out of breath. And Byron is unhurt from his fall, as the smoke heals any cuts or bruises instantly. An army of boys on foot could outpace soldiers on horseback."

"Very good, Edyon." Thelonius nodded and clapped. Many of the lords joined in, though Edyon noticed that Lord Hunt and some others near him did not.

"We'll demonstrate the spear next," Edyon said.

"Will we need protection?" Lord Hunt asked.

"Step back, everyone," Lord Birtwistle joked.

Edyon smiled and ignored them. "I've chosen the spear to demonstrate how the smoke gives power without reducing accuracy. As you can see, there are targets painted on those gates. I don't think even the best spearman in the Calidorian army could get his spear to fly that distance, but Byron and Ellis will hit the bull's-eye."

Byron and Ellis picked up their weapons and launched their spears as Edyon muttered, "Please don't miss. Please don't kill anyone."

But the spears flew with perfect accuracy, landing so hard that they almost split the wood of the targets.

Some of the lords whistled and there were a few comments of "impressive" and "impossible."

"And just once more," Edyon said. "Though Ellis and Byron could do this with the same force and accuracy a hundred times, our gates would not stand it." And the throws were repeated with the same results.

Thelonius clapped again, and now most of the lords joined in.

"And how are they with a sword?" Lord Hunt asked.

"We're doing that next, Lord Hunt," Edyon replied. "Ellis and Byron will spar for you, showing their speed and agility."

"It would be more relevant to see how they'd fare against an ordinary soldier," Lord Hunt said.

"It would be too dangerous, I'm afraid," Edyon replied.

"Well, I'd like to think I'm not that ordinary a soldier, but I'll risk a bruise or two," Regan said, stepping forward and drawing his sword. "I want to feel the boys' strength.

Byron, come at me. Just don't kill me, and I'll do you the same courtesy. I've only just recovered from one stabbing."

Regan didn't mention that the stabbing had been at the hands of March and his compatriot, Holywell. He didn't have to.

"I'm delighted you're entering into the spirit of the demonstration, Lord Regan." Edyon looked over to Byron and nodded. "Lord Regan wants to feel your strength, Byron. Let him feel it."

*Please don't hold back. But please don't kill him either.*

Byron smiled. "I'll just disarm you, Lord Regan. I don't wish to—"

Regan slashed at him with his sword, hoping to catch him unawares, but Byron parried the attack, retaliating with a hard swing to Regan's raised sword, knocking it from his hands, and then somehow Byron was standing, dagger at Regan's throat, making a pretend slice across it. Byron held the position for a moment before moving back gracefully and bowing to Regan. It was all terribly quick but rather beautiful.

*Goodness me. Byron's someone to watch.*

Regan rubbed his hand, clearly in a little discomfort, though he was trying to hide it. The lords were clapping and laughing.

"Byron's strength is impressive, but his speed is amazing," Thelonius said. "Normally he wouldn't get close to you, Regan."

Edyon was delighted.

"And what's this about healing?" Lord Hunt asked. "Are we going to get to see that too?"

They hadn't rehearsed this, but it was important.

Edyon said, "Injuries heal faster when you've inhaled smoke, but the fastest way to heal is to apply smoke directly to the skin. Perhaps if I have a cut, Ellis can heal it." Edyon really didn't want to cut himself. But Byron had a dagger at the ready, and he stepped forward, already slicing the blade across the palm of his own hand, saying, "Your Highness, allow me."

*Byron really is rather heroic. And, yes, I most certainly will allow it.*

Byron was now holding out his hand, dripping blood, to show the audience. Ellis inhaled the smoke and bent his head to Byron's hand, while Edyon commentated: "It looks a little strange, but Ellis is holding the smoke in his mouth and putting his mouth over the wound. The smoke is in contact with Byron's broken skin. And Ellis will hold his position there for as long as he can and then, when he releases . . ." At that, Ellis lifted his head, blood on his lips and cheek, and Byron held his hand out. There was blood around the wound, but the cut itself was already healed and scarred over.

The lords murmured to one another and passed around the bottle, all wanting to feel its strange heat and weight.

"How much of this do the Brigantines have?" someone asked.

"I don't know exactly," Edyon replied. "But that's the smoke of just one demon and, as you can see, it can provide enough for many inhalations. There are many demons in the demon world. If Aloysius can capture and kill them all, he'd have enough smoke to fuel a huge boy army. They'd have the strength to take over the world."

"And he'll try, if I know my brother," Thelonius said. "He's a threat to us and to the Pitorians."

Edyon was so heartened by this response to the demonstration that he went one step further and added, "This is why King Tzsayn asked that Calidor join with Pitoria to work as one. Together we have a better chance of standing against the Brigantines."

"Together?" Lord Hunt asked. "With Pitorians?" He looked around at the other lords with an exaggerated expression of disgust on his face.

"Yes, together," Edyon said. "Working with others who are threatened by Aloysius."

"We don't need to work with them. We can defend ourselves."

"Not against an army fueled by smoke," Edyon replied.

Thelonius stepped to Edyon's side. "I fear my son is right. Against a conventional army, even the Brigantine army, I believe we can hold firm. We've done it before. But this demon smoke changes things."

"But, Your Highness, we've spent the last decade building our defenses." Hunt turned to Edyon. "The demon smoke gives strength and speed, but does it protect from fire?"

"Um . . . I don't think so. I've not actually tried that."

"We need to see it. That is a key part of our wall defense strategy."

"And that is what I will now demonstrate," Regan said, striding forward.

"But we didn't agree to this, Lord Regan," Edyon said.

Regan ignored him and addressed Thelonius and the lords. "It's all very well seeing Ellis and Byron run after horses, but I've set up an example of what invaders will have to overcome at our wall. This will be a truer test of the power of the smoke."

Regan led the group over to his soldiers, who were standing by two stone walls divided by a wide ditch. The ditch was full of broken wood that was being lit, and there must have been pitch or oil in with the wood, because the flames were soon leaping high. Edyon had heard much about the huge defense wall along the northern border of Calidor, which had been built since the last war. This appeared to be of the same design, and though not as big, it still looked formidable. Clearly Regan had spent some time putting this together, and clearly he had avoided telling Edyon anything about it.

"All Byron and Ellis have to do is cross from that side—Brigant—to this side—Calidor," Regan said.

"No," Edyon replied, looking at the flames. "It's too dangerous, and we shouldn't ask them to try."

"The walls here are far lower than those on the border and the ditch isn't as wide or deep, and you're already saying this is too formidable?" Regan scoffed. "Suddenly this all-powerful smoke is not so powerful."

Ellis, however, was eyeing the flames. "I can make it."

"No, you can't," Edyon said, moving to block Ellis's

path. "This is what happens: the smoke makes you feel invincible, but you're not."

Regan smiled. "Interesting. *Now* we're learning something useful."

"I can do it!" Ellis said, and he nimbly ran round Edyon and sprinted toward the wall.

"No! Ellis. Stop! I order it!" Edyon shouted after him. But it was too late. Ellis was already bouldering on to the first wall, from which he made a huge leap up and over the flames. Edyon held his breath as Ellis flew through the air. It seemed for a moment like he would make it the whole way across. He reached close to the far wall—but not close enough, and he came down into the ditch with a crash of splintering wood.

The flames rose around Ellis. He was up to his thighs in burning timber and yet somehow, thanks to the power of the demon smoke, he clambered out of the ditch, his clothes burning and his hair aflame. Byron ran to Ellis, patted him down, and helped him roll on the ground to put out the fire.

"He'll heal, I suppose," Regan said, looking down at him.

"Yes, but he'll still have scars," Edyon muttered. And to Ellis he said, "I'm sorry."

Ellis lay back, the wounds already healing as he said, "No, I'm sorry, Your Highness. I didn't listen to your order. I didn't even make the leap."

"I'd like to see Aloysius send his boy army across our wall!" Lord Hunt shouted over them, ignoring Ellis's plight. "I'd like to see them all burn."

A few other lords shouted their agreement.

Lord Regan spoke to the audience. "Prince Thelonius, my lords, I'm sure we're all grateful for this informative demonstration of the demon smoke by Prince Edyon. It's clear that the smoke gives strength and speed, but it doesn't protect from fire, and it also impairs judgment and discipline. We don't need to join forces with the Pitorians. We need to ensure our defenses remain strong."

"Indeed so, Lord Regan," Lord Hunt agreed. "We can beat it." And he began to clap. "Well done, Prince Edyon, for your enlightening demonstration."

*But that isn't what the demonstration was meant to show at all.*

# MARCH
## BRIGANT

MARCH AND Sam walked together, mostly in silence. When Sam did talk, he fantasized about the future, which was always wonderful, and March, when he did talk, mused about the present, which was far from wonderful. The most pressing issue was food and how to get more. The rabbit traps had yielded two rabbits. They'd eaten them and all the food March had stolen, but they were hardly growing fat.

They avoided the few villages they passed and both hid as soon as they saw a cart coming along the road. March suspected Sam hid because he had committed some crime, possibly hurt the owner of the clothes he was wearing, which he assumed was Sam's master. But March wasn't that interested in finding out, and Sam certainly wasn't going to volunteer the information. March hid because he wasn't sure how any locals would take to him, an Abask, as the territory of Abask was part of Calidor and thus the enemy. He expected the reaction of most Brigantines would be similar to that of the farmer he'd stolen from.

Another lesson March had learned from that farmer was how stones could be used for protection. As he walked, March picked up stones from the side of the road and threw them at randomly chosen targets, such as a tree trunk or a bush. Stones were the only weapon he had, but they were better than nothing and might protect him if they got into trouble.

Sam did make his presence known to fellow travelers twice to ask the way to Hornbridge, which was where he'd been told that the boy army was camped. After two days they eventually reached the outskirts of the village, but there was no sign of a boy army.

"If they were ever here, they're not anymore." March kicked at a cow pat.

"Should we ask someone?"

"Be my guest." March waved his arm toward the village.

Sam hesitated but then set off toward the houses. March hung back and hid in the trees, feeling like an outlaw but not sure why.

A short while later Sam was running back, a smile on his face. "They were here a week ago. Just a small number of them. Boys our age. Not a full army but definitely part of one."

March smiled too, though he suddenly felt nervous. He knew his plan to be a boy soldier, gain information, and help Edyon was absurd, but suddenly at least part of it was becoming more real.

"They went west into those hills," said Sam. "Come on. We'll be with them soon. I can feel it."

But they saw no sign of an army or a brigade or even one boy other than themselves. They finally stopped as it was getting dark and made a fire but had little to eat.

"When we find the army, at least we'll have food," Sam said, poking at the fire.

March nodded. "Food and fighting."

Sam frowned at March. "What's wrong with that? I want to fight for Brigant and Aloysius. It's my country; he's my king. Why do *you* want to fight for him?"

March had been thinking of this. He needed a good story, and he'd have to convince more people than Sam of his new allegiance. "I'm homeless, Sam. I've no family, no country. Nothing. But I hate the Calidorians more than any other people. I want to fight against them." He remembered that people said he sounded evil when he spoke Abask, so he added in his old language, "And I made a mistake and I must do what I can to remedy it, even if it's in vain, even if I die."

March looked toward Abask, the hills dark against the sky. He might have had a home in those hills, living a peaceful life, if it wasn't for King Aloysius and the men who fought for him. And if it hadn't been for Prince Thelonius and his betrayal. The two royal brothers hated each other, but together they had caused the death of March's whole family, his whole people. They had torn March's life completely from what it might have been. He'd never get that back. All he could do was take each day and try to do what was right. He'd do what he could to help Edyon. Edyon was the only loyalty he had now.

As he looked to the hills, March saw a faint spot of light.

He got to his feet, and as he watched, two more lights appeared. *Fires?*

Sam came to stand next to March. "Do you think it's them?"

"Dunno, but it's someone. And if we can see them, they can see us." March stomped on their own fire, putting it out. "We'll go over there when it's light. I don't think it's a good idea to wander into someone's camp in the dark."

Sam was grinning with excitement. "We could be joined up by this time tomorrow."

"Let's hope they want new recruits."

"Every army wants recruits."

*Let's hope they want me.*

As soon as it was light they set off. By midmorning they found the remains of the campfires they'd seen in the night, but all the boys—if it was the boys—had gone.

Sam walked around, peering at the ground. "I'm sure it's them. There were a lot of people here, and, look, they've left footprints going that way."

"Yes, funny how they've done that. And how they lit fires for us to see. Almost like they want us to find them."

But Sam was already following the trail. March hurried after him, scanning around all the time. Soon they entered a narrow, wooded valley that was still and silent. They continued alongside a stream, making slow but steady progress, until Sam stopped abruptly and pointed up to his left.

A boy was silhouetted against the skyline. He pointed his spear across the valley—and there was another figure, also holding a spear. They both gave quick, short, whooping shouts and ran down the valley sides. It was an impossibly dangerous and stupid thing to do. *They'll trip and break their necks*, March thought.

But that didn't happen. Instead the boy on the right leaped off a rock, turning in the air and hanging upside down, so it looked like he'd land on his head.

Sam gasped.

The figure flipped upright at the last moment, landing on his feet and speeding away, up the far side of the valley. The other boy leaped down, performing a cartwheel in the air, and then he too was running away. A moment later they had both vanished into the distance.

"Did you see that boy on the right? It was almost as if he was flying! I can't wait to do that."

"We're joining the army, not the circus, Sam."

"I know. I know, but still—they looked great." Sam set off after the boys. "I think they're showing us the way to go."

March looked behind and saw another boy high up on the valley side. He had a feeling there was no going back now. But almost immediately Sam came to another halt. "Shits. The trail leads up that cliff."

"We'll have to find another way." March looked around and was reminded of something. The silence and stillness— it was as if they were being watched. No, it wasn't *just* that they were being watched. It felt like when the sheriff's men had been following him and Edyon and Holywell. Just like when Holywell got killed with a spear. Nothing happened. Not a leaf moved, not a bird sang.

Nothing.

Perhaps March was just imagining it all.

But then he heard a bird.

No, not a bird—a flapping noise.

Sam yelped and grabbed March, pulling him to the side as a spear pierced the ground a pace away. Attached to the end of the spear was a piece of fabric. It had flapped as the spear flew and made the noise. On the material was the figure of a bull's head.

There was more flapping coming from March's left.

March pulled Sam back as another spear with a flag hit the ground where Sam had been standing.

Then another flapping noise from behind. Now Sam pushed March out of the way and a spear landed at Sam's feet.

They moved to the cliff. More spears were coming all the time. They were being forced up to the rock face.

"We have to go up. That's what they want us to do." March found a handhold in the cliff and began climbing. Sam followed. The handholds became harder to reach the higher March climbed. And he felt totally exposed. The boys might throw a spear into his back at any moment. His life was theirs to take if they wanted.

March cursed but continued on, his fingertips finally reaching the top of the cliff. His legs were shaking with the strain as he reached up, felt around, found a tiny hold, and, gripping it desperately, pulled himself up.

Standing ahead of him at the cliff top was a boy, no older than himself and as thin, though his bare arms were muscled and wiry. He wore a sleeveless leather jerkin with a red and black badge depicting a bull's head sewn over the heart. And attached to his leather belt was a leather-covered bottle, a cut in the leather revealing a sliver of purple glow. Most importantly the boy was holding a spear, which he now lowered so that its sharp tip was a finger's width from March's right eye.

"Silver eyes. Nice! Thought you Abasks were all dead or slaves."

"You thought wrong, then."

"Not the first time." And the boy lowered his spear and held his hand out. "Here, let me help you."

March ignored the hand, not trusting the boy at all, and pulled himself to standing.

"Lovely day for a bit of climbing. My name's Rashford, by the way."

"I'm March." He turned and looked over the cliff, adding, "That's Sam."

Rashford peered over the edge too. "Seems that Sam's struggling a bit."

March wasn't sure what to do. "You could help him."

"You mean catch him if he falls?" Rashford smiled and stepped back, raising his spear to March's chest again. "I'm not really the helping sort. What sort are you, March?"

"Generally pissed off. And really pissed off when people point spears at me."

"I can see that." Rashford pushed his spear toward March so that he had to step back to the edge of the cliff. "But I get pissed off too. Pissed off by people following us." And he jabbed the spear at March, who wobbled on the cliff edge. "Spying on us." He jabbed the spear again and March had to grab it to stop from falling.

"We're not spying. We heard about an army of boys. Me and Sam want to join up."

"An army of boys? Only boys? No lords? No men?"

"They're strong, fast, good at throwing spears." He waved down to the ground and saw that the spears had been picked up by many boys who stood below him. "Good at sneaking up on folks. Good at hiding their trail when they want to."

"I like the sound of them already." And Rashford moved back a little, giving March a bit more space. "But what is it *you're* good at, March? What can you offer this army of boys? Are you strong? Fast? Good with a spear?"

March shrugged. "I'm good at pouring wine."

Rashford laughed. "Not got much wine on me and I reckon if I did have, I could pour it myself."

"I poured wine for Prince Thelonius. I've traveled in Calidor and Pitoria. I know about the purple demon smoke. I know it makes you stronger and faster. And I know it heals too. I've been healed myself by it. I'm betting that's what's in that bottle you've got there."

Rashford raised his spear so the point was just in front of March's right eye again. "You certainly know plenty, March. Maybe a bit too much for your own good. And I wouldn't go bragging about Prince Thelonius. You're in Brigant. Thelonius is the enemy, you know."

"And I'm Abask. Everyone's victim, everyone's slave. But Abasks aren't victims or slaves at heart—we're fighters.

I won't be made a victim or slave to anyone anymore, but I will fight."

Rashford smiled. "Now that's what I call attitude. Course, if you want to join us, you're going to have to prove yourself. We're gonna have to see some fighting spirit for real." Rashford backed off, adding, "Why don't you give your friend a hand up? You shouldn't leave him dangling there."

Just then, Sam's fingers reached the top of the cliff, and March grabbed his wrists, pulling him the rest of the way. When March turned back to Rashford, he saw that the other boys had joined him. They were wearing leather jerkins with red and black bull's head badges, all holding spears with flags, some with short swords and knives strapped around their waists. Some seemed to have red and black war paint on their faces, some grinned, some scowled; all were skinny, none looked old enough to shave.

"Come forward, March. Don't be shy!" Rashford shouted.

One other boy called out, "Don't look so scared. We won't hurt you—much." There was laughter, jeering, and some wolf whistles as the boys closed in around them—there was no escape, though really, with the speed of these boys, there was never going to be a chance of escape. March and Sam were now surrounded by a ring of boys—perhaps a hundred of them.

Rashford stepped forward. "As leader of the Bulls, the best and most honorable of the boys' brigades, I invite you to demonstrate your fighting skills to see if you're worthy of joining us."

Sam nodded and smiled. "Yeah, sure. How?"

Rashford smiled back. "By beating the shit out of each other, of course!"

The boys around them had started up a chant. "Fight. Fight. Fight."

Sam turned to March. "They're serious. You up for it?"

"I don't think we've got any choice. Just don't use your knife. We stick to fists."

"Definitely. I'll try not to hurt you too much," Sam replied, and backed away, getting in a rather absurd stance with his fists stiffly raised.

"You serious?" March asked.

Rashford, who was walking around the inside of the circle of boys, yelled, "Come on, March. My money's on you."

March raised his guard and moved forward. He was older and taller than Sam. He'd win this easy.

Sam grinned at him, rolled his head, and beckoned March forward.

*Cocky little shit!*

March drew his fist back and sent a hard punch to Sam's jaw. But Sam dodged his head to the side. March punched again—Sam moved and punched March in the stomach, and he doubled over in pain.

The boys were cheering louder. Rashford was shouting, "March! You'd better not let me down here."

Sam sent a punch to March's jaw. March staggered back. The boys were shouting louder. March put his guard farther up, but another punch hit his ear. And then another to his stomach bent him over. Sam danced back and March could just see his feet moving around. Somehow Sam knew how to fight and March had nothing to offer in return. He had to show his toughness, though. He straightened up and ran at Sam, who dodged out of the way. March tried again and the same thing happened. Rashford came to him and turned him round to face Sam, shouting, "Don't make a fool of me as well as yourself, March." Then quietly added, "Get him this time. On the nose."

And this time, two boys had hold of Sam and pushed him to March as Rashford pushed March to Sam. March just raised his fist, and it was more like Sam's face hitting his fist rather than the other way round. But the result was the same—blood exploded from Sam's nose. Sam staggered to the side, grabbing his face, and March leaped at him, knocking him to the ground and kicking him in the back.

Sam rolled over and tried to get away, but March fell on him, pinning his arms down with his legs and punching his face again and again. Eventually Rashford shouted, "Enough, March. Enough." And he was dragged off Sam, who rolled over and tried to get up, but then collapsed again.

Rashford ignored this and said, "We can see that both these boys are fighters. They can join us. There's just one thing left to do."

And faster than March could think about these words, Rashford's fist hit him and pain filled his head, blood filled his mouth, and the sounds of the boys' laughing and cheering faded as he let darkness fold around him.

# TASH
## DEMON TUNNELS

FIRST COMES a vision. Shades of red are wrapping you up, soothing your muscles, and warming your bones. It makes you feel wanted, makes you feel strong. And it makes you want to go back. You want to reach out as you tumble through it, through the red smoke. You are returning.

Returning where?

You open your eyes. There is no red. There is only black.

Black envelops everything, blacker than the blackest night. But this is not night, not day, not anything.

And it's cold. Stone, stone cold.

And silent. Not a sound.

Except . . . except for this sound, this voice in your head.

But do you even have a head?

Do you have a body?

Can you feel anything?

Are you alive?

How do you know what you are when there is nothing to see or hear or feel?

Perhaps this darkness, this coldness, this silence is death.

*It's certainly shitting bad enough.*

# CATHERINE
## NORTHERN PITORIA

*Money is as vital as swords in any war.*
War: The Art of Winning, *M. Tatcher*

THE SIDES of Catherine's tent were drawn back so that she could make use of the early morning sunshine as she sat at her desk. She could also look out over the camp, which had been moved to open, green meadows uphill from the old one. It lay between two streams, which provided clean water but no risk of flooding. Davyon had selected the location and organized the move, ensuring the prince was disturbed as little as possible and keeping Catherine informed of progress. At least that had gone well.

Catherine dragged her gaze from the view and back to her desk, which was covered with papers. She picked up the first and glanced through it—a bill for provisions. And underneath—another bill, more provisions. And another under that. Running a war wasn't only about fighting and tactics; it depended on food to ensure all the men were well fed, and that depended on money.

And then there was the issue of the men's health—so far the Pitorian army had lost more men to disease than to fighting. The red fever had spread through the camp quickly, killing several hundred. But the move had been the right decision. The new camp was cleaner and better organized, with animals and latrines away from the sleeping quarters. There were fewer new cases of fever reported every day. But no sooner was that problem dealt with than Catherine had to move on to the next one, and the next . . .

This was her job now—to take each problem, deal with it as well as she could, and then move on to the next. Logically, she knew that if she could just keep going, then—step by step—she'd get there. But the steps seemed never-ending and the problems needed solving two or three—or twenty—at a time. Catherine's mind was overloaded. She needed help to think straight. She looked over to her maid.

"I'm going to give you a new job title, Tanya."

"Lady Tanya of Tornia?" was the reply, said with a smile as she gave an elaborate curtsy.

Catherine smiled but shook her head. "No. I said *job* title."

"Chief dogsbody? Head dogsbody?"

"You are the chief of my maids. In fact, you are much, much more than just a maid and you are definitely not a dogs-body. I want you to do what you've always done for me, only under a different title."

"So what title will I receive?"

"Dresser."

"Hairdresser? A vital role in a country so obsessed with hair as this one."

Catherine smiled again. "No, Tanya, your new title is not

hairdresser. I said *dresser*. The same title as General Davyon."

"Oh, I see. Thank you." Tanya nodded thoughtfully, then added, "Sounds like I'll get a pay raise."

"Why does everything come back to money?" Catherine snapped. "Do you want to take my last kopek too?" She felt tears of frustration fill her eyes. She wanted to knock the whole pile of papers on the floor and just walk out.

Tanya stepped closer. "I apologize, Your Majesty."

"No, I apologize. I'm tired. But I shouldn't take it out on you." She'd been sitting with the king most of the night, but Tanya had hardly slept either.

"I'm honored that you've given me any thought at all," Tanya continued. "And I'm honored to have a new job title. And dresser is a good one. If I can be thought of anywhere near as highly as Davyon, I'll be doing well."

"The point is that I already think of you as highly as him, and I want everyone to do the same. We have been through so much together, Tanya. I want the world to know how much I value you."

"So, I'm your adviser?"

"Indeed."

"On anything in particular?"

Catherine sighed and rolled her shoulders. Where to begin? "War . . . money . . . marriage . . . love."

"The little things."

Catherine laughed and kissed Tanya on the cheek. "Yes. But first it must be war. Come. I'm due at the war council."

Catherine had been absent from the daily meetings the

last few mornings as she'd been at Tzsayn's bedside, but she was determined not to miss another.

Ffyn, Davyon, and Hanov, the most senior of Tzsayn's generals, led the war council. As Catherine arrived, General Ffyn, newly promoted to replace Lord Farrow as leader of the Pitorian army, beamed at her across the map table.

"Good news, Your Majesty. A delegation from Calidor arrived this morning. They will be joining us shortly."

"At last!"

It had been a month since Edyon had set sail for Calidor with Catherine's warning about the threat posed by the boy army and her request for an alliance against her father, and the silence since had been so deafening she had begun to fear that the message had got lost.

"Perhaps you can update me on the general situation while we wait for them to arrive?"

"There's no change, Your Majesty. The Brigantines are holding their positions around Rossarb and on the Northern Plateau."

He pointed at the locations on the map, almost as if he didn't expect Catherine to know where they were.

"But under there is where most of the action is," Tanya said, gesturing to the Northern Plateau. "In the demon world, I mean."

Ffyn looked at Tanya and then to Catherine with raised eyebrows. Tanya was not officially on the war council.

As matter-of-factly as she could, Catherine said, "I've promoted Tanya to position of dresser. I welcome her views on all matters."

The general cleared his throat. "Of course. Whatever you think best, Your Majesty."

"And Tanya's right," said Catherine. "My father is consolidating his position on the plateau and busily farming the demon smoke. He has exactly what he wants—a secure supply of smoke and time to train his boy army. When that's ready, we won't stand a chance."

"I like to believe we'd put up a little more resistance than you seem to expect, Your Majesty," General Ffyn replied stiffly.

"You've seen how the smoke works, General. We all know an army fueled by demon smoke is unbeatable, even if it's an army of boys. There's no shame in admitting it. The shame would be in not having a plan to deal with it."

Ffyn shook his head. "Our numbers may be down due to this damned fever, but we are over that now. We have a good position on high ground. I believe we can hold this line if the regular Brigantine army attacks."

"However, one of my men returned from Brigant last night," General Hanov, who controlled the spy network, interjected. "He reports sightings of boys' brigades—"

"The boy army?"

"Not exactly, Your Majesty. The brigades are small units—there's at least ten of them, with a hundred boys in each. These boys are brutal, strong, and fast . . . and improving their fighting skills all the time."

"And where are these brigades?"

"At least three are with Aloysius near Rossarb."

"And the rest?"

"We think they're near the border with Calidor."

Catherine looked up from the map. "Calidor? Do you think they're preparing to invade?"

Hanov shook his head. "That's just a few hundred boys. All of Aloysius's best troops are still at Rossarb. There are no signs of them moving south."

"Even if the boy army were to go in first, Aloysius can't take Calidor without support from his regular army, Your Majesty," Ffyn explained. "He needs boots on the ground to occupy the country once the fighting is over. I still see nothing to indicate an imminent attack against either ourselves or Calidor."

"I agree with you, Ffyn," Davyon said. "Except there's the matter of the Pitorian Sea."

"The sea?" asked Catherine.

"The Brigantines may not be confronting us or the Calidorians on land, but they are attacking our ships," he said. "We've had to bring most of our fleet into port. The Brigantine ships are bigger and faster than ours and now have almost total control of the waters between us and Calidor."

Catherine inwardly cursed the meetings she'd missed. She'd been busy with Tzsayn and the finances, but her father was never still. What was his grand plan? She looked at the map again. "If the Brigantines are free to move anywhere around the Pitorian Sea, they could invade at any point along our coast! We must regain control."

Ffyn looked irritated. "Yes, but how? We can't take control of the sea if we don't have the ships."

"So we must get ships—better, faster ships," Catherine

said, but even as she spoke her heart sank. It was all very well shouting at her generals about it, but where could they get them from? How long would it take to build them? How much would they cost to build?

"The Calidorians have a strong fleet," Hanov said thoughtfully. "They've built it up since the last war to defend themselves against Aloysius."

"Then we must ask the Calidorian delegation to loan us some ships to protect our coast and patrol the Pitorian Sea. It's a solution that will benefit us both." *Could it really be that simple?*

"You're right, Your Majesty," Davyon said. "And we must protect our coast as you say. But smoke is the key to this war. That is what Aloysius needs for his ultimate victory. It's why his forces are concentrated in the north, which is his greatest strength but also his greatest weakness."

Catherine smiled. "A weakness! You're giving me hope, Davyon. Explain."

"It's a question of logistics, Your Majesty. Aloysius's army is a long way from home. Some of his supplies can come along the northern coast road between Brigant and Pitoria, but the army is too big to be supplied exclusively by land, so most comes by sea. That's fine in the summer, but it'll be different when the winter storms begin."

"But winter is months away," objected Ffyn. "And meanwhile the Brigantines have superiority on the water and are strengthening the land route all the time."

Catherine nodded. "But with naval support from Calidor we'd have a chance to disrupt their shipping and maybe even attack the northern coast road, cutting their overland supply lines."

"Leaving Aloysius trapped in Rossarb and starving," Davyon finished.

Catherine smiled. "Draw up plans."

Davyon bowed. "Your Majesty."

"In the meantime," Catherine continued, "how can we stop the farming of the smoke? You're right, Davyon, that the smoke is the key to everything. I feel that we have some knowledge of the demon world and we're not making use of it."

"I do have one suggestion, Your Majesty," said Davyon slowly. "We could send a special unit behind enemy lines to disrupt things. A small group of select men who can travel fast and strike hard. It would be a dangerous mission, but it would cause the Brigantines some headaches."

Catherine nodded, her thoughts already going to Ambrose. He'd be the perfect leader for such a mission, and sending him away would have the added advantage of quashing rumors that still swirled around the camp about the nature of the relationship between the queen and her bodyguard. But, because of those rumors, Catherine didn't even dare suggest his name to Tzsayn's closest aide.

"Find a way of doing it, Davyon. Without smoke, the boy army is just a bunch of boys."

An aide stepped into the tent with a formal bow.

"Your Majesty, may I present the Calidorian delegation?"

Catherine came out from behind the map table and

smoothed her skirts. This was a historic moment: the start of an alliance between Pitoria and Calidor. She had to look like a queen.

"Lord Darby and Master Albert Aves."

The aide stood aside, and two old men entered and bowed. Catherine nodded graciously, waiting for the aide to announce the rest of the delegation.

The silence stretched.

Finally, after what seemed like an age, Catherine realized that this was it: Lord Darby, an old, frail man with a cloud of snow-white hair, and his assistant, who wasn't much younger. It was hardly a delegation meant to impress.

"Lord Darby," she said hastily. "Welcome to Pitoria."

"We are honored to meet you, Your Majesty." Lord Darby bowed again stiffly. "But I was expecting to have an audience with King Tzsayn."

Catherine's jaw tightened. Of course he was. "Alas, the king is indisposed today, but whatever message you have for my husband you may tell me and have confidence that I will share it with him."

Lord Darby looked a little uncertain. "Perhaps the king will be available tomorrow?"

"I fear not. But I am available now, Lord Darby. I am queen and have equal status to my husband."

Lord Darby's assistant muttered in his master's ear. Darby nodded and pulled a smile across his face.

"My apologies. I was instructed to present my message to the king, but of course if that's not possible . . ." He took a scroll from an inner pocket and held it out to Catherine. "A message for Your Majesties from Prince Thelonius of Calidor."

Catherine accepted the heavy scroll with a smile. She carefully broke the seal of green wax, conscious that all eyes were on her. This scroll would contain Thelonius's offer to join forces with Pitoria against Brigant and turn the tide of the war. It was a significant moment, and she read aloud so all those present could hear:

"His Royal Highness Prince Thelonius of Calidor sends his greetings and thanks to King Tzsayn and Queen Catherine of Pitoria for their gracious assistance to his son, Prince Edyon, Prince of Abask. Prince Edyon is to be formally invested in Calia as heir to the throne of Calidor, and King Tzsayn and Queen Catherine are invited to attend the ceremony and the celebrations that will follow as special guests of honor."

*We've asked for a military alliance and they're inviting us to a party?* Catherine took a breath. *Surely there will be more about the war. Thelonius is merely beginning with his thanks.*

"Prince Edyon has demonstrated to us the power of the purple demon smoke and we thank our Pitorian friends for providing us with an example of this strange substance."

*Good. More thanks, but good.*

"We also thank you for your warning about the imminent threat from the forces of King Aloysius of Brigant. In Calidor we are constantly aware of our northern neighbor and the threat he poses to our freedom and security. We have prepared our defenses well and will continue to hold firm against him should he attack our borders. Lord Darby has many years of experience fighting the Brigantines, and we are sending him to you as our special emissary to provide advice on how you might deal with our common enemy. I again send you my most grateful thanks, Prince Thelonius of Calidor."

*Special emissary? Advice? And more thanks than I can shake a stick at! Is that all he's offering?*

Catherine let the scroll roll up as she turned her attention back to the men in front of her.

"How many men have you brought with you, Lord Darby?"

Darby looked confused. "Just Albert here. He sees to all my needs, and Prince Thelonius felt we would travel faster without a full military escort."

Catherine swallowed a sudden burst of anger. This was the Calidorian effort—two old men and a letter of hollow thanks, when she needed men and ships and an offer of alliance. What was Thelonius playing at? Edyon had demonstrated the power of the smoke—the letter said as much. How could Thelonius not see the threat? This response was either madness or an insult.

"Well, if you have been sent to provide advice, perhaps you could advise us on the question of ships. We have urgent need of naval support and—"

Lord Darby cleared his throat softly. "Forgive me, Your Majesty, but it has been a very long journey, and I am not as young as your dashing generals. Might we discuss this to-morrow?"

"The war will not wait until tomorrow, Lord Darby."

"No, of course not, Your Majesty. But perhaps I'll be more able to assist then."

Catherine was in serious danger of saying something un-diplomatic. With a supreme effort, she forced herself to smile again.

"Of course. Someone will show you to your quarters."

Darby bowed as he left the tent, leaving Catherine to wonder whether any assistance would be coming at all.

# AMBROSE

"IT LOOKS good," Geratan said, ruffling Ambrose's hair, which had been dyed brilliant white and cut short at the back but left long at the top—the same as Geratan's. Only Ambrose's wasn't quite long enough to stay tucked behind his ears, so it kept flopping into his face.

"It would've been easier to get a hat."

"But this shows your loyalty." Geratan twirled his wooden practice sword and then pointed it at Ambrose. "Very important if you've got Brigantine blood in you." Geratan continued swishing his sword around. "There are more white-hairs each day. More blue too. Everyone's keen to show their loyalty to Tzsayn and Catherine. There's a lot of enthusiasm for them as a couple."

"This week, yes, but it ebbs and flows."

Ambrose couldn't forget how Catherine had arrived in Pitoria on a wave of enthusiasm, only to have to flee the capital in fear of her life after Aloysius's invasion.

"For Tzsayn it's constant. In fact, since his father died, it's grown even more."

Ambrose knew that was true. And he only ever heard good things about Tzsayn. The new king had led his troops bravely in defense of Rossarb, choosing capture rather than fleeing and leaving his men behind. "Yes, everyone loves Tzsayn."

Geratan peered at Ambrose. "Everyone?"

Ambrose ignored the question. "As much as I'd love to continue this conversation, we're here to practice." With that, he swung his wooden sword at Geratan, who knocked it forcefully back.

"So you're not going to be gentle with me?" Ambrose asked. "I'm only just out of my sickbed. My shoulder's stiff and I can hardly walk."

"You can limp well enough." Geratan darted forward, aiming a cut at Ambrose's thigh, but Ambrose parried automatically. Geratan nodded. "And it seems your instincts aren't too bad."

"This toy sword is useless, nothing like the real thing. A stick would be better." Ambrose swung the wooden sword left and right, feeling the balance of it—and his own rustiness.

"Stop whinging and put a bit of effort in."

Geratan thrust forward at Ambrose's other leg, but again was countered by Ambrose, who replied, "Careful what you wish for, Geratan," as he slipped under his opponent's guard and slapped him hard on the left thigh. "Or you'll find yourself beaten by a cripple."

"Or talked to death," Geratan replied, attacking again.

Ambrose defended himself with ease. "But I want to talk. You've still not told me what you discovered up north."

Geratan had returned that morning from a scouting expedition on the Northern Plateau to assess the Brigantine positions.

"Any sign of Tash?" asked Ambrose, though he knew if there had been, Geratan would have said. There had been no word from her since she had chosen to go back into the demon world to discover more about that strange, underground realm. Perhaps there never would be.

"No. Just a few Brigantines and a lot of midges."

As he spoke, Geratan left himself open and Ambrose counterattacked, driving Geratan quickly back and knocking his sword out of his hand on the third strike. Ambrose struggled to hide his glee, but forced a frown as he rotated his shoulder, muttering louder, "Yes, I'm still very rusty."

Geratan growled, "Again. I won't be so easy on you this time."

Ambrose grinned. "Ah, you let your guard down on purpose. I see that now. It was a kindness to an injured man."

"You don't seem to have lost your technique, Sir Ambrose," Davyon called as he approached them. "How's the leg?"

"I'm limping faster every day."

"You're planning on rejoining the war? Or is this swordplay merely for fun?"

"I'm a soldier, Davyon. As soon as I'm well, I'll return to my position as Catherine's personal guard."

*If she ever wants to see me again, that is.*

Davyon nodded. "A vital role, of course, but we have other plans for you. If you're fit and able."

"Other plans. Far from Catherine, I'll wager. That would suit you and Tzsayn just perfectly, wouldn't it, Davyon?"

Davyon smiled but his gaze was cool. "Actually, this plan comes from the queen, Sir Ambrose. Come with me and I'll explain."

Davyon led Ambrose into a large marquee. Inside were two tables covered with maps. On one, the positions of various troops were marked by stone figures like tiny chess pieces, with flags to denote their nationality. On the other table were more detailed maps of the Northern Plateau and the area around Rossarb. Ambrose quickly took in the positions of the Pitorians and Brigantines. "I don't see any Calidorian forces anywhere. I would have expected them to have started arriving by now."

Davyon gave a strained smile. "Actually, a delegation from Calidor arrived yesterday."

"And?"

"They are standing side by side with us in heart and in spirit."

Ambrose couldn't help but give a short laugh. "In heart and spirit but not in body, you mean."

"That's pretty much it."

"So they've sent no men?"

"Two graybeards who have done nothing but eat and sleep since they arrived. Mostly sleep. However, it's not men we need from Calidor at the moment but some of their ships.

The ground war is currently static, but we need to regain control of two locations: the Pitorian Sea—hence the need for ships—and the demon world—hence the need for you."

"Ah, I get the easy option!"

"Yes, the mission is going to be challenging, even for you."

*Challenging or impossible?*

"What's the objective?" Ambrose asked.

"To stop, or at least disrupt, the supply of smoke."

Ambrose frowned. "But don't the Brigantines already have all they need? When Geratan told us they were farming the smoke, he said they were getting two bottles a day. They've occupied the Northern Plateau for more than a month now. That's plenty of smoke to keep their boy army going."

"Actually, we don't think it is. There are a thousand boys in their army. They need smoke to train with and to use for the real battles to come. We don't believe they've got enough yet."

Ambrose nodded. "So, what's your plan?"

"You and a team go up to the plateau and into the demon world through a demon hollow. Geratan's group have found one they think you can use. Once inside, you find a way to disrupt the production of smoke."

"That's a little thin on detail, if you don't mind me saying."

"None of us knows exactly what's happening in there. You'll have to react to the situation you find. You'll have the best men and equipment—whatever you need. And Geratan, of course. You've both been in that world. You know what it's like. Get back in there and do whatever you have to do stop the Brigantines from getting the smoke out—destroy any stockpiles, kill the soldiers, take control of access to the demon world if possible."

"Oh, is that all?" Ambrose muttered.

The plan was stupidly dangerous and almost certain to fail, and yet Ambrose was already calculating how many men would be needed. A small force might be better in the demon world, where communication was so difficult. But how many Brigantines would they be facing? And, just as importantly, how many demons . . . ?

"How soon do you want us to go?"

"Yesterday."

# CATHERINE
## NORTHERN PITORIA

*Love, passion, desire—they'd all be terribly straightforward if people weren't so terribly complex.*

Queen Valeria of Illast

"OF COURSE we wish to cooperate with you, Your Majesty." Lord Darby nodded and smiled. Albert, his assistant, nodded and smiled as well. "And now that I have a thorough understanding of the various strengths and weaknesses of the forces, I feel I can give you my advice."

Catherine had to bite her lip. "I'm most grateful for your advice, of course, Lord Darby, but what I need most is ships."

"Ah, the ships."

"Indeed. The ships. To protect our coastline."

"Yes, indeed. And the very same ships that Calidor needs to protect her own coastline."

"If you help us now, we could help you in future."

"But we may not have a future if we make ourselves vulnerable by moving our ships from their defensive positions."

"So not even one can be spared?"

"Each ship is doing a vital job for Calidor."

"Really? So how many ships do you have? Where exactly are they all along your coast? What, precisely, are they all needed for?"

Darby looked to Albert, who replied, "We'll have to look into it."

"*How?*" Catherine exclaimed, her patience finally exhausted. "How *exactly* will you look into it?"

Albert paled. "I'll . . . I'll send a request for information to Calia, Your Majesty."

"Well, let's hope it gets across the sea safely—if only we had the ships to protect the message!"

Catherine swept out of the tent, muttering to Tanya as she went: "Another delay, another evasion. What we need are the ships."

"I spoke to Albert earlier."

Catherine turned to her. "You did?"

"He's as frustrated as we are. He says that Thelonius wants to help, Lord Darby too, but many Calidorian lords fear us as much as Aloysius."

"Fear *us?*"

"Well, fear that an alliance will mean a loss of independence. Pitoria is so much larger than Calidor—they think we'll take them over."

Back in Catherine's tent, Tanya plopped into her chair and almost instantly fell asleep—Catherine wasn't the only one working long hours. But Catherine couldn't afford to rest. There were more papers to go through, more money to be found, and surely there was an answer somewhere to the ship problem . . .

Catherine paced around her tent, passing the chest that contained her bottle of purple demon smoke. A small breath of smoke would do her a world of good—relax her and give her energy for the afternoon. Looking across at Tanya, who was snoring lightly, Catherine carefully lifted the lid of the chest and took out the bottle, warm and heavy in her hand. She let a wisp of purple smoke slide up and out of the bottle, and inhaled it deeply, waiting for a hit of energy.

Nothing happened.

Catherine blinked. She felt a little lightheaded but nothing more.

She mustn't have taken enough. She took another, larger breath. Now she felt the warmth of the smoke fill her nostrils, her throat, and her lungs. Her head swam and she felt slightly dizzy, but she had no spike of energy, no feeling of strength or power.

She sat on the bed. She could weep. Even the smoke wasn't working now.

But why? Only a few weeks ago it had given her strength enough to fight a man twice her size. She knew that the smoke didn't work on adults, but she was still seventeen. A girl in many ways, though with the responsibilities of a woman—of a queen. Catherine lay back and stared up at the canopy above her. She couldn't be too old for the smoke. She needed it. It was her protection. It had saved her life, more than once. Without it, what was she?

She felt heavy sleep crowding in on her.

Catherine dreamed she was in a small boat on a flooded river, bailing out water while everyone else in the boat slept on. A man with bright green hair told her it would cost a thousand kroner to fix the boat, and she bent down and tried to fill the cracks in the boards with paper bills, but it was all too much and she was sinking, sinking . . .

Catherine jerked awake. She was unsure if she'd slept a few moments or the whole afternoon. Her mouth was dry and she was desperately hungry. Tanya was no longer in her chair and Catherine got up to look for her. As she left the royal tent, a familiar figure caught her eye and stopped her in her tracks.

Standing in the flap of the marquee where the war meetings were held was Ambrose. Catherine was not supposed to meet him, except on official business—she'd agreed to this with Tzsayn.

*He's commanding a mission to the demon world. Which is quite official.*

And she wanted to see him.

*I'm queen. I should be able to do some things that I like.*

Ambrose withdrew into the marquee.

*He's expecting me to follow. How long has he waited there?*

She remembered the excitement, the yearning she used to have to glimpse his hair in the distance; the beauty of his hands as he held them out to lift her on to her saddle; riding along the beach at Brigane, the sun on her back, leaping into the water and swimming in the cool sea, the water pressing at her body, pulling at her clothes.

She felt none of that excitement now, and none of the intense passion they'd had in Donnafon. Instead she felt nervous. That fearful nervousness she used to have in Brigant. The fear of being found out.

*Well, I'm not doing anything wrong. I'm just going to talk to him.*

She entered the tent. Ambrose stood by the maps, as if looking at them.

*He's still so handsome.*

And now he came toward her. He had a slight limp.

*He even makes a limp look good!*

Ambrose bowed and kept a short distance between them. "Your Majesty. I was just reminding myself of some of the plans."

*But he's a terrible liar.*

"How long have you been reminding yourself of them?"

"Most of the afternoon. And I've been keeping watch for you, hoping to see you. In fact, I've been hoping to see you for weeks. Since the battle of Hawks Field."

Catherine nodded. "I'm sorry I couldn't visit you when you were injured. I agreed with Tzsayn that I'd only see you in formal situations. My reputation . . ." Catherine blushed, unsure what else to say, and glanced to the tent entrance.

"This is more formal than when we were in Donnafon."

"Most things are more formal than when we were in Donnafon." Catherine's mind flew back to her rooms there, all the times they had contrived to be alone together, the kisses they'd exchanged and the embraces that she couldn't get enough of. "But things have changed since then, Ambrose," she said firmly, though she was still drawn to

Ambrose—there was something about his physical presence that pulled her to him. And she stepped closer to him now.

"What's changed? How so?"

The world had changed, but seeing him here, Catherine still felt a connection to Ambrose. He was her guard and her love. He had risked his life for her many times and would be risking it again. But she couldn't put that into words, and instead she found herself saying, "Thank you for agreeing to lead the mission into the demon world."

"It's an honor." He stepped closer to her. "But I asked how things have changed. Have you changed?"

*Yes. No.* Catherine was suddenly not so certain. "I'm older."

"And wiser? Is that what you mean?"

"No. I'm . . . I'm not sure what I mean. I didn't expect to see you today. I'm not sure what to say."

"Do you have to rehearse everything? Can't you just speak from your heart? Tell me something of what's going on in it? I've been thinking of you every day but I've not spoken with you since before the battle."

"That seems a long, long time ago."

"It *was* a long time ago, but I always thought of you."

"You've gained a limp."

"Yes."

"Had a haircut."

"Everyone comments on the hair."

"That's Pitoria for you."

"But I've not changed inside . . . have you?"

"I . . ." Catherine knew she had changed and her circumstances had definitely changed, but what about her feelings toward Ambrose?

He took another step closer. "My feelings are the same, Catherine. I love you still. May I?"

And he bent and kissed her hand. His lips were soft and gentle on her skin, his breath warm, and the physical pull to him was wonderful . . .

Catherine leaned toward him and murmured, "Sir Ambrose . . ."

"Sir Ambrose!" Tanya hissed.

Catherine jumped back, pulling her hand free as if burned.

"Tanya," said Ambrose, standing upright. "Good afternoon."

Tanya put her hands on her hips and looked from Ambrose to Catherine. "Discussing the mission, were you?"

"Actually, yes," Ambrose replied. "Communication without words is something we need in the demon world."

And he came to Catherine and lifted her hand again, pressing his lips hard against her skin, letting her feel his breath. Then he raised his head, slid his hand from hers, and walked out of the tent.

Catherine watched him leave.

What would they be doing now if Tanya hadn't appeared? How could something be wrong when it felt so wonderful?

# TASH
## DEMON TUNNELS

YOU'RE ALIVE—POSSIBLY. Maybe you're dead, though. All you know is that it's black, silent, and stone-cold.

The black is the darkest black. There's stone all around, except you can't see it. It's the same whether your eyes are open or shut—black.

The silence is total.

Shut-in-a-box-and-left-alone silence.

But inside . . .

*It's shitting noisy in my head. Shitting, shitting, scary noisy. And I can hear my own breathing, which has to mean I'm still alive, doesn't it, but this is no way to be living and the voice in my head is so loud at times—LIKE NOW—that I think I'm going MAD, MAD, MAD, or dreaming it all and I'll wake up, but I don't ever wake up, and maybe this is just the start of madness and maybe madness is better than death. And that's when I know for sure that I'm not mad or dead, I'm shitting trapped in stone and really, really, really shitting cold. No one should be this cold. Cold to the bone.*

*Though I've been colder.*

*There was that storm when me and Gravell were stuck for three days in a snow hole with just Gravell's farts to keep us warm. It certainly wasn't silent then, with him letting off.*

Tash tried to laugh, but tears ran down her face and she sobbed.

*Black, silent, cold, AND alone.*

*I'm not afraid of dying or even going mad, but I don't want it to hurt and I want someone with me to hold my hand and I hate this. I want Gravell and his stinking farts so, so badly.*

The demons had left her here and let the stone walls creep in on her, trapping her in this tiny space about the size of a coffin.

*Why did they do this to me?*

The walls had crept toward her but they'd long since stopped moving in. Tash had no idea why. She wasn't sure if the demons wanted her to die or just to imprison her. She clung to a hope that they hadn't allowed her to die—so perhaps this was a punishment.

*And maybe they know I'm really, really sorry and I really, really don't ever want to hurt a demon ever again. And if they know that, then maybe they'll let me out.*

*They've got to let me out soon.*

*Haven't they?*

# AMBROSE
## ARMY CAMP, NORTHERN PITORIA

IT HAD taken a few days but, with Geratan's help, Ambrose had chosen fifty men for his mission and they were standing before him now, all fit and healthy, a mix of white-hairs and blue-hairs.

"Congratulations on being selected to join my brigade, men. I've seen each of you fight and had the pleasure of facing a few of you on the practice ground." Ambrose had done this partly to test the men but also to show them his own skills; the men needed to believe in him, and needed to believe their leader could fight despite his limp.

"We have a special mission. The Brigantines are collecting purple demon smoke. Our task is to stop them. To do that, we will have to go into the demon world. It's a strange and dangerous place, but I have been there and come back safely, and I'm going to bring you all back too."

The faces of the men showed no fear. In fact, most were grinning and one called out, "Let us at 'em!"

"The demon world itself is not to be feared, but it is not a world like this one. There, sounds are different—words are like clanging cymbals, a footstep sounds like a bell. So we must be silent. Our clothes, our boots, our equipment must make no noise."

"What do farts sound like, sir?" Anlax asked—a typical Anlax question. There was some sniggering and comments about the smell being of more concern than the noise.

"Actually, you've raised a good point, Anlax," Ambrose said. "In the demon world you don't need to eat. So you won't be scoffing beans for breakfast, lunch, and dinner, and thus, hopefully, we'll never discover the answer to your question."

"We really don't eat anything, sir?" a man named Harrison asked.

"No. You will get thirsty, though. The demon world is very warm. You'll need large skins for water, and enough provisions to get on and off the Northern Plateau—that's four days' basic rations. We travel fast and light. We take weapons to use in confined spaces: short swords, daggers, and clubs. Finally, and most importantly, and this will be especially hard for some of you"—here Ambrose looked at Anlax—"from the moment we enter the demon world until we come out again, we don't speak a word."

There was a bit of laughter and Geratan said, "No laughing either. Sounds will give our presence away. We must all learn to be silent."

"Though, if we can't speak," continued Ambrose, "we must communicate in a different way. In the demon world you can hear someone else's thoughts if your skin is touching theirs. So I can pass on orders by thinking them while I'm touching Geratan. If he is touching Anlax at the same time,

Anlax will hear the order too. That's useful, but it can also be problematic. We can hear things other than orders. We can hear other people's thoughts by mistake. I've chosen you men for your fighting skills but also for your temperaments. We cannot afford to work as anything less than a perfect team. We must trust and respect each other. You might inadvertently tell another soldier your deepest secret—or hear another man's. You must be ready for that, and be able to stay calm. We can't risk a failure in teamwork or discipline."

The men looked solemn and a few nodded, but Ambrose was pleased that no one made a joke.

"So we must learn to be honest with each other. And I'll begin by sharing some truths about me. I was born in Brigant, but Pitoria is now my home. I love Pitoria, and I cherish its freedoms and many of the people I've met here. But, in truth, I still love Brigant too.

"It is the home of my father and his father; it is the land where I grew up, where I learned to play with my brother and sister. It has beautiful mountains and rugged coasts. But it also has an evil and cruel king. It is a country where many are persecuted. It is a country where my brother was tortured and killed, where my sister was executed because she learned secrets that the king didn't want anyone to know." Ambrose had to take a breath; he rarely spoke of this to anyone. A vision of his sister on the scaffold and his brother's severed head came to him, but he had to focus on the men in front of him—he had to think of them. "And that's why, even though I still love my home country, I'm jealous of you men. I'm jealous of each of you because you have a good king. You have a ruler who is honest and fair, who does not torture and maim his own people, but who would gladly sacrifice his life for them. I'm jealous of that and hope that one day the same may be said of the ruler of Brigant. Aloysius must be stopped. Together we can achieve that. Together we can end his reign of terror."

A few of the men clapped, and Anlax shouted, "Thank you for your honesty, Sir Ambrose."

Ambrose raised his hands for silence. "And that brings me to the most serious subject of all." He surveyed the group with a smile. "Hair."

"White—it has to be white!" someone shouted.

"No, fuck off, it's got to be blue!" Anlax replied, shaking his own blue locks.

"I thought this might be a bone of contention," Ambrose interrupted. "But we are a team, and we must be able to recognize and trust each other. We are the Demon Troop and, by permission of the queen, we will have our own hair color."

At this, Geratan pulled off his hat to reveal a shock of bright crimson.

There were a few wolf-whistles and cheers.

"After our mission is complete you may change your hair back to whatever you wish, but while we are working together, this is our color."

Ambrose looked around the group and was pleased that they all appeared eager, already feeling part of a special team.

"Finally, I have one more thing to say and then I really

can shut up. There will be situations in the demon world where we need to communicate when we can't touch one another. The best way to do that is by hand signals. And, to help us, I've asked an expert to teach us all. She has also been into the demon world and come through it, so she knows exactly what we'll have to face."

And, with that, Tanya stepped forward.

# EDYON
## CALIA, CALIDOR

EDYON SLID slowly off the cool marble and sank down into his warm bath. He put his head back, feeling his hair float out in the water. On the ceiling was a painting of a garden full of flowers and fruit trees with distant, snowcapped mountains. It was beautiful. Everything around Edyon looked beautiful, sounded beautiful (there was the tinkling of chimes in the window), felt beautiful (warm, warm, warm), and even smelled beautiful (the almond oil in the bath had an aroma delicious enough to eat). Everything was designed with his comfort and security in mind. Or at least it was designed for *someone's* security. This room was the same as the one next door. They had been the rooms for Thelonius's two legitimate sons, Castor and Argentus, who had died earlier in the year. Were they still alive to inherit the throne, Edyon would never have come to know his father.

Had Castor lain back in the bath like Edyon was doing now?

*Undoubtedly.*

Had he, too, submerged and floated and breathed in the almond oil?

*Possibly.*

Castor had expected to be the next ruler of Calidor. Now he was gone, and who was bathing here?

*A bastard son from another land.*

Edyon felt sorry for them, his dead half brothers, and a little sorry for himself. He was now in their shoes—well, in their bath anyway—and though he was surrounded by riches, he was also surrounded by intrigue, doubt, gossip, and lies.

The lords were a constant problem. Thelonius relied on them: they provided income from taxes and men to fight in the army. Thelonius had sent a delegation of just two men to Pitoria, because none of the other lords would go. Thelonius had reassured Edyon, "Lord Darby is old and frail, but he's experienced in war. I trust his judgment. He'll advise us well."

From his bath, Edyon could see out of the wide windows to the blue sky filled with fluffy white clouds. Even the sky was pretty.

Talin, his short, chubby personal servant, appeared holding some towels. "It's time, Your Highness."

"Already?" Edyon felt a squirm of nerves in his stomach.

He stood, and while Talin patted his body dry with a large towel, Edyon dried the gold necklace that he wore round his neck. He never took it off, not even in his bath. The chain no longer held the gold ring that was the prince's seal— the ring was lost somewhere in a river in Pitoria. But the necklace was all he had from his old life. The necklace reminded him of his past and linked him to his future. It also reminded him of March, who had rescued the chain from the river. March, who should be drying him now. March, who should be dressing him. March should be massaging his shoulders and calming him with his witty conversation. March, his one friend.

But March had betrayed him. March had lied to him from the start.

And, anyway, who was Edyon kidding? "March was awful at conversation."

"I'm sorry, what was that, Your Highness?"

"Nothing, Talin. Nothing."

But somehow March could always calm Edyon, had always helped him, had always . . . believed in him.

*March wanted to kidnap you and sell you to the Brigantines. Stop thinking of that wretched boy!*

"There's a lot of oil in your hair still, sir," Talin said. "I can rub it and wave it with my fingers. Your hair is at its most attractive when it's waved." And he set to work on Edyon's hair, while Edyon allowed himself to be primped and clothed and positioned.

At the end of it, Edyon looked in the mirror and was surprised by what he saw. A handsome-ish young man with a soft face and a sad look in his eyes. His hair was waved and shiny. His clothes were beautiful—silk and soft suede.

There was a knock at the door.

"How exciting! They're here for you," Talin said. "But your boots are more important than them. They can wait a little." He disappeared for a few moments before reappearing, carrying a new pair of black leather boots that had a gold trim at the top and round the ankle. They were beautiful too, of course.

Edyon sat and pulled them on as there was another knock on the door. Edyon's stomach tightened. "You'd better let them in."

Talin bowed his head and glided to the door. The chimes chinked, and the room seemed to be growing darker. Edyon glanced out of the window—the sky was filling with large, heavy clouds. A summer rainstorm would clear the air, but for the moment it was still hot.

Edyon checked his appearance in the large mirror again. His cream silk shirt was heavily embroidered in gold at the neck and cuffs. His tight jacket was black velvet and suede, with gold beads sewn onto it in a random, scattered design. His trousers were black suede and rather tight without looking absurd. The boots were shiny, soft, and comfortable. Edyon pulled out his gold necklace to hang at the front of his jacket. It was perfect—just the right amount of gold and just the right amount of black.

Talin said, "Prince Thelonius asks that you join him, Your Highness."

Edyon swallowed and forced a smile. "Yes. Great. Thank you, Talin."

His servant leaned closer and added quietly, "You look the part. Just believe in yourself, Your Highness. Your father will be proud of you."

"Thank you, Talin." Edyon pulled his shoulders back and lifted his chin.

*Think like a prince. Act like a prince. Walk like a prince.*

He followed the guard of four men out of his quarters and along the wide, marble corridors to the Grand Hall. The distant buzz of conversation grew as he approached. Through the large doorway ahead, Edyon could see his father, and by him, on a table, the crown Edyon would wear.

The crown was a symbol of position and power. The boy who'd not been allowed to study at university because of his birth would wear it. From now on, Edyon would be allowed anywhere.

The trumpets began to sound a fanfare. The guards moved forward and Edyon went with them into the Grand Hall. All eyes turned to him. Edyon's heart was pounding so loud and hard it seemed to drum through his body in time with the trumpets.

For a moment Edyon thought he saw March at the far side of the room—that same profile and eyes of silver. Edyon strained to look again, but it was a trick of the light. The young lord he'd noticed was nothing like March.

The guard escorted Edyon all the way to Prince Thelonius. Edyon bowed to his father and took his place next to him, on his right side. They'd practiced all this the previous day, but then the hall had been empty and now it was full of strangers. Edyon looked out at the faces watching him and recognized only a few of them. He felt more alone than ever. He'd love his mother to be here, and March.

*Stop thinking of March. Think of being with your father. Think of being a prince!*

Thelonius addressed the room. "We're here today to

make right what should have happened years ago. My son, my firstborn, Edyon, stands with me now, and I couldn't be prouder. His lineage has been confirmed. His position is clear. He is my only living son. He is my rightful heir. Today he will be crowned and will take the title Prince Edyon, Prince of Abask."

A table was carried across to Thelonius and Edyon. Ink and quills were brought over on a cushion. The chancellor laid out the parchment, which Edyon had been shown the night before. It was beautifully written in swirling black ink with gold, silver, and red patterning. Edyon glanced through it again to the part where it said "son and heir to Prince Thelonius Melsor." The prince signed it, and then Edyon signed it with his new name: *Edyon Melsor.* The chancellor poured out the wax, and Thelonius stamped it.

There was some polite clapping at this point and Edyon looked up. A number of young lords were watching intently, all smiling at him. All hoping for favors, all grateful that his claim to land hadn't taken anything from them. His father had explained that he had to be careful to choose land to give to Edyon that took from no other lord, that offended no one. Abask, it seemed, would offend no one, except perhaps March, but March wasn't here.

*Stop thinking about that bloody boy!*

The table had already been removed and replaced by a low, padded velvet stool. A servant approached, carrying a large cushion on which rested the finely wrought gold crown.

Edyon looked at the crowd. The smiling faces genuinely and falsely happy. All of them strangers.

*Not all of them. There's Byron.* Byron, the handsomest of the young men in court, who had handled the smoke demonstration so well, was far to the back.

Edyon knelt on the stool. His father took the gold crown and held it above Edyon's head.

"I crown my son, Edyon Melsor, as Prince of Abask and the future prince and ruler and defender of Calidor." And he lowered the crown onto Edyon's head.

Edyon stood. The chancellor passed the symbolic sword and shield to Prince Thelonius, who in turn passed each one to Edyon.

Edyon had to hold the sword upright and the shield out while the trumpets blared. Edyon held his position firmly. The chancellor stepped forward and Edyon repeated the words the chancellor spoke, swearing his allegiance to truth, honor, and his father. And also swearing that he would guard the independence of Calidor with his life.

That done, Edyon just had to hold this position while each of the twenty-three lords were presented to him. Lord Regan's name was called first. He strode forward quickly, bowed, turned, and moved away.

Lord Brook was next. He was the oldest of the lords and could barely walk. It seemed to take forever for him to arrive.

*Good grief, hurry up, man!*

Brook bowed and then slowly stepped back and walked away.

*Twenty-one to go.*

Edyon could feel the sweat building on his forehead. They hadn't practiced this in full the night before, and already Edyon's arm was aching and a small shake began that was only subdued by holding the sword even tighter.

*This sword must be the heaviest in all Calidor.*

Edyon lowered his sword arm for a brief, blissful rest, just as Lord Arnan was called, and almost immediately he had to raise the wavering sword again. His jacket was now feeling too tight and too warm. Sweat had broken out across his chest and he felt a drop roll down his forehead and into his eye. It stung horribly, and Edyon tried to blink it away. Then he realized it wasn't just sweat but the oil from his bath. Even worse, the oil was making his crown slip down. And though Edyon was keeping his head as still as possible, the crown was a terrible shape and horribly heavy. Another dribble of oily sweat ran down the side of his face. And the crown seemed to slip even further.

By the sixth lord, the crown was down at Edyon's eyebrows and the oil was running down his nose.

Edyon's hands were full with the sword and shield, so all he could do was use willpower and his facial expression to halt the crown's descent. He raised his eyebrows as high as possible, pausing the crown's slide and diverting the oil's track down the side of his face. Another few lords went by.

*Where are we up to? Tenth? Twelfth?*

*Hurry up, you old fool.*

By the time the twentieth lord, Lord Grantham, was presented, Edyon had his head tilted back, with his eyebrows at maximum strain.

By the time the twenty-third lord's name—Lord Haydeen—was called, Edyon's arm was shaking and his eyebrows were at the breaking point. Lord Haydeen moved forward smartly but then looked at Edyon and seemed surprised at Edyon's expression. It took a moment for Edyon to realize that Lord Haydeen was imitating his own raised eyebrows. Was this an insult, a joke, or an effort to curry favor? Edyon didn't know or care.

*Just hurry up and bow for goodness' sake!*

Haydeen gave a stiff bow, holding his lowered position for an eternity as Edyon's arm shook and his crown began to fall down over his eyes. He couldn't hold his eyebrows up a moment longer. Haydeen stood and turned away just as Edyon dropped his arm and the crown slid down, bringing with it a pool of oil that ran into Edyon's eyes. The stinging pain was nothing compared to the relief of lowering his eyebrows. Now Edyon had to get rid of the sword so that he could raise his crown.

He stood with his eyes closed and heard a muffled laugh before someone took the sword. At last! Edyon pushed the crown up off his face. But with the strain in his arm he pushed too hard, and, with the oil on the crown, it slid off his head and tumbled with a clatter to the ground.

There was a gasp and then silence.

But the silence didn't last long, as it was filled with a low rumble of distant thunder.

# MARCH

BRIGANT

MARCH LAY on the ground, staring up as stars filled the darkening sky. This was the position he was in most evenings—on his back, flat out and too exhausted to move. Around him the other members of the Bull Brigade were talking, and there was the occasional overly loud laugh from one boy or another. There was also a delicious smell of roast meat—some of the boys had successfully hunted down a boar. But it was quiet compared to what March had seen of army camps in Pitoria. There were no lords, no servants, no horses, no hangers-on—just boys, one hundred of them including Sam and March. It was small and contained but also violent and hard. There was huge pride in being a member of the Bull Brigade. March had no real memories of his Abask childhood, but this was how he imagined the Abask fighters to be. And March was surprised to find that he liked the brigade life. He wasn't a servant or a lackey. He had to do the same work as everyone else and no one lorded it above him. He was called names, but no more than anyone else, and they were joking and admiring at heart.

Rashford, the leader, and Kellen, his second-in-command, were the ones who made the Bull Brigade the positive force it was. They were good fighters who led by example and gave the other boys encouragement and opportunities to shine. Rashford in particular was admired, if not actually worshiped, by some of the younger boys. He was broad-shouldered but wiry, without any fat on his body. Kellen was a little taller, with small dark eyes that seemed to be constantly surveying the group. They couldn't have been more than seventeen or eighteen, and yet they somehow seemed much older. March hadn't enjoyed getting knocked unconscious by Rashford, but he respected why he'd done it. It was a rite of passage, a way of proving who belonged.

Most of the boys came from the west coast of Brigant, all from poor families or no families at all. The Bulls were their family now—and March could see why they liked it. They were brothers-in-arms.

Over the last few days, the Bulls had moved from place to place. The boys rarely used the smoke, as it was too precious. They knew the army leaders were working on securing more for them, but they didn't know how long it would take. In the meantime, they were constantly practicing with swords, spears, and bows. The sword was the weapon that required the greatest skill and the one that most of the boys struggled with. Rashford was the best, though March wondered how even he would fare against someone like Sir Ambrose or King Tzsayn, nobles who'd trained with these weapons from childhood. March hated the sword, and today in practice he'd been beaten with that, and then twice more in boxing and wrestling. His nose, which had only just healed from Rashford's blow, was bloodied and broken again, and he was fairly sure he had two black eyes to match.

Sam was a natural with most weapons. He was thriving as part of the Bulls, as if he'd truly found a home at last. Tonight he was, as usual, sitting with some of the younger boys. They formed a little unit. March sometimes sat with them, but mostly he formed his own unit of one, practicing with the one weapon he liked—the stones that he threw with increasing accuracy. Sometimes he imagined he was aiming at a particular face (the man who'd tortured him in Rossarb, Lord Regan, or the various people who'd insulted him over the years—but not Thelonius, as his face was too similar to Edyon's).

"How you feeling?" Rashford peered down at March.

March dragged himself up to a sitting, or at least a slumping, position. "Like I've been kicked by a donkey, then trampled over by him and his friends."

"You calling my boys donkeys?" Rashford sat down next to March.

"If the hat fits . . ."

"Don't know what that means."

"It's an expression from Pitoria."

"You been there too?" Rashford asked, picking at the worn leather of his tatty boots.

"Yes, just a month or so ago." March had told Rashford a little of his life in Calidor, but he'd not spoken about his adventures in Pitoria. "I wish I was there now."

"How so?"

"It's peaceful. Rich. Good food. Not many donkeys."

Rashford sniggered.

"I went up on the Northern Plateau. Where the demons live."

"You see any demons?"

"A couple. We were attacked by one. I slept with the dead body of another in a snowstorm to keep warm."

Rashford frowned and stared at March. "You serious?"

"Always. The smoke's serious too. And the demons. And the war. Not sure I'd want to rely on the smoke, though. Or the king who fuels his army with it."

"That's treasonous talk there, March. You're new to the Bulls, so I'll let you off this time." But Rashford sounded like he really didn't care. He pulled the bottle from his waist holder and held it out to March. "Take some. It'll heal your nose."

The bottle was heavy with purple smoke. All the other boys carried similar bottles with leather covers, which hid the smoke's luminous purple glow. March slipped the cork to the side, letting out a slight wisp of smoke, then sucked it in. The smoke went straight to the roof of his mouth and March pressed on the sides of his nose, straightening it as best he could while it healed.

Rashford said, "I'll let you fill your own bottle soon, when we get our supplies."

Rashford had given March and Sam empty bottles on the first day, and March had been giving this a bit of thought. He asked, "Whose bottle did I get? I'm guessing that you've lost two of the brigade and that's why you had empty bottles for us."

Rashford squinted ahead, then shrugged. "Seems I've forgotten the old men's names already."

"So they manned up?" It was a phrase he'd heard the other boys use a few times—a phrase that seemed to fill them with fear. It meant that someone had become too old for the smoke to work anymore. When that happened, they'd be out of the Bulls. March remembered that the smoke worked for Princess Catherine, Edyon, and himself, but not Sir Ambrose or King Tzsayn, who were only a few years older.

"It ain't hard to work out, March. We're all getting older. But you can't ever really tell when you'll man up. Seventeen, eighteen, definitely by nineteen."

March nodded and wondered when it'd happen to Rashford. He was the oldest of the boys, after all. "So, what happened to them? I mean, did they just leave?"

"My commander found them different positions. They're regular soldiers in the regular army now."

"Your commander? Who's that? When do you even see him?"

"Not very often, which is often enough. But, as it happens, we've all got a new commander now, and I'm going to see him in a few days. You and Sam will have to come with me. He wants to see all new recruits. There'll be a little test to prove your worth."

March had heard some of the other boys talking of this too. It sounded like a race, and, although it apparently always turned into a fight at the end, it didn't sound any worse than what they did every day in training.

"Will the other brigade leaders be there?" March had

heard much talk of the other brigades too—all consisting of a hundred boys. The Bears, Hawks, Stags, Lions, Eagles, Foxes, and, not forgetting the Wasps, who had a particularly young membership and were reputed to be as tiny and vicious as their name suggested.

"They'll be there."

"And anyone from the main army? The man's army, I mean?"

Rashford snorted. "We don't have anything to do with them."

"But they should be arriving soon. I mean, I assume we're here for a purpose and we're not just beating the shit out of each other every day for the fun of it. We must be going to attack Calidor, which means the Brigantine army must be on its way."

Rashford shook his head. "No, March. You've got to think differently. This is a new world we're in now. And the way we boys' brigades fight is different from anything anyone's seen before. We can leap over ten soldiers, then turn and kill them all with a few sword strokes. Even you'll be able to disarm another swordsman. You'll break his arm if your sword clashes with his. All this practicing we go through gives the boys a bit of confidence, but the smoke gives us the power to win. With the smoke we're unstoppable. We can do what we want. The old mans' army just gets in the way. Well, actually, they're left behind. They're a joke. They fear us showing them up." He leaned forward and whispered, "They fear us fucking them up too."

And March, for the first time, realized Rashford was

right. The boy army didn't need support from the normal fighting force—they'd only slow the boys down. "But wouldn't Aloysius want to come and see the carnage he's made?"

"You mean the carnage *we've* made." Rashford shrugged. "I don't know about that."

"He'll want to see it at some stage. I'm guessing we run in, kill everything in our path, and then hold the fort until the men arrive. Which sounds fine . . . until we run out of smoke. How much smoke do they give you? Enough for days? Weeks?"

"Ten days, tops. They're tight like that. Our relationship isn't like a normal army; ours is based on trade—they give us smoke, we give them dead bodies."

That sounded right at first, but March thought about it for a few moments more and shook his head. "No. They give you smoke. You give them certain victory. You have more power than you realize. They're right to fear you."

They sat in silence for a few moments before March asked, "But what happens at the end of it all?"

"We win." Rashford grinned, his white teeth shining in the dark.

March disagreed. "You only win when you have smoke. If you don't have smoke, you lose. That's why they ration it. At the end of the war, or when you man up, at best you'll be given a shit job in the regular army. The sort of job that goes to people like us, who aren't nobility, who have already served our purpose. I reckon King Aloysius won't want you hanging around like a bad smell."

Rashford looked at the sky. "Well, I've no intention of hanging around, March, when that time comes. I'm no fool. I haven't been to fancy Calia or bloody Pitoria. I've never slept with a dead demon or poured wine for a prince. I've lived in Brigant all my life, and I've seen worse things than you could imagine: men hung, drawn, and quartered for nothing; people starved; children run down by men on horseback. I don't know what'll happen to me, but I do know, for the first time in my life, I have the power to do whatever I like. I'm going to enjoy that while I can. And I look at you and see someone much the same as me."

"But you're not thinking beyond ten days of smoke?"

"I didn't say that, March. I'm making my own plans. But I'm certainly not going to share them with you." He leaned close and whispered, "I like you, March, but there's something about you . . . You're holding something back. I'm not sure I can trust you yet—with my secrets or with my life. But I hope there's nothing too bad going on in your head, 'cause from what I hear, my new commanding officer will suss it out."

"I'm not worried, Rashford. I've nothing to hide."

"Good job. 'Cause you don't want to get on the wrong side of Prince Harold."

# EDYON

## CALIA CASTLE

EDYON SAT beside his father in yet another meeting with the chancellor and Lord Regan. He hoped this one would go better than the last. He was trying to be quiet this time. Trying to be a dutiful son, one who did not enrage his father and who proved his loyalty to the country.

Thelonius was reading a message that had just arrived from Lord Darby.

"The Pitorians are holding their position in the north of Pitoria. Aloysius is still with his main army in Rossarb. The Pitorians believe he's farming the purple demon smoke but have no idea of the quantity he has. Lord Darby says the Pitorians are convinced of the power of the smoke, and also convinced that the Brigantines plan to attack Calidor as well as Pitoria, and even beyond. Darby is impressed by Queen Catherine, who is firm but reasoned, but concerned because he has not yet seen King Tzsayn, who is still ill from the wounds he suffered when a prisoner of Aloysius. The Pitorian army is a considerable force, even though it has been depleted by a sickness in the last few weeks."

Edyon was pleased that Lord Darby was impressed by Catherine. His thoughts briefly went back to when she was a judge for Edyon's murder trial. "Firm but reasoned" summed her up perfectly. That sounded all to the good, but Tzsayn had been healing for weeks, and yet he still hadn't met with Calidor's delegation? Why not?

Thelonius looked up briefly and then began to read again. "Lord Darby's assessment is written thus: 'The Pitorians are vulnerable to an attack from the Brigantines in the north—they should hold against normal forces, but the boy army is an unknown factor. They are also vulnerable to an attack in the south—if the Brigantines sent a force by ship, the Pitorians would have to split their army, and the north would likely fall.' It is Lord Darby's assessment that such an attack is likely."

And if the north were to fall, the Brigantine army would have clear access to the whole of Pitoria, the Northern Plateau, and the demon world, and they could transport the smoke to their boy army as fast and as often as they wanted. They would be unstoppable. Edyon was itching to speak, but should he comment? What was he supposed to do or say?

Thelonius looked to Regan. "Our own reports are that the Brigantine fleet is massing."

Regan nodded. "A naval attack seems inevitable. But will they attack us or the Pitorians?"

*Both, probably.* Edyon wanted so much to speak, but he pushed his fist over his lips. *Don't say it. Don't say it.*

Thelonius tapped his finger on the scroll. "Aloysius wants revenge for Boris. I'm sure of that. He wants his daughter to suffer. I suspect he will attack the Pitorians first, but we won't be far behind." Thelonius continued to read through to the end of the message. "Lord Darby recommends we send assistance to the Pitorians, not with men but with boats."

*What?! Darby recommends helping our enemy's enemy! Shocking.*

Regan scowled. "But if they have our ships, we are vulnerable."

The chancellor was frowning too. "The lords will oppose such a move."

Regan continued. "We need all our boats for our own defenses. The Brigantines could attack our coast first—or even if they come for us second, as you said, it won't be long. It's not our fault that the Pitorians haven't prepared their own fleet as we've prepared ours."

Edyon wanted to scream. If they didn't help to protect Pitoria now, then it would be impossible to stop the boy army later! What did it matter whose "fault" it was?

Edyon was surprised to see his father smile. "Lord Darby has quite an ingenious plan. He suggests we send fifteen scullers. The loss of just fifteen small boats should not affect our defenses."

"Then how will it help the Pitorians?" the chancellor asked.

"They can use the scullers to steal ships from the Brigantines, thus depleting the Brigantine fleet while adding to their own."

Lord Darby was turning out to be both astute and clever.

"Won't they need training in their use?" the chancellor asked.

"Yes," Lord Regan replied. "The scullers are our design. They ensure our waters are safe. If we give away their secrets to the Pitorians, then we have no advantage, should they ever come for us."

*Oh, that's ridiculous. Why would they do that? They've never threatened Calidor.* If Regan said another thing, Edyon would have to chew off his own tongue to stop himself from speaking.

Thelonius shook his head. "Regan, you go too far. The scullers are our design, but they're no secret weapon. We either give them boats and train the Pitorians, or give them boats *and* men. And I know you won't want to do the latter."

"Nor do I want to do the former. We should give them nothing."

"*Nothing?*" Edyon couldn't not say it. But it came out as a strange kind of squeal, forced through his lips, and he tried to cover it with a cough.

"This is not the thin end of the wedge that you fear, Lord Regan," Thelonius said. "This will not lead to Pitorians coming to fight on Calidorian land."

"The boats are Calidorian and will have Pitorian men on them," Regan countered.

Thelonius muttered, "And if you say it, the other lords will too."

"The boats won't be Calidorian if we sell them to the Pitorians," Edyon said. Regan and Thelonius turned to him.

"Just thought I'd make a small suggestion. I mean, it's just an idea. And presumably we can charge a high fee for these scullers, whatever they are."

Thelonius nodded. "I like that idea, Edyon. The lords can share equally in the revenues. It will offset some of the burden of financing the army, and the building of the wall and sea defenses."

"I thought the Pitorians were broke," Regan said. "After they paid the ransom for Tzsayn, Aloysius has all their money. They won't be able to pay us a kopek."

"We can give them a loan," Edyon said. "Charge them interest. We do it all the time in Pitoria."

The chancellor was nodding as well now. "That would be an excellent source of income for the future."

Regan's scowl deepened. "Yes, until the Pitorians default on the loan and use our boats against us. Then the deal will not look so excellent."

Thelonius sighed. "I understand your concerns, Regan, but while we're all nervous of potential enemies, our one known enemy is Aloysius. The letter from Lord Darby explains clearly the threat he poses, and we have to deal with that threat. If the Pitorians show any threat to us in the future, then we will react to that."

"So you're going to send boats and men?" Regan asked.

"We are going to send fifteen scullers and a few men to train the Pitorians. We will charge for the boats and the training, as my son wisely suggested. We will not be fighting alongside the Pitorians on the boats. This is a business transaction. The men we send will only be to train. No Pitorians will come to Calidor."

"And I will calculate a price for the boats, the service, and the interest on any unpaid amounts," the chancellor said.

"Excellent," Thelonius said, nodding. "Can't you see this benefits us all, Regan?"

"I merely wanted to raise awareness of the risks. But of course, as always, Your Highness is correct." Regan bowed deeply and added, "There are benefits to us all, indeed."

# CATHERINE

## NORTHERN PITORIA

*A woman must know her own mind before she can act on it.*

*Queen Valeria of Illast*

"THE KING has asked for you, Your Majesty."

Catherine looked up from her desk at Doctor Savage. "He's awake?"

"Awake but weak. If you could encourage him to rest, Your Majesty, that would help."

"I'll do my best, but he has a will of his own."

And he always claimed he was well even when he was clearly feverish or in pain. What was it about Tzsayn that made him unable to admit to weakness, even to himself? Catherine remembered the first time they had met, on her arrival in Tornia, how proud and aloof Tzsayn had appeared. She'd learned a little more about him since then—and, yes, he was proud, but he was not aloof at all. He loved his family and his country. He was intelligent, witty, extremely brave, and aware that his life hung on a thread that could snap—or be cut—at any moment.

It was Ambrose who had talked about life being held by threads, though now Catherine couldn't remember how that conversation had come up. But she liked the analogy. Yes, threads could break, or be cut, but they could also be strengthened by being bound with others.

"You are a welcome sight," Tzsayn said as Catherine entered his bedchamber.

The king was propped up in bed on a mountain of blue pillows. It was over a month since his release from captivity and the wounds to his neck had healed over, but his face remained drawn and there was still a haunted look to his eyes. It seemed to Catherine that although he was no longer being kept in a cage, forced to watch his men being tortured to death, he was still seeing it in his head. She sat down close to him and took his hand, feeling how thin it had become.

"How are you feeling?"

"I'm feeling fine. Very fine. Even better now you're with me."

"Your leg?"

"I don't want to talk about my leg anymore. Savage has bored me to death about it today. Tell me about you . . ."

"I'm fine also. Working hard. Getting jobs done."

"I wasn't thinking of jobs; I was thinking of you. Dealing with all the pressures of state as well as those of life . . . and death."

Catherine frowned. Which death was he thinking of?

Tzsayn seemed to read her mind and he added gently, "I mean your brother. We've still not spoken of that."

In her head, Catherine saw again the spear leaving her arm, flying through the air low and fast, Boris turning to her, their eyes meeting at that last moment as the weapon pierced his chest.

"I don't regret what I did."

Tzsayn's eyes were on hers, as if he was looking for something. "Not at all?"

Catherine shook her head. "He was my enemy. He would have killed me without hesitation. He would have tortured me and shamed me. When I think of that, I know that there is nothing wrong with me being glad he's dead, glad I killed him. I'm sorry that he was a bad person. I'm sorry for my mother who loved him. But I have no regrets about my actions. I'd do it again. Sometimes I wonder if I should have done it sooner—found a way to kill my father and brother in their sleep." Catherine looked at Tzsayn. "Do I shock you?"

Tzsayn raised an ironic eyebrow. "With your Brigantine lust for blood?"

"With my lack of femininity. The violence of my feelings. The brutality of them."

"I admire your honesty." He smiled at her for a brief moment, as if to reassure her. "I always have. And I'm grateful for it. Honesty is a rare commodity. As for what is supposed to be femininity, being gentle and kind toward someone who is a bully, a brute, and inhumanly evil in his treatment of others—well, being gentle and kind to someone like that seems more like stupidity. It's weakness, it's failing to support those who are suffering, and that sort of gentleness and kindness aren't to be admired—certainly not in a queen."

Tzsayn kept doing this—surprising her. She'd half expected he'd be horrified at the coarseness of her feelings. Did she *want* him to be horrified, to push him away?

"You're not weak, Catherine, but I still worry about you, about what is required from you. The work, the war."

"Please, let's not talk about that either. You've had enough discussion of your leg, and I've had enough about food supplies."

Tzsayn smiled. "I can tell you that, after lying in bed for weeks, the thought of a discussion about bushels of wheat is exciting."

"Well, you can talk to Tanya, then, because I will not say another word on the subject."

"So what shall we discuss?"

"I was thinking about our first meeting—"

"Ah, yes, I remember that day."

"How you scowled at me." Catherine was teasing and was also vaguely aware that she was playing her usual trick of making light of her troubles, but realized that, for once, she was happy to play at being happy.

"Scowl? I didn't scowl once. I went to great lengths to show utter disdain for the whole charade. That was my look of disdain." And he did a good imitation of it now.

Catherine shook her head, smiling. "A fearsome scowl. It came shortly after your sneer."

"I never sneer. It's an ugly look. And everyone knows that King Tzsayn of Pitoria is never ugly." Tzsayn turned so she could only see the burned side of his face, the one that looked old and wizened, the skin drawn over his eye, and no eyebrow.

Catherine leaned over and kissed it. "That's true."

Tzsayn's eyes met hers and she blushed, realizing she'd never kissed his face before. He cleared his throat and said, almost formally, "But now we must decide what to do about *our* little charade."

Catherine felt her blush deepen. She didn't want Tzsayn to think of their marriage as a charade. It was a lie, yes, but a necessary one. After his capture, she'd had to declare that she'd secretly married Tzsayn, so that the Pitorian lords couldn't put her aside, or send her back to her father— although it had only delayed the latter. Since his return, they'd been together—not exactly as man and wife, as they had separate bedchambers off their shared living quarters, but that could be explained by Tzsayn's ill health, and Catherine knew that when he did improve, things would have to change.

"It's hardly a *little* charade."

He took her hand again. "And I'm not sorry about it. The lie kept you alive. But I don't want our lives or our marriage to be a charade."

Catherine nodded. The dreaded question of love and marriage.

"On most subjects you are quick to share your opinion with me, and yet as soon as I say the word 'marriage,' you go silent. But we can't ignore it, Catherine. We can marry— make the lie true. Or . . ."

"Or?"

"You wait for me to die of my wounds."

"What? No! Don't say such a thing."

"Why not? I've been close enough to death these last weeks. Felt it creep up on me and put its cold fingers round my heart."

"Why are you saying these things?" Catherine dropped his hand. "I never wanted that. And I have always wanted you to live and want that now, despite how heartless you are to me."

"I'm not heartless, Catherine."

"And neither am I." She leaned over and looked into his eyes. "Please believe me when I say that while you were gone, I never once hoped for anything other than your safe return. And, while you have been ill, for nothing but your recovery. And I still want that."

"And if your hopes are fulfilled and I do recover? What then would you choose? To stay as my wife or divorce?"

"Divorce? Is that even possible?"

"It would be a first for the king of Pitoria, but given our countries are at war and your father has assassinated mine, I'm sure my lawyers could find a way. I want us to be married—I can say that simply and honestly. But I'd like a simple and honest reply."

"They're simple options, but that doesn't make the choice simple. And I'm not used to being given choices. I'm used to being told what to do with my life."

Tzsayn frowned. "Perhaps that was true once, but now you are clearly quite capable of making your own decisions."

Catherine knotted her fingers together. What was she to do? She wanted to be queen. She was ambitious to rule, to prove that she, a woman, was just as able as any man. But did she want to be a wife too? And, if so, to whom? It felt like the answer should be obvious, and yet . . . every time she thought about it, she was drawn in all directions.

She'd been sent to Pitoria to marry Tzsayn, accepted that as her fate, and been pleasantly surprised when she met him. He was attractive, amusing, clever, kind, and nothing like any man—any person—she'd ever met. Would Tzsayn make her happy? Would this life make her happy? Was it the right choice? It seemed like the right choice until she thought of Ambrose. Just a few weeks ago her heart had been set on him.

"This *is* my scowl," Tzsayn said. "I reserve its use for when you sigh in that way."

"What way?"

"That way that you do when you think of Sir Ambrose."

"I wasn't thinking of him. I was thinking about you."

"I praised you for your honesty earlier, so don't lie now, Catherine." Tzsayn frowned. "And don't scowl at me either." But now his frown turned to a wince.

Catherine half rose. "Oh dear, I'm not good for you. I'm vexing you."

"You're very good for me. My leg is throbbing that's all." He shifted position, wincing again. "Do you know what I want, Catherine? Apart from a good leg, of course. I want *everything*—peace, happiness, prosperity, love. I want them all and I want them with you. I believe I can give them to you. But can you give them to me? Or do you want to give them to someone else? I need to know, Catherine. Together we may rule this country and rule it well. We can defeat our enemies and live happily ever after. But you must decide if that is the life you want."

What was the alternative? Ambrose. A quieter life. Travel. Freedom. Which was right for her?

"Another sigh," Tzsayn commented. "Tell me, how is Sir Ambrose?"

"As I'm sure Davyon has already told you, he's recovered from his injuries and is about to lead a mission to the demon world."

"And I genuinely am glad for his recovery and wish him success on his mission. He's a good soldier and a good man. He'll wait for you to make your decision, if he's worthy. And I will too, Catherine. But neither of us will wait forever. Which brings me to another subject I wanted to discuss. I'm king now and I must have a coronation, the formalities must still be followed even in war. I should return to Tornia for the ceremony."

This time Catherine rose completely. "You cannot travel in your condition!"

"Calm yourself, Catherine. I was about to say that I'll have the ceremony here instead. It'll be a good opportunity to bring together the people of the north in celebration and recognition of all they have done in the last few months."

"As long as you're well enough."

"I'll be fine. We can keep the ceremony short and simple. What's there to arrange but a few words and a crown?"

Catherine wasn't totally convinced but she tried to joke. "Well, I suppose that'll keep costs down, and we must watch every kopek."

"Apart from that, there *is* something else to consider," Tzsayn said. "Should there be one crown or two? If I am crowned king, then you should be crowned queen at the same time. But for that we must be married. I mean *really* married. If that is what you wish, I would be honored for you to be my wife and my queen. But I need to know, Catherine. And soon."

# TASH
## DEMON TUNNELS

IT WAS still black, silent, and stone-cold. Tash had just enough space to turn over to lie on her front or her back, her shoulders and hips scraping the roof of her space. And she had to move regularly, as her legs kept cramping and her back was aching.

At first she'd been afraid of running out of air, but somehow air was coming to her. And water was trickling in through a fine crack near her head. She could lick at the water like a dog.

There wasn't much else she could do, though.

Except think—she could do a whole lot of thinking. She'd done more thinking here than in her whole life, it seemed. She'd gone right back to her earliest memories—of sitting in the rain in a muddy puddle, her brothers stomping around her so that the water splashed her face. She had other memories too—mostly miserable—of her father beating her brothers or her, of his shouting and cursing.

Her memories of Gravell were different, though. Those felt real—they warmed her and made her smile and cry (why did thinking of Gravell always make her cry?). Yes, he'd shouted at her, but somehow even his angriest words never filled her with dread like her father's footsteps had. Tash remembered the first night after Gravell had taken her from her family. He'd given her shoes and food, and an extra blanket when she'd begun to shiver and cry. Over the following weeks she'd cried lots more, not with fear or cold but with a mix of relief and sorrow—sorrow for her old self that had suffered and hadn't known any different. Gravell was always a wonder to her. He was big and shouty on the outside, but inside he cared for her, and she knew that from the first day. No one had ever done that before and it had changed her world.

Tash wished she'd hugged Gravell more and wished she could hug him again.

Well, perhaps she'd see him again soon, if there was a life after this one. Gravell had never believed in that sort of thing, and perhaps it was wishful thinking, but she smiled at the thought of it.

"But we won't hunt no demons," she muttered.

And in her head, she wagged her finger at Gravell, standing in front of him on the most beautiful part of the Northern Plateau, snow heavy on the branches of the conifer trees. "We can hunt for food, but nothing else. Not to sell stuff for money, not so you can have your women and your pruka."

And Gravell belched and said, "You just don't appreciate the finer things in life. What is life without women and pruka . . . and pies?"

"We can swap some meat and skins for a pie in Pravont."

Gravell grinned. "They have the best pies, the best food in the whole world."

"I'm not sure we're in the world anymore, but I think we can have the pies."

Gravell picked up his harpoons and said, "Let's go hunting, then."

And Tash was happy to imagine being with Gravell. Happy to have lived her life knowing a man who'd cared for her.

She squirmed round to lie on her stomach, and wiped the tears from her face as she did. She carried on her daydream, imagining the hunt: running through the forest, finding deer tracks, and then closing in on the prey. Gravell sending her round to the right, to scare the deer toward him. She knew by instinct where to go and made her way forward, but to her surprise she didn't see a deer. There was something else ahead of her.

It was a demon. A huge red demon sitting on his haunches.

Tash dropped to the ground.

What was it doing?

The demon was using his hand—no, his finger—to make marks in the earth.

Tash crept closer, to get a better look.

The demon glanced up. Tash expected it to be Twist, the demon she'd freed from the Brigantines, but it wasn't him. It was another demon she recognized—the one that had attacked the group led by Princess Catherine. This was the demon that had tried to kill Geratan before Tash had intervened and stabbed the demon, which had then fallen on her. The red smoke that had escaped from the demon's mouth as it was dying had seemed to travel through Tash's body and, more than that, seemed to carry her to the center of the demon world—to the core where the smoke lived and where it all seemed to return. And, remembering that now, Tash felt something inside her chest stir. As if a small wisp of the smoke was somehow still inside her body.

Could it be so? Was that what was keeping her alive? Preventing the stone from crushing her completely?

She felt a connection with this demon, but would he be able to explain what the connection was? The demon had been as scary as shit when he was dying, but now he seemed quite calm and focused on what he was doing, which was making a hole in the ground by moving his finger across it. The hole was shallow and small, but now he used four fingertips and the hole deepened, then he used the palm of his hand.

Tash leaned forward and saw the hole went deep into the earth and was full of red smoke, and it looked like it was opening up beneath her. She screamed and jumped back—

And hit the back of her head on the hard stone.

She was surrounded by blackness again. There was no hole, no forest, no demon.

It was a dream.

*Just a dream.*

She dropped her head back down. But now it fell into a dip in the stone.

A dip that had not been there before. And . . .

*I can see my hands!*

There was a faint red glow in the space before her.

Her hands were lying in a slight hollow, about the size of her head and as deep as her fist.

Was the stone moving again?

*Or have I moved the stone?*

She'd dreamed that the demon was making a hole with its fingers. But her own fingers were sore, as if she'd been doing the same movement in her sleep.

*I must have made the hole.*

And, like any prisoner, her next thought was of escape.

*If I can make a hole, I can make a tunnel.*

# EDYON

## CALIA, CALIDOR

EDYON WAS late. He was supposed to be in the main courtyard for the procession, but he'd got himself lost in the castle's corridors. A servant had given him directions, but somehow he'd ended up near the kitchens. He'd asked for guidance from there and ended up near the library. He was beginning to think the servants were doing it on purpose. But he could now hear noise from a crowd. He turned a corner, and ahead was the archway to the main courtyard, which was full of people. As Edyon drew nearer he heard some snippets of conversation. "He's late. Probably doing his hair." "I wonder if he's just a bit simple."

Edyon turned and went round the other way, hurrying as much as he could. He was aware that the whole procession was waiting for him, and aware that, yet again, he'd messed up. He walked as quickly as he could to his horse, which was being held for him, and did his best to mount smoothly. He hated riding and the cobbles in the courtyard were slippery with rain. The horse was the tamest thing in the royal stables, however, and Edyon was grateful that it stood solidly unmoving.

And with the blast of a trumpet, the procession was off. Edyon rode beside his father at the head of the long line of lords, soldiers, horses, drummers, and trumpeters.

"I'm sorry I was late." He had to shout to be heard above the fanfare.

Thelonius waved it off. "You're a prince, Edyon. The people can wait for you. Now, let's tour our country."

Edyon was supposed to wave to the crowd from his horse, but all he wanted to do was cling to the saddle. The last thing he needed was to fall from his horse and be even more of a laughingstock, even more of a disgrace. The lords were in the procession behind him, all staring at his back. Edyon could almost feel their gazes, all assessing him and all finding him wanting.

When the procession had taken them out of the city, his father said, "You're very quiet, Edyon."

"I was thinking of the lords. And the coronation ceremony."

"Oh?"

"It was a disaster."

"No. You were crowned. You took the oath. You did all that was required."

"It looked like I threw the crown to the floor."

"I didn't see it like that."

"The lords saw it. All of them. They had front-row seats. The chancellor has already warned us that my loyalties were being questioned. It doesn't look good to throw the Calidorian crown to the floor."

"It was an accident." Thelonius turned to look at Edyon. "You're young and, yes, you'll make a few mistakes—haven't we all?"

"But one of the first things you told me was that we must learn to balance the power of the lords—having them scorn me doesn't seem the right way to go about it."

"They won't scorn you when they get to know you a little better, and this tour will give the opportunity for just that." Thelonius patted Edyon's shoulder and then gripped it. "It's also an opportunity for you to get to know your new country. I'm pleased beyond words that my son is riding with me." He glanced at Edyon and added, "There is another purpose too. I'm sure you're correct about the threat from Aloysius. We'll inspect our defenses, the main ports, and the northern wall. The lords will see how serious we are about maintaining our strong borders and defenses."

Soon they arrived in the fortified harbor town of Gaross, the hometown of Lord Regan, which had the honor of being the first stop on the tour. It was only a short distance from Calia and renowned for being picturesque. The castle was impressive, set on numerous terraced levels looking out over the blue sea. The stonework was practical, forming a strong defense, but also attractive, as it was softened in appearance by plants and flowers. On each terrace there were ponds and fountains.

Regan proudly showed a small group, including Edyon,

around the main terrace. "It's certainly very beautiful," Edyon said.

"My architect is a genius. We have excellent views along the coast. He has built beauty into functionality," Regan replied. "We are a strong defense site, protecting the coast up to Calia and down to the South Stacks."

One of the other lords was looking back at the castle and commented, "Your famous architect hasn't sorted out your ruin yet, Regan."

Edyon had noticed the crumbling stone walls covered with vines to one side of the castle but thought they looked quite attractive. "A ruin?"

Regan smiled. "It's a bit of a joke among some of the lords. The walls are not a ruin. I had begun extending the castle years ago, to add another meeting room, a gallery, a few bedchambers, and more servant quarters, but when the war intervened, building stopped. Then the stonemasons were needed to build the great wall at our borders, and I decided the extra rooms weren't necessary—the workers and the money could be put to better use. One must make some sacrifices for one's country."

Edyon looked at the extent of Regan's home and thought that there weren't too many sacrifices being made. But still, Edyon had to court the lords, and that included Lord Regan. A bit of flattery would do no harm, and on impulse Edyon said, "Well, I think it's all wonderful. Perhaps your architect could design a home for me one day in Abask."

Regan smiled. "Of course. I'd like to see you tame that

land. And I'm sure that would bring you much pleasure—bringing culture to the uncivilized Abask."

And somehow, from the way Regan looked at Edyon, he knew he was referring to March.

*I wasn't trying to tame March or civilize him . . . He didn't need me to. He didn't need to change at all. He was perfect as he was. It's you who needs taming. It's you who's barely civilized.*

Edyon had to get away from Regan. The man made his blood boil.

*March never had this wealth or position. He'd lost everything: home, family, friends. And now even Calidor has been forbidden to him. Yes, I know he tried to kill you, but . . . but . . . he lost everything . . . even me.*

Edyon stormed away, into the castle, escaping down a long corridor and snatching up a small vase from a cabinet that he passed. Holding it in his hands made him feel better. Calmer.

This was the second time he'd taken something in the last few weeks—he'd stolen Regan's gloves on that awful day when he'd seen March in Calia's dungeons. Edyon was dismayed that the urge to steal had overwhelmed him again. But he didn't put the vase back.

Edyon went onto another terrace overlooking the sea. The view was framed by lemon trees and flowering plants that attracted birds that hovered around, darting in to taste the nectar. It was all beautiful and all Regan's. He looked down at the vase in his hands. It was made of glass, blown so that it had bubbles within it, and the colors were the blue-green of the sea. It was beautiful. Edyon hated it. He threw the vase out over the terrace, and it disappeared onto the rocks below.

That evening there was a banquet hosted by Regan in a magnificently decorated hall. The food was as beautiful and plentiful as it was delicious—and so was the wine, which Edyon sampled generously.

The next morning Talin woke Edyon at dawn and dressed him. This day would be the same as the one before—a journey to the next castle and another assessment of the defenses there. However, today was different in that Edyon's buttocks were sensitive from the previous day's riding and his head was sensitive from the previous evening's wine. He managed to mount his horse with some assistance, though he was horribly dizzy. He'd just got his reins untangled when a trumpet blared in his ear, and he almost slid out of his saddle in shock. Trumpets, Edyon had discovered, were a large part of royal life and one he'd happily get rid of.

The sun was blinding, his jacket too hot, and his mouth was as dry as a baker's oven. The trumpet blared behind Edyon again and he thought he couldn't feel any worse. But then, just as the procession set off, his stomach began to revolt.

*Do not throw up. Puking is not princely.*

Edyon couldn't turn his head or open his eyes more than slits. The only way to get through the morning would be to somehow ride and sleep at the same time, but the noise around him was unbearable.

"May I ride with you, Your Highness?"

It was Byron, the lord's son who had taken part in the smoke demonstration.

"If you get rid of that man with the blasted trumpet, then perhaps we could talk."

"It shall be done, Your Highness."

Byron had a word with the trumpeter and returned in relative quiet to ride beside Edyon. Byron was broad-shouldered, dark, and handsome; his beautiful long plait, which was woven with a silver thread, was hanging down his back. At the smoke demonstration Edyon had discovered he was also empathetic and brave, but, sitting on his black horse, Edyon could see that Byron's thigh muscles were even more impressive.

"How are you finding the tour so far, Your Highness?" Byron asked.

"Better without the trumpet. I've got a stinking hang-over, truth be told," Edyon said. "And I can't stand riding; I'd much rather walk. My buttocks feel like dough that's been pummeled by a master baker."

Byron laughed. And it seemed he had a full set of perfect white teeth.

"I'm afraid there will be much more riding before the tour is over," Byron said. "Probably a hunt or two as well."

"I will not hunt anything. I might watch, from a distance, and cheer for the deer or the boar or whatever poor animal has to flee for its life."

Byron flashed a smile. "Then I shall join you and eat no meat, only turnips."

"No turnips. Ever. I have an aversion to them." Edyon

recounted his arrest in Pitoria just a couple of months earlier. "We'd fled across the Northern Plateau, fought demons and Brigantines, and *then* I was arrested and dragged in chains behind a horse very like this one by a sheriff's man and had turnips thrown at me."

Byron laughed and frowned and squinted at Edyon. "I never know if you're serious, Your Highness. Your speech last night amused us all, though most thought you were exaggerating your experiences."

"They did?" Edyon frowned. He vaguely remembered Regan boring on about pride in Calidor and the coastal defenses, though Edyon couldn't remember much and could remember even less of his own speech—he had a feeling he'd spouted something about friends and neighbors, Calidor and Pitoria. He asked Byron, "Which parts in particular did they think I was making up?"

"Well, I think sleeping with the body of a dead demon was the most surprising, but then you talked about other places you've slept—your vast experience of prison cells. You compared the merits of each."

"Oh shits, did I?"

"King Tzsayn's was the most comfortable and Lord Farrow's the most disgusting."

"Please, don't say any more." Edyon wondered if he'd mentioned March, but surely he hadn't.

"Perhaps I would be allowed to speak if we chose a different subject?" Byron asked.

"Please. Take my mind off my awful hangover. Tell me about yourself, Byron."

So Byron spoke of his life as the third son of Lord Harris. A happy family living in some comfort, with sun and orchards, vines and river fishing. Byron's stories did indeed help Edyon forget his headache and even his buttocks until they approached their next destination.

That evening, as he entered the banqueting hall and saw another feast laid out, he muttered, "Shits, I'm going to have to do this every night?"

Lord Regan was just behind him and replied, "Indeed, Your Highness. And I'm curious as to what subject you'll educate us about this evening. Another treatise on prison life? Or another attempt to heap acclaim on your 'friend' who helped you face the trials of your journey?"

Edyon winced. Byron hadn't mentioned that, though perhaps only Regan noticed, as he knew who March was. He knew who March was, of course, because March had been part of a plot to kill him.

*Well, damn them both.* Edyon poured himself a large goblet of wine. *The hair of the dog will help, and I'll make as many ridiculous speeches as I like.*

And that night he made another speech, this time passionately talking of the demons and their powerful smoke, how it can make boys strong and also heal. "The threat from Aloysius and his boy army is something we all must face one day," he said.

When he'd finished, their host, Lord Haydeen, thanked him with a smile. "The smoke certainly is powerful, as is this wine!"

Edyon looked around the room and wondered if anyone had actually listened to him, if anyone believed anything about the demon smoke or the jails or anything at all.

Edyon made his excuses about being tired after his journey and left the hall to go to his bedchamber. As he got there, he saw a servant leaving the room next door with Regan's boots. "What are you doing with those?" Edyon asked.

"Taking them to be cleaned and polished, Your Highness."

"Take mine too," Edyon said, and he showed the servant to his room, where his riding boots were. All the time Edyon had that old feeling buzzing in his head, his arms, his fingers. "Shits," he muttered to himself.

He watched the servant leave. Regan's room was a few steps down the corridor. He could be in it in a moment. No one would know.

Edyon went to his bed, sat on it, and muttered to himself, "No. I mustn't. I must resist. Stealing is bad. Even though it's Lord 'I'm curious as to what subject you'll educate us about this evening' Regan. He won't even take the threat of the smoke and the boy army seriously! He's got off lightly so far. He's lost a pair of gloves and a shitty little vase. He could lose everything." And, before he knew it, Edyon was out of his room and entering the one next door.

Regan had been given a large room, with a seating area and the bed at the far side. Edyon wandered around, his fingers twitching.

Regan's clothes were laid over the stool and a very nicely embroidered nightshirt lay on the bed. "I somehow can't imagine Regan in a nightshirt," Edyon whispered to himself and held the shirt up. It was of fine fabric and very soft. "Who'd have thought it?" He threw the nightshirt to the floor, resisted the urge to stomp on it, and went to the stool. Regan's riding trousers and jacket were there, as were his knives. Edyon drew one out, inspecting it—long and slender, it caught the candlelight brightly and looked to have the sharpest of blades. Had this knife fought against March?

Edyon dropped the knife and it speared the floor. He picked it up and put it back in the sheath.

There was a large, heavy chest of drawers, on which was a small mirror and two silver hairbrushes. The mirror was made for traveling, it seemed, as it folded apart to make a stand and then together again to be compact and to protect the mirror itself. The silver surround was finely engraved with the picture of a tree by a river.

Edyon had to have it.

"It's too beautiful to belong to Regan." With that, he slid it into his jacket's inner pocket. He was opening the door to leave when he heard footsteps approaching. And a voice.

*Regan! Shits!*

Edyon shut the door quietly and ran back into the room. But now what?

*Under the bed? Out of the window?*

Too late. The door was opening and all Edyon could do was slide behind a large, solid wooden corner chair and crouch down, hoping the blankets that were draped over its back helped conceal him.

Regan entered, followed by two others, and the door closed.

Edyon curled up tightly and tried to breathe silently as Regan offered port to his guests, whom Edyon recognized from the smoke demonstration as Birtwistle and Hunt. Someone sat heavily in the chair, pushing it farther back into the corner and trapping Edyon completely.

"I'll be brief." Regan's voice was curiously quiet, not his usual manner at all. "I've been thinking about your proposal, as I said I would. And, as I said before, this is not easy for me."

"We understand that, Regan. It's not easy for any of us."

"I admit that I haven't been happy for some time. Thelonius is . . . changed."

"Weaker," Hunt added.

"The death of his wife and children strained him," Regan said. "It's understandable."

"Understandable, but that doesn't mean it's acceptable. He has to be fit to rule. And putting that illegitimate fool in line for the throne is not acceptable."

"Nor is forcing you to perjure yourself, Regan." That was Birtwistle's voice.

"That's what hurts me the most," Regan said in a pained voice. "Thelonius, my oldest, closest friend, asks me to lie under oath for him. He says it's for Calidor, but at heart it's for him."

"And for that fool of a boy."

"And you nearly got killed trying to bring the boy back."

"We all agree," Hunt said. "We'd give our lives for

Calidor. We've already given much: lost family and friends in the last war, paid huge taxes to build the wall and the sea defenses. None of us wants to lose more. And this alliance with Pitoria will be just the start of it. Mark my words."

"He's sent boats. After promising to send nothing," Regan said. "Contrived to do it with the help of the bastard boy, who seems to know about borrowing money better than anyone his age ought to."

"If Thelonius can't be trusted to keep a promise such as that, a promise about the defense of our country, then what else will he renege on?" Hunt asked. "And what will the future hold for Calidor if a boy who's born and raised in Pitoria, who's half-Pitorian, takes the throne?"

No one dared answer.

"So, Regan?" Hunt asked. "What do you say? We need you. We've taken a bloody risk talking to you, but you know we're loyal to Calidor in our bones."

"Yes, I know. And it gives me no pleasure to agree with you. I'm reluctant but I'm willing to accept your proposal."

Thanks and congratulations were given in muted tones, and then Hunt said in an even quieter voice, "So we agree on what. The next is how."

Regan said, "It's difficult. Thelonius will still have many supporters."

"We've been thinking along the same lines," Hunt said. "Force can be opposed; indeed it almost invites opposition, but an accident . . . Well, that leaves the future open to whoever is best able to take the country forward."

"An accident that removes Thelonius and his ridiculous

offspring in one simple and quick—and obviously tragic—manner."

*What?!*

"No one will oppose it; no one *can* oppose it. The fates have stepped in . . ."

"And put power into different hands."

"It's for everyone's benefit."

*Except mine and my father's. They really are plotting against us!*

"With Thelonius gone and no heirs, Calidor's future lies with the lords. The chancellor will go along with anything as long as it keeps the money rolling in. And the money will keep rolling in."

"The people love Thelonius, though."

"They'll forget him soon enough. The history books can be rewritten."

"But he saved Calidor."

"The lords saved Calidor. *That* is the history that should be told. We sacrificed our children and many gave their lives."

"So . . . the big question remains . . . *How?*"

"We go to your castle as the final stop of our tour, Birtwistle," Hunt said. "Isn't it a little old, and isn't the masonry a little weak in places? A balcony could collapse at any moment with the weight of people on it. A tragic accident for the perpetually unlucky Prince Edyon."

"And his father."

"The country will mourn briefly and then the lords will rule with you, Regan, as our leader."

# MARCH
## BRIGANT

RASHFORD, SAM, and March set off at dawn.

"How far is it?" March asked.

"We've only just left, and you're already on with the questions?" Rashford joked.

"Is there a law against asking questions in Brigant?"

"Probably," Rashford muttered.

And March did have lots of questions, like: how did Rashford know where to go, and was Prince Harold really their commanding officer, and would he really be there?

"Well, there can't be a law against talking, and I've heard plenty of it in the camp over the last week," Sam said. "Some talk is that Prince Harold is our commanding officer and heir to the throne of Brigant because Prince Boris was killed in battle against the Pitorians."

"There *should* be a law against gossip," Rashford replied. "That'll be from Frank and Fitz, I'm guessing."

"I can't believe Boris is dead." Sam shook his head. "I thought he was invincible. I saw him once. He was on the biggest, blackest stallion you've ever seen. I couldn't hardly look at him for the shine on his armor. The Pitorians have to pay for killing him."

"Aloysius will make them pay. Don't you worry about that, Sam," Rashford replied.

"So it's true? Boris *is* dead?" March asked.

"I believe that the honorable Prince Boris was killed in battle," Rashford said. "However, I don't believe it was the pathetic Pitorian army that killed him. I have it on good authority that he was killed by a spear thrown by his own sister, Princess Catherine. And if that's so, then I'm betting she took some purple smoke to do it."

"I've met Catherine. She's petite and delicate. She'd need the smoke for sure, and I know she uses it," March replied.

Rashford laughed. "Well, of course you're pals with her, March. Hang around in the same smoke den, did you?"

"Not actually, no."

Rashford turned to Sam. "Do you believe March's stories, Sam?"

Sam stared back, almost in surprise. "Sure. Why not?"

"Your innocence does you credit. Me, I'm not so innocent. And March sure ain't. He's poured wine for Prince Thelonius, slept with a dead demon, and now he's taken smoke with Princess Catherine."

"Actually, she watched while I was healed by the smoke. Prince Tzsayn was with her," March interjected.

Sam gawped in delight.

"Oh, of course. I took that for granted." Rashford smiled.

"Who *hasn't* hung out with Prince Tzsayn? Me and him go way back. But tell me, March, have you met Prince Harold of Brigant?"

"Not yet."

Sam asked, "How old is Prince Harold? I thought he was just a little boy."

Rashford laughed. "Like us all, he just keeps getting older."

March tried to remember what he knew. "He's three years younger than Princess Catherine, so that means he's fourteen."

"Younger than most of us Bulls," Rashford said.

"I wonder if he likes a bit of purple smoke," March said.

Sam looked shocked. "Not a prince!"

"Why not? Who wouldn't want all that strength and power, Sam?"

"But he's a prince. He doesn't need it."

March laughed. "Maybe he needs it more."

Rashford agreed. "You might be right there, March. He's head of the boys' brigades now. He wouldn't want us to show him up."

It was midmorning when they saw smoke rising from a camp in the trees ahead. This wasn't like the Bulls' camp. It was bigger and noisier and a whole lot fancier. There were lots of grown men and horses, and also a few carts and some mules. One huge cart, which two blacksmiths were working on, had some kind of metal bars and chains on it. In the center of the camp were two large marquees with black, red, and gold pennants—the colors of royalty.

They made their way to an open area near the tents, where some other boys were already gathering. All were wearing the jerkins of the boys' brigades. Rashford greeted some of the other boys as they stood and waited. Sam muttered, "I can see Bears, Foxes, Lions, Hawks, and even a few Wasps."

Rashford nodded and added thoughtfully, "No Eagles or Stags, though."

There were three, four, or more representatives from each brigade: their leaders and their new recruits. It was easy to tell them apart. The recruits were the ones who looked nervous.

Sam gasped and dug his elbow sharply into March's ribs. "It's him. It's actually him! Prince Harold."

It was, without doubt, the prince. He was wearing a fine golden crown that was woven with his hair to hold it in place. His immaculate clothes were black and gold—leather boots and trousers and a silk shirt, with a leather jerkin similar to that worn by all the boys, except that the prince's had a black sheen, and over his heart he had a different badge—a golden sun.

Sam was muttering, "This is the best day of my life. Look at him. Look at him. He's like a god!"

And it had to be said that Harold did look impressive. He stood with his legs apart in a patch of sun that pierced through the trees. He held a long sword, which caught the light—its blade sparkling silver and the hilt a bright gold. The sword was massive and must have weighed almost as much as Harold, who looked small and delicate—very much like his sister, though Harold's hair was more red-blond. But he was still very much a fourteen-year-old boy, and he was most definitely using demon smoke to give him strength to lift the weapon.

Behind him were two aides, grown men, immaculately dressed. One of them stepped forward and welcomed everyone, and asked the leaders of each brigade to come forward with their new recruits. The Bulls were the first to be summoned, which was an honor—it seemed that Rashford's brigade was highly thought of.

"What do we do?" Sam muttered.

Rashford replied under his breath, "Bow. Look strong. Don't stare and, whatever you do, don't wet yourself, Sam."

March followed Rashford and Sam. He kept his head bowed as the prince spoke to Rashford. "So, Bull leader, how goes the training with your boys?"

"Excellent, Your Highness. They are fit, healthy, and tough. They're learning sword and spear."

"I hope to see them for myself soon. But today is for the recruits. How many boys have you brought?"

"Two new recruits to replace two who manned up last month."

"Two to replace two—you're confident they're good enough?"

"The other brigades always bring more boys than there are places, but I select the boys to bring first. I won't waste your time on any others."

"You. Lift your head." Harold pointed at March, who did as he was told. The prince stepped closer and stared into

March's eyes. "So much silver in those eyes. I've seen a few like them before. But how come they're not at work in our mines in the north?"

"I have lived most of my life in Calidor, Your Highness. As servant to Prince Thelonius."

"And you dare to come to Brigant after living with our enemy?" He glanced at Rashford. "Have you brought a spy into my camp, brigade leader?"

Rashford looked alarmed. "No, Your Highness."

"I'm no spy, Your Highness. I hate Calidor." And that was the absolute truth.

"And yet you brag about coming from that place! The home of our enemies!" The prince grabbed March's hair and wrenched his head to the side and down. It was all March could do to not cry out. March looked up into Harold's face and saw no anger or irritation, merely a curiosity.

Harold held March's hair tight and leaned close to whisper, "Do you think I'm a fool? You're clearly a spy. Or worse: you're an assassin."

March had to think of something to convince Harold. "If I have spied for anyone, it was for your father, Your Highness. I had been providing information to another Abask man called Holywell. Holywell worked for your father."

This was all true as well.

At the mention of this name, Harold's face lit up and he released March's hair. "Holywell! Ha ha. I know him. I remember seeing him thrashed years ago. He was a fighter. A true Abask. A true hard man."

"He was a friend to me but, alas, he's dead now."

"How so?"

"I was with him on the Northern Plateau. We had got something for your father and were fleeing to Brigant." The "something" they'd got had been Edyon, but March would not reveal this to Harold. "We were attacked by Pitorians and a demon," March went on. "The Pitorians got Holywell. The demons got the Pitorians. I escaped."

Harold was grinning now. "What a tale! Your stories are as wild as Holywell's. I was never sure how much of Holywell's talk to believe, nor am I sure about yours yet, but I see something of him in you. Do you fight as well as him?"

March shook his head. "Alas, no, Your Highness. Holywell was an expert with knives, and I witnessed him using them on a Pitorian, a sheriff's man, whose death was bloody but very quick."

"Yes, that's right. I saw him use his knives. You *did* know him!" Harold nodded in approval. "What's your name?"

"March, Your Highness."

"I'll be watching you, March. I expect great things of all my boys and especially of you."

The Bulls were ushered away and the next brigade was brought forward.

Sam was in awe of March having had a conversation with Harold. "I wouldn't have been able to say anything if he'd spoken to me. But you were chatting with him as casually as you'd talk to the baker!"

"The baker doesn't pull me by the hair. Or have the power to have me executed."

"Shits, I thought we were in trouble then," Rashford

said. "But you recovered it well, March. I think he likes you. Just make sure he keeps on liking you, that's all." Rashford looked around as the other boys were being presented to Harold. "Right, listen up, you two. The test will start soon. The best recruits are selected, the rest rejected. You'd better not let the Bulls down."

They didn't have to wait long to find out what the challenge was. As soon as all the boys had been presented to Harold, one of the prince's aides called out, "And now for the test of the new recruits. Your commander, Prince Harold, has taken the opportunity to improve the challenge and has personally designed this test to make it more realistic."

And a man was dragged from behind a marquee. He was covered in cuts and bruises, wearing no shirt or boots, just tattered trousers. The man looked half-dead already and could hardly stand. He had dried blood on his chin and neck.

"He's had his tongue cut out," someone behind March muttered.

*So this is the prince's idea of realism*, March thought.

"This man is a thief and a traitor," the prince's aide continued. "He is to be executed. He has no value except as part of your test. The challenge for you recruits is simple. You must race to retrieve the prince's sword, which will be by this traitor. First to reach the sword and return it to the prince wins. All recruits will be assessed for speed, agility, and fighting spirit. There are weapons to be found along the route that you can use if you wish." And with that, the man was dragged away.

Rashford stared after the prisoner and swore under his

breath, before turning to Sam and March. "Right. Forget about the prisoner—think about each other. Whatever happens, work as a team, look out for each other, and keep your wits about you. Don't be distracted by getting the weapons. Let the others waste time on that. Use your stones well, March. Remember you heal with the smoke and so will the others. So don't hold back, 'cause no one else will."

All the recruits were now given their smoke rations, swapping their empty bottles for full ones. March watched the other boys inhale their smoke, some taking huge amounts.

"Don't take so much," Rashford advised. "You need to have some sense still. Inhale once. Remember to keep focused. I'll follow, but I can't interfere."

The recruits were separated from the leaders. Sam stretched and limbered up. March was nervous but the smoke was filling him with strength, and confidence too. Some of the boys began joking and shoving each other. They were keen to get going—all had too much energy to be waiting around.

The prince and his aides rode past on horseback and the prince shouted, "Good luck, boys. Show me what you can do."

Another aide on horseback now took over. "Right, boys. The prince's sword has been stolen. You have to get it back. Follow the trail out of the woods and up the hill to the thief. Recover the sword. Show us what you're made of. Are you all ready?"

The boys shouted their replies.

"I said, *Are you ready?*"

The boys were shouting even louder now.

"I said: ARE. YOU. READY?"

The reply was long and loud, with swearing and whoops thrown in. March found himself joining in, bellowing as loud as he could.

"Then you must GO." And the man kicked his horse and set off.

With hoots and shouts, the boys started running, quickly passing the man on the galloping horse. March and Sam were in the middle of the pack of thirty boys. The great thing about the smoke was that running was easy, and with the boys around it felt good; it felt like a bit of fun. But March had to remind himself, *This isn't fun. A man's had his tongue cut out. This is real.*

Some of the boys peeled off. One boy leaped up to retrieve a spear that was lodged high in the branches of a tree. Another boy had already picked up a shield. But March couldn't see the point of the weapons. He wasn't going to use a spear on another boy; he'd punch and kick and use his stones if he needed to. And he did need to. The boys were getting more aggressive, tripping one another, pushing and shoving. A brawl had started to one side. The smoke was making them more violent as well as competitive.

A shout to March's right alerted him just in time to leap over a pit. Another two boys were not so quick and fell in. And then the group was out of the woods and in a meadow, which rose before them to a rounded peak far ahead. On the peak was a platform with the wood and metal contraption that the blacksmiths had been working on. The prisoner was standing on the platform with his arms out. The sword was stuck into a wooden beam close to his head.

But getting to the sword wasn't going to be easy—a boy near March screamed and fell, an arrow in his leg. The boy ripped the arrow out, shouting a curse. The archer now fled, but he didn't stand a chance—some other boys chased him and brought him down.

Those boys had got distracted from the main task, but March and Sam stuck to it. They were at the front of the group now. March slowed a little to scan around for more bowmen, but that was a mistake. Pain shot through his back—not from an arrow but a punch. "Too slow, White Eyes." A tall boy with the badge of a Fox ran past him and grabbed Sam, who had turned to check what was happening. The Fox lifted Sam by his jerkin and swung him round, tossing him through the air. Sam rolled nimbly to his feet, dodged an arrow, and gave chase, but they had lost precious moments. The Fox was nearly at the platform. March shouted to Sam to keep going while reaching into his pocket, pulling out his stones, and sending three in rapid succession at the Fox's head. The boy screamed and slowed as blood poured down his neck. Sam ran past him, punching him in the face. They were nearly at the platform, but more arrows rained down, and March and Sam had to run back to avoid them. The boys behind were approaching; one sent a spear whistling past Sam's head. March defended Sam with his stones, cursing as he threw. But Sam was there. He climbed on the platform and shouted, "I've got it! I've got the sword."

And Sam stood on the platform above them all, hand on the hilt of the sword.

March was below him, ready to defend the position with his stones, but the other boys slowed to a halt as the prince and his soldiers rode up.

It was over. Sam had won. And March had hopefully done well enough that he could stay in the army.

Prince Harold called out, "Well done to the Bulls: the first to reach the platform. But to win, you must return the sword to me."

March smiled and looked up at Sam. But then he realized the test wasn't just a matter of getting the sword.

It was stuck into a wooden beam and was holding a rope in place. The prisoner whose tongue was cut out was tied to a wooden cross—no, not tied: his hands were nailed in place. And above the prisoner was a metal contraption with a huge blade attached to it. It was clear that when the sword was removed, the rope would be let loose, the blade would swing round, and . . . and March wasn't sure, but it looked like it might cut the man in two, across his stomach.

The prisoner's face was full of hate, his eyes staring at Harold.

"Come on, Bull. I want my sword back," Harold said.

Sam looked to the prince. His mouth worked, though no words came out. It seemed that he said, "Yes, Your Highness." And, with shaking hands, Sam pulled the sword free.

For a moment, nothing happened. Sam gave a brief smile of relief and held the sword up. But, as he took a step to the prince, the contraption whooshed down, almost taking Sam's arm before it slammed into the prisoner's stomach, cutting across his body. The man was sliced in two. His eyes still stared ahead.

Sam stood in shock, staring ahead too.

The prince rode forward and took the sword.

Sam jumped down to March, not looking round once to the body behind him. "I had to do it. I had to."

"Yes, I know, Sam. The prisoner was dead anyway. The prince did it, not you."

March put a hand on Sam's shoulder, but Sam shook it off. "Don't touch me. I'm not a baby. I can handle it. The man was a traitor."

And all the boys except for Sam stared at the prisoner's body as his lower half slithered slowly to the ground and the upper half was left nailed to the cross.

"Now that's what I call a good spectacle," Harold said with a smile. "Lift up the blade."

The prince's aide ran up to the contraption and pulled the rope but couldn't move it. He pointed at March. "Help me here, Abask."

March climbed onto the platform and pulled the rope, and, with the strength the smoke gave him, he raised the blade. It swung back into its upright position, splattering everyone with spots of blood. And then the innards of the man ran out, blood running in rivulets across the platform, an awful smell following. March didn't want to look at it, didn't want to think. He focused on the rope and tied it securely before jumping down to the ground, getting away from it all as quickly as he could.

The prince was still staring at the man's body. "It's perfect. Quite beautiful. Imagine my uncle's body being displayed like that—the cart being driven from town to town in Calidor. Carts for all his lords too, and that bastard son he's claimed. It'll be quite a parade."

March shuddered. He'd not thought much of his original plan to help Edyon in the last few weeks, but this reminded him of his true aim. The Brigantines were not his friends. The idea of Edyon being treated like this was horrific. As much as March liked Rashford and being a member of the Bulls, they were part of the Brigantine army, and so too, it seemed, were horrors like this device. March would stay with the Bulls and help Edyon in any way if an opportunity arose to do so. But he couldn't wait to get away from Harold.

The prince then raised his sword and shouted, "The Bull recruits have won! They worked fast and together. As a special honor they will be the first in my elite Gold Brigade. They will stay with me."

# TASH
## DEMON TUNNELS

THE SPACE around Tash was bigger. Not much, but bigger. It was also lighter, as a faint red glow filled the air. Tash felt the warmth from the light and felt the light inside her too. She couldn't make sense of it, but she was sure now that some of the red smoke from the dying demon had remained inside her, and it was allowing her to make a tunnel.

She'd started off on her back, gently rubbing the stone in front of her face. Slowly the space above her became bigger. Eventually she'd made enough room to sit up. Now the space was wide enough to stretch her arms out.

*And it feels so, so, so good to stretch.*

She took a break to roll her neck and her shoulders, then flex her legs and feet, but she had to get back to work. She leaned forward and breathed on the rock as she rubbed her hands over the surface. She was concentrating on the rock, thinking about making a tunnel, and slowly the rock dissipated and she edged forward. It was slow and difficult, her arms were aching, and the skin on her fingers was raw, but she was doing it.

*At this rate, perhaps I'll have tunneled out of here by the time I'm a hundred.*

As she worked, Tash thought of her old freedoms that she'd taken for granted—running through the snow in sunlight, looking up at a starry sky, leaping over frozen streams.

The more she thought of good things, the faster she shuffled forward.

She tried to think of the human world, how beautiful it was, and how wonderful it would be to be back there, but as she got more tired, she could only think of the depth of rock between her and the world above, and how painful the raw skin on her fingers was.

It was too much to do, too far to go.

*It's impossible.*

Her arms dropped to her sides, and Tash leaned her forehead against the stone and cried.

She wished Gravell was with her. She'd fall asleep in his arms and never wake up. Tears ran down her face as she imagined him holding her against his chest, his heart beating loud and steady as he put his arms round her. She imagined being on the Northern Plateau with him beneath a pale blue sky.

And then she was falling forward. The tunnel wall seemed to be receding without the use of her hands. But how?

*Doesn't matter how. Just keep doing what you're doing. Think of Gravell.*

She pictured Gravell standing in front of her, holding his spears.

Nothing happened.

She thought of Gravell in the snow, walking through trees.

The stone seemed to recede again.

*That's it! Think of the human world. Oh, I've got it. Think of where you want to go.*

The stone dissipated, laying out a path for her to follow. She was doing it. Making a tunnel—a tunnel filled with a faint red glow. She raised her arms and the floor began to slope upward.

And Tash began to laugh as she walked up toward the world she knew.

# CATHERINE
## NORTHERN PITORIA

Ultimately you must choose: right or wrong,
any choice is better than none.

The King, *Nicolas Montell*

CATHERINE TIPTOED into the king's bedchamber.

"Is he sleeping?" she whispered to the doctor sitting at his bedside.

The doctor nodded. "Yes, Your Majesty."

"No, I'm not. I've slept enough." Tzsayn's voice was rough but weak. "And I'm bored out of my mind." He tried to sit up while the doctor hurried to help. "I can do it myself," Tzsayn muttered, though he clearly couldn't. "Leave me alone."

Catherine took a step back.

"No, not you, my darling." Tzsayn gave her the briefest of weak smiles that turned into a grimace as the doctor pulled him upright. Finally the pillows were arranged to the king's and the doctor's satisfaction, and the doctor took his leave. Tzsayn put his head back and closed his eyes. His face was damp with sweat.

"Shall I sit here?" Catherine asked, stroking the bed beside Tzsayn.

"The chair is best. I wish you could be closer but . . . my leg is giving me a lot of pain. I'm starting to think I'd be better off without it."

Catherine cast her eyes over the outline of the frame that had been put over Tzsayn's leg, holding up the covers so nothing could touch the injured limb. She wasn't sure if he was being serious or not.

"What does Savage say?"

Tzsayn mimicked the doctor's deep, slow voice: "*I will not let your leg defeat me, Your Majesty. If you would allow me to apply several lotions, an ice compress, a hot compress, a heavy compress, an herb compress.*" He looked at Catherine. "He's given me every kind of bloody compress going, and my leg's just getting worse."

"Should we get a different doctor?"

"He's the best. I'm just tired."

"Do you want to be left alone?"

"No!" Tzsayn seemed surprised by the strength of his own reply and repeated it more quietly. "No. Absolutely not. I've had enough of my own company. Just don't come near me with a compress."

Catherine held her hands out. "I'm unarmed, no compresses about my person."

"And so you must stay. I command it!" Tzsayn said with a smile, then he added, "Is this visit about the marriage question?"

"You said you needed an answer soon, but it's only been four days."

Tzsayn looked a little sad. "Indeed. Don't rush. Take longer."

Catherine frowned. "Why do you say that? What's wrong?"

"Nothing. Nothing. Cheer me up. Tell me news."

"That I can do."

"Good news first, then the bad. I'm assuming there is *some* good news, of course—or is that presumptuous?" He looked sharply at her as he said this, as if to judge her expression rather than the words of her reply.

"Good news . . . well . . ." Though Catherine struggled to think of anything. "I've given Tanya a pay raise."

"Good for Tanya."

"And she's spending her money on—well, I'll give you three guesses."

"Hmm, it won't be ribbons or shoes—not Tanya things at all. How much of a raise did you give her?"

"More than I intended."

"How so?"

"Somehow I was persuaded that, since she has the same title, she should be paid the same as General Davyon. I'm still not sure how that happened."

"I'm beginning to think Tanya should be my chief negotiator."

"She wouldn't be a bad choice."

"You are still my first choice—you evaded answering

my question very neatly by pretending Tanya outsmarted you, which I'm absolutely sure she did not. Anyway, as you won't answer my question, I guess she spent her money on . . . a horse."

Catherine laughed. "She does like riding, but no."

"Armor, like yours. She'd be terrifying."

"I will ensure I never suggest it."

"Am I even warm with that guess?"

"Freezing cold."

Tzsayn frowned and shrugged. "Books."

"Now you're being absurd."

"I give up."

"Three words I'd never thought you'd say."

"So put me out of my misery. What did she spend it on?"

"She gave it to the farm widows. Women who've lost their land, as well as husbands, to the war. Their children are destitute."

"She puts us to shame with her generosity. But Lord Eddiscon should be caring for his people, not Tanya."

"I've raised it with Eddiscon but there are always excuses—the lack of money he's getting in taxes; the amount of money he's paid to the crown. I have a certain sympathy, actually. I'm trying to raise money to pay for soldiers, food, horses, weapons, ships, repairs, tents . . . the list goes on. I don't have enough for that, never mind helping those who are left behind in the wake of the war. I'm emptying your coffers faster than a Pitorian greyhound. We'll soon have to borrow more."

"I thought we were doing good news first."

Catherine smiled. "My apologies. You're correct. Let me think . . ." But she was at a loss.

"You're a true Brigantine at heart still. There is no good news in your eyes."

"We're at war. There's disease, there's—"

"What about the sunshine? It's sunny today—is that not good news?"

Catherine sighed dramatically. "Yes, but we Brigantines know only too well that sunshine brings flies, and with the sun comes heat, which means the meat and milk go off faster."

"You sound more like a farmer than a queen."

"I sound like a woman who hears farmers' complaints all day."

"Fine. So the sunshine is a problem. How about the war? Has your father sent his army against us?"

"No. He's still holding back, building up his stockpile of smoke, no doubt."

"It's a grim situation indeed—sunshine and peace." Catherine snickered.

"And you laugh at this dire situation!" Tzsayn scolded her.

"My apologies again, Your Majesty."

"So give me the really bad news then." His face was serious now. "The red fever?"

"There have been no new deaths from it for three days now, and most are recovered, but some are still weak."

"Is that almost good news or is there a punch line?"

"It's almost good news. Just not all good yet."

"Is Sir Ambrose ready to go?"

"The day after tomorrow. I was going to ask you about that. It would be useful if he attended the war briefing tomorrow, so that he understands the overall situation." Catherine hesitated, then plunged on. "And I'd like to wish him well. He's my oldest friend. He's helped me and protected me for years. This mission is incredibly dangerous. There is a good chance he may not come back. I confess I've met him once . . . by chance. But I shouldn't have to confess it. I need to set my own standard of behavior."

"You think I'm a dictator? That I've gone too far in my concern about appearances?"

"No to the first question. And perhaps a little to the second."

Tzsayn nodded. "You should see him. Give him my thanks for all he's done." But he couldn't seem to resist adding, "But meet him in a public place. With Tanya, Davyon, and half the army . . . no, the whole army, present."

Catherine smiled. "It'll be Tanya, Davyon, and the generals at the war meeting—actually not that far off your request."

"Good. Any more news? How are our friends the Calidorians?"

"Lord Darby and his aide are actually more experienced than I initially expected. They fought Aloysius in the last war and their insights are useful, but dealing with them is even harder than negotiating with the farmers. However, they have agreed to sell us some ships, though we're having to pay for them at vastly inflated prices. I'm going to take delivery of them next week and sign Pitoria up for years of loan repayments."

"That's tomorrow's problem," Tzsayn said. "At least we'll have the ships today. You've done well with the Calidorians. Thelonius has always had a problem trusting others. That comes from having a brother like Aloysius, I suppose." Tzsayn held his hand out to her. His skin was hot and his fingers felt thin, but his tone was as comforting as ever. "You astound me, Catherine. To come from that family—to have Aloysius as a father, Boris as a brother—and to be so loving and caring. Not to have been corrupted by that shows how strong you are."

"You're too generous. I was lucky in one respect: being female, my father took no interest in me. I rarely saw him, was rarely in the company of Boris or any man. At the time I felt imprisoned, but now I'm glad I led a sheltered life. I was protected from the worst of my father's ways. I fear for my younger brother, Harold." She hesitated before adding, "He was on the battlefield after Boris died, and sent a message to me."

"Really? I didn't hear of this."

"I didn't want to bother you with it. He maimed a Pitorian—after the battle and for no reason other than his own evil pleasure—and left a message that I should flee before he leads the army against us." Catherine recalled Harold before she'd left Brigant—standing on the quay, watching her ship leave, a small boy in the shadow of his older brother. "I try to imagine him now. But we spent so little time together. He was always trying to copy Boris or my father.

He's just turned fourteen. From what the soldiers say, he had the strength of a grown man, so I'm sure he must have taken some purple demon smoke. But I'm more concerned that he's changed in his heart as much as in his body. He was a little boy just a few months ago, but I know my father will be training him—perverting the way he thinks."

Tzsayn gave her fingers a gentle squeeze. "At least you're safe from your father now."

"As are you." Catherine leaned forward and kissed his hand.

"You have no idea how I hate him. A man like that doesn't deserve to rule; he doesn't deserve a family."

She nodded, thinking of her mother, who had lost Boris and Catherine and probably no longer saw Harold.

"I'm sorry I'm not more help." Tzsayn's eyes began to close.

"You are a help. But you're tired. Shall I leave you now? Do you want to sleep?"

"Stay for a while longer. Hold my hand. Tell me something good."

And that's when Catherine realized how much Tzsayn needed her to take his mind off what he'd been through at the hands of her father's torturers. So she described the tree that grew outside her window in Brigane, how the breeze ruffled the leaves so they shimmered and the sun would change its leaves from pale to lime green, which reminded her of something else, and she described tasting a lime for the first time and how delighted she was with the flavor, and after that she talked about her favorite fruit—raspberries—and the berries she used to eat in Brigant. And by the time she'd described them all, Tzsayn was sleeping, his head turned to the side so she could see his old burn scars.

Catherine kissed his hand once more, laid it back down on the bed, and tiptoed out of the room.

# AMBROSE
## NORTHERN PITORIA

AMBROSE MARCHED across the camp, doing his best to walk without a limp. It was the day before he was due to leave for the Northern Plateau, and he'd finally been invited to the war council. But he took no pleasure in the summons. It undoubtedly meant Tzsayn would be there. The invitation must have come from him. There was no way Ambrose would be allowed near Catherine outside the king's presence, not after being caught with her by Tanya.

The previous day he had tried the sympathy card on Catherine's maid, but received short shrift. "I might never see her again, Tanya. The mission is absurdly dangerous."

"And you put Catherine in danger when you see her. She . . . she changes with you, Ambrose. She forgets herself."

He had liked hearing that, though he preferred to think that it was her work and role that Catherine forgot. That with him, she was her truer self.

"You're not good for her," Tanya continued. "Her position is precarious. It would be best if you didn't 'accidentally' meet her again."

"Catherine came into that tent looking for you, I believe. I just happened to be there reminding myself of the army's positions. If I was invited to the war council, I wouldn't have had to do that."

"Davyon briefs you personally. You've no need to go."

And that was the end of it.

Until this morning, when Davyon had sent a message— Ambrose was invited to the council where, no doubt, Tzsayn would be pontificating and posing in one of his absurd blue outfits while Catherine was pushed into the background to deal with the bills like a good little housewife.

Ambrose strode past the guards and into the tent, his leg only bothering him slightly. Davyon greeted him with a formal bow and introduced Ambrose to General Hanov and General Ffyn.

"So, we're just waiting for Tzsayn, are we?" Ambrose said.

Davyon opened his mouth to comment but then turned away.

Hanov replied, "No. Queen Catherine attends for him."

"For herself, I'd say," Ffyn muttered.

"Well, if Tzsayn won't come, she has to, I suppose," Ambrose countered, a little surprised. *Would she be here? Why didn't Tzsayn come?* "Perhaps the king is too busy with his latest fashion, designing some new silk trousers."

Davyon turned back, his body rigid with anger. "They're going to amputate his leg, if you must know."

*What?*

The general's eyes seemed full of pain and anger.

Ambrose started to apologize, but Davyon's gaze had already moved past him, to the entrance of the tent. Ambrose turned and saw Catherine in the doorway, her face ashen.

"Is that true?" she demanded.

Davyon nodded reluctantly. "My apologies, Your Majesty. The king didn't want you to know until after the operation."

"Well, I certainly know now."

The silence seemed to go on. No one moved.

Catherine's eyes filled with tears, and she turned and left the tent.

Ambrose wanted to curl up in a hole, or rewind time and take his words back. But it was too late. "Davyon, I apologize. I—"

"I'm not interested in your apology," Davyon seethed. "This isn't about you, Sir Ambrose. You're here to discuss the war and to make sure you don't fail in your mission. Now let's get on with it."

# CATHERINE
## NORTHERN PITORIA

*Love is madness; love is free; love rarely
lasts for eternity.*

*Pitorian saying*

CATHERINE LAY on her bed, holding the bottle of
purple smoke to her chest. She wanted to speak to Tzsayn but
didn't know what to say to him. What could she say? Losing
a limb would be bad enough, but if the best doctors in Pitoria
couldn't save his leg, there were no guarantees they'd save
his life. Why hadn't he told her?

"Have you used any of that stuff?"

It was Tanya, standing in the doorway, hands on hips.

"Not yet, but I'm going to." Even if the smoke no longer
gave her strength, it might help her forget her misery.

Tanya marched over, saying, "Not if I have anything to
do with it," and she snatched the bottle out of Catherine's
grasp.

"Give that back!" Catherine sat up and held her hand out.

Tanya didn't move.

"That's an order."

"No," Tanya replied, holding the bottle out of reach. "And that's a refusal."

"Shall I call the guards and have them take it from you?"

"Well, as you're the queen and I'm merely the dresser, you could do that."

Catherine was half-tempted just to show Tanya . . . but show her what? She flopped back on the bed. "Please leave me alone."

"Can't oblige you there either, Your Majesty. I've spoken to Davyon."

"Good for you."

"And Savage."

Catherine tensed. Did she want to know what the doctor had said? Was there worse news? She raised her head. "What did he say?"

"They've only just decided to amputate. It's the only route to take—medically, I mean. As you were due to go to the coast to see the Calidorian ships, Tzsayn wanted it done while you were away. He wanted to save you from distress."

"Well, it hasn't saved me from anything."

"No, but it might save the king some distress if he thought you still didn't know."

Catherine's eyes filled with tears. "So I'm supposed to go off to look at some boats and hope my husband is still alive when I get back?"

Tanya raised an eyebrow. "Your what?"

"You know what I mean."

"Whatever Tzsayn is to you, at this moment he's trying

to save you some pain. I'm sure he's feeling helpless and wants to have some control over something in his life."

Catherine thought Tanya was right. But she was still hurt and angry. "Just last week he talked to me about being honest. Ha!"

She thought back to that conversation and then to their most recent one. He'd not pushed her for a marriage decision and even said she could have more time. More time until after his operation. "He . . . he knows he may not survive." Catherine looked at Tanya, tears in her eyes.

"I can't imagine he wants to lie to you, but he's trying to do what he thinks is best. He cares for you very much."

"And I care for him."

"Enough to play along with his plan?"

"I don't know." Catherine was due to leave for the coast the following day. She'd be gone for three nights. Davyon would be here with Tzsayn. He was Tzsayn's closest friend and companion and would be at his side. Still, it felt like she was being pushed out. "Davyon will be with him and I'll be looking at ships." She felt it should be the other way round—she wanted it to be the other way round.

"Savage says the operation will take some time, and the king will be given a sleeping potion," Tanya said cautiously. "He'll not wake at all for over a day. Then they'll keep him sedated until the pain lessens."

"But what if he doesn't wake at all?"

"Savage says there's a good chance that all will go well."

"A slim chance it'll go badly, then."

"You can't do anything to change that by remaining here."

"I know that."

"So . . . shall I set out your traveling clothes for tomorrow?"

Catherine curled up on her bed and mumbled, "I don't know. Let me think."

Tanya left and Catherine lay quietly for a while. She had to go and see the ships; that was her duty, but not her only duty. The Calidorians could wait two days, but if she delayed her departure until after the operation, then she'd be away when Tzsayn was awake and recovering, and she'd hate to leave him at that time too.

She had to make a choice. And linked to that choice was the other choice between Tzsayn and Ambrose.

Catherine gazed up at the canopy above her.

*I have to see Ambrose.*

# AMBROSE
## NORTHERN PITORIA

AMBROSE PACED outside the war council tent, cursing his own stupidity.

*Idiot! Idiot!*

The rest of the meeting had been a disaster. Catherine had not returned, and Davyon would barely speak to him, while Hanov and Ffyn hardly knew where to look or what to say.

Why had he made that joke about Tzsayn's health? Admittedly it irked him that Tzsayn seemed to have Catherine's favor. But to let that rivalry affect his behavior so much as to shame himself with thoughtless, childish comments? *Unforgivable.*

Ambrose imagined that he and Tzsayn might have been friends under other circumstances. He admired the king's bravery and kindness. And Tzsayn had been tortured by Aloysius just as Ambrose's brother and sister had been, so shouldn't Ambrose feel extra sympathy toward him? But he didn't. What was wrong with him? Was he inhuman? Was his love for Catherine driving out whatever noble qualities he might once have possessed?

He was still pacing when Tanya hurried up to him.

"Catherine wants to see you."

"Now?"

"Yes, now."

"What's happening?"

"I don't know, Sir Ambrose, but you've certainly set the cat among the pigeons."

Ambrose followed Tanya through the royal enclosure and into an open marquee by a stream, where she left him alone. The table was laden with papers, indicating that this was where Catherine worked. The location was beautiful—the stream bubbling through the camp, the arrangement of silk carpets and curtains, water, grass, ferns. And now he saw that Tanya was walking to the other side of the stream, as if he was on a playhouse stage and she was there to watch.

"Sir Ambrose."

He turned to see Catherine. Her skin was pale and her eyes were red from crying.

"Your Majesty." Ambrose bowed. "Please, may I speak first?"

Catherine nodded.

"I can only apologize for my behavior earlier today. I was unpardonably rude and insensitive. I'm ashamed of myself."

"We all make mistakes, Ambrose. We all say things we shouldn't," she replied.

"I'm sorry if I've caused you any pain."

"I was shocked at first, but you weren't to know Tzsayn's situation. After all, we have deliberately kept secret the severity of his wounds. And now it seems even I didn't know the full story. But I've had the morning to think about it, and that has made me think of other things too. Of my feelings for Tzsayn . . . and for you."

"I've ruined the good opinion you had of me, haven't I? I can see it."

Catherine shook her head. "My opinion of you hasn't changed, Ambrose. I don't think it ever will. You have always been a dear friend to me. You've seen me through so many troubles; it would be stupid of me to let one small mistake undo all that."

"I've been more than a good friend to you, I hope." Ambrose wanted to step closer, but something about her poise kept him back.

"You have been my first love and my most faithful friend and supporter."

*First but not last?*

Ambrose had to say something. "Your lover and your fighter. That was the phrase we used."

Catherine blushed a little. "And I will always love you. Always. You're part of me, my history, my journey here." She put her hand on her heart. "And here." Then she smiled and put her hand on her head. "And here too. And I would not change that, even if I could. I do not wish to hurt you, but as much as I love you, I also love Tzsayn."

Ambrose swallowed, dread filling him. It wasn't so much her words but the way she spoke them—with a certainty that he'd never heard from her before. But still, he had to ask.

"And you choose Tzsayn?"

"He's right for me, Ambrose. I finally realized it this morning after hearing what was going to happen to him. It's Tzsayn that I truly love. It's Tzsayn that I want to be with."

*Tzsayn, Tzsayn, Tzsayn.* "He kept you away from me. Even now he contrives to do it. He plays with people like they're chess pieces."

"No, Ambrose. Circumstances kept us apart. Society, appearances . . . whatever you want to call it. But, much as I missed you, I was able to endure our separation. If I'm apart from Tzsayn, if anything happens to him now, I know my feelings will be . . . deeper."

"And you know too that he may not survive the week." Ambrose felt cruel saying it.

"I do. But I'll risk that, because I can see that the future with him, if we're allowed it, will be best for us both. We're alike; we want the same things; we can make each other happy. And that's the difference. I was never sure I could make you happy by being me. With Tzsayn, I know that the more I become my true self, the more our relationship blossoms."

It was over. There was no way to argue or plead. Ambrose had run out of words. He looked across the stream at Tanya, who was standing, watching. This place and these people were a part of him. He'd fought for them, bled for them. His brother had been killed, his sister executed too. His father was probably dead. His lands lost forever. Everything seemed to be lost.

*What was it all for?*

Ambrose had an overwhelming urge to get on his horse, ride out of the camp, and keep going.

As if Catherine was reading his thoughts, she spoke again. "Ambrose, I have a feeling you're thinking of leaving us. But I ask you to resist that urge. You've saved my life and Tzsayn's too. If it weren't for you, all of Pitoria would be lost. We owe you so much and I know you've given so much already, but I still ask that you fight on with us. Lead the mission to the demon world. You are a great soldier, but you're an even greater leader. Help us and continue the fight against my father."

Could he do it? Did he want to do it? Ambrose felt like gathering Catherine in his arms and sweeping her away. But this wasn't the Catherine of even just a few weeks ago. The girl had gone, and now there was a woman. Well, he was a man to match her. He stood straighter, his head up. "I'll fight, Catherine. I'll lead the attack into the demon world. But not for you, or for Tzsayn, or even for Pitoria, but for me, my family, and Brigant."

And, as he said it, he knew it was the right decision and there'd be no changing it.

# CATHERINE
## NORTHERN PITORIA

*Truth is like a diamond—precious and hard.*
*Pitorian saying*

CATHERINE NEEDED to calm down after Ambrose left. He'd been upset, obviously, and was probably angry and very hurt and many other things, but she had to believe that he could cope with his feelings. She was upset too, but she'd managed to master her emotions, though tears filled her eyes as she remembered the look of hurt on Ambrose's face. But her responsibility now was not to Ambrose but to Tzsayn. She wanted to be with him more than anything. She ran out of her tent and to Tzsayn's bedchamber, slowing as she approached his sleeping figure, and sat close to him, taking his hand and kissing it.

"That's good to wake to."

Catherine smiled and kissed his hand again. "I leave at dawn for my journey to the coast. I thought I'd sit with you for the rest of this afternoon. If you don't mind."

"I definitely do not mind."

She kissed his hand again.

He squinted at her. "You seem different."

"Do I?"

She had to find a way of telling him about her decision.

"And how did the council go this morning?"

"The war council?"

"Yes, the war council. The one Sir Ambrose was invited to. I assume he attended?"

"He most certainly did. He's had his hair dyed crimson. Who'd have thought anyone with such brightly colored hair could still be so . . . manly."

"Who indeed? And was anything discussed at the meeting besides Ambrose's hairstyle?"

"Actually, I don't know what was discussed at the meeting. I didn't stay."

"What? Why not? What's been going on?" Tzsayn frowned.

"The truth has been going on."

"You're talking in riddles."

"By chance I heard the truth. A difficult truth, but one I needed to hear." Catherine lifted his hand again and kissed it. "The truth that they're going to . . . that your leg is worse than I realized . . . than you told me. That Savage is going to operate." Tears filled her eyes.

Tzsayn struggled to sit up. "Who told you?"

"No one told me. I overheard Davyon saying something. But don't blame him. You should have told me."

"I judge differently. And Davyon should have kept his mouth shut. He's supposed to be discreet. That's his job."

"Well, sometimes even Davyon makes a mistake. He cares about you very much."

"That's no excuse."

"And I care for you very much too. I care that you planned to deceive me. I know that you did it for the best of reasons, but when we spoke last week you talked about honesty, and yet you chose to hide this from me. I wasn't sure what to do about it, if I should play along and go and buy some ships."

"Obviously you decided against that sensible course of action."

Catherine ignored his comment and continued with her speech.

"I don't want you to deceive me, ever. And I won't deceive you. On anything. Big or small. I won't pretend I don't know about this—it's too important. It's hurt me that you thought I'd be better off not knowing. I don't want us to have a relationship with any lies or pretense . . . not if we're going to be husband and wife."

Tzsayn went very still. "Husband and wife?"

"Indeed."

"So . . . are you saying that you agree to marry me for real?" Tzsayn asked, a half-smile playing on his face.

"Yes, that is what I'm saying."

Tzsayn pulled her hand to his lips and kissed it. "I want to take you in my arms but I'm too weak."

Catherine gently leaned forward and kissed his lips. "You asked me to choose my future. I choose a future with you."

"Really? Even though . . . my leg."

Catherine kissed him on the lips again. "I love you. With or without the leg."

"You know I lied because I was trying to . . ." Tzsayn

stopped when he saw her look. "Fine, I won't make excuses about that. But I don't want you to cancel your trip."

Catherine nodded. "I wish I could. I wish I could be with you. It'll hurt me to leave, but I have to sign the loan agreements. Only the royal seal will suffice, or, knowing the Calidorians, they'll sail their ships away again. And every day we don't have them means we're vulnerable."

"I wish you could stay, but we're both strong. We'll get through this."

*But are you strong enough?*

Perhaps. Catherine stared at Tzsayn's thin face, and it seemed to her it had already changed. He was smiling and there was delight in his eyes.

"Yes, we're both strong," Catherine repeated. "We'll get through this."

"And when you return, we'll have the coronation." He leaned forward and whispered, "And, before that, the marriage ceremony, which I long for much more."

"I love you very much."

Tzsayn smiled. "And I love you. I will do my best to be the husband you deserve. I won't lie or deceive—and I will get out of this damned bed and, even with one leg, I'll stand with you."

# TASH
## DEMON TUNNELS

TASH CLIMBED up the slope, the stone parting before her. In her mind she held an image of the Northern Plateau, of sunlight and trees and a stream. She was thirsty and tired but suddenly the darkness around her was no longer a red-dark but a blue-dark. There were little spots of silver light above her—stars.

Tash put her arms up, hardly daring to believe it.

*Please don't be a dream.*

She scrambled up the slope and her hand touched cool earth—not stone but soil, which she dug her fingers into. The air was chillingly cold and she collapsed on the ground, rolling onto her back, then crawling to a tree to put her arms round it like an old friend. The bark scratched her cheek.

"It's real. I've made it."

Tash ran her hand over the ground. All she wanted to do was marvel at the beauty of the plateau. She lay back and stared up at the stars, wept silently, and eventually slept.

It was still dark when Tash woke, chilled to the bone.

"At least it's not that horrible total black-dark. This is the lightest dark possible," she muttered. "And muttering to yourself isn't a sign of madness. It's just a sign of . . . being a normal, talkative type of person. I'd talk to the trees if I could. Shitting shits, I'm cold."

She got to her feet and jumped around to get warm. "Need to make a fire. Then get some water and food. Then . . ."

But she wasn't sure what would come after that.

"Who cares? Fire first."

Tash set off, picking up old dried branches and some moss that was good to get the fire going. She found a stream nearby and drank and washed her face. As she walked, she noticed a faint red glow in a slight depression in the ground ahead of her. She froze. A demon hollow?

Then she realized what it was and smiled.

"I've walked in a circle. It's my demon hollow. I made that."

She started the fire and wondered if someone might see it. Brigantines or Pitorians. Geratan maybe? But she could see no other fires anywhere. The only light was from the stars and moon.

She lay by the fire, warm at last. "Tomorrow is for setting traps for food. Easy enough when I'm rested." And she closed her eyes and slept again.

The next time Tash woke, the sky was a pale blue and the sun was over the treetops. Her fire was out, but she was lying in a pool of sunlight. It felt wonderful to have the warmth of the sun on her skin. She got up and stretched—oh, the joy of stretching. That would never get old.

Her stomach made a loud, groaning noise. She hadn't been this hungry in a long time. She'd have to set some rabbit traps and then go and get her bearings—where exactly was she?

*Food first.*

She made traps, set them, and started her fire up again, then sat by it, looking over to her demon hollow. It was still there, still glowing faintly red. She had thought it might close—after all, there was no demon alive to keep it open. Somehow, though, it was staying open for her. It was her tunnel, her demon hollow.

*But I'm not a demon.*

At that thought, Tash looked at her own skin to check.

*Definitely human.*

But the demon hollow—her hollow—was still there.

*There's a wisp of smoke still in me. That's why. I've still got a bit of demon smoke deep inside that came out of the demon when he was dying. It was heading back to the core of the demon world, but somehow some of it got left behind.*

Tash turned away from the hollow. "I may have a bit of demon in me, but I'm not a demon. I'm human. I don't belong in there. I belong up here in the human world."

She thought of the human world farther south. Civilization. She really should go back there, back to civilization.

"I should get a job, food . . . a bed to sleep in." She picked at the worn leather of her shoes. "New boots. The ones I wanted in Dornan. The most beautiful boots in all the world."

Though now she thought about it, Tash no longer wanted

the boots. She wasn't sure what she did want, other than to sit here by her fire and do nothing.

It was a beautiful spot. The stream was clear and gentle, forming a lovely pool just right for bathing in. It was similar to a pool she'd bathed in last summer, with two flat boulders, one submerged so that you could sit on it comfortably in the water, the other out of the water for drying on. She could do with a good wash now. It would be the perfect place. She got up and went to the pool.

As Tash approached, she could see the two boulders weren't similar; they were *exactly* the same shape as the pool she remembered.

*Is it the same one?*

Impossible, surely.

Of all the millions of places to emerge on the surface of the Northern Plateau, she'd come out at a place she'd been to before?

But it did look exactly the same.

*If it's the same place, then . . .*

Tash turned round and walked to the west and, within a short distance, she found what she was looking for. It was partly filled in, one side collapsed, but two of the sides were straight. It was a demon pit that Gravell had dug.

She walked back to her demon hollow and realized it was where she and Gravell had made their campfire. The same spot where they'd sat and talked and . . . and it was the place she'd imagined when she was tunneling.

The tunnel hadn't just brought her out to the Northern

Plateau—it had brought her out to the very spot she'd been imagining.

*The exact same spot.*

"Shits."

*That's amazing. I mean, moving rock is amazing, but moving rock so you can travel wherever you want to be—that is really amazing.*

And now Tash had another idea.

*If I think of Twist, can I tunnel to him?*

She wanted to see Twist. He was the one demon who had tried to help her and she knew he hadn't wanted her to be encased in stone.

"But Twist will probably be with all the other demons who *do* want me encased in stone. Not that they can do that to me again, ha ha. Not now that I'm the queen of tunneling."

But they might not encase her in stone next time. Next time . . .

*They might just pull my head off.*

Tash knew she should forget about the demon world and head south.

*I should get a job, a safe job, with money and . . . and. But I don't want that. I want to see Twist. I want to learn about the demon world.*

She looked back to her demon hollow. Frost, the girl she'd seen down in the demon world, seemed to know it better than anyone—at least, anyone else human. Tash wanted to know about her as well, and why she was helping the Brigantines.

*I wonder if she can make tunnels too. But she'll be with lots of Brigantines, who aren't noted for being any nicer than demons, so I can't really ask.*

Tash began pacing up and down. She wanted to test her skills. But how?

She stopped pacing.

"Simple. I head to the central core. Once I'm there, I can decide about Frost or Twist or just leaving for good. But first I have to see if I can really do this."

# EDYON
## ABASK, CALIDOR

EDYON HAD remained hidden behind the chair in Regan's room, crouched and fearful, long after Hunt and Birtwistle had left. Regan took time over his ablutions, blew out the candles, and went to bed, but it was only when he was snoring lightly that Edyon dared to carefully push the chair forward, crawl out from behind it, and creep to the door. Edyon did not immediately go to his father to report the conversation he'd overheard. Instead, he returned to his own room.

Why didn't he report the treason immediately? Well, in truth, Edyon had a feeling his father wouldn't believe him. And he wasn't sure he believed it himself. The whole incident seemed unreal, and this feeling of unreality wasn't helped by the fact he had been more than a little drunk when he'd hidden behind the chair. Edyon left it a day, and then another, and with time, the more the whole event seemed more unreal and the more he began to wonder if he'd misheard, or misinterpreted, or indeed imagined the whole thing.

Birtwistle's castle home was the last stop on the tour, so

Edyon had some time to decide what to do, but time was running out. He asked his father one day, with practiced casualness, "Do you trust Lord Regan?"

"Absolutely," Thelonius replied without hesitation. "He is my oldest friend and confidant. I would trust him with my life, and I did trust him with yours. Why do you ask?"

Edyon could only look away. "No particular reason."

What he needed was proof. Something he could show his father so it wouldn't just be his word against Regan's.

Were more lords in on this assassination plot, or was it just Regan, Hunt, and Birtwistle? It seemed that Regan hadn't been the instigator, but it hadn't taken much time or effort to draw him into the plot.

The irony was that Edyon could understand some of the motives of the plotters—they believed Edyon was illegitimate, which was true. He himself had not been able to lie about his parents' being married, and yet Regan had been pushed by Thelonius into perjuring himself.

Then, of course, there was the issue of money. Edyon had learned from the chancellor that all the lords had been taxed severely to finance the building of the huge border walls. Regan, Hunt, and Birtwistle had been taxed most and continued to pay. And, finally, there was the issue of the aid to Pitoria, and thus also the issue that Edyon himself, their king-to-be, was half-Pitorian.

However, none of this was reason enough for a coup nor could it excuse murder. And the traitors were with Edyon and his father every day and every evening. Edyon watched them closely, listened to them speak, and observed their

mannerisms. He wondered if he could draw them out in dis-
cussions, but they were all careful to talk only of defending
Calidor and supporting, if weakly, any decision Thelonius
made.

The tour had progressed to the border wall and they rode
westward along the southern side of it, camping beneath its
looming presence for a night. The wall was, as everyone had
promised, impressive. Even Edyon could see that a lot of men
and a lot of money had been needed to construct it. The huge,
first wall was formidable, the ditch wide and deep, and the far
wall thick and solid.

Edyon woke early and lay on his bed, thinking about the
traitors, the wall, Aloysius, and, indeed, his whole life. He
recalled Madame Eruth's foretelling: *This is the crossroads.
Your future divides here. There is a journey, a difficult one, to far
lands and riches, or to pain, suffering, and death.*

He'd chosen a path, and, after much time with death all
around him, he was now in a land of riches. But was death
just the other side of the wall? Was death around him in the
form of the traitors?

Madame Eruth had also foretold a handsome foreign
man. Where was he now? Where was March?

Edyon couldn't stay in bed any longer. He rose and
climbed to the top of the wall.

"No sign of the boy army yet?" Byron asked as he joined
Edyon in the early morning light.

Edyon shook his head. "Brigant's a lot less forbidding
than I'd anticipated. I expected to look over the wall and
see . . . oh, I don't know, half-starved people and barren

fields." He gazed at the rolling green fields on the Brigantine side. "But will the wall do its job? Imagine an army of boys running toward us, Byron. Would they be able to scale these walls and attack our army?"

Byron's gaze followed Edyon's. "It wouldn't be easy. Even with smoke. And once you're in the ditch, you're vulnerable, a sitting target. Of course, that doesn't mean the Brigantines won't try it."

Edyon knew he was right. Death was there to the north, but, turning to look at his father's camp, he saw Regan and Hunt walking together, and he had a feeling that death was there too.

The royal tour left the camp and headed into the rugged territory of Abask. As they threaded their way up the jagged mountains, Edyon tried to take it all in. There were stunning views back down the valley, a series of waterfalls with the faint colors of a rainbow in the mist at the bottom. But there were no people, no villages, not even any proper roads.

"So, what do you think of your land, Edyon?" Thelonius asked as he rode beside him.

"It's very beautiful," Edyon replied.

"Beautiful and empty. I know you think I feel nothing for the Abasks who were here, Edyon. But I do. This was their home, and they fought hard and died for it. They were a brave people."

Edyon nodded but didn't know what to say. It was true—March was perhaps the bravest person he'd ever known.

"During the last war, the Abask people were trapped here, surrounded by the Brigantine army. They clung on as long as they could, until the Brigantines overwhelmed them, killing most and taking the ones left alive as slaves. There were so many Brigantines—they'd trapped us in Calia. But at least we still had routes out via the sea. The Abasks didn't even have that." Thelonius added, "We could have fled, of course, but I'll never leave."

Edyon remembered what March had told him about Abask. The Brigantine army had killed many, but what had defeated the Abasks was hunger. This had been their land; they'd not fled either. They'd been killed or taken. That was true of March too.

Thelonius continued, "I received news last night from our spies in Brigant. They report that the main Brigantine army is still in the north, and they have no significant troops to the south. My assessment is that the ships they are massing will attack Pitoria, and the Brigantine ground troops will strike there too."

"I'm glad you sent them the ships."

"Let's hope Tzsayn can make use of them."

"And what if Aloysius defeats the Pitorians and turns on us?"

"We'll be ready for him. The ports are protected. The north wall is well fortified. Even with all its might, the Brigantine army will struggle to breach it."

"And what of the boy army? What of their powers when they have the smoke?"

"They will be formidable. You've shown us that, Edyon. Lord Darby reports that the Pitorians are sending men to disrupt the production of demon smoke. We can only hope they are successful."

"Didn't Lord Darby say that the boy army was in the south of Brigant?"

"The Pitorians believe some of these boys' brigades are. I've had various reports and it seems some are in the south—actually not far from here, just over the border." Perhaps seeing the look of concern on Edyon's face, Thelonius said dismissively, "But they aren't an army—they need a leader and a real man's army behind them. They have neither."

"But wasn't the latest rumor that Harold—"

"Harold is a boy. Younger than you and just as inexperienced. He's no leader. He's no Boris, no Aloysius. I'd be delighted if he was in charge. I hear he's fond of fashion and changes his hairstyle daily."

Edyon brushed his hand with a small feeling of shame over the new, rather showy, velvet jacket he'd put on that morning. "But won't he have advisers who do have experience?"

"Yes, Edyon, and he'll learn in time, as you will. But for now, he's just a boy."

So that was how Thelonius thought of Edyon. Just a boy? At times that was all he felt like. A boy trailing along, following his father, a man who had been a stranger to him until recently and often still seemed like a stranger. And how could he tell this man that his oldest friend was plotting against him? It would sound ludicrous.

When they reached a confluence of two rivers, they

stopped and made camp for the night. Tables were laid out with wine and food. The warm light from the setting sun gave everything a golden glow. Edyon stood by the water, watching the sun fall behind the mountain. The camp lanterns began to shine out.

Again, Byron joined him, saying, "Abask really is surprising. There is beauty everywhere I look."

Edyon glanced at Byron, catching his eye for what seemed like a long moment. *Does he mean me? Is Byron flirting with me?* Edyon couldn't help but smile. *No! Don't be ridiculous.*

Byron continued, "Will you make a home here? Castle Edyon? It could be stunning."

"I'm not sure. Perhaps. But everything here is so . . . so empty. There's not a village, not even a house left standing from when the Abasks were here."

"They all lived in mud huts," Regan said, joining them and immediately dispelling whatever flirtation might have been in the air.

"I'm not sure that's true," Byron muttered to Edyon.

"They were a primitive bunch. Inbreds," Regan continued.

"I'm not so sure about that either," Byron muttered again, and more loudly he replied, "My father has much respect for them, Lord Regan."

"Does he now? And have you met any Abasks yourself, Byron?"

"Um, no."

"Alas, I have . . . as I said, evil-looking inbreds."

Regan looked at Edyon as if waiting for him to admit to

knowing at least one Abask. Edyon had never wanted to punch anyone so badly before.

"Still, it's certainly an impressive location," Regan continued. "It would be a magnificent place for a castle. And it's not so impractical. It's only two days' ride to Calia if you go over the pass. And you could have the roads improved. The land in the river valleys is fertile for farming. There are plenty of forests for wood, for hunting. There's also some old copper, tin, and silver mines, which could be reopened."

It almost sounded like Regan was planning on taking Abask for himself when his plot came to fruition.

"It's a huge amount of work. And a huge amount of money," Edyon said, wondering if Regan would say more.

Byron added, "But it could be wonderful. Perhaps you could utilize the mountainside to create waterfalls, pools, and gardens."

Edyon nodded. "They might even surpass Lord Regan's fountains and terraces."

"That would be a commendable venture, Your Highness," Regan replied. "I could see that this would be a place of wonder."

*Yes, but who do you imagine living here? Me or you?*

And then it seemed Regan couldn't resist adding, "It certainly would be a wonderful place for you and your family to live—a wonderful place for your children to grow up. Your wife would be a lucky woman indeed."

Edyon pasted a pleasant smile on his face. "She would be. Though I've yet to find the right woman for me."

"The chancellor is keen to help," Regan said. "He's

already drawing up a list of potential wives for your father to review."

"Well, I'll make my own choices. And I won't be picking off a list."

*I won't be picking at all.*

"Tell me, how did you make your choice, Regan?" Edyon asked. Regan's wife had died young, Edyon had learned. She had been from a rich family—richer than Regan's.

"Purely from my heart," Regan said. "We had a short but happy time together." And he put on a pained expression of grief, adding, "I wish all could be so happy as I was."

"She sounds quite special. I wish I could have met her."

"Indeed. Excuse me, Your Highness." And Regan, overcome by his memories, bowed and left.

Edyon watched him go. "She must have been a remarkable woman, to have been able to make Regan happy."

"She was remarkably rich, they say," Byron replied.

"I sometimes wonder about Lord Regan. He's given a lot of thought to the wealth of Abask."

"He gives a lot of thought to his own wealth."

"Do you trust him?"

Byron frowned. "I . . . in what way?"

"Is he loyal?"

"Yes. Undoubtedly, Your Highness. He'd die for Calidor."

Edyon replied, "All the lords are loyal to Calidor. They know their future is tied to this country and their lands. They'd rather die than lose their land. So they fight to the death. It's self-interest."

Byron shook his head. "I think you do many of the lords

a disservice, including my father. He loves his land, but also the people on it."

"I'm sorry, Byron. I spoke rashly. Please forgive me. I meant no insult to you or your family."

But Edyon looked around. This place didn't feel like his land—he wouldn't want to die for it. It felt like a lie. "I don't know if I belong here. I could build a castle and a village, but the people who moved here wouldn't be Abask people. *I'm* not Abask."

"You're the Prince of Abask, Edyon. It *is* your land. You can do with it what you want. Make it what you want."

Edyon forced a smile. "You're a good person, Byron. Sometimes I don't know what to believe. I'm not sure what is the truth and what is a lie. But perhaps one day I'll build a home here—a place to retreat from the world."

"Whatever you choose, make it your truth, Edyon." And Byron reached across and lifted Edyon's hand and kissed it.

To Edyon's surprise, tears filled his eyes. He felt that someone truly cared for him. And immediately his thoughts turned to March. What he'd have given for March to say that to him, to have March kiss his hand again.

# CATHERINE
## NORTHERN PITORIA

If the ship leaks, everyone gets wet.
*Pitorian saying*

CATHERINE RELEASED Tzsayn's hand as dawn
broke. She had spent the whole night with him, talking, kissing, sharing their hopes and plans, but now she had to leave.

She whispered to him, "Be strong. Once this is over, we'll be
together." Then she kissed him on the cheek, then on the lips.

Tzsayn caressed her neck. "I'm feeling stronger already,
thanks to you. Savage knows what he's doing. I'll be glad to
be rid of this darned leg if it means we can start our future life
together."

Catherine kissed him again. "I'll be thinking of you."

"Think of me some of the time, but also think about your
own safety. Do as Ffyn says. He's there to take possession of
these ships but also to protect you."

"Once I've signed a loan agreement so huge all the finan-
ciers in Calidor will be cheering, and I'm totally safe, then
I'll think only of you. Is that acceptable?"

He smiled. "That is definitely acceptable."

"I have to go. One more kiss, then I'm leaving." But it was at least ten more before she managed to tear herself away.

Catherine left the camp on horseback with General Ffyn and a hundred soldiers, her white-hairs as well as Tzsayn's blues. The men were immaculate, their armor and horses gleaming. Catherine's own armor glinted in the sun and, with her white dress below it, she looked, according to Tanya, "like someone from another world, someone invincible."

As they passed through villages along the way, people ran out to watch and cheer, and Catherine and the men waved back. It was all part of the performance of being a queen. So much of life seemed to be a performance that it was sometimes hard to know where that ended and the real Catherine began. Here she was, dressed in armor and looking invincible, but inside she had never felt so afraid. Afraid for Tzsayn, the pain he was in and the pain yet to come. And yet very few people even knew he was ill.

"The people are delighted to see you, Your Majesty," Ffyn said.

Catherine blinked her tears away and turned her thoughts from Tzsayn as she'd promised to do. "Yes. Incredible, isn't it? The war front is only a day's ride north and yet these people carry on with their lives."

"They have no choice," replied Ffyn. "Their farms and livelihoods are here. But seeing you gives them hope, Your Majesty."

Catherine smiled tightly. "I want to give them more than hope. These ships had better be the answer we're looking for."

They joined the coast road and made their way south. This was the route Catherine had ridden with Ambrose weeks ago as they'd fled Tornia. How much had changed since then—King Arell had died, Aloysius had invaded the Northern Plateau, and so much more. And Catherine had changed too. She was older and wiser, and—she smiled to think of it—her heart was finally fixed on Tzsayn. And although she wasn't supposed to think of him, she allowed herself a few happy memories of his smile.

It was noon the following day when they arrived at the coastal town of Crossea. The harbor was bustling with sailors, laborers, and tradesmen. A small delegation ran to meet Catherine's group and guided them to the quay, where Lord Darby and his assistant were waiting. Catherine looked around as she approached, wondering where the ships were. There were many small boats in the harbor and two larger vessels, but no sign of fifteen Calidorian ships. Her heart sank. Had the ships been delayed or sunk by the Brigantines? Had her journey been wasted? Could she have stayed with Tzsayn after all?

But Lord Darby greeted Catherine with a smile. "Good day, Your Majesty. I'm delighted to report that the crossing went well. Your ships are ready, as are their crews, to train your soldiers and sailors."

He stepped to the side and gestured grandly toward the dozen or so tiny vessels moored in the harbor. "It is a historic moment of cooperation."

*What? That can't be them!*

Catherine felt sick. No, she felt furious. Tears of rage and frustration filled her eyes. The things tied up to the dock were not ships. They were no more than fifteen paces long—they were barely boats. She stared and stared, as if by looking hard enough she might find a real ship hidden among them. It was a historic moment all right—a historic moment of foolishness on her part for ever trusting these Calidorians. She had no words.

General Ffyn, however, did. "Is this some sort of joke?"

Darby looked confused. "Joke? I'm not here to joke."

General Ffyn stepped closer to the quay, his voice now dangerously level. "You promised us ships. These are . . . well, I don't know what they are. But they are not ships."

Darby smirked. "You have the same reaction as many who know little of the sea."

"I have the same reaction as someone who has been duped!" Catherine exclaimed, finally finding her voice.

"Duped!" Darby's eyes boggled in outrage. "We're not here to trick you. We're working together."

"Ha! Not once have you offered unconditional support," Catherine said, her voice rising. "Not once have you offered anything but words, not once have you offered anything real or free. You only agreed to giving us ships after we agreed to *buy* them, priced over the odds and at high interest rates. Everything has to be pulled from you like rotting teeth, and these boats are the most rotten trick I've ever come across."

"Those are strong words, Your Majesty," Darby snapped.

"They match my feelings. This is an outrage. We're at war. We need your help and you send us these . . . *toys!*"

Ffyn advanced on Darby. "Are you working with Aloysius? Planning on letting us fail—*helping* us fail? Because that's what it looks like. I should have you thrown in the local dungeon and left to rot."

Darby stepped forward to meet him, his bent back straightening. "You will do no such thing. Our ships can beat the Brigantine ships. Your problem is that your men can't beat the Brigantine men."

"Sedition! Sedition in front of Her Majesty. I can have you arrested for that!" Ffyn shouted.

Albert, Darby's aide, stepped forward. "Please, Your Majesty, let us explain. These ships are called scullers. Yes, they are small. But they're a special design that our navy has perfected over years. They're lightning-fast, stable in all weathers, and incredibly maneuverable."

"You forgot to mention that they are extremely expensive as well," Catherine retorted.

Lord Darby cleared his throat. "You asked for vessels that will allow you to take control of the Pitorian Sea. And the scullers will allow you to do that," Darby said. "That is what you're paying for."

"Let us at least prove to you what they can do," said Albert. "I think you'll be impressed when you see them in action."

Catherine doubted it, but she had no other option, other than returning to the camp empty-handed. If the scullers were a disaster, then she'd wasted a lot of time, but at least she wouldn't have to pay for them. But then how would they protect the Pitorian coast?

"This afternoon. And it'd better be *very* impressive."

Later that day, Catherine rode with Ffyn and her men to a nearby headland, from which they could see a wide bay called Hell's Mouth.

Lord Darby was already there, and, in frosty tones, he explained what was going to happen. "This bay is a good test for the scullers. The currents are strong, waves high, and winds variable. Most small boats would struggle, but you'll see how they ride over the waves smoothly. Also, the beach is narrow and sandy, very like the beach west of Rossarb, so a landing there can be simulated here."

Catherine wrinkled her brow. "Landing?"

"Scullers have multiple uses, Your Majesty. They can allow you to take back control of the Pitorian Sea, or at least prevent the Brigantines from dominating it. Their second use is as landing vessels to carry large numbers of soldiers short distances—across the Bay of Rossarb to land on the north shore, for example . . . That was your plan, wasn't it?"

"It is our plan, Lord Darby," Catherine replied cautiously, though she had rowboats that could do that job. And surely these boats couldn't do both tasks? She looked at the bay, where the small ships were sailing up and down round one large ship. She had to admit they were swift and agile. "But what is happening at the moment?"

"There are to be two demonstrations, Your Majesty," Darby said. "You need large ships that can patrol the

Pitorian Sea, but you have no time, or indeed money, to build them. So my suggestion is that you take them."

"Take them . . ." Catherine began to smile. "Take them from the Brigantines?"

"Indeed. Not easy, of course. But the scullers can do that for you. As long as your men can do the fighting."

"Show me."

Darby nodded to Albert, who waved a huge red flag. Darby pointed out to sea.

"You see the ship now sailing away? It's called the *Emerald*. A large vessel, much like those used by the Brigantines. You might think it's in no danger from such small vessels as the scullers. But now watch them speed past the *Emerald* and turn quickly."

And they did turn quickly.

Then they converged on the *Emerald*.

"Because they are so maneuverable, they can coordinate their attack so they all reach the target at the same time."

As he spoke, four scullers ran alongside the *Emerald*, the men on board throwing grappling hooks.

"The *Emerald* sits much higher in the water, so the men must be agile to board her quickly. This is the moment of danger. But with four boats attacking at the same time, the chances of failure are much reduced. One boat alone would easily be repelled, but four will overpower them."

And already the men were climbing the ropes and swarming onto the deck of the *Emerald*.

"The scullers can carry fifty men and still operate at that speed. They are the best vessels for your tasks. They are not built for comfort—there are no sleeping quarters except for the deck—but they are the perfect attack boat."

Catherine was smiling. "I like them."

"With fifteen scullers and the element of surprise, you can defeat the Brigantines and build your own fleet in days."

"And my father will hate it even more because it turns his own ships against him. I like your plan very much, Darby."

"Thank you, Your Majesty," replied Darby, thawing somewhat. "And now for the second part of the demonstration."

Albert waved a yellow flag. The men who had boarded the *Emerald* quickly returned to the scullers as Lord Darby began his commentary again.

"As you see, the scullers are now sailing at speed directly to shore. There are fifty men on board each boat. Again, they coordinate their arrival for maximum protection of their own forces and maximum impact on the opposition."

"It's the impact on the shore I'm concerned about," said Catherine. "Won't they break up when they hit the beach? They're going very fast."

"Please keep watching, Your Majesty, and you'll see . . ."

Racing to the shore, the boats rode smoothly up the beach, coming to a gentle stop as the men leaped out and into the shallows.

"The shallow draft and a liftable keel mean the scullers ride the surf and glide up the beach. Disembarking soldiers hardly get their knees wet."

"Do they have no faults at all?" Catherine asked.

"Like all ships, they need wind. If there is no wind, they

rely on oars, and if that happens near a Brigantine ship, your men will have to row fast in the opposite direction. But in all other circumstances the scullers are the better vessel."

Catherine could see how quickly the men had landed and were running ashore, weapons in hand.

"What do you think, Ffyn?" she asked.

"They do seem better than I first thought."

"Yes." Catherine nodded. "I think so too. I want the scullers working immediately. I want to capture some Brigantine ships."

Catherine felt a strange sensation in the pit of her stomach that she was surprised to recognize as hope. With these ships it *was* possible to turn the tide of the war, to beat her father at sea and then cut off his forces on land. And if Ambrose could cut off the supply of smoke to the boy army, they could beat Aloysius once and for all.

Catherine wished she could tell Tzsayn the good news. The sun was setting now, and Catherine allowed herself to think of Tzsayn. Had the operation been a success? She didn't want to think of the pain he must be suffering, or—worse—that he might not have survived. For the moment, all she could do was assume the best. She looked at the sea, the unlikely beauty of the place called Hell's Mouth, and hoped one day she could share it with Tzsayn in a time of peace. But she'd be leaving here at the first sign of dawn to ride back to the man she loved.

# AMBROSE
## NORTHERN PITORIA

THE DEMON Troop were ready to go. They'd trained intensively for a week in narrow, steep-walled ditches to simulate the demon tunnels, practicing close-quarters combat. Ambrose stood above their small training ground, watching his men go through one final drill. They looked good, but still, a wave of doubt and depression was looming over Ambrose's thoughts. It was the same feeling he'd had after the battle of Hawks Field, that feeling of hopelessness, of being alone and detached from the people around him.

He'd lost his sister, Anne, and had to stand by while his family denounced her, then he'd had to denounce her too before watching her execution. Then Ambrose had been accused of being a traitor and fled his homeland. Tarquin, the most honorable of men, Ambrose's brother and closest friend, had been tortured and killed. Ambrose had no idea what had become of his father but suspected that he too was dead. Ambrose had lost all his family and his home, but throughout it all Catherine had been his shining light, the person that had kept him hopeful. He'd clung to Catherine as they'd escaped Tornia, and clung to her even more as they'd crossed the Northern Plateau after leaving Rossarb. She had been his rock when all else was lost. And now he couldn't hold her anymore. He wasn't sure what else he had to anchor him.

"May I join you?" Davyon came to stand beside him, his voice formal and his face expressionless as usual. They hadn't spoken since the war council two days earlier.

"Of course, General Davyon." Was Davyon here to see him or the men? Ambrose almost didn't care. "How is the king?" he asked.

"The doctors are operating now. I couldn't bear to be there. But Tzsayn is the strongest person I know. He'll get through it."

Ambrose nodded. "I sincerely hope so." And that was true: he didn't want Tzsayn to die; just didn't want him around, and didn't want him with Catherine. "I can only apologize again for my shameful remarks the other morning."

"I accept your apology, Sir Ambrose. I think we were both at less than our best."

Yes, Ambrose had been at less than his best. He'd been jealous and impulsive. Would things be different if he'd kept quiet? Ambrose felt wholly adrift. Tzsayn had Catherine. Ambrose had nothing. Nothing except a bunch of men with crimson hair and an almost impossible task ahead of them.

Davyon nodded down at the men in the ditches. "They're looking good. You've done well with them in a short time."

The Demon Troop had already all been excellent fighters, but now they could communicate with hand signals and move silently at high speed. "I know it's taken longer than you'd have liked, but it was necessary to give us the best chance of success." Ambrose had agonized over this. A week of training was another week of smoke production, but Ambrose and Davyon both knew that the mission would be their only chance to cut off the supply. They needed to balance preparation with speed.

"Though really . . ." Ambrose shook his head, unable to stop himself from saying, "the whole mission is absurd—the Brigantine army is formidable, the demons are wild, and I've got fifty men."

Davyon looked at Ambrose. "Are you saying you want to cancel the mission? That you shouldn't lead it?"

"I'm saying . . ." Ambrose wasn't sure what he was saying. "I'm sorry—it's been a strange few days. We'll do the task we've been given." But he had a feeling of doom. "If . . . if I don't return, I'd like to think that there will still be justice for my brother and sister, Tarquin and Anne. I'd like history to record how they fought for truth and died for it, and how lies have been told about them. Justice for them, and my hope that no one else suffers the same fate." It hurt more than anything knowing that people might believe his brother and sister were criminals, when the real criminal was Aloysius, but Ambrose wasn't sure he could deal with it anymore. It all seemed too much, and he seemed too small. "Can Tzsayn do that?"

Davyon nodded. "He knows of your sister and brother.

He knows of their bravery and yours, Ambrose. And, when this is over, everyone will know it. They'll learn the truth of each person's bravery and sacrifice. I'll tell Tzsayn and Catherine your thoughts, but I hope that you will speak with them yourself on your return."

# TASH
## DEMON TUNNELS

*THECAVERNTHECAVERNTHECAVERN...*

Tash repeated the mantra in her head as she tunneled. She was moving at a slow walking pace. She'd no idea how long she'd been going, though it wasn't her body that was tired but her mind. She had to keep thinking of the central cavern of the demon world and not let her mind drift, but it was beginning to get a little boring.

*Boring—get it? Boring through stone.*

*That's a joke.*

*Not very funny but it's a joke.*

*Boringly boring through stone.*

She came to a halt. The tunnel had stopped growing.

*Shits. Concentrate! Think of the cavern.*

*Thecavernthecavernthecavern...*

The tunnel started to move forward again.

Tash forced her brain to focus on an image of the mid-level terraces of the central cavern, the ones between the Brigantines and away from the demons. It wouldn't do to come out among either of them.

*That wouldn't be boring. That would be a disaster. Mid-level, please. Direct route preferably. No twists, no turns. Just straight in. Thecavernthecavernthecavern . . .*

The light around her was red and the tunnel warm. Just like any other demon tunnel. In her chest she could feel the heat of the smoke from the dying demon—its desire to return to the core. It was like a living thing, and it wanted to get back. Tash might not be a demon herself, but while she had the red smoke in her, she had some of their powers.

*Thecavernthecavernthecavern . . .*

And suddenly the stone that was retreating in front of her dissipated altogether to reveal a huge, open space.

*Shits. It worked. It shitting worked!*

The hole was just large enough for her to stick her head through.

*I'm on the shitting mid-level terrace too!*

Tash jumped up and down with excitement, clamping a hand over her mouth to stop herself from shouting in glee.

Once she'd calmed down, she thought of moving the tunnel three paces forward and the remaining stone in front of her slowly dissolved. Tash dropped to her knees and crawled forward. Looking up to the stone bridges crossing the cavern above and to the terraces all around, she could see no one—either human or demon. Peering over the edge of the terrace, down to the core of purple smoke rising from the center of the cavern, she could see that the scene was the same as when she'd first seen it however many days or weeks ago that was—the Brigantine soldiers were still farming the demon smoke.

There was a body with blue hair lying on the lower terrace—presumably the next to be thrown into the core to be reborn as a demon. And, farther away, there was a larger pile of bodies—perhaps six or seven of them.

*It's shitting horrible.*

There were a lot of Brigantines on the lower terraces. The ones not on duty seemed to be playing dice or sleeping. There were others on guard by the entrances to the various tunnels that opened onto the lower terrace. Tash had seen how these tunnels closed up when the demons who had made them died, and it looked like many more had closed since she was last here—most terraces, like the ones the off-duty soldiers were relaxing on, had no tunnels at all. Tash twisted round to check the terraces above her, but it was impossible to see from her position if the tunnels there had closed too.

*And where are the demons?*

Tash crawled back a little and got to her feet, keeping close to the wall and out of sight of the Brigantines below. She ran up a ramp to the terrace above and then up another, but there was still no sign of them. There were fewer tunnels here too.

*Where are they?*

She turned into the next tunnel she found, looking for the markings on the wall that would show where it led. She and Geratan had managed to decipher the signs that showed the way to the demon war room and to the human world. What would this tunnel's sign be?

But there was no sign at all.

*Strange . . .*

Tash moved along the tunnel, wondering where it would lead, slowing as it turned sharply and descended. She moved down the slope, trying to creep forward and breathe without making a sound. And then she was in a small, open area—a room that was familiar but different.

*This is the demon war room.*

But it had shrunk. It still had a number of tunnels branching off it, but they were smaller too. There was a general air of abandonment.

Tash frowned. Had the demons left? Where could they have gone?

She checked each of the tunnels for signs but found only one—a sign Tash hadn't seen before.

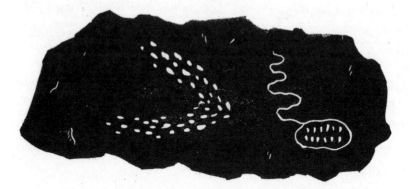

*I've no idea what that means, but I'm betting this tunnel leads wherever the demons are.*

Tash headed along this larger tunnel, which corkscrewed downward as if it was drilling into the center of the earth. Tash had a bad feeling about it, but also a strange urge to go on, her feet carrying her down the slope faster and faster until she finally forced herself to stop. She closed her eyes and realized she knew what was ahead. It was the core of smoke. The wisp she had inside her knew it. It wanted to go there. It *needed* to go there.

Was that what the new sign meant? That this was the way to the core?

Tash, slowly and silently, moved down the tunnel until it straightened, and she could see far ahead.

*Shits.*

At the end of the tunnel was a wide chamber filled with lots of demons. They all stood together in a line, holding hands, with their backs to her. The room sloped away from her and, at the very front, Tash could see a bright purple light.

It was the core—the base of it, the source of the smoke.

As Tash watched, the demon at the furthest end of the group let go of his neighbors' hands, leaped into the core, and instantly vanished.

*They're returning to the core. Returning to the smoke.*

And Tash could feel inside herself an urge to follow them.

*No. Do not do that. Turn round and get out.*

And yet a part of her wanted to join the demons.

*I'm not a demon. I'm human.*

Tash put her hands on the stone walls and forced her body to turn. She ran back up to the terraces, only able to think clearly when she was away from the core.

What were the demons doing? It made no sense. They should be fighting the Brigantines, not giving up.

As she reached her tunnel entrance, she spotted a demon's face peering over a ledge far above. Then she saw another. Then a third. She scanned for more but that was all—three.

*So not all of them are going back into the core—at least not yet.*

Had they spotted her? And if so, what would they do? Tash moved back out of sight, but as she did, another familiar figure came out of a tunnel far below.

*Frost.*

The girl who had been helping the Brigantines was with the same soldier Tash had seen her with the first time. They went to the central core and walked round it, the soldier touching Frost's arm—communicating something. Then Frost pointed up, high above Tash. The soldier looked where she pointed and shook his head, then suddenly seized Frost and dragged her close to the edge, as if he was going to throw her into the core. She kicked and struggled, and the soldier laughed—a harsh, clanging sound—and threw her to the ground before walking away, back into the tunnel he'd come out of.

Frost sat on the ground and rubbed her face. Then she picked up a bottle and went to stand at the edge of the core, wafting her hands toward it, as if she was trying to capture the column of smoke in the bottle. But the smoke slipped away from her. For some reason it couldn't be bottled up like that; it had to be caught as it escaped from the body of a demon.

*But wait. That's changed.*

Tash stared at the core, thinking back to when she'd first seen it.

*The smoke wasn't anywhere near as high then.*

She closed her eyes and tried to remember her first view

of the cavern. It was huge—half of Rossarb could fit in it. And the hole in the center had had a red and purple swirling glow, with wisps of purple smoke rising from it.

Tash opened her eyes. The cavern was definitely smaller now. Still huge, but not nearly as big as it had been. The glow from the smoke was brighter too—and there was more of it, billowing from the core and rising far higher into the cavern.

Was that what Frost had been doing? Pointing out that the cavern was closing in?

*More smoke means more dead demons. And if the cavern is closing in like the tunnels, that must be because the demons are dead too.*

But why would the demons be doing this?

Tash looked down at Frost. If anyone had the answer, she did.

*Right, missy. I'm coming to get you.*

# EDYON
## BIRTWISTLE, CALIDOR

EDYON STILL hadn't told his father about the assassination plot, and now the tour was departing for Birtwistle. He'd hoped that he'd somehow find proof, but he'd found nothing and time was running out.

The tour wound its way along the coast road, arriving at Birtwistle in the early afternoon. The castle was built on the cliffside, and as they rode up to it, Edyon could see some balconies stretched out over the sea. Edyon remembered Lord Hunt's words: "A balcony could collapse at any moment with the weight of people on it. A tragic accident . . ." A fall from any of them would mean certain death.

When they arrived at the castle, a tour of the building and its defenses had been arranged as usual. Birtwistle showed them from the hall, through the portrait gallery, along corridors with glimpses of the Birtwistle lands, and then he led them up one of the towers to see the coastline. On the highest turret was a small balcony.

The breeze here was strong, but the sound of waves crashing on the rocks below could still be heard. Birtwistle stood by the side of the balcony and said, "I believe the view from here is the best in Calidor. If you stand out there, you can see as far north as Brigane and as far south as Calia. Please, Your Highness, take a look at the view and give me your opinion."

Thelonius took a step forward.

Edyon had waited too long. He had wanted to find the right time and the right way to tell his father what he knew. Instead, he had been a coward and told him nothing.

It was not very different from March never telling Edyon the truth about where he was taking him, even when he'd had so many chances to do so. There was never a good time to tell someone news that would hurt them. But Edyon could be silent no longer.

"No! Stop!" he shouted. "Don't do it."

Thelonius paused. The entire crowd, including the three traitors, turned to stare at Edyon.

"Father, the balcony will collapse if you step on it," Edyon said, locking eyes with his father. "I know it."

Birtwistle looked shocked. Regan looked impassive and said, "Perhaps Prince Edyon doesn't have a head for heights?"

"I don't have a head for treason. You and Hunt and Birtwistle are in on this. This is a plot to murder my father and myself."

A few in the tour party frowned in confusion or surprise, while many looked from Edyon to Thelonius to Regan, but all remained silent.

Thelonius was frowning too. "What is this about? What are you saying, Edyon?"

"They plan to kill you. And me too." Edyon's words seemed to be carried away by the wind.

But Regan had heard them well enough, and his eyes blazed. "These are serious allegations, Your Highness. Perhaps you've had a little too much sun, or even more wine than usual, in which case, if you apologize now we can . . . accept your feelings of regret and move on."

"No. I will not apologize. You are plotting my murder and that of my father."

Regan's face changed to a look of disgust. "Even too much wine cannot excuse that accusation. I demand that you retract that statement now, and apologize to Hunt, Birtwistle, and myself."

Edyon didn't care if Regan was furious with him. He cared only that he and his father were safe. "I stand by my words. You, Hunt, and Birtwistle are planning a coup, but without even the bravery to admit it or to attack us openly. You're planning an 'accident.' My father and I will fall to our deaths, and you will take over Calidor."

"These are wild accusations," Hunt said. "Where's your proof?"

"That's my proof." Edyon pointed to the platform. "The balcony will collapse if we stand on it."

"You're talking nonsense," Hunt replied.

"Then *you* step out on it," Thelonius spoke up.

Hunt's face seemed to quiver in fear.

"I support my son," Thelonius said, coming back to stand beside him. "He would not make accusations without reason.

You asked for proof? Well, let's see who is telling the truth here."

Hunt swallowed and stepped cautiously onto the small balcony, stood still for a moment, then began to return to Edyon.

"You don't have the weight of two people," Edyon shouted.

Regan said, "I'll be the second, if it's to clear my name." And he strode onto the platform beside Hunt and held his arms out.

Now Birtwistle came forward. "I'm accused too. I'll stand with my fellow lords to show we are innocent." He was not a small man, and he joined the other two and jumped heavily up and down.

Nothing happened. The balcony didn't move a fraction.

Edyon felt ill. *Did I imagine the whole thing?*

Thelonius looked horrified. "My lords. My friends. It seems that you are true and my son . . . my son has been misguided." He turned now to Edyon, adding, "I'm sure he will apologize immediately and unreservedly. And explain himself completely to me later."

All eyes were now on Edyon. His mouth was dry. He looked like a fool once again, but now a dangerous one. He held his head up and said, "I apologize only to you, Father, for not being able to prove my words." Then he turned and left. Byron stepped toward him, but Edyon ignored his friend. He fled to his rooms.

*What have I done? How could I be so mistaken? Was it all a trap? Did Regan know I was hiding in his room and say wild things to lure me into disgracing myself?*

Edyon got to his room, shut the door firmly, then sat, then got up, walked to the window and back. And then to the window again.

*I should have apologized. Why didn't I? What was I thinking? I'm a fool. An absolute fool.*

He'd messed up completely. He went to the washbowl, bent over, and threw up.

Edyon couldn't sit. He paced around as the thoughts whirled in his mind. They were stopped only by a loud bang on his door. It was a guard.

*Am I to be arrested for slander?*

The guard carried a message that Edyon was required immediately in the presence of his father.

*Oh shits. I'm going to be thrown in the dungeons.*

"Just one moment," Edyon said. He closed the door and went back to the washbowl to throw up again. He took a sip of water and turned to see that the guard had opened the door and was watching him.

Edyon was escorted to Thelonius's rooms and was relieved to find that Regan, Hunt, and Birtwistle weren't there. It was just his father and the chancellor, Lord Bruntwood.

"Prince Edyon, you have made the most serious allegation against three lords. Three of the most senior and powerful lords," the chancellor began. "But it's not too late to resolve the situation. An explanation to your father. A sincere and full apology to all concerned . . ."

"No," Edyon said. "I will not apologize, but I will explain myself."

The chancellor looked from Edyon to Thelonius. "Well, that's something, I suppose. And I do have many questions, but perhaps we start with a simple one. Why did you accuse these three senior lords of plotting treason?"

And now Edyon saw what was happening: he was on trial.

"Why? Because it's true. They believe my father is taking the country in the wrong direction by aligning too closely to Pitoria. They believe I'm ill-equipped to rule after him, and they believe themselves to be much better equipped. Regan's feelings were hurt because my father had asked him to perjure himself. And, rather than saying no, he blames my father. I'm sure there are many more reasons too, but greed and evil natures seem to be at the base of it all."

"That explains your view of their position but not your accusation," the chancellor said. "Why did you accuse them?"

"I heard them plotting. Regan, Hunt, and Birtwistle were discussing it after a banquet one evening, as casually as if they'd been planning a boar hunt."

"This is very hard to imagine, Your Highness." The chancellor frowned. "How did you overhear this? At the dinner table?"

"No. In Regan's room, on the second night of our tour."

"And you were invited there?" the chancellor asked, trying to work it out.

"No. I . . . I happened to be in the room."

"I don't understand," Thelonius interrupted. "How were you in Lord Regan's room? You'd been drinking heavily, I seem to remember. Did you confuse the rooms? Explain the circumstances clearly."

Edyon wanted to lie, but it seemed pointless. He wasn't a prince; it was all a fraud anyway: he didn't belong here at all. He pulled the silver mirror from his jacket and slammed it on the table. "I was in Regan's room stealing that. I was about to leave when Regan, Hunt, and Birtwistle returned. I hid and I overheard the conversation."

Thelonius frowned and picked up the silver mirror to inspect it. "But why? I really don't understand."

The chancellor looked equally confused.

"I'm a thief. I can't help it," Edyon said. "I was a little drunk as well; I won't deny that either. But neither will I change my accusation. I heard what I heard. They were plotting murder."

Thelonius put the silver mirror back on the table. "I don't know what to say, Edyon. Are you so lacking in morals? Do you care nothing for honor? This is not the behavior of any son of mine."

Tears filled Edyon's eyes. "I'm sorry, Your Highness, if you think I'm not worthy of being your son. I may be a thief, but I do have some honor. I'm being honest with you about what happened. I won't lie about that. And I won't apologize to three of the worst sort of men, men who truly have no honor."

"Then I'm not sure what we can do for you," the chancellor said.

# MARCH

MARCH WAS pouring wine for a prince again and finding it less enjoyable than ever.

Prince Harold was fourteen, and he had the wine more as an accessory to his appearance than for the taste or to quench his thirst. Today Harold's goblet was made entirely of gold, though some days he preferred the glass with the gold stem. Most things of Harold's had gold on them, even though he was in an army camp. "Most things" included March, who now wore a white shirt with a sleeveless jerkin that had a gold badge over the heart to show he was in the Gold Brigade. The day before, Harold had complained that March's eyes were silver and didn't match the gold pitcher March was holding, and for a moment it really did feel like Harold would skewer out March's eyes for clashing with the tableware. Harold considered March to be just another of his possessions, and not much more valuable than his gold plates and goblets.

Sam was in the Gold Brigade too, but he was not treated like a servant. As Sam had no aptitude for or experience with waiting on a prince and, as he'd won the trial, Harold took pleasure in giving him arduous physical tasks to test his strength and speed. Sam was also being trained in the proper use of weapons and was already much more proficient with the sword. He was quickly turning into an able soldier and was once even allowed to spar against Harold. "Just remember to lose, Sam," March had muttered under his breath as he'd watched the bout.

The Gold Brigade was slowly increasing in numbers as Harold selected the best from the other brigades to build the ranks. It now comprised twenty boys, whose main roles were to act as Harold's personal guard, and in March's case, his personal assistant.

The prince's camp was spread through the forest, extending farther every day as more people heard of their location and came to provide services. Food provisions—the store of flour and vegetables, as well as pigs, geese, chickens, goats, and even a herd of cows—were on one side of the camp. The horses, saddles, and armory took up space on the south side. And here also was the farrier, and by him, the other blacksmiths constructing the strange metal contraptions that Harold delighted in. The prince had designed the machines himself, and twice a day went to see the progress on their manufacture.

The morning's inspection was now over, and a new man had arrived in camp. He seemed to be a soldier, in that he wore a sword and rode into camp with his own men, and he sent a nervous panic among some who recognized him. He was slim, fit, stylishly dressed, and old enough to be

Harold's father, but it was the way he held himself that struck March—he was a man who could blend into the background or be center stage with a simple change of posture. This man had a rare confidence that March had only ever seen in royalty, a few nobles, and, indeed, Holywell.

March stood at the side of the marquee by a table laden with fruits, nuts, and—Harold's favorite—preserved ginger. He looked ahead as he'd been trained to, but out of the corner of his eye he could see Harold and the new man.

"I sent for the Eagles and Stags. Where are they?" demanded the prince.

"Your father wanted them near him."

"But the boys' brigades are mine to command."

"And you are your father's to command, Your Highness."

"And what about the smoke? Where is that? We were promised more."

"It will be here when it's needed, when all is in place." The man's voice was soft as butter, and he appeared to be as slippery.

"It is needed. All *is* in place." Harold frowned. "So, why are you here? You bring no boys and no smoke. Are you here to spy for my father, Noyes?"

So that was the man's name: Noyes. And March recalled a few things he'd heard. This was King Aloysius's dreaded spymaster and chief interrogator. He had a reputation for being intelligent and ruthless.

Noyes sauntered over to the table by March and surveyed the food, not even looking at Harold as he replied: "The king merely asks for my reassurance that all is well. You're still a young man, and, though naturally gifted, you are relatively inexperienced."

Harold came to stand by Noyes, and he did indeed seem like a small boy in comparison. "I've watched my father all my life. I've been on campaigns with him since I was a baby. I know I can win this. Brigant needs a victory."

"That's true, Your Highness. But your father also needs an heir. And he doesn't want to risk losing another son. It's only because of his love for you that he demands caution and that he asks for my reassurance."

"*Love?* From my father?" Harold rolled his eyes. "Is he still mourning Boris?"

"Your father has much grief and anger to deal with. Boris's death has diverted his attention from Calidor. Thelonius took land from Aloysius, but your sister and her sickly husband have taken his first-born son. His top priority now is to rid the world of them. And the attack will begin soon."

"Meanwhile Thelonius sits in his castle eating honey. He'll be laughing with delight."

"There's no rush. Calidor will be ours in time." Noyes picked up a segment of candied orange and seemed to swallow it down whole.

"I say the time is right now. I say my brigades are ready. I can do it. My boys will be victorious."

"Getting over the wall won't be easy, even for your boys."

"I know the exact dimensions of the wall—it was *your*

spies who gave us all the information we need, as you know, Noyes. And I've sent my own scouts out too. I have a way across." Harold went to the central table and picked up a small metal contraption, a bit like a series of ladders that could be pulled out and then slotted together. "This is a model of it."

Noyes took the model. "It spans the distance between the walls?" He opened it out and weighed it in his hand. "The real thing must be huge. And heavy."

"I'm having my blacksmiths make four of them. We carry them to the wall ahead of the attack. They lie there hidden. Three are already made; just one more to complete."

Noyes traced his fingers across the model. "I assume the boys will run across these, but there will be fire burning beneath them from the pit. You're sure the construction will be strong and stable enough?"

"We'll be over the pit and the walls in a blink of an eye. And, once over, I can make it to Calia in a day."

March went cold.

"A day to get there, perhaps, and possibly to take it," Noyes allowed. "But can you hold it and still be there in two months?"

Harold smiled. "If we take the leaders, yes. We go in hard and fast, straight to the heart of Calidor, and kill or capture Thelonius and his bastard son and every one of his lords. Their bodies will be on display for all to see as we parade through the towns and villages of Calidor. When the people witness what the boy army is capable of, they'll crumble."

Harold looked at Noyes. "You know my boys can do it, and you know I can too."

"I don't deny your ability, Your Highness, but your father won't allow it. He wants to fight his brother himself. He wants to ride into Calia at the head of the army. That's been his chief desire for years."

"And yet you yourself say that he's lost his focus."

"I would never say that, Your Highness. I say that his focus has changed to another enemy for the moment. But it will return here, and he will be the one to lead the attack into Calia."

March didn't care terribly much if the Brigantine army was led by Aloysius or Harold or a pack of dogs; if they reached Calia, they would kill Edyon either way.

"But, as you said, my father will have dealt with the Pitorians soon enough, Noyes. I can attack the wall now and hold it until he is ready to lead the army into the capital."

"Perhaps." Noyes returned to the map. "Where's the Calidorian army positioned?"

"They're thinly spread along the wall and concentrated in camps in the west and east, here and here." Harold pointed at the map.

"If you take the wall, the Calidorians will come to you. How will you fare?"

Harold grinned. "I'll try to resist destroying the army completely so that my father has someone to fight when he arrives."

Noyes nodded. "I suspect the Calidorians believe all our focus is on Pitoria. If you can take and hold the wall, and then dismantle it to allow your father's army through when they're finished with the Pitorians, your father will see the merit in such a plan. But your father will want at least one section of the main army here to support your attack. And your father will wish to know you're safe."

"Then tell him I'll be out of harm's way at the rear. I'll be taking smoke, and with that stuff I'm invincible."

"Alas, not totally, Your Highness."

"But you see the plan can work. And the longer we wait, the more likely that Calidor will learn of our positions and strengthen the army at the wall. We need to advance. Send me the smoke. And some troops from the old man's army if you must."

Noyes gave the slightest of nods. "I'll summon Lord Thornlees and his troops down here from the north. They can provide the support of the traditional army, and they can bring the smoke. Thornlees can be here in a week."

"And where will you be, Noyes?"

"Alas, I will miss the spectacle of your brigades taking the wall. I must return to the north to support your father. The attack on Pitoria will begin soon."

Harold and Noyes both seemed pleased. They had reached an agreement. March let no emotion show on his face. He stared straight ahead, as he always did, and he thought about Edyon, imagining him safe in Calia, happy with his father, but how much longer would that last?

# EDYON

## BIRTWISTLE, CALIDOR

EDYON SAT in his room, tears in his eyes. He felt more alone than ever. He needed March to give him confidence, to reassure him that he wasn't a complete idiot. March had always believed in him. And, even if March couldn't actually help, Edyon still wanted him. "I miss you," he muttered as tears ran down his face. "What I'd give for you to be here."

At that moment the door opened, but it was just Talin, carrying Edyon's best jacket.

Edyon wiped his face. Talin must have noticed his tears but held up the jacket and said, "I think you'll need this for tonight's banquet, Your Highness."

There was, of course, going to be another banquet. No misbehavior on Edyon's part could stop the proceedings.

"I don't want to go." Edyon realized he sounded like a spoiled child and added, "I don't think I'll be required. My father . . ." But he ran out of words.

"I heard there was an incident at the tower."

"Indeed. The incident was me being a fool, once again. I

accused some lords of treason and failed to provide the proof."

"Which is why you should go to the banquet, Your Highness. If you don't mind me offering my opinion, you'll have to face them all at some point, and it's perhaps better sooner than later."

"I'm not sure I can face my father, and I'm not sure he'll want me there. And I'm fairly certain Regan, Hunt, and Birtwistle won't. I've messed up completely. One of the first things my father told me was to handle the lords carefully, and now I've set them against him. Well, against me, anyway, and him because he supported me. He believed me."

"And you can face them or hide here."

"Hiding sounds like the easier option."

"Possibly it is, for now. But I think some lords will admire you more if you are not scared off by the likes of Lord Regan. Not all lords are the same as those three."

"They'll want me to apologize, and I don't think I can do it."

"A prince must do what is necessary to rule. You'll find a way. And hiding is not the way."

Talin was right. Edyon pulled his shoulders back. "I must face my enemies." But would he apologize? He still felt sick at the thought.

Just then there was a knock on the door. Edyon muttered, "Probably my father telling me not to come to the banquet, not to come to anything."

But it was Byron. "Are you all right, Edyon?" he asked.

"Guess!"

Byron looked sad and concerned. "I'm sorry. I would stay with you, but I have to go straight back to your father. He sent me to get your bottle of demon smoke. And said I shouldn't speak with you."

Why did he want the smoke? Did Thelonius think Edyon might use it against the lords? Was Edyon now considered dangerous?

"Did he tell you anything else? About me, I mean . . . about the silver mirror?"

Byron looked a little embarrassed as he nodded. "Yes."

"I see. Well, you'd better get back to him."

"Yes." And Byron left.

So that was it. Edyon had no friends left at all, and soon he'd have to face his enemies.

Edyon went to the banquet dressed in his smartest clothes, looking like a true prince, but inside he was a bundle of nerves. He dreaded what Regan, Hunt, and Birtwistle would say, but mostly he dreaded facing his father again.

The sounds from the banqueting hall swept down the corridor. The musicians were playing and the talk was lively—at least until Edyon stepped into the room. Then all eyes turned to him, and the hubbub quieted. The room was full; the meal already started. Thelonius was sitting at the head of the table, and next to him was an empty chair and a place setting.

Edyon bowed to his father.

Thelonius ignored him.

Edyon sat in the empty chair and looked down the long table. At the far end, sitting directly opposite, were Birtwistle, Regan, and Hunt. They ignored him also—no greeting, no bow. This was the point when he should apologize. Edyon cleared his throat, but no words came. Around him, talk gradually got back up to speed. Edyon looked down at his plate. A small fried fish lay there, its eye burned black. He put a forkful in his mouth. It tasted of nothing. He glanced around him, but he was being ignored by all except Byron, who was sitting halfway down the table. Byron caught Edyon's eye and gave him a nod and a small smile.

*Perhaps I still have one friend, then. One, but no more.*

He leaned to his father. "I know I handled the situation badly, but I feared for your life and I had to tell you what I heard. I chose the wrong way to do it, and for that I apologize. But I acted sincerely."

"I don't know you well, Edyon. And I've known Regan all my life. He's my closest friend. You're a thief, and some say a fool, with no loyalties to Calidor. For whatever reason, you've taken a dislike to Regan. March has poisoned your mind against him. But that doesn't excuse stealing from him or accusing him of treason. This is your chance to publicly apologize. At the end of the meal you must do it, or your future is . . . well, I'm not sure what it is."

Before his coronation, his father had said Edyon's future was Calidor's and Calidor's future was Edyon's. Now Edyon didn't seem to have one unless he apologized. Edyon thought back to Madame Eruth's foretellings, but they didn't seem to cover this.

Edyon returned to his fish in silence. And without the distraction of conversation, he heard a strange noise. It was coming from above, where the musicians were standing, but it wasn't a musical sound. He looked up and realized that they were seated beneath a large stone balcony, on which musicians were performing.

Could it be that he'd got the wrong balcony?

Could it be that he and his father weren't going to be *on* a balcony as it collapsed, but *under* it?

He looked across at Regan, who was drinking from his goblet, his eyes on Edyon.

*I can't challenge him again. No one would believe me. I'm not sure I believe me.*

Had he even heard a noise? The sounds in the hall were a mix of talk and music.

But then he heard it again.

"Father, I'd like to continue this conversation with you outdoors in private." Edyon began to stand. He had to get them both out. But then there was an unmistakable *crack*, and the balcony began to tilt toward Edyon's head. Cries came from above as the stone began to fall. It was too late—Edyon and his father were trapped below. But Byron leaped onto the table and ran at Edyon as fast as the stone was falling. He launched himself at Edyon, shoving him and Thelonius back to the wall and standing on the table to hold up the falling balcony. There were screams from the musicians above, and Byron shouted for them to get off the balcony.

"I can't hold it much longer!"

Guards ran up and dragged Thelonius and Edyon to safety, and Byron stepped back. The balcony gave way, and masonry and musical instruments fell, crushing the end of the table under a huge block of stone. A cloud of dust lifted as the noise and shouts continued.

Edyon was gasping for air. He was alive. His father was alive. Incredibly, no one appeared to be harmed. "So that was why you wanted the demon smoke," he said. "For Byron to take, in case he needed to save us. So you did believe me."

Thelonius shook his head. "I believe in being prepared." Covered in gray dust, he bellowed out, "Hold my enemies! Hold Regan, Hunt, and Birtwistle." And he pushed and scrambled his way over the rubble. There was much shouting from the other side of the dust cloud. By the time Edyon emerged, Thelonius was standing opposite Regan.

"I have done absolutely nothing wrong here," Regan said. "Thelonius, my friend. Do not let your son poison your mind against me."

"You haven't even the honor to admit it!"

"Admit what? The masonry in Birtwistle's castle is old. The balcony collapsed. I'm grateful that you're safe."

Byron shouted from the back of the room. "It collapsed because someone cut into the stone to weaken it. I can see a block has been removed from here."

More quietly to Thelonius, Regan said, "Even if that *is* correct, we don't know who cut into the stone. It could have been anyone."

"It could have been anyone, but I know that it was you,"

Thelonius snapped back. "Hunt and Birtwistle have been against me for a long time, but you, Regan, you have always seemed to be my friend. Well, enough of your lies."

"*My* lies? What about your lies?" And he pointed to Edyon. "What about him? Your son."

"This is not about Edyon."

"No, you're right. It's about your marriage. Or lack of one."

The silence in the room was palpable now.

"Another lie, Regan. Another lie. No one can trust you." Thelonius stepped back. "Guards," he said. "Take Regan to the dungeon."

Regan drew a dagger from his belt and leaped at the first guard, stabbing him and taking his spear. Regan thrust the spear at Thelonius, who dodged it just in time, as another guard thrust his sword into Regan's side.

Regan took a step back, dropping the spear and putting his hands to his wound as blood ran through his fingers. The guards grabbed his arms, but he was no longer a threat—his knees were buckling; his face had paled. He stared at Thelonius and said, "I was your friend."

"You *were* my friend, but now you're nothing to me. Your treachery shames you." With that, Thelonius turned from him and told the guards to take the traitor away.

Edyon watched, half expecting Regan to struggle, but he was weak from his wound, and Edyon wondered if he'd survive to face trial or even get through the night.

Hunt and Birtwistle had been cornered but hadn't

resisted the guards, and they too were led away, with Hunt shouting, "We're loyal to Calidor!"

Thelonius came to Edyon and embraced him. He turned to the lords. "My son was brave enough to risk his reputation—and indeed his life—to stand with me. I couldn't hope for a better son, and Calidor couldn't want for a better future than with him. I owe him my life."

And Edyon stood with his father, his knees shaking with shock. As he looked around the room at the lords, his eyes fell on the bloody body of the guard Regan had killed, and Madame Eruth's words came back to him.

*I see death all around you now.*

# CATHERINE
## COAST ROAD, NORTHERN PITORIA

*Fly to your love, as your love flies to you.*

THE RIDERS met Catherine on the road halfway between the coast and the camp, three blue-hairs from the king's own household. Catherine slowed her horse as they approached. They carried urgent news; that much was clear. But was it good or bad? The lead rider came straight to her, nodded respectfully, and handed her a message.

"From General Davyon, Your Majesty."

Catherine's fingers were clumsy as she broke the seal and opened the letter.

*The operation went well. Savage is pleased. The king is resting, but his first waking thoughts were of you.*

*Davyon*

# AMBROSE
## NORTHERN PLATEAU, PITORIA

AMBROSE LED the Demon Troop out of the camp at first light and headed north. Their departure was low profile. Catherine had not yet returned from the coast, Davyon had already said his farewells, and hardly anyone else knew of their mission, which was just as Ambrose wanted.

It had felt as if a wave of gloom had been towering over him in camp, like a huge weight of water was building up, ready to fall, but the wave receded the farther north Ambrose rode. The farther he was from camp, from Tzsayn, and from Catherine, the more he felt like he could breathe again.

They rode fast to the River Ross and along the river road to Hebdene, where they left their horses, crossed the old wooden bridge, and began the steep climb up to the Northern Plateau, heading for the demon hollow that Geratan had located on his previous sortie.

The men were fit and the weather was fair, and they made excellent time. Once on the plateau, Ambrose sent four men ahead to scout and arranged the rest in two parallel columns. They marched in silence, as they'd trained to do, but from reading their hand signals Ambrose knew that most of the men were hoping they would run into some Brigantines before reaching the hollow. They were spoiling for a fight, and who better to fight than the invaders of their homeland?

"It'll happen soon enough," Ambrose muttered to himself. "Kill or be killed." That was an old Brigantine motto. And he'd kill his fellow Brigantines; he'd kill anyone who stood with Aloysius.

"Think of Tarquin," he muttered to himself. Though he hated to picture Tarquin's tortured body, he forced himself to do it. "I can't be weak. I can't let these bad moods swallow me up. I have to fight on. Think of Anne. Think of all the people Aloysius has hurt. Tarquin should be helping Father oversee the harvest now, guiding all the people who live on our land. Anne should be traveling, or studying, or falling in love."

*Love . . .*

And Ambrose couldn't help but think of what he felt he should be doing. "Protecting the woman I love. Protecting the princess. Except she's a queen now, and she doesn't want my protection."

Geratan fell into step beside him, a quizzical look on his face.

"Was I talking to myself?" Ambrose asked.

"Yes, but in Brigantine."

"Shits." *I tell the men they've got to stay silent, and I end up talking out loud to myself.*

"Do you want a rest?"

"No. I want to go faster."

Geratan grinned. "Then let's get moving." And he set off at a gentle run. Ambrose followed. This was what he lived for—action, purpose. It was what he needed now more than ever.

They made very good progress and rested the first night without lighting a fire. Ambrose shared the first watch, then lay down to sleep, but woke again just as it was getting light. His first thoughts were of the mission, not Catherine, which was a good sign. He also didn't feel the wave of depression hanging over him, another good sign.

He got to his feet and walked around the small camp, checking that the watch had changed as it should and that all was well, then went to the stream. He crouched down to scoop a handful of water when a small deer stepped into view. Ambrose froze. The deer eyed him. Perhaps it had never seen a human before. Ambrose remained motionless as the deer drank. Then the sudden noise of a dropped helmet came from the camp, and the deer leaped away.

"So much for me and my silent soldiers," Ambrose muttered.

They set off again, and by afternoon they were approaching their destination. Geratan pointed and signaled to Ambrose:

*Demon hollow. Three hundred paces.*

*Good*, thought Ambrose. *But now for the hard part . . .*

A demon hollow meant a demon. And Ambrose needed to get into the demon world without killing it. He intended to lure the demon out and use strong nets and ropes to trap it. This was how the Brigantines had gained access—captured a demon and caged it in the hollow to ensure the tunnel didn't close. It didn't feel good to be doing the same things as the Brigantines, but neither Ambrose nor Geratan could think of another way. The troop had practiced this, though never with a real demon, of course. But they needed to get it right—the tunnel had to remain open as an escape route for when their mission was over.

"Set up the trap. You know what to do. Lure the demon this way, Geratan, and we'll do our best not to hurt it."

Geratan nodded. He'd volunteered to lure the demon out—he knew how to get into the demon world and what to expect in there. But would he be able to run fast enough? Geratan was strong and agile, but not the quickest of men.

The men set up the nets, and Geratan checked over everything. Then he shook hands with Ambrose, saying, "Seems like there's nothing more for me to do except go and see this demon."

"We'll be ready."

The men waited silently in their positions as Geratan crept toward the demon hollow and out of sight.

It was quiet. No birdsong. No wind.

Ambrose waited. And waited.

And waited.

Why was it taking so long? Was Geratan struggling to get in?

*Perhaps he's already been ripped in two by the demon.*

But then Ambrose heard footsteps.

*He's done it!*

Geratan came into view at a jog. Not the sort of speed to flee from a demon. What was going on?

"We've got a bit of a problem," Geratan said. "The hollow isn't there anymore. I've looked all around, thought perhaps I'd missed it, but I've checked the whole area. It's gone."

Ambrose cursed. They'd have to find another way into the demon world.

"How did you originally find the demon hollow that was here?"

"We crisscrossed the whole of this part of the plateau until we came across one."

"How long did that take?"

Geratan grimaced. "A week."

Ambrose cursed again, thinking of the week he had been so insistent on spending training the men before they set out. He hadn't factored in the possibility that they might need to find a different hollow. Now they were up on the plateau with a few days' rations and no idea where to start looking.

# TASH
## DEMON TUNNELS

TASH WAS tunneling again.

This time she was holding in her head an image of Frost alone and asleep. The tunnel grew differently now, in short bursts, as if it only worked when Frost was asleep or on her own. It was slow going.

*It's not a race. The important thing is to get her on her own, not with half the Brigantine army around her.*

So Tash tunneled when Frost slept and rested while Frost was awake. And while Tash rested, she planned what she'd do when she found her.

*I'll sneak up on her while she sleeps. Put my knife to her throat. Wake her. Question her. Find out what's happening to the demons and why.*

It sounded unlikely to work, but then again, Tash reminded herself, she was tunneling through stone with the magic power of the demons, so who knew what she was capable of?

The tunnel had wound steeply down at first but was flat now. Tash sensed she was close, the image in her head of

Frost asleep changing as if the tunnel was showing her what really was ahead. In the new vision, Frost was asleep on a blanket on the ground, some sort of cage behind her, and—

The stone before Tash opened up.

*It's worked! She's there!*

Tash took a step back; she needed to compose herself.

*Right. Take it slow. Check there's no one else nearby.*

She slowly leaned forward to peer through her hole.

It opened into a stone chamber of sorts, lit by the same glow as all the demon tunnels, but here it was purple rather than red. There was one small, low entrance on Tash's right, and at the far left was a cage with thick bars and a massive lock. There were no soldiers. The only person there was Frost, lying asleep on her blanket, just as she had been in Tash's vision. And stacked high inside the cage . . .

Bottles. Bottles with a purple glow.

*Shits! This is their smoke store!*

Tash took another step back.

*Right. Keep calm. Think this through. This changes things. If I can get past her, I could get to the bottles and release the smoke.*

Tash imagined the hole in the stone expanding, and it immediately did so. She stepped slowly forward, checked right—no soldiers—and moved slowly and silently toward the cage.

Frost lay in front of it, a thin blanket over her bony shoulders. Her face was relaxed, though she was pale and had dark circles under her eyes. Close up, she seemed older than Tash had thought—perhaps a bit older than Princess Catherine;

she only looked young at a distance because she was so small and scrawny. She was lying close to the cage door, which had a huge padlock on it, and there wasn't a key left handily on a hook nearby.

*I bet the commander has the key.*

Tash stood still, uncertain what to do.

*Even without opening the cage I could try to smash all the bottles from the outside.*

*Or, if I take a bit of smoke first, I could get strong enough to force the bars open! That'd be easier. And helpful if any of those soldiers poke their noses in.*

She'd taken smoke only once before, in Rossarb Castle, when she'd thrown a spear farther than anyone else. The feeling of strength it had given her was amazing, but also strange and somehow unnatural. However, a small amount now would do no harm.

Tash lifted her right foot over Frost and put it on one of the cage's horizontal bars. She steadied herself and bent forward, stretching her arm as far as she could into the cage. Her fingertips grazed the nearest bottle.

*Just a bit farther!*

Tash stretched and touched the bottle again. It wobbled alarmingly.

She pulled her arm back. She couldn't reach from here.

Carefully, she tried again and managed to get her fingers round the neck of a bottle. But she'd forgotten that the smoke was heavy, and her hands were sweaty with nerves and the heat. The bottle began to slip.

*Shits!*

Tash lowered the bottle gently to the ground inside the cage and tried again with a better grip on it. She pulled the bottle to her, but it wouldn't fit through the bars.

*This isn't funny.*

She tried again, turning the bottle, but it was still just a bit too wide. And now the bottle was slipping out of her fingers again. She tried to lower it gently, but this time it touched the ground with a gentle chime.

Tash froze.

Frost turned in her sleep. And rolled into Tash's left leg.

In an instant Frost was sitting up, a cry that sounded like a bell coming from her lips. Tash fell on her, pushing her back to the ground and clamping one hand over her mouth, grabbing her knife with the other, and holding it to Frost's throat.

Tash shot a glance at the entrance, bracing herself for soldiers to come running in. But no one appeared. It was silent again.

Tash turned back to Frost, who wasn't resisting her, but merely staring at her and scowling. Her eyes were brilliant silver—more startling even than March's.

*Who's March?*

A cutesy, little-girl voice filled Tash's head, almost making her drop her knife.

*Never you mind who March is.* My *name is Tash and I have a knife at your throat.*

*I can see that, Pea-Brain.*

*Make a sound and I'll kill you.* Tash moved her hand from Frost's mouth to put her weight on Frost's shoulder.

*Are you trying to get the smoke? Need a little fix, do you?*

*No. I hate the stuff. I want the key to the cage. So that I can let the smoke out.*

*Now why on earth would you want to do that?*

*It's not yours. It's not for you to take.*

Tash waited for a reply, but there was only silence. She had to look down to check her hand was touching Frost's shoulder. It was touching skin to skin. Why couldn't she hear Frost's thoughts?

*Strange, isn't it? Silence? But you're not silent at all. Your little pea-brain is racing around. You're like a headless chicken.*

*If I'm headless, I can't have a pea-brain, so shut up about that.*

And suddenly a vision came to Tash—a headless chicken racing around in circles.

*Stop that!* Tash pressed the knife harder against Frost's neck, but she merely smiled, and in Tash's vision more chickens joined in, all headless, all racing round and round, dozens of them.

*Stop it! You'll be the one without a head if you're not careful.*

*If you were going to kill me, you'd have killed me. I don't know what you really want, but you're not very good at getting it. You're not good at anything are you, Pea-Brain?*

*I can tunnel through stone.*

At that Frost frowned and her eyes flitted to the tunnel Tash had made.

Tash raised her eyebrows. *Not such a pea-brain after all, am I?*

But she got no reply—there was nothing but a sort of strange emptiness. It was as if Frost was deliberately cutting all her thoughts off from Tash while she thought about this. Finally, she spoke again.

*So, you like the demons, do you?*

*Yes. And I want to know what's happening to them. You know, don't you?*

*There's a special one, isn't there? I can see you trying not to think of him. Oh, right, you've given him a name—Twist. How sweet. Do you call him that because that's how he kills people— by twisting their heads off?*

*No! He's called Twist, 'cause of the markings on his face. He . . .*

*He's what? A nice demon? Oh, but I see he imprisoned you in stone. Maybe not so nice then?*

*Twist didn't imprison me. And anyway, I got out.*

Silence again, but not for so long this time.

*So how do you do it?*

Tash smiled. She'd been wondering why Frost hadn't called for help or tried to get free—she wanted information from Tash as much as Tash wanted information from her.

*I can get information out of your head without those buffoons. If they come, they'll probably slit your throat.*

*Maybe you can get the information out of my head, but that doesn't mean you'll be able to tunnel like me. I guess I've just got the knack.*

*So what's this knack?*

*You tell me about the demons first. How many are left? What are they doing?*

*We've killed a few, but mostly they're hiding. It's all very dull. The soldiers throw dead bodies into the core pit; new demons come out. They're killed, and the smoke is collected and piled up here. Commander Fallon is happy.*

*Fallon. Is he the soldier you go around with?*

*I don't go around with him; he goes around with* me. *He'd know nothing if it wasn't for me. He's another pea-brain. He just wants smoke, smoke, and more smoke.*

*And you help him get it.*

*They need the smoke to fight their war—and lots of it. You should have seen the cage last week. It was full to the roof before they sent it off to the boys' brigades. It's getting easier too—the amount of smoke in the core is growing, and the new demons are being born out of it faster and faster. Which I can see is something you're interested in . . .*

Frost smiled. Her teeth were rotten, and her eyes glowed lilac in the light, just like a demon's. Then she frowned. *My teeth aren't rotten.*

*Are too. But the demons are putting themselves into the core of smoke. I've seen them. Why are they doing that?*

Frost grinned. *Now* that *information is a bit too valuable for the likes of you.*

*Tell me, and I'll teach you how to tunnel.*

*No deal, Pea-Brain. I'm sure tunneling is fun, but I'm getting out of here soon, and then I'm never going in a tunnel again.*

*After you've killed all the demons, you mean? You and these horrible soldiers.*

*If I didn't help them, they'd just find someone else. Anyway, why shouldn't I? At the end of this, they're going to pay me so much I'll never have to work again. I can eat and drink whatever I want, never work, never get hungry, and even have a pony to ride.*

*People are dying, the world's at war, and you want a* pony?

Frost sneered. *People are always dying. The world's always at war. The Calidorians betrayed us Abasks, and my people were destroyed. But we kept our history alive in our little community of slaves. I've worked in the Brigantine mines for years, slaved for mine owners from as soon as I was old enough to crawl. I got out and I'm not going back. And I reckon if I want a pony, I'll have one.*

Tash wanted to get out too.

*There's a slight problem with that, though, Pea-Brain. You're not going to get away from the Brigantines. The soldiers will cut you to pieces. And I'll watch as they throw your body into the core and wait until a puny, pea-brained demon comes out, and I'll kill it myself.*

And, with that, Frost gripped Tash's arm and shouted. The noise filled the cavern with a horrible clanging.

Tash twisted free of Frost's grip and darted to her tunnel, just reaching it as a Brigantine soldier appeared. Tash ran on, the shouts of the Brigantine soldier echoing behind her.

Tash had the advantage that the tunnel was made by her and for her, so it was small and narrow, and the sound of the soldier soon faded behind her. She made it up to the mid-level terrace where she'd started and peeked into the cavern. There were Brigantines just below, heading her way. She had to find her tunnel back to the surface. She had to get out.

She almost reached it when she heard a loud, high-pitched clanging. Across the cavern, Frost was standing with Fallon, the Brigantine commander, pointing at Tash with a look of delight on her face.

Tash darted into her tunnel and ran for her life.

# CATHERINE
## ARMY CAMP, NORTHERN PITORIA

*Love and friendship make the best marriage.*

*Pitorian saying*

CATHERINE HAD hardly been parted from Tzsayn since her return to camp. He was recovering well, though Catherine suspected he lied about the amount of pain he was in. But it was also obvious that he was happy, and so was she. The country was at war, there was much to fear, and yet Catherine felt a lightness that she'd never known before. She knew that her future with Tzsayn was right, and together they'd get through whatever lay in their path.

Of course, that didn't mean there were no arguments.

"We don't need to marry immediately," Tzsayn said.

"But you were the one telling me I had to decide quickly!"

"We were going to wait until the coronation, and I can't go through with that ceremony until I'm fully healed. Savage says he'll chop my other leg off if I try."

"But I want to marry now. It won't be a public ceremony. It will be just us. Privately making it . . . legal."

"Ah, I know how keen on the law you are, Judge Catherine."

"Are you trying to get out of it now? Why so reluctant?"

Tzsayn shook his head. "I'm not reluctant."

"Yes, you are."

"I'm . . . I'd like to feel a little more like myself. I want you to love me, not pity me."

Catherine took his hand and kissed it. "I love you. Totally. I don't pity you at all. We said we'd be honest and I am. I worry that you're in pain and that life will be harder for you with one leg, but I know you'll find ways to cope—and I'll do all I can to help. But I need you to trust me on this. Marriage now is the right thing."

"Now?"

"Tomorrow. I'm having a dress made. It'll be ready in the morning."

And so, the next morning after the war council, which had to go ahead as if nothing unusual was happening, Tanya helped Catherine put on her new dress and presented her with a platter of fruit, honey, and cheese.

Catherine felt her eyes fill. In Brigant, the bride's mother would bring her the wedding breakfast—her last meal as a single woman.

"Thank you, Tanya, I'd forgotten about this tradition. It's good to have something of home here with me."

"Not all things from Brigant are bad."

"But it's strange to think my mother doesn't even know I'm about to marry."

"She knew you were to marry Tzsayn. Even if the circumstances are somewhat different from those we expected,

I'm sure she would wish you a very happy life together."

A messenger came to say that the king was waiting. And Catherine's heart was suddenly beating hard.

"Let me check from all angles," Tanya said, running round Catherine and tweaking the hang of the simple white and silver dress.

"Can we go now?"

"Yes, you're looking perfect."

They walked together to Tzsayn's bedchamber where Tzsayn, General Davyon, and the chancellor were waiting.

Catherine was delighted that, for the first time since the operation, Tzsayn was out of his bed and dressed. In fact, he looked stunning in blue silk and leather with a fur trim at the collar and cuffs. To his jacket was pinned a white wissun blossom—the flower that Catherine had chosen as her emblem. He was sitting on one of two throne-like seats and he got to his feet with the help of a crutch and Davyon as Catherine entered.

Tanya escorted Catherine to the other throne and Catherine sat down, knowing that only then would Tzsayn return to his own seat. She smiled at him, and he smiled back and took her hand in his.

The marriage documents were already drawn up and laid out on a table. The wording was ambiguous enough that it could be interpreted that the marriage was a confirmation of the earlier, rushed ceremony that was supposed to have happened in Rossarb, while also being binding in and of itself.

Catherine confirmed her name and watched Tzsayn as he

confirmed his. She promised she'd be a loyal wife and love her husband always, and Tzsayn returned these promises in kind. Then Tzsayn signed the document, and Catherine picked up the quill and put her name next to his.

Tzsayn took her hand again and kissed it.

"I'm happier than words can say, Catherine."

Catherine wanted to laugh with happiness, and whispered, "I love you."

"And I love you." Tzsayn pulled her to him and nearly toppled from the chair, but he was laughing too as Davyon held him up.

The chancellor cleared his throat. "Well, I'll leave you now, Your Majesties."

Davyon too excused himself, as did Tanya. A dinner was served for Catherine and Tzsayn alone.

"Do any of the servants suspect, do you think?"

"As far as anyone is concerned, this is a meal to celebrate my return to health, and your purchase of some ships."

Catherine put on an exaggerated frown. "No mention of ships this afternoon, please."

"Agreed, as long as you don't ask about my leg. Which is fine. Savage has done his job well."

"You're not even tired?"

"I'm delighted to be out of that damned bed and wearing clothes again. But yes, as I must be honest with you, I'm a little tired, but very, very happy."

They talked until evening, when more food was brought, the candles lit, and rose petals strewn across the floor.

"Everyone seems particularly attentive," she said, though she felt like she was almost in a dream.

"I should hope so. I'm king. You're queen." Tzsayn smiled broadly. "And husband and wife too." He leaned to her and kissed her lips. "And happy, I hope."

"Very happy. I can't quite believe it's true, though."

The war council that morning seemed like a lifetime ago, and she'd mostly managed not to think of the fighting. Time spent not thinking of war felt like a precious gift. She looked at Tzsayn and said, "If I'm being honest—which I must be—I'm a little nervous."

"I'm nervous too."

"Impossible!"

"It doesn't happen often," he said, leaning over to kiss her. "And I'm hoping this will help. You're mine. I'm yours. We belong together." He put his hand on her waist and pulled her to him. "Forever."

Catherine stroked his cheek with her fingertips, the good cheek with perfect skin.

"For all my father's faults—and I won't waste our time by listing them—he did choose you as my husband. And he was right to do so. He did it for all the wrong reasons, but he chose the right man for me."

Tzsayn shuddered. "I don't want to think of him this evening. One night free of that monster would be good."

"You're right. This is not the night to talk of him. This is for us." She smiled and stroked his cheek, this time the scarred one. It was smooth but uneven, like melted wax.

Tzsayn turned his head so their lips met and they kissed again, their tongues touching, his arms holding her body to him and her hands reaching up his back.

Tzsayn began to unbutton his jacket with fumbling fingers.

Catherine giggled as she tried to help, saying, "The candlelight is very atmospheric, but I can't see well enough to undo the ties."

Eventually Tzsayn undid the last one and slid his jacket off. He raised his shirt over his head, revealing his body, half-scarred as his face was.

"Not so pretty, but I hope you can bear it," he said.

Catherine smiled at him and traced the line down his slim stomach between the scarred and unscarred skin. His muscles twitched. He was beautiful.

And now he turned her round and slowly undid the ribbons of her dress, kissing her neck after every pull. And all the while, Catherine could feel her dress loosen.

"I love you," she said as he undid the final bow.

# AMBROSE

## NORTHERN PLATEAU, PITORIA

IT WAS pouring rain, and Ambrose was up to his knees in mud. The mission had gone badly wrong and was getting worse. It had been two days since they had reached the demon hollow—only to discover that it wasn't a demon hollow anymore. Since then, they had been marching across the Northern Plateau in search of another, to no avail. The men were tired, cold, and hungry, but all they could do was keep plodding on. Ambrose wanted to scream with frustration, except he was too exhausted.

By the light of a low fire that night, Ambrose looked at his soldiers and could see that they had begun to lose their belief. They were quiet, and even Anlax had run out of jokes. Was this where Ambrose's fight would end? Lost on the Northern Plateau and starved to death?

Geratan looked particularly miserable as he approached Ambrose. "I'm sorry I've led you into this mess."

Ambrose shook his head. "You couldn't have known that the hollow would close up." And Ambrose hadn't even thought it might happen. He was the leader; he should have considered all possibilities when he was planning the mission. He was responsible. Had he been too caught up in his own misery, his own personal problems?

It was up to him to find a solution. "We have just enough food to make it back to the camp if we turn round now. But if we reequip and come out again, it could still take a week or longer to find a demon hollow. We'll be too late to prevent the Brigantines getting the smoke to their boy army. However, if we stay out here, we risk starving before we find another hollow."

Geratan winced. "Poor choices both. Which way are you leaning?"

"I don't know," Ambrose replied. But he did know. They'd have to head back. His mission had failed.

# EDYON

## CALIA, CALIDOR

EDYON WAS standing with Byron on his terrace, which overlooked the sea. The white of the buildings of Calia stood out brightly. He looked out and then to Byron. It was a glorious day and a glorious view—Byron was incredibly handsome. "Thank you again for taking the smoke and saving our lives," Edyon said to him.

Byron smiled a little shyly. "Your father asked me to. He said it might not be necessary. I'm sorry that it was."

"As am I," Edyon agreed. Though perhaps not very sorry. He was now the hero of the day, and his father was safe from the traitors.

"There's something I still don't understand about your side of the story," Byron said.

"What's that?"

"The bit about stealing the mirror. I mean, why were you really in Regan's room? Did you suspect him?"

Edyon shook his head. "Alas no. I really was in there stealing a mirror."

"But . . . I can't believe you're a thief! Did you not have a mirror in your room?"

"You believe in my vanity more than my thievery?"

Byron smiled and shrugged.

"The truth is that I have a compulsion to steal." Edyon hated to even admit it. "Obviously I'm not proud of it and it's hard to explain, but I get an urge to take things sometimes. And I don't know if it's because I'm so weak, so flawed, but I give in to it. Every time. I'm never sure when it'll happen. But I've stolen for a long time—since as early as I can remember. I stopped recently, for a brief time . . . There was a person . . . He helped me to not steal."

Byron raised his eyebrows. "A person?"

Edyon took a breath. Now he had to be really honest. Now he had to say it out loud. "A boy. I loved him."

Byron didn't scream in horror, so Edyon continued. "He used to be a servant to my father. It's a long, complicated story, but fate threw us together in Pitoria. We went through many trials, and I fell in love with him."

Edyon watched Byron for his reaction.

Byron's eyes showed interest and concern. "The friend who helped you in all your trials. The one who escaped with you across the Northern Plateau."

"That's him. His name is March."

"And you loved March, but did he not love you?"

"That's a very good question. I think he did. He wasn't quite as open with his feelings as I am."

"Not many are, Your Highness."

"He was quite the opposite to me, in fact, but he saved

my life on several occasions, and I'm proud to say I helped him through terrible suffering too." Edyon's eyes filled with tears at the memory of March lying in pain after being tortured in Rossarb.

"And where is he now?"

"I'm not sure. He was banished."

"Ah . . . him. I've heard rumors."

Edyon nodded and felt sick. "I'm sure all the court gossips about me and him."

Byron shook his head. "No. Not about you and him, but about him attacking Regan. I heard that it was Thelonius who felt compassion for March, that he valued him as a servant, but had to send him away."

"The truth is that I asked my father to spare him. He did try to kill Regan—not such a serious crime, it would seem now." And Edyon thought of Regan in the cells at Birtwistle. He'd died that first night of his wounds, and Edyon felt some pity for him, alone in a cold, miserable cell. *How the world turned, and no one could predict the future!*

"Perhaps March could return now?"

Edyon tried to smile. "I'd like that, but the truth is that he is gone, and I don't think he would want to return."

"May I ask if he was your first love?"

"Not the first. But . . . the only one to stop me stealing." Then Edyon asked Byron, "And you? Has your heart been broken?"

Byron nodded. "Once. I was much younger and perhaps my heart is stronger for it. It was a simple break—to the relationship and to me. He left me for another."

*He! Well, I had guessed, but still, that's not unpleasant news.*

"I'm sorry for the pain you suffered, Byron. And perhaps my heart will be stronger in the end too."

Byron was a good person, Edyon thought. Brave, thoughtful, and, of course, handsome. Would it be so wrong to form a close relationship with such a man? Edyon blushed as he said, "I love March still, but that is over, and I need to find a way out of the loneliness I feel. Will you stay with me, Byron? Keep me company?"

Byron turned to Edyon, bent down, and kissed his hand, and said, "I will do all I can."

# MARCH

SOMEWHERE IN SOUTHERN BRIGANT

SINCE NOYES'S visit to camp, Harold had spent more time on his metal contraptions. The bridges were now all made, but they had to be tested. The brigades had discovered, then perfected, the best technique to raise, expand, and drop them almost as one movement. They could do it so quickly now that, even as the ladders were settling in place, the first boys were already leaping in the air to land on them and run across.

The "rungs" of the ladder were flat metal slats that were widely spaced, and the ladder was narrow to keep the weight of the machine down—as March had learned from Harold's discussion with the blacksmiths who were making it. On the first practice the boys had leaped from rung to rung, but that had caused the ladder to bounce, and the whole thing had flipped up and out of place, sending boys flying through the air. The technique they then used was to run smoothly up the side of the ladder, which was narrow but flat—with smoke in you it was simple.

All the boys grew increasingly aggressive with the use of

smoke, and fights between them broke out frequently. However, with all the practice, smoke was running short and
Harold's patience, which was minimal at best, was approaching zero.

Finally, a week after Noyes left, Lord Thornlees arrived
with his troops. They kept a quite separate camp from the
boys, which seemed wise. Lord Thornlees came to Harold's
camp to deliver the smoke and March poured them both
wine.

Harold told Thornlees, "When my brigades attack, your
job is to follow us. We will take the wall and then you hold
it."

Thornlees frowned. "Yes, Your Highness. We will hold
it together."

"Yes, yes."

"Though I'm not sure we can use the metal bridges that
your boys are using. I watched the boys' brigades practicing,
and, well, the agility required may be beyond many of my
men. And we need to bring our horses, obviously."

"That's your problem. Do you want me to do everything
for you?"

"Not at all, Your Highness. I intend to dismantle the
wall. I have the men to do it."

"Fine. Knock your way through and make a path for the
old men to use."

And Thornlees was dismissed. He hadn't even had the
chance to sip his wine.

Now it was the morning of the advance. The smoke had
been dispersed to the brigades. The ladders were hidden at

the wall. Thornlees was holding position farther back from the boys' brigades. His men were ready to join the attack, but, if Harold had his way, March suspected it'd be over before Thornlees arrived.

March helped Harold to dress. The only armor the prince wore was a breast- and backplate, as these pieces helped his chest look wider and shone blindingly in the sunlight. There was a gold sun over Harold's heart—assuming, of course, that he had a heart. Harold carried two flasks of purple smoke—one on each hip.

Harold inspected the Gold Brigade, as they had to complement the prince's appearance. Harold even checked that Sam's sword was sharp and clean, and gave him a spear to carry. "Yes, yes, yes. You're my star boy, Sam. Now you look the part." And Sam's grin almost broke his face open.

Harold turned to March and said, "You're hopeless with a sword, March. And not much better with a spear. So I've had a few of these made especially for you." Harold held out his hand, on which rested three small pieces of metal, each the shape of a lemon but the size of a large chestnut.

"Thank you, Your Highness." March wasn't sure what he was supposed to do with them.

"I've seen you practicing with your stones. You used them to good effect against the other recruits in the race. These are my design, a good shape to fly fast and true, with more weight to add to the impact."

March took the metal shot from the prince. "Thank you, Your Highness."

"Let's see what you can hit with them. Take a sip of smoke and throw one at . . . my chest."

"Your chest!" March wasn't sure what to think of this idea. "But, Your Highness. I don't want to miss."

"Then don't."

March backed away. Was this his one chance to end the attack? Kill Harold and end it all? He licked his lips.

"Farther back," Harold called.

March moved away, feeling the weight of the shot in his hand. But also feeling sweat on his palm.

"I hope you're going to look more fearsome in battle, March. You look like you're going to pee in your pants."

March bent down to rub his palms on his trousers and muttered, "Fuck you, Your Highness," before standing upright, hauling his arm back, and throwing.

The shot zinged through the air, flat and hard, flying to Harold's face. But Harold had smoke in him too, and he simply moved his head quickly to the side. "Your aim's lousy. I said to hit my chest."

March threw again, before Harold had time to say more. The shot hit Harold's chest with a sharp *bang* so that he staggered back. "Ho, ho! March. That was a good aim and much more like it." Harold looked down. "Shits, you've dented my armor. Right on the heart."

March froze—spoiling the prince's armor and appearance was possibly more dangerous than hurting him.

But Harold laughed. "I rather like it. Shows I've seen a fight. I've got a bag full of shot for you, March. You'll be deadly with them."

March had one last piece in his hand. He could kill Harold now. He could do it; he pulled his arm back.

"Hey," Sam said as he grabbed March's arm and wrenched him round.

"Hey yourself, Sam. Don't you like me getting even a little praise for my skills? It can't always be about you, you know."

"It's not that. I thought you were . . ." He let go of March's arm. "Never mind."

March could attack Harold, but actually Sam was right to stop him now. Thornlees would still want to take the wall; the Brigantine army would still come and attack Calidor. March's one hope of being useful to Edyon was to stay alive and to use his privileged position in the Gold Brigade somehow.

Harold rode out of camp with the Gold Brigade jogging behind his horse. Ahead, the boys' brigades were lined up. The Bulls were in the middle, Rashford at their head. Many of the boys had war paint on and their hair shaved into strange shapes. They had already taken their smoke, it seemed, and had been worked up into a frenzy by their leaders.

Harold pulled his horse up and shouted to the boys. "Today is a historic day. Today is the day when we boys show the world what we're capable of. We don't need old men to lead us or tell us what to do. We *know* what to do. We know our power, our speed, our strength. And now the world will learn about it too. The world will learn to fear us. The world will learn to ignore us no more. Today we invade Calidor. We take the wall, and the Bears will hold it. I will run with the rest of you to Calia."

*What?* That wasn't the plan at all. That wasn't what Harold had promised Noyes. He had agreed to hold the wall until his father arrived with his own troops. He had promised not to go on to Calia.

The boys were cheering and whooping. But March was silent, trying to take in this news. He turned to Sam, who was waving his spear in the air. "We're going to go to Calia? He's going to leave Thornlees at the wall?"

"Sounds like it. We can do it too. We'll show them." Sam's eyes were bright with excitement.

Harold continued, "Calidor will be ours. Everyone in our path will learn to flee, or they will die. We boys will take Calia. We boys will take Calidor."

The shouts and cheers were deafening.

Harold was standing in his stirrups, his arms out, his armor shining. "Are you ready to show the world what we can do?"

The shouts grew louder still.

"Are you ready?"

But March could hardly hear what Harold was saying now, the shouting was so loud. Harold leaped from his horse and ran ahead of the boys. March and Sam ran close at his heels, and the other boys were following as fast as the wind and on toward the wall.

The first wall was the lower one. Though it was solid and imposing, with smoke in his body March saw it as an easy obstacle. The thing he feared was the pit. If he fell in when it was on fire, then getting out would be almost impossible.

The place where Harold had chosen to breach the walls was between two lookout points, and the boys were hidden from them by the undulating land until they were nearly at the wall. But once the boys were in view, speed was essential.

The boys raced forward faster and faster. Ahead of March the first of the four ladders was being raised. The Bears and Wasps were working together on it. The Wasps scaled the lower wall with ease, and the Bears raised their ladder, scaling the wall and then pulling the ladder in an arc. As the ladder swung, it opened out to land with a huge clang across the pit between the two walls.

Calidorian soldiers were already running along the top of the main wall to meet the invaders. They unleashed their first arrows at the Wasps, who were crossing the pit on the first ladder. A second ladder landed across the span with a crash. The third was arcing down as one of the guards hurled a flaming torch into the dividing pit below the Wasps. More flaming torches followed as the last ladder fell into place.

Arrows zinged down on the crowd of boys as they threw grappling hooks over the first, lower wall. March was with them at the base of the lower wall and protected from the arrows, but not for long. Harold climbed up a rope and March had to follow. At the top he had a view of the battle. Flames in the ditch had already taken hold and were licking the bottoms of the ladders.

Calidorian soldiers were using their spears to lever a ladder over, tipping boys into the ditch. Archers were targeting other boys on the wall. Harold drew his sword and ran across

the nearest ladder, showing no fear, no hesitation. The Gold
Brigade followed, shouting as they went, even though the
flames were round their ankles.

March ran across and could hardly see where to put his
feet for the smoke rising from the pit. The ladder sloped upward and his boot slipped, but he regained his balance and
ran on. Then he was through the smoke and on the second
wall. Harold was ahead, swinging his sword into a Calidorian soldier who towered over him, but was no match for
Harold's speed or strength. Harold moved along the wall,
cutting down each soldier he met with ease. The boys
followed, and it was clear that the opposition was quickly
crumbling; some Calidorians were already fleeing.

Was it really that easy? The wall had taken years to build,
and hundreds if not thousands of men to construct, and so
much money—March remembered how the Calidorian lords
had complained—and now a few boys had breached it in moments.

Harold was shouting, "Kill them all! String their bodies
up for all to see." There was a scream as a Calidorian soldier
was dragged forward. A young boy ran him through with a
spear, then hoisted his body into the air, the boys around him
laughing and cheering.

Harold shouted, "Bears, hold the wall. Give assistance to
Thornlees if he needs it. We are off for Calia." And, without
waiting for a response, the prince was lowering himself down
a rope and leaping onto Calidorian soil. Sam followed. March
looked back. In the distance he could see the pennants of the
Brigantine army—Lord Thornlees was coming.

Rashford joined March. "Well, that was easy."

"I was thinking just the same," March replied. "But we'll see what happens in Calia. Getting past the castle fortifications will be harder than climbing this wall. And they'll have been warned we're on our way. The beacon is lit as well as this ditch." March nodded toward a flame burning high on one of the Calidorian forts. "They'll be ready for us."

March looked toward Calia. Edyon would be there. Perhaps he'd be safe. If Edyon stayed inside the castle, perhaps they'd hold out. And if not, March would do all he could to protect him. He knew that might mean killing Harold. And if it came to that, then he also knew he'd not escape with his life.

# EDYON
## CALIA, CALIDOR

EDYON WAS half-asleep, wrapped in a sweaty tangle of sheets. It had been a long and leisurely afternoon of lovemaking, and now it was evening. Byron was gentle, tender, and possibly the most handsome human Edyon had ever lain with. It was lovely, but it wasn't love. Byron was beautiful, but he wasn't March.

*But I can never have March, and so I need to stop thinking about him.*

*Especially when I'm lying with another man!*

Byron was asleep, breathing softly, and Edyon stroked his finger down his chest. Could he love Byron? Could his heart move on from March? Certainly Byron was a worthy partner. But was Edyon worthy of Byron? Edyon was supposed to marry—a woman—and sire children—future heirs. The future of Calidor rested on him. He looked down at his naked body. The future of Calidor rested on this body.

Edyon got out of bed and went to the window. The view took in the sea and coast to the south. This was his land. As Madame Eruth had foretold, he'd made a difficult journey to a far land and riches. She'd not spoken of happiness, though. He'd assumed the riches would make him happy, but now tears filled his eyes, because it was March, only March, who had made him happy.

Below him, in the streets, some revelers began shouting, disturbing his thoughts.

*At least someone's happy.*

Then Edyon noticed the light on the distant hillside. And he heard more shouting, closer, inside the castle.

"Master! Master!" Talin burst into his chamber, and, seeing Edyon naked, turned to the bed, and, seeing Byron naked, turned to the door. He spoke, his voice breathy and desperate, his arms flapping strangely as he hopped up and down. "Prince Thelonius has called for you, Your Highness. You're required to be with him immediately. The beacons are lit. We're being invaded."

And Edyon knew that for all the wealth and riches he had, death was still all around him.

Byron was out of bed and pulling his clothes on. He came to the terrace to look. "It's true. The city beacon is lit."

Edyon dressed as quickly as he could, and they ran to his father's meeting room. Edyon had expected the chamber to be full of panic and clamor, but it was surprisingly quiet. Several lords were there, but most had returned to their own estates after the tour. Edyon went to stand with his father.

Thelonius spoke in a clear, serious tone to the whole room. "The beacons are lit. Brigantines are attacking the wall. Once again our northern neighbors want to take what isn't theirs. However, it seems that my brother's tactics have changed from those he used, and failed with, in the last war. I have received a report sent by bird that the wall was taken by the Brigantine boy army, eight hundred strong. Behind them are conventional troops led by Lord Thornlees, but that too is merely two thousand men. Aloysius and his forces aren't in sight. Our army is five thousand. We have the strength to beat them."

"They must be sending more of the main army," the chancellor said.

Thelonius replied, "The most recent reports from our brave spies in the north of Brigant say that the main army is not yet moving. It would appear that this attack is intended to take the wall and hold it. If they do that, then Aloysius can come south whenever he likes. We must act swiftly to counter this attack, retake the wall, and secure our borders. The ports are safe, and there are no signs of an attack by sea. However, as we are now in a state of war, all towns and cities must activate their defense procedures—all people must take shelter within city and town defenses, and all members of the army and defense are on full alert."

Thelonius turned to Edyon, saying, "I ride out immediately, but you must stay here, Edyon. Your life must not be put at risk. Stay inside the castle until it is safe."

"Father, I'm aware you know much more about war than I do, but please be aware of the risks of the boy army."

"I remember your demonstration, Edyon. And I remember Byron's strength at Birtwistle. But I have confidence in my men too. However, you must take care. They may send a small force south to Calia, aiming to assassinate you and other key individuals, but as long as you stay within the walls of the castle you'll be safe. However, should anything happen that would threaten you directly, we have boats prepared to take you back to Pitoria."

Edyon was surprised to find himself saying, "No. I won't flee. I'll fight."

Thelonius shook his head. "You're brave and true, Edyon, but you're not a soldier. The boats are only to be used as a last resort—you won't need them, but they're there." He looked to Byron. "Stay with Edyon. You saved us before, Byron, and I know, should anything unexpected happen, that you will do all you can to protect Edyon."

Thelonius embraced Edyon, and they said their good-byes.

Edyon watched from the ramparts as Thelonius rode out of the castle with his men. At the same time, the first of the townspeople began to arrive to take shelter. None were empty-handed; all seemed to be carrying what they could— food, clothes, chickens, some leading cows, others herding goats. It was as if the people knew what to do already. They'd been through it before, as had his father and many of the soldiers. They'd survived before and won, and Edyon had to believe they'd do it again.

# TASH
## DEMON TUNNELS

TASH WAS running for her life again. This time from Brigantine soldiers and along her own tunnel through the demon world.

*Just keep going. Get to the surface and head south. Find the Pitorian army—that can't be too hard, can it? Find Princess Catherine or Sir Ambrose or General Davyon or Rafyon or anyone who isn't a Brigantine. And warn them that the first load of smoke has already gone, and they might be attacked any day.*

Tash stopped to listen but couldn't hear anything behind her. Her tunnel was low and narrow—a huge advantage for her and a huge disadvantage for them.

*They won't give up—they're Brigantines. But I need to think about where I'm going.*

She put her hand on the stone walls of the tunnel, her tunnel.

*Perhaps I can use the smoke in me to help me find the others. If I think of them, maybe it will guide me to them, if they're here.*

*Right. So. Think of General Davyon.*

Tash thought of the general: grim face; serious eyes; glossy, gleaming blue hair.

Nothing happened. The stone didn't change.

*Right. So now think of Rafyon.*

Tash imagined Rafyon: handsome, broad-shouldered, and slim.

Again, nothing happened.

*I'm losing my touch! Or they're not on the Northern Plateau. Try again. Think of Geratan.*

Tash pictured him: smiling face, white hair tucked behind his ears.

Immediately she felt the stone beneath her hand disappear. A new tunnel was forming. *It's working!*

The new tunnel continued to grow, branching off her old one.

*But I'm going to make sure this one is even smaller and more of a squeeze for those Brigantines behind me.*

Tash bent down so the tunnel was low, and smiled to think of the huge Brigantine soldiers trying to even walk through this new tunnel—they'd certainly not be able to run.

*Concentrate! Think of Geratan. Geratan. Geratan. Geratan. White hair. Calm face. Great dancer. Strong. Brave. Polite.*

And, as she thought of him, the tunnel opened faster and faster, until she was jogging along in her half-crouch. As she ran, the vision she had of Geratan began to sharpen, and she realized that his hair wasn't white.

*Crimson! What's that about?*

And she could see he was among other soldiers—all with the same colored hair. And Sir Ambrose was there. But not Davyon and not Rafyon.

*This is like the vision I had of Frost. The smoke is showing me my destination. I must be nearly there.*

And, at that thought, the tunnel turned sharply upward. Tash scrambled up the slope as it formed ahead of her, the air changed, and she took a breath of wonderfully cool air as she pulled herself out, back into the human world.

It was night; the sky was full of stars and tall pine trees. And ahead was a small fire with figures sitting round it.

And then someone grabbed her, pinning her arms to her side, a rough-skinned hand over her mouth. She could hardly breathe.

"And what have we got here?"

"Wee gahr shirring shirring shir!" Tash shouted, and kicked viciously at the man's shins.

"Bloody hell. She's a wild one. Look at this, Geratan."

"Geraghaan!"

"Don't know what she's—OW!"

Tash shook her teeth out of the man's hand and shouted, "Geratan!"

"What's going on? Silence!"

It was Sir Ambrose's voice, rushing toward her from the fire. And with him, Geratan.

"It's me, Tash!" she shouted, giving the man holding her another kick in the shins. He swore loudly but still didn't let her go.

"You can release her, Anlax."

"Gladly."

And the man dropped Tash, and she was in Geratan's arms, being hugged. His smile was something to see.

"You're alive, Tash. You're alive!"

"Course I'm alive."

Tash sat by the fire with Geratan, Sir Ambrose, and his men—the Demon Troop, as she'd discovered they were called—and told them everything she'd done in the demon world. Some of it sounded daft even to her own ears, but by the way Geratan looked at her and nodded, she was reassured that he trusted everything she said was true. And if he believed it, then Sir Ambrose did. And if he believed it, then—well, the Demon Troop would too.

She was just explaining how she'd made her way back to the surface when she remembered something.

"Oh shits! The tunnel. The Brigantines will be coming!"

"Anlax, take two men and keep watch outside the tunnel. If you hear or see anything, sound the alarm." Anlax nodded and hurried off. "Thank you, Tash," Ambrose continued. "Your information is incredibly valuable. So the Brigantines have shipped out some of their smoke but still have a lot stored down there. We need to destroy it, if we can."

"But I want to hear your story too," said Tash. "What happened after Geratan and I got separated from you and the princess?"

Sir Ambrose gave a weak smile. "I'll tell you all our adventures properly when this is over, Tash, but I'm afraid there's some bad news in them." He hesitated. "I'm sorry, but

Rafyon was killed. Not by demons, but by an assassin. He died saving Princess Catherine's life."

Tash could feel the tears coming. She hated war. Hated how one moment her friends were alive and well and loving you, and the next moment, gone.

"And everyone else?" she asked. "The princess?"

"Alive and a queen now. Married to King Tzsayn."

"Queen, eh? And are you still her . . . what was it?"

"Personal guard. No, I'm head of the Demon Troop now. Somehow I don't think King Tzsayn is going to want me around."

"And you've been sent up here on a mission to kill the Brigantines and win back the demon world." Tash pursed her lips. "Well, lucky for you I found you. I think I can help you with that . . ."

# AMBROSE
## NORTHERN PLATEAU, PITORIA

AMBROSE WAS feeling positive again.

Thanks to Tash, he had access to the demon world and a guide to show them the way to the smoke store. Armed with Tash's information about the numbers of the Brigantines and the lack of demons, their chances of success had soared. Even with just fifty men, he felt he could take the central cavern. From there, they should be able to capture and destroy the smoke store. First, however, they had to deal with the Brigantines who would be coming along Tash's tunnel.

Ambrose said to Geratan, "If we meet them in the tunnel, some will escape and warn the others, and the element of surprise will be lost. We have to wait for them all to come out here, lay a trap for them; none can be allowed to return to the central cavern to warn of our presence."

He positioned the men in the trees surrounding the tunnel, making sure that the only footprints visible were Tash's leading off to the south. Then they settled in to wait.

They didn't have to wait long, as just a few moments

later, a long-haired Brigantine, covered in scratches and growling with anger, emerged from the tunnel. His sword wasn't drawn, and he was clearly not considering he might be surrounded by Pitorian soldiers. Another Brigantine soldier appeared and more joined them. One began looking for tracks, easily finding Tash's footprints. Soon the Brigantines had gathered together—eight in all—and Ambrose could hear the leader giving orders.

"Hugo, you go back and inform the commander that the rest of us are following the girl. She can only be a short way ahead of us. We'll be on her by the end of the day, now we're out of that fucking tunnel."

Ambrose glanced over to Geratan and gave the signal to attack.

It was brutal and swift. The Brigantines fought to the end, but the end came quickly. Only one of the Demon Troop was wounded, with a cut to his arm. While this was bandaged, Ambrose congratulated the troop on their first victory. But there was no time to waste. Now, finally, the real part of their mission was to begin.

Ambrose knelt on the rim of the hollow, lowered his head, and pushed forward.

He'd almost forgotten how hot it was in the demon world, how strange and red-tinted the light was. However, it was nothing like the demon hollow he'd been in before. There was no room to move. He could hardly fit his shoulders through Tash's tunnel. He returned to the human world and asked Tash, "Any chance you can make the tunnel a bit bigger? Anlax has lost a bit of weight in the last few days, but he still won't get his stomach through there."

"I'll try," Tash replied. "If I lead the way, I might be able to widen it as I go."

Ambrose followed her, curious to see what she did, expecting her to touch the tunnel walls, but she didn't even need to do that. She spread her arms out wide and the stone walls retreated from them, and as she walked forward, the tunnel widened and the ceiling rose.

Ambrose followed Tash and looked back to check that the rest of the Demon Troop was following. He felt a touch on the bare skin of his hand and heard Geratan's voice in his mind:

*Everyone's in.*

Their pace wasn't fast—more of a stroll than a march— but it was quicker than trying to squeeze through a narrow tunnel. They walked on and on until the tunnel joined another. Ambrose touched Tash's arm.

*What's this?*

*This is my original tunnel. If you go right here, it takes you back to the surface. The way to the left goes down to the central cavern. We're probably about halfway there.*

*That's great, Tash. If you sense anything that feels wrong, stop and tell me.*

Ambrose sent the message back up the line to his men that they were halfway to the cavern. They proceeded slowly, Tash still widening the tunnel, but everyone was even more careful about not making a noise.

After a time, Tash stopped and lowered her arms.

*Sorry. I'm just a bit tired. I've got to concentrate so hard.*

*That's fine, Tash. You're doing brilliantly. Rest if you need to.*

Tash nodded and sat down. Ambrose looked back at his men. They too were resting, preparing themselves. They knew the fight wasn't far ahead.

When she was ready to move again, Ambrose and the Demon Troop rose as one and followed.

Now Ambrose noticed a change in the light—it had a more purple glow. Surely it was coming from the central cavern.

Tash grabbed Ambrose's arm, her warning loud and clear.

*Brigantines! Guarding the way into the cavern.*

Ambrose nodded, his heart beating faster as he drew his dagger. *Let me get past.*

Tash shook her head. *There's too many. Someone will raise the alarm. Back up and I'll make a new tunnel so we can come out farther down.*

Everyone moved backward, calmly and silently. Tash set to work making a new tunnel that cut off to the right, then swerved to the left and opened up into the cavern. Ambrose wanted to laugh at how easy Tash made it seem. She checked left and right before dropping to her knees and crawling out onto the terrace. Ambrose followed, signaling the others to wait.

Geratan had described the cavern to him, and Tash had told him the cavern was shrinking, but it still took Ambrose's breath away. It was huge. The sides were covered with terraces—on the very highest one he spotted the red figure of a demon. Farther down, some Brigantines were guarding a few tunnel entrances, but others seemed to be relaxing. And in the center of it all was a deep hole with a column of purple smoke swirling out of it. The core.

*That's changed again*, Tash told him. *There's more smoke than before, and it's moving faster. The demons are making it happen. Far below us, beneath the core, they're throwing themselves back into the smoke. Making it bigger.*

*The Brigantines don't seem bothered by it*, said Ambrose, looking at the relaxing guards.

Tash wrinkled her nose contemptuously. *The Brigantines just think they're going to get more smoke, but I wonder where it'll end.*

*I don't know, Tash. But I do know we have to destroy the smoke store if it's still there. First, though, we need to mark this tunnel so we can find it again—it's our way out.*

Tash nodded. *I can maybe make it a slightly different shape. Give it a lopsided look?*

*That'll do fine. Then we need to get to the smoke store. Can you make a tunnel to it?*

*Easy.*

*Good. Five of my men will go with you and Geratan to destroy it.*

*What are the rest of you going to be doing?* Tash asked with a frown.

Ambrose grinned. *Causing chaos.*

# CATHERINE

ARMY CAMP, NORTHERN PITORIA

Advantage must be exploited swiftly and decisively.

War: The Art of Winning, *M. Tatcher*

TZSAYN STILL wasn't well enough to go to the war council, but he was well enough for the war council to come to him. The king sat in a comfortable chair, his bandaged stump covered by a blanket, while Catherine, Hanov, Davyon, and Lord Darby stood round the map table as Ffyn made his report.

"For weeks the Brigantine invasion force has stayed put in their camps around Rossarb, but our spies have learned that Lord Thornlees and his men are in Brigant." He looked at Lord Darby. "That's two thousand men on foot and horse. They are heading for Calidor."

"Only Thornlees's men?" Darby asked.

"We believe it's just his force that is on the move, and we're sure that Aloysius is still in Rossarb. But it looks like the war is entering a new phase."

"I'll send word immediately to Calidor," Darby said.

"Your message might not get there ahead of the Brigantines. I'm afraid the information is a little old," Hanov said, looking miserable.

"But at least the message will get through," Ffyn added, picking up a model boat from the map. "The scullers have enabled us to break Brigantine control of the Pitorian Sea. Several of their ships have been picked off, and the threat of a naval invasion of Pitoria has been almost eliminated."

"Indeed," Catherine said. "And now we need to put the scullers to their other use. We must attack the northern land route while Aloysius is still at Rossarb."

"A bold move," Ffyn commented. "But risky. Aloysius will bring all his forces to bear against them."

"Not if he's also being kept busy to the south," Catherine replied. "The scullers will carry one force to the north shore of the Bay of Rossarb. These men are to take the forts and hold the road to prevent Aloysius from retreating. Meanwhile, the other prong of the attack is by land—the blue-hairs and white-hairs converging on Rossarb, one from the south, one from the east."

Tzsayn spoke now. "Queen Catherine's white-hairs will travel north from here to the Ross River Road before cutting west. Ffyn, you will go with that force and ensure that the queen is safe at all times. Davyon, you will lead my blue-hairs, who will advance from the south. You will coordinate your attack on Aloysius's forces just outside Rossarb."

Davyon said, "What about the boy army? Any details about their location?"

Hanov stepped in. "Information on the boys' brigades is sparse, to say the least. They move quickly and with minimal support—no horses, no baggage, no camp followers—so tracking their location is almost impossible. However, we believe Prince Harold has taken overall command of them, and we believe he's somewhere in the south of Brigant. I don't know if all the boys are with him, but that would make sense."

Tzsayn nodded. "With Thornlees moving south, it looks like the Brigantines are intent on beginning an offensive, spearheaded by the boys' brigades. If so, the attack has probably already begun—our information is days old."

"And yet the conquest of Calidor is so personal to Aloysius," Darby said, "I can't believe they would launch a serious offensive without him."

"Which is another reason why we must not delay our attack," Catherine said. "We want my father trapped in the north. This is our chance. His forces are weaker for the loss of Thornlees and the boy army. But if they are able to conquer Calidor and then reunite, we will be outnumbered again."

"You haven't mentioned the mission to the demon world," Hanov said.

Catherine held her breath. It had been a week since Ambrose had set out. Every day she asked for news but so far there had been nothing.

Davyon replied, "We didn't expect to hear from them, but I have confidence that Sir Ambrose and his men will be doing whatever they can to stop production of the demon smoke."

Catherine's mind went back to the demon world and her time there with Ambrose. He'd hated it. He'd have much preferred to be in the battle aboveground. Tzsayn took her hand and leaned into her, whispering, "Sir Ambrose has more lives than twenty cats. He'll be back."

Catherine nodded and smiled. She thought again of how Ambrose had talked of lives being held by thread. Each of the men in his Demon Troop was another thread that was supporting him. And, somehow, she still felt bound to him herself. That thread would never break—they were always going to be connected.

"Anything else?" Tzsayn looked around the group, but no one spoke. "Then the army will move out to their forward positions tomorrow morning. The scullers will attack tomorrow night, the land army at dawn the following day."

Once the others had left, Tzsayn said, "I wish I could be with my men. It doesn't feel right to be sending them into battle while I lounge here in my tent."

"I doubt you'll be lounging. And it wouldn't be safe," Catherine replied, refraining from adding that it was practically impossible. Tzsayn was improving every day, but he wouldn't be fully fit for weeks, and even then would have to relearn how to ride with only one leg.

He took her hand again. "The queen needs to be safe too. I know you want to ride out with your men but I'm still not happy about it."

"I'll remain well back, don't worry. I can't fight, but perhaps I can inspire."

"You won't be tempted to throw a spear again?"

Catherine shook her head. "I confess I've tried the smoke, but it no longer works for me. I must be getting old."

Tzsayn smiled. "You're not old. Though I'm glad you're not going to be tempted to use it. I'm still frightened of losing you."

Catherine kissed him. "I'll be careful. My future with you is too bright to risk."

In bed that night Catherine clung to her husband and hardly slept. She wanted to savor every moment with Tzsayn, feeling his body next to hers. But all too soon it was morning and Tanya was helping her to dress.

Catherine wore a simple white silk shift, over which was her skirt of chain mail. Then came the breastplate, which still contained the small bottle of demon smoke secured inside. She considered removing it but decided against it. The smoke had always brought her good luck. Maybe it would again. She held the breastplate firmly to her body as Tanya positioned the backplate and strapped the two tightly together.

"I don't see why I have to stay in camp," Tanya complained, tugging on a strap. "You should have a maid with you."

"I'm not out for a pleasant jaunt through the countryside, Tanya. I'm leading an army."

But in truth, Catherine was thinking back to how she had lost Sarah in Tornia and Jane outside Rossarb. Maids didn't fare well in battles and she couldn't bear to lose Tanya.

Outside, the men were ready. Tzsayn made a short appearance before the troops to much cheering and shouting. Catherine was delighted to see how just the sight of her husband lifted the spirits of the Pitorian army.

Tzsayn turned to her and said, "Don't do anything rash. If you are hurt, I won't be able to bear it. So, for me, please, please stay safe."

He kissed her and the men cheered, but Catherine hardly noticed. She stroked his cheek and promised, "I will."

Davyon was sitting astride his huge horse at the head of the blue-hairs, who outnumbered the white-hairs standing beside them ten to one. They would bear the brunt of the fighting, with Catherine's men providing support on the flank.

Catherine mounted her own horse and they set off together. They split at the stream just outside the camp, Catherine's white-hairs heading due north to the River Ross, Davyon and the blue-hairs turning west to the coast road before they too swung north. Once over the shallow stream, Catherine took a last glance at the camp and Tzsayn. She was sure he was there somewhere, looking back at her. Then she turned away and set her gaze forward, toward the far gray wall of the Northern Plateau.

# MARCH
## ABASK, CALIDOR

THE BOYS swarmed down the steep-sided valleys of Abask. March was in his home country, the land where his mother, father, and brother had died, slaughtered by Brigantines, by Aloysius. And now March was running with Brigantines and servant to Aloysius's son. And this, more than anything, hurt and shamed him. But what surprised him was that Harold was aware of how he might be feeling. As they ran, the prince said, "You're in your old country, March, but now you're fighting with your father's enemies. What's that like?"

March found it was more and more of a struggle to slip back into his blank servitude, but he tried. "Abask died years ago, Your Highness. This land is empty now and times have changed. I must fight for my own future."

"Times have changed indeed. Now we boys will rule the world."

*We? No, you want to rule. Anyone who gets in your way will be killed. All I can do is try to ensure Edyon never crosses your path.*

Harold looked down at Calidor before him. The view was an idyllic scene of woods and green farmland; wherever the Calidorian army was, it wasn't here. "Thelonius is hiding in his castle, I can feel it. He's terrified to meet us."

"Perhaps he thinks you will stay at the wall and await the main Brigantine army."

"Like my father wanted me to do. Those old men are out of touch with modern warfare. Their days are numbered. I am the future. The boys' brigades are the future. Nothing will stop us. I'm going to make history."

And on they ran. Some boys inhaled more smoke as they went. They didn't stop to eat or drink—the smoke was all they needed. They ran south down the hills, crossing fields to join the road to Calia. The first Calidorians they saw were at a village on the road. An old man stood in front of his cottage and stared at them. In the distance March saw some villagers fleeing for the trees. Harold gave the order for them to be killed. March was shocked that the boys didn't hesitate. These were ordinary people, not soldiers, but Harold didn't care.

At the next village more were killed, but Harold was already getting bored of it. It was a diversion from his real task, and it was slowing them down, so the boys ran through the villages, but they didn't chase those who fled.

The boys ran all day, and it was only when the sun was low in the sky that March saw the sea and Calia Castle before it. As they neared, the sky darkened as night fell, and torches were lit on the highest battlements. Somehow the walls of the castle looked taller than March remembered, even though he'd lived much of his life here. Mostly he'd been inside looking out. Now, looking up, even with smoke flowing through him, he couldn't see how Harold could take these walls. If Edyon was in there, he was safe.

March had expected that Thelonius and his army would be waiting for them outside the castle, but they met no opposition.

Harold muttered, "He's gone to the border wall. He'll be on the coast road, plodding up there to join the bulk of his army and confront Thornlees."

March tried to make out the flags at the very top of the castle. It was hard to see in the dark, but he was sure that Thelonius's flag was not flying. Harold seemed to be correct: Thelonius would be heading to the point of invasion, not expecting the boys' brigades to move so quickly through the mountains.

So Thelonius was not here, but what about Edyon? Was he up there looking down on March? March was sure Edyon wouldn't be involved in any fighting—Edyon was so hopeless he wouldn't even try. All March could do was hope that the Calidorian army and the castle wall would do their jobs.

Rashford came over to report to Harold. "Your Highness. There's no sign of opposition outside the castle. We've been through the city. It's mostly empty."

"Everyone's withdrawn into the castle. They're like women—too frightened to come outside. Well, we'll just have to go in after them."

Harold positioned the brigades around the castle and

tasked them with finding a way up onto the ramparts. The boys set to work using grappling hooks and ropes attached to spears. But, even with the power of the boys' throws, few hooks reached the ramparts and, although the spears did reach, most were quickly thrown back down. The Calidorian guards were lined along the castle battlements and seemed to be having fun, even shouting encouragement to the boys who were climbing the few ropes that stayed in place, and allowing them to get partway up the ropes before cutting them. All the while, arrows rained down on the boys— sometimes in thick volleys, then nothing, then just a few arrows aimed at boys throwing spears, followed by another thick volley. Although the boys had shields, some were hit.

The night wore on and Rashford reported to Harold that many boys had been hit by arrows; some had healed with the smoke, but seven Bulls had been killed, along with forty other boys. "The Calidorian tactics are working nicely for them," he complained. "They're sitting up there laughing at us." Rashford looked angry and added, "Eventually we'll run out of smoke or boys."

"And have you a better plan, Bull leader?"

Rashford shook his head. "No, Your Highness. My apologies, I shouldn't let my emotions get the better of me."

"No, you shouldn't. Now do something useful and bring me the leader of the Wasps."

The boy, Tiff, soon joined them. He was smaller and younger than Harold, with thick black hair and deep-set eyes.

"Your boys are the best climbers, Tiff. Can any of them climb that wall?"

Tiff squinted at it. "There are narrow fingerholds in the stone. If it's like that the whole way up, it's possible, but it ain't easy. Not many could do it. Perhaps me, Ned, and Shardly."

"Then take them and do it while it's dark. We'll withdraw, make them think we've given up for the night. You go to the south side. Find a way to the battlements, and once you're there, hold the position. We'll throw ropes up to you on spears. You'll have to defend the position while the rest of your brigade join you. It's an opportunity for the Wasps to show the other brigades that you are the best."

Tiff grinned. "We'll show 'em."

"Yes, you will have the glory. The Bulls are not so brave as you." Harold gestured to Rashford. "Their leader is quaking with fear." Rashford looked aghast, but raised his chin as Harold continued: "You can take your Bulls on the night patrol. Or is that too frightening, Bull leader?"

"My boys can do that, Your Highness."

"Ensure the Calidorians don't counterattack from the castle. Check again that they've no troops hidden in the surrounding area."

Rashford bowed his head. "Yes, Your Highness." And he turned and ran back to his brigade.

The boys withdrew out of range of the arrows and set up camps, lighting fires, eating food stolen from the homes in Calia. It appeared that they didn't expect the Wasps to succeed in their assault, at least not anytime soon. But Harold couldn't rest; he went to watch the Wasps, and Sam and March, of course, had to go with him.

The three climbers were each trying different routes but all seemed to be stuck at different points about a third of the way up the wall. There was a slight overhang at that level, and getting past it seemed impossible. One boy fell with a faint cry. Harold cursed him for making a noise. The boy wouldn't make a noise again, though, as the fall had certainly killed him.

Tiff was stretching up past the overhang when his legs slipped. March winced; he didn't want them to get in, but he didn't want to watch Tiff die. But then Tiff was moving faster. He'd made it. He'd found a route. The second boy now climbed across to the same place. After a bit of a struggle, he made it up to join Tiff.

"Well done, Wasps." Harold pumped his fist. "Go and tell the brigade leaders to prepare their boys and get them to join me here, Sam. The Wasps will do this."

And the two Wasps began moving up together, slowly and steadily heading for the ramparts above, but had the cry alerted the Calidorians? March stared at the silent castle and willed it to be so.

Tiff reached the rampart, swung onto it, and was out of sight for a moment; then he reappeared and helped the other Wasp up as the brigade leaders joined Harold.

A spear with a rope attached was sent hard and fast up to the rampart. The throw was perfect. The spear skimmed up past Tiff, and he reached out and caught it as it slowed at the top of its flight. Another spear was sent up as Wasps began to ascend the first rope.

*They're going to make it. Where are the Calidorian guards?*

And, as if in answer to March's question, a shout went up from the castle. A guard had spotted the Wasp boys. It was impossible to see what was happening on the ramparts. There were only two small Wasps up there, but two boys on smoke were worth about six men.

There was more shouting from the Calidorian guards, but more Wasps were climbing the ropes at speed, and the ropes weren't cut down. Whatever the guards were doing to try to stop them, it wasn't working. The Wasps were climbing over the ramparts. Tiff appeared and waved.

*They're in. They've made it.*

But the Calidorians would counterattack. Could the Wasps hold it until more boys joined them?

"Bring everyone to this point," Harold shouted. "Send up more ropes! I want more boys up there now." He ran to the castle wall to climb a rope himself as a body fell from above. It landed with a horrible, dull crunch on the paving in front of March, who jumped back, swearing and shaking. Harold didn't flinch, but merely stepped over the body of the Calidorian guard that was bleeding and broken at his feet.

Harold started to climb, and March and Sam followed. March pulled himself up in the same way that he'd climbed the border wall, but this was different; this was much higher, and, although the smoke made him strong, looking down was terrifying. As March reached the top and leaped over the ramparts, Harold had already joined the fight, killing three men with the first three strikes of his sword. Sam was close to him. Their strength and swordsmanship together were making all the difference. The other boys pressed after them and March followed at the rear, stepping on bodies that now lay two deep on the ground. March wasn't entirely sure who to cheer for. He wanted the Calidorians to win but didn't particularly want to be tossed over the ramparts to the ground below.

However, the Calidorians weren't winning. They were falling back. They weren't outnumbered, but they couldn't put more men on the narrow battlements, and Harold and the boys were cutting through the defenses. Soon there was no one left to fight, at least not at this level, but the boys were still far from taking the castle. They were merely in possession of an outer ring. They had to move up and in, but the boys had gained confidence, and it seemed the more they fought, the more they wanted to fight, as if the smoke fed the desire. As for March, he hadn't thrown even one of his metal shots. All he did was walk over the bodies of the fallen, his thoughts with Edyon.

*Just stay safe, Edyon. And please, let the Calidorian guards inside do a better job.*

Harold was enjoying himself. "We're nearly there, boys. We can do this. We can destroy our enemies. A famous victory for my boy army and for Brigant. Calia Castle will be ours."

*More like a famous victory for Harold.*

March thought of using his shot. Could he get Harold in the back of the head? Probably, but the boys would turn on him if he tried anything. Then he'd have no chance of helping Edyon at all.

By now some boys were copying the Wasps and trying their climbing skills. A few failed and fell back, but it wasn't long before the first boy reached the battlements above and sent a rope down. He'd met no opposition. The Calidorians must have retreated farther into the castle keep. That was where they'd have their final defense.

Harold knew it too. "The castle is nearly ours. Calia is nearly ours. They're terrified of us, boys. One more assault and the victory is ours. Kill them all. Kill them all!" The boys screamed with delight as March followed Harold up another rope and then along the terrace, where there was open access. It had never been imagined that anyone could climb this high. The boys ran past March—coming to the main group of guards, who fought together. The men towered over most of the boys, but the boys were too fast and too strong. The men were brought down one by one. Some tried to run, but it was hopeless. The boys swarmed across the rooms and terraces, children cutting adults to pieces and shouting with glee as if at a fair.

And it wasn't just soldiers who were killed but unarmed townsfolk and servants. The boys didn't care—they attacked anyone in their way. Men's heads were sliced from their bodies; blood made the floor slippery; shouts and screams came from all over the castle. It was mayhem, and the boys were loving it. March was horrified. These people weren't soldiers. But there was nothing he could do for them. The only thing he could do was try to ensure Edyon was safe if he was here, but how he'd do that, March had no idea.

*He'll have gone. He can't possibly be here. They'd send him somewhere safe.*

But March had to be sure. In the mayhem, hoping no one would be keeping close track of his movements, he ran to the private quarters, to the rooms of Thelonius's eldest son. This room would surely now be Edyon's. And it looked that way: the clothes and boots seemed to have been made for him, a parchment on the table was addressed to him. This was his room. The bedsheets were in a tangle as if Edyon had just risen, as if his servant had had no time to make the bed.

*That means he's been in the castle recently. He's still here somewhere. Oh, no, Edyon.*

March ran from room to room. He knew this place intimately. Knew the quickest way through. The bedchambers were all deserted; Thelonius's rooms were also empty, but as he ran, three other boys arrived, gasping with delight at the riches around them, riches they'd never even seen before. One boy was throwing silk cushions in the air, another was pulling on tall black boots, while the third was marching through the rooms, shouting, "Where are the crowns? I want a crown!" The boys were delirious with success and didn't know what to do with it. March was shocked. He had no love for this place, and yet he'd grown up here and had a respect for its order and calm and beauty. But there was no time to think of it now; he had to find Edyon.

Throughout the castle, hacked bodies lay sprawled on the bloodied floors. Some rooms appeared untouched, and in one March stopped to get his breath—then he turned and spotted a body lying in the corner, the wavy brown hair exactly like Edyon's.

*Oh, no. Please no.*

March stepped forward to see the face. It was another young lord. One who'd always scorned him, but March took no pleasure in seeing the man dead. March turned away. He had to think. Edyon must have escaped. There was a safe room, but there was also a secret tunnel from the castle out to the beach. Would he risk that route? Edyon would be exposed along the way.

There was a staircase to the tunnel from one of Thelonius's rooms. In his panic, March hadn't checked it. He ran back there and pulled aside the silk to reveal the secret door; he turned the handle, but the door wouldn't budge. It was locked from the other side.

*He's gone through it. He's escaped to the beach.*

That was a start. But still, March had to ensure Edyon had got away. The quickest way to the end of the secret tunnel was down through the kitchens, the courtyard, and the side entrance to the town. March moved faster than he thought possible, but in the kitchens he slowed. He didn't know where to look. He gagged at the sight before him.

The kitchen was horribly still and silent. And yet it wasn't empty. It was full of carnage. The servants here had tried to defend themselves with whatever was at hand—knives and pans, cauldrons and meat hooks. But the weapons had been

turned on them and men, women, and children were now lying dead. March saw faces he recognized, people he'd grown
up with—and he had to look away.

*Just find Edyon.*

But something made him turn back. There was a movement. One of the maids, a young girl, was looking at him. He
didn't know her name, but she clearly recognized him and
looked at him with dread.

March went to her slowly, crouching down to whisper, "I
won't hurt you. I can help if you let me." And he pulled out
his bottle of smoke. "Don't say anything, just do what I say
and do it quickly."

The girl stared and didn't move.

"Inhale the smoke. It'll heal you and give you strength."

The girl shook her head.

"Copy me."

March inhaled a wisp of smoke. And let another wisp out
for the girl. She hesitated but then did it.

"You'll have to be careful. Hide here for a while. Then
find a way out through the stables. Go through the fields.
Stay away from buildings. Find some others—find adults."

The girl nodded. The bruise on her forehead was already
fading.

March could do no more for her. He had to find Edyon.
He ran across the courtyard to a side door. It was barred, but
newly powered by smoke, he ripped it open and sprinted
down the alley to the town. He was dismayed to discover the
boys had already been here. There was a body on the corner,
and a few people, having escaped from the castle, were

running away. They were heading toward the sea too, probably hoping to find a boat to escape in. Nearer the quay were more people rushing down the hill, all strangely and desperately quiet.

Turning away from the road to the quayside and off to the far side of town, where the prince's tunnel came out on the beach, March kept going. There would be a rowboat to take Edyon, and whoever else had escaped, to a ship anchored round the bay. All small, all distinctly not royal in appearance, all secret. He ran past the last house, then between the high rocks, his feet ankle-deep in seawater, then out of the rocks and onto the beach. There were two small rowboats pulled up on the sand and a ship anchored offshore. If Edyon was escaping this way, he hadn't yet left. Along the beach, his feet slower on the soft sand, March made it to the small stone hut where the tunnel from the castle came out. He stopped to the side, hidden in the dark shadows, his chest heaving. He would have to wait. He wasn't sure if he wanted Edyon to appear or not.

*Just let him be safe. Please.*

His breath had calmed completely when he heard the voices.

"The beach is ahead."

"We'll wait here. Let Byron go first." It was Edyon's voice.

And a young man appeared. He had a long black plait down the side of his head. He looked around but didn't see March. Then he beckoned the others behind him to come out.

Edyon appeared, as did a soldier supporting a chubby man. Behind them were five or six others.

March hesitated. He could just hide and watch Edyon escape. He had to speak. He stepped forward to Edyon. But the young man with the plait spotted him and darted forward, swinging his sword with such speed that March knew he'd taken smoke.

# EDYON

## CALIA, CALIDOR

AFTER HIS father had ridden off to the border wall, Edyon had followed all the instructions he'd been given.

"Stay in the castle"—he'd stayed in the castle.

"Let Byron protect you"—he'd definitely let Byron protect him.

"The castle is impregnable"—he'd heard that one before.

"Only as the last resort, if the castle is taken—which won't happen—then you use the secret staircase, follow the tunnel, and head to the ship."

Edyon had watched from the ramparts as the boy army drew near. Not a large army but not the few boys his father had thought might make an assassination attempt. It was clear that their intention was not just to attack swiftly and retreat, but to attack and hold the castle.

His guard reported that over forty Brigantine boys had been killed. "They can't scale the wall, Your Highness. We just have to hope they keep trying and we can keep picking them off."

Edyon had tried to eat, tried to sleep, but he could do

neither. It was a dark night and he stared out from his terrace. He remembered the last time he had been in a castle under siege. Then, Rossarb had been surrounded by Aloysius's huge army. This seemed quite a different battle, and yet Edyon had the same tension in his stomach and in his chest.

Another difference was that Byron was with him and not March. Byron stayed quietly by Edyon's side, looking out across the land. Edyon looked up to the sky and wondered where March was now. Hopefully he was somewhere safe, somewhere away from war and fighting.

The chancellor stood behind Edyon, constantly talking, considering likely outcomes—Thelonius would send troops back to attack the boy army. The boy army would flee back north. This might have been a plan to draw the army from the wall and send the main Brigantine troops through. Edyon must have heard the chancellor come up with a hundred options of what might be happening.

And, just as Edyon was beginning to believe that they might be safe for a while, a guard ran in. "The boys have scaled the walls to the lower level."

Edyon knew it was over. The boys would be too strong. If they'd scaled one wall, they could scale more. But still he was told to remain in his rooms. Byron stayed with him, as did the chancellor and Talin, who almost died of shame as his bowels couldn't hold up to the tension.

But it wasn't long before the guard returned. "They've broken through to the upper levels. You must leave, Your Highness. Now. Immediately. There's no time for hesitation." And while Edyon was still trying to absorb this, Byron was leading him by the hand, following the guard, picking up speed as they heard shouts and screams, running through Thelonius's rooms, sliding on the marble floors, Talin panting behind. The guard held up the silk curtain that hid the door and Byron pulled Edyon through. Edyon kept asking who was with them, and Byron was just saying, "Don't worry about that, Edyon. The guards know what they're doing. They'll lock the door behind us. We must concentrate on moving as fast as possible."

And Edyon *did* have to concentrate. It was dark, and the stone spiral stairs were narrow and steep. Down and down and down they went. Edyon heard Talin cry out and the guards told him to be silent. As they descended, he heard other noises through the walls—the screams and shouts of fear and war. But then they were down on level ground in the damp darkness of a tunnel. It was silent except for the heavy breathing of the group. Everyone gathered together while torches were lit. There was urgency, but not panic.

Talin was limping, as he'd fallen on the steps, but he took Edyon's hand. "Thank you for not leaving me, Your Highness. Thank you." As if Edyon would leave anyone behind. He squeezed Talin's hand, which was damp with sweat, and reassured him that they'd soon be on a ship sailing to safety.

And then they were off again, running along the tunnel, the ground underfoot turning from stone to sand. At the end of the tunnel was a heavy wooden door, a key found hanging inside its lock. The door was stiff and it creaked open and they were out of a small building built into the cliff, and onto the sand and into the half-light—it was still well before dawn, but the dark blue sky seemed light after the tunnel.

There was someone ahead—one of the boy army—and he was coming at Edyon. And then it all happened so fast. Byron leaped in front of Edyon to protect him, swinging his sword at the assailant. The other guards drew their swords, surrounding Edyon, expecting more attackers. Edyon couldn't even see, but he heard a shout. "Edyon! I'm here to help!" It was a familiar voice. A voice Edyon would know anywhere.

*March?*

"Let me past," Edyon shouted, forcing his way through his guards as Byron slashed his sword down toward March's body.

"No! March!" Edyon screamed. "He's a friend, Byron! Don't hurt him!"

But it was too late. Byron's sword was sweeping down.

Edyon stumbled forward and Byron moved immediately to his side. He held Edyon back but kept his sword pointed at March's prone body on the sand.

"March?"

And, to Edyon's amazement, March raised his head. "Yes, it's me."

Had Byron managed to divert his sword at the last moment? Or had March dodged to the side? It didn't matter; March was safe.

"I came to help. If I could," March said falteringly, getting to his feet and glancing from Edyon to Byron and back.

"But I see you have help. Just get away. There's no hope for anyone here. Harold's taken the castle. He'll kill everyone."

Edyon tried to take it in. Calia was lost, people were being slaughtered, and yet somehow March was here. "But what about you, March? Are you in the boy army?"

"Edyon. Your Highness. We don't have time for this." Byron took his arm. "You mustn't stop. This could be a ruse."

Edyon looked at March, looked into his beautiful silver eyes. March had lied to him in the past. Their entire relationship was based on a lie. But March had also saved his life more than once and risked his own to do it. Edyon shook his head. "It's no ruse."

"But we still can't stop!"

"Then we all go," Edyon said, grabbing March's arm. "March, come. Tell us what's happening."

They set off again, running along the beach to a rowboat that was pulled up between some rocks. March spoke quickly: he'd joined the boy army; Harold had made him his servant; they attacked the wall on the border near Abask, then came south to Calia. But before March could explain further, they were at the boat. Edyon clambered in. "Hurry, March."

But March hesitated. "Where's Thelonius?"

Byron said, "It doesn't matter. We don't have time for this."

"My father's with his army near the border, March. But get in the boat and we can talk more." Edyon needed March to be with him.

March didn't move. "Thornlees is leading the conventional army south. Just his men, not the whole Brigantine army. Your father has a chance against them, but not against the boys."

"But the boys are here."

"They won't be for long. Harold wants to take all of Calidor. He'll do whatever he can to kill Thelonius. And all the nobles, including you, which is why you must flee. Get to Pitoria."

"Yes," Byron said firmly. "That we agree on."

"No, we don't," Edyon replied. "Not until March gets in the boat."

"No." March shook his head. "I can't go. Harold's mad. Worst of the lot of them. He has to be stopped. I think I can do it. Maybe. Anyway, I have more of a chance than most."

"March. You're not a fighter. Not a soldier."

"I'm an Abask. I can do it." And his eyes lit up. He looked terrified and yet defiant. "I have to do it. I can get close to him. Without Harold, there may be an end to this."

Edyon remembered Madame Eruth saying he'd meet a foreign man who was in pain. And March's pain was so acute that it seemed to be radiating out of his eyes.

"He's destroying people. He won't stop. I should have done it before now."

Edyon knew he'd not change March's mind. He grabbed his hand. "Don't let him kill you. Get through this, March. Please." Tears filled his eyes; he pulled March to him into an embrace. "I loved you before and love you still. You're my hero, always."

March buried his head in Edyon's shoulder, then stood back, tears in his eyes too. "And I love you too. Always. And you are my hero, Edyon. Be a prince. Be whatever you want. But never change. You're perfect as you are."

Edyon kissed March's cheek, tasting the tears, and before he broke down entirely, he turned and stepped into the boat. Byron told them to push off and, when Edyon turned to look to shore, March was walking away.

# MARCH
## CALIA, CALIDOR

MARCH WALKED away from Edyon and couldn't bear to look back. He'd break if he saw Edyon leaving again. Edyon and his new companion—the most handsome young man in the world, it seemed, and clearly extremely protective of him. But that wasn't even important. It was a good thing that Edyon had protection. He'd get away. He'd go on to live his life. March could have left with them, but he knew now that he had to do what he could to end this war. After seeing the bodies in the castle, he was certain that was his destiny. Perhaps all his life was coming to this point and to this realization.

March despised Thelonius for keeping him as a servant, for betraying the Abasks, but he'd done it to protect others. What March hated most was that Thelonius never admitted it, never expressed regret, never said what an impossible choice it had been, never showed any humanity, only a regal certainty that what he'd done was for the best. It was an awful choice, but why not admit it?

But, for all Thelonius's faults, compared to his brother he

was a saint. Abask and its people would still be there if it weren't for Aloysius. And Harold was his father's son, only worse—madder, badder, and on demon smoke. March had seen Harold was capable of pure evil, of doing to the Calidorians what his father had done to the Abasks. But Calidor wouldn't be left empty like Abask; it would be colonized by Brigantines.

March had to find a way to stop Harold. "I'd just rather not die in the process," he muttered.

"What's that?"

March looked up. Rashford was standing ankle-deep in seawater, blocking the path between the huge rocks. March had been so caught up in his thoughts, he'd not even seen him. He glanced over Rashford's shoulder. There was no one else with him. "Just thinking about life and death. What are you doing here?"

"A question I was just about to ask you."

March looked back. Had Rashford seen Edyon? The beach was mostly out of sight.

"Fancied a paddle to wash the blood off my boots," March said.

"Me too."

*What was Rashford up to?*

"Is the fighting done yet?" March pushed past Rashford.

"The fighting's over. The castle is ours," Rashford replied, following him. "The boys, however, have not stopped killing just yet."

"Or burning." March nodded to the sky above Calia,

which was beginning to lighten with dawn as fast as it filled with smoke from fires.

"Whereas we're just two boys who prefer a stroll on the beach to looting and killing."

March ignored the comment and walked on. "Where's Harold?"

"In the castle somewhere. Why?"

"He's my master. I should report to him."

"And what will you say you've done in Calia? How many have you killed?"

March shrugged.

"More than you've helped escape?" Rashford grabbed his arm, but March pulled away. "You've never been one of us, have you, March?"

March turned to face Rashford. "And you? Are you really one of them, Rashford? I know you love the Bulls, but do you love your king? Do you love Harold? Do you love all this killing and destruction?"

Rashford opened his mouth but no words came out.

"If you were truly one of Harold's followers, you'd have called your men by now and had me killed. Or you'd kill me yourself if you had even the slightest doubt about my devotion. I have access to Prince Harold, after all. I'm a danger to him."

March found that now he'd started, he couldn't stop. All the anger and frustration of weeks—years possibly—was pouring out. "But you haven't, have you, Rashford? You know all this is bad. It's wrong. It's evil. But you don't want to starve; you want something from life other than a pile of shit and a beating. This smoke seems a good way to get it, but you know it won't last. You know your days are numbered. And what will you have at the end of it? At best, a job as an ordinary soldier, fighting for Aloysius and probably dying of wounds or the shits, or just being killed in battle and forgotten. You want something more, and you think the smoke can give it you, but you're not sure how."

"Maybe all I need to do is tell Harold the truth about you, and I'll get to be his new favorite," sneered Rashford.

"For half a day, if that. You know not to trust Harold—ever. None of us interest him any more than an ant."

"So what's your plan, March? Do you have one, or are you just letting off a bit of steam?"

In truth, he didn't have a real plan other than to wait for an opportunity. But he kept waiting and kept putting it off. "Steam, mostly," he replied.

Rashford grinned, reached over, grabbed March's bottle of smoke, and pulled the cork out.

March snatched after the bottle, but it was too late. The purple smoke drifted out and up and away. "What did you do that for?" he yelled.

"Sometimes you look so angry, March. I wouldn't want you to lose it when you had smoke inside you and get ideas that you could fight Harold. Even with the smoke, you'd lose, but you might be tempted to try. I've just done you a favor."

March pushed past him to make his way back to the castle, but Rashford stayed with him. They passed the bodies of two old women lying in blood on the street. March said, "This isn't war. This is carnage. These people weren't soldiers."

"Harold wants one in ten dead," Rashford said.

"Who's doing the counting?"

They reached the castle, where the body count was higher still.

They stopped talking now and made their way inside, conscious that other boys could hear their conversation. Someone told them Harold was in the Throne Room and Rashford muttered, "I'll leave you to it."

Harold was sitting on Thelonius's throne. There was a chair next to it that hadn't been there when March had last served Thelonius. It must be Edyon's place. They'd been ruling together—Edyon's dream had become a reality, for a few weeks.

"There you are, March."

March stopped and bowed. "Congratulations on a great victory, Your Highness."

Harold grinned. "The first of many."

"The first of many," March echoed, approaching Harold, wondering if he could attack him from behind while they were alone. "Is there anything you need, Your Highness?" he asked.

"Yes. Lots. Food. Immediately. And prepare my bedchamber."

March had no alternative but to turn round and go out. When Harold said *immediately*, he meant it.

March went to the kitchens and was sickened again by the

sight of the bodies there, but relieved to see that the girl he'd given smoke to had gone. He collected as much food as he could carry and took it back up to the Throne Room, but Harold had already left. March took the supplies to Thelonius's rooms, which he assumed Harold would want as his. Just like old times, March would sleep in his old, small chamber nearby. The perfect place from which to creep up on Harold. It would be much harder without smoke, but that was just one more excuse for inaction, and March had been excusing himself for long enough.

*Perhaps I can do it tonight. Perhaps while he sleeps.*

But Harold didn't return for the food or even to sleep. He was in a state of euphoria. He'd had his first victory. He'd done what Aloysius had never managed, and done it quickly—absurdly easily. He'd taken Calia. He spent the day walking the city, with Sam and some of the other boys trailing after him. March joined them for a while but kept his distance. The celebrations were empty to him, he was exhausted, and he had no smoke to give him any strength.

The revelries were finally over by the time dawn came to March's second day in Calia. The harsh light of day was not kind. Bodies lay in the streets, and gray smoke from numerous fires hung in the still, hot air. March wandered around the castle. He had no idea where Harold was. Or Sam. Or Rashford. People moved around and met in different rooms, sleeping on floors, eating what they could.

At midday riders arrived—Commander Pullman, one of Lord Thornlees's senior officers, and ten men with him from the old man's army. They were taken to the Throne Room, where they waited. Someone said that Harold had been sent for but finding him would be hard. Pullman paced around the room, looking at March, who shrugged. "He's a prince. He'll come when he likes."

"He's leading this campaign, and we're at war. He's already messed up. The boys' brigades were supposed to stay at the wall and help us hold it, and now Thelonius's army is attacking our men."

"They are?" March tried not to sound hopeful.

Just then Harold strode in, looking surprisingly smart and tidy, still in his armor, his hair a different style from the day before. He flung himself onto the throne and called out, "March, bring me my wine."

Pullman bowed and stepped forward to speak.

*Oh dear, no. That's not the done thing, Pullman. You have to wait to be invited.*

March could already see that the meeting would not go well. He could help smooth things over, but why should he? He poured Harold a large goblet of wine and stood by his shoulder.

"Your Highness. Lord Thornlees has sent me with—"

"Is someone speaking, March? Did you hear a noise?" Harold asked, taking his wine.

Pullman realized his error in speaking without invitation. He added to it by apologizing profusely.

"Still an awful noise. Do you hear it, March?"

"There was something, Your Highness."

"Something rude and unpleasant hurting my ears."

Pullman opened his mouth to object but apparently had second thoughts.

"Who's that before me?" Harold asked.

March replied, "That is Commander Pullman, Your Highness. Sent with a message for you from Lord Thornlees. A message of congratulations on your famous victory, no doubt."

"Let him speak, then."

Pullman hesitated for a moment, glanced at March, and pulled a smile across his face, taking March's words as his cue. "Congratulations, Your Highness, on your victory here in Calia. All of Brigant is joyous at your success."

"They've already heard of it?"

"Well . . . I mean, they will be joyous when they do."

"Is that Thornlees's message?" Harold asked.

"Lord Thornlees hadn't heard the news when he sent me either, Your Highness. He is holding the wall but is under attack from the Calidorians, who vastly outnumber him. He asks that you send your boys' brigades to his assistance."

"So *that's* where Thelonius has sneaked off to."

It was hardly sneaking off to be fighting your enemy, but Pullman wasn't quite so foolish as to contradict Harold.

Harold turned to March, who would have far preferred to be left out of this conversation. "You know Thelonius better than us all, March. What's in his mind? Why has he left his castle to go to fight at a wall?"

"I'm no strategist, Your Highness."

"Answer me!"

"While my knowledge of strategy is limited, my knowledge of Thelonius tells me much." March struggled to think of things to say. "He will do everything to defend his country, defend his borders. He trusts in his castle. I'm sure he never expected you to take it. He possibly didn't even know we were coming, as we ran so fast through Abask. He probably knows it now, but too late, as he's committed his forces to the attack on Thornlees. If he wins the wall back, he believes you will be trapped in Calia . . . with limited smoke . . . and when that runs out . . . he will only have to fight fewer than a thousand boys."

Harold's face was impassive. "Sometimes, March, I do believe you're not as vacant as your pale eyes imply." He lifted his boot and flicked a speck of dust off it. "It looks like we'll have to return to save Thornlees and show Thelonius what we can do."

The relief showed on Pullman's face—relief and regret that he was somehow dependent upon the whims of this boy.

Harold stood and smiled. "It was getting very dull here. March, tell the brigade leaders to get their boys together. We return to the wall. We'll show these old men how to win against the Calidorian army."

# TASH

## DEMON TUNNELS

JUST THINK *of the smoke store.*

Tash tried to focus but nothing happened. It was hard to concentrate, but she had Geratan and Ambrose and the Pitorian army depending on her. She had to forget about the danger, even forget about what they were trying to achieve. All she had to do was concentrate . . .

*Think of the cage.*

Still nothing happened.

*Bottles in a cage.*

*Bottles, bottles, bottles!*

The stone before her didn't change at all.

*Shits.*

She took a breath and rested her head on the stone. She'd had to widen the tunnel all the way back from the surface. And she'd got herself to the surface before that. She'd found Geratan, which was great, but Rafyon was dead. And lots of images were swimming in her head; she was exhausted.

*Are you all right?* Geratan asked, gently putting a hand on her shoulder.

Tash stood upright. *Yes, fine. Just need to concentrate.*

*Of course. Yes. We're all grateful for what you're doing, Tash. You're amazing.*

*I'm alive—that's amazing. In a demon tunnel in a demon world. Who'd have thought that?*

*Tash, I'm trying to give you a compliment. When someone praises me for my dancing, I take their words into my heart. Bringing someone pleasure is a wonderful thing to do. Please take my compliment into your heart.*

She had no idea how to do that. *Sure. Right.*

*You can thank me for it too, if you like.*

*Oh. Right. Thanks.*

*It's a pleasure.*

Tash was still uncertain what else to say, but it did feel good. No one had ever said nice things about her before, not even Gravell.

*I've got to think of the smoke store now.*

*Of course.*

*Thanks, though.*

*I'll be right behind you if you need me.*

Tash felt a little stronger. A little happier. She held the vision of the smoke store in her head. A specific place too— she wanted to come up from below, *inside* the cage.

And finally the stone began to move away—almost like a curtain being drawn aside—and the tunnel sloped down, swinging in a wide arc and then beginning to rise.

The vision in Tash's head was getting clearer—they were close to the store. She closed her eyes and thought of coming up inside the cage, and almost as soon as she thought it, the stone above her opened up and a bottle of smoke fell toward her. Tash caught it, then slowly raised her head up through the hole. She was inside the cage. She could see a guard at the entrance to the main cavern, but he had his back to her and didn't seem to have heard anything.

Tash dropped back down to Geratan.

*We're in. There's one guard at the entrance.*

He squeezed past to take a look and then dropped back down, touching her shoulder.

*Can you make another tunnel to come up just behind him?*

Tash did as she was asked, thinking of a place a few paces behind the guard. As soon as the stone opened fully, Geratan moved past her with three of the other crimson-hairs. Tash didn't want to see what they were going to do. Whatever it was, they did it silently.

Geratan dropped back down to her again.

*Ambrose will start the attack on the main cavern soon. Stay here until the fighting's over.*

Almost immediately there was a distant sound of clanging. The attack had begun.

*Stay safe, Tash!*

Geratan and his men ran up the slope and into the cavern, out of sight.

Tash went back along her tunnel and climbed up into the smoke store. She couldn't fight, but there was something just as important she needed to do. She picked up the nearest bottle and pulled the top off. The smoke escaped out of the bottle and swirled around her, but then it seemed to choose a direction, sinking to the floor of the tunnel and flowing out to the main cavern.

Tash put the bottle down, picked up a second and released its smoke, which again swirled down the tunnel and out. She opened a third bottle, and a fourth. But there were still so many. It was taking too long. She picked up a fifth and dropped it. Then a sixth—dropped. Seventh and eighth—smashed against each other with a laugh. The ninth she threw at the bars of the cage.

Glass and smoke flew around her. She could hardly see the bottles at her feet for all the purple smoke. She kicked at them as it swirled around her, getting in her face and up her nose, into her head. She was surrounded by it, breathing it in as she threw and kicked and laughed and shouted.

# AMBROSE
## DEMON TUNNELS

AMBROSE CREPT along the terrace, keeping low against the walls, his men silently following. Across the cavern Anlax mirrored him, moving down toward the unsuspecting Brigantines. Glancing up, Ambrose saw several demons peering down from the higher terraces—*they* had noticed something was happening, even if the Brigantines hadn't.

*Well then*, thought Ambrose, *let's give them a show . . .*

Giving the signal to attack, he ran at the nearest Brigantine, drawing his short sword. The blade sliced into the man's neck, blood spraying onto Ambrose's hands and face, but he was already on to the next Brigantine and thrust his sword into the man's shoulder. Clanging noises rang out, reverberating around the cavern. The Brigantines grabbed their arms and raced up to join the fight. Ambrose leaped down the ramps to meet them, cutting down two more men and was then in the clear. He ran along the terrace and down another ramp, checking his men were following, then glancing across to check on Anlax's progress. That was when he saw Frost, the girl Tash had spoken about, racing into a tunnel, leading some Brigantines.

*She knows the tunnel network*, Ambrose thought. *They'll try to come at us from behind.*

He signaled five of his men to go back up to intercept Frost, as a group of Brigantines charged up to him. The man in the lead was huge and Ambrose couldn't match his strength, so he dodged to the side, slicing at the man's legs as he jumped down to the terrace below, two Brigantines immediately coming after him.

His fighting was pure instinct now. His eyes saw and his body reacted. He cut into the neck of one man, used the Brigantine's body to shield himself for a moment, then rolled low to slice at his next opponent's legs and up into his groin. Ambrose rose to his feet again as his men leaped down to join him.

Purple smoke was flowing out of one of the lower tunnels and swirling around the cavern.

*Tash! She's destroying the smoke store.*

He caught sight of Frost again, higher up now, above Anlax. Following the girl was a stream of Brigantines, racing down to attack Anlax's men from the rear. But the men Ambrose had sent up to intercept them were already there, ambushing the Brigantines from the mouth of a tunnel.

At the base of the cavern, the Brigantines were falling back, purple smoke swirling around them ever more thickly. Ambrose ran at them, yelling his battle cry—a deafening, clanging sound. His men joined in, shouting with him as they ran down the ramp and crashed into the final group of Brigantine soldiers. Ambrose's sword arm was aching, his hand slippery with blood, his head full of noise and clamor, but he wouldn't stop until they'd won.

# TASH
## DEMON TUNNELS

THE NOISE in the cavern was like nothing Tash had ever heard before. It was madness. The purple demon smoke she had released from the bottles flowed over the bodies of dead soldiers and around the living, turning the fighting men into silhouettes. The smoke in the core was rising even higher, the whole cavern glowing more purple than red. It was hotter too, much hotter. Like being inside a fire. Tash's eyes were drawn upward, toward the roof. Somehow she wasn't surprised to see demons looking down, watching the battle. And one demon in particular.

*Twist!*

And then, a few terraces below him, she spotted another familiar face peering out from a tunnel. Frost was staring down at the smoke in the core, before ducking out of sight.

*Oh no, missy. You're not getting away . . .*

Tash ran faster than she'd ever run before, feeling the power of the purple smoke flowing through her as she leaped over dead bodies and discarded weapons. Up and up. Higher and higher. At the higher levels, stone bridges crisscrossed the cavern and Tash glimpsed Frost running across one and leaping down to another, her eyes on a tunnel to her right.

Was it a way out? Whatever it was, Tash didn't want her to reach it.

*I've got to get there before her.*

Tash ran and pushed off hard. She flew through the air and landed on the next bridge, going so fast she had to brake hard so as not to fall off the other side. She ran onto the terrace and blocked the tunnel entrance, just as Frost ran up a ramp, her chest heaving with the exertion. She slowed on seeing Tash, then shook her head and held her arms out as if defeated.

*If you think I'm falling for that, it's you who's the pea-brain.*

But then, behind Frost, another shape appeared—the huge red figure of Twist. Frost glanced round, her face changing to one of fear. She ran to Tash and grabbed her arm desperately.

*Let me through. I need to get out.*

*You're not going anywhere.*

*If you let that demon get me, he'll kill me.*

*What's that to me?*

*I'll tell you about the smoke. Why it's changing. And it's changing even faster now. I know what'll happen next.*

*If I protect you from Twist, you'd better tell us what's happening. If not, I'll hand you over to him myself.* And Tash grabbed Frost by the hair and let go of her arm so her thoughts couldn't be heard, and she stepped forward toward Twist.

Twist stood very still. He didn't look angry or violent, just curious. He was even smiling a little.

Tash wasn't sure what to say, and she knew demons spoke in pictures, not words, but she held her hand out, and Twist slowly put his hand in hers.

*It's good to see you, Twist. Even if you can't understand me. But I need to take Frost to Ambrose.*

She tried to show with her mind what she was going to do, but before she had formed the images properly, she felt Twist's grip on her hand tighten and she knew he was glad she was alive, that he was happy to see her.

*I've got so many questions, Twist. So much to say. But I really don't know how to say any of it.*

Again she felt a wave of something good, almost like an invisible hand lifting her and comforting her. And Twist was smiling.

Then he took his hand away and stepped aside.

# AMBROSE
## DEMON TUNNELS

AMBROSE WAS breathing hard, his sword arm shaking. The purple smoke that swirled over the ground was thinning to reveal bloodied bodies at his feet. The Brigantines had fought to the last at the base of the cavern, but they were beaten. However, there was still work to do—he needed to ensure the tunnel entrances were secured and then check on his losses. He turned to look for Geratan, and instead saw Tash pulling Frost toward him by her hair.

Tash touched his arm.

*This is Frost.*

*I gathered that.*

*She can't hear me. I'm just holding her hair. She says she knows what's happening to the cavern and demons. She says it's important.*

Ambrose shook his head. *She'll say anything—her life depends on it. But I'll deal with her, Tash. Thank you.*

Tash released the girl and Ambrose took her arm, but the girl didn't try to escape. Rather, she put her arms tight round his waist, clinging to him.

*Thank you for rescuing me from the Brigantines. I've been so afraid.*

The voice in Ambrose's head was soft and desperate. Frost looked up at him. Her eyes were beautiful. Silver, like March's, but shining lilac in the purple light of the cavern. But Ambrose wasn't interested in their beauty.

*We haven't rescued you. You're a prisoner. You've been working for the Brigantines.*

*They forced me. I was their slave. I'm Abask. A slave's life is all I know. The Brigantines would have killed me if I didn't do as they demanded. But I see you already know how cruel they are. They killed all my family too.*

Ambrose shook his head. *You're looking into my thoughts? My past?*

*Your thoughts are open. As are mine. See—I'm not hiding my suffering from you.*

And a vision filled Ambrose's head of Frost working in a mine, dragging carts of stone. Beaten, starved, watching her fellow Abasks die.

*Yes, you suffered. But still you worked for them,* Ambrose replied.

*And so did you. You were a guard to the royal household. And I see you were a favorite of Princess Catherine.*

Frost released her hold a fraction and looked up in surprise. *Oh, now I know who you are. Sir Ambrose Norwend. I've heard of you.*

*I don't have time to compare past horrors. Tash said you have useful information about the demons and the smoke. What is it?*

*Yes, I do have information. And now that I have seen your*

*thoughts and memories, I know it will be more than useful—it will be vital. I know what's going to happen here in the demon world. And I know what's going to happen to the smoke. I can help you.* Frost smiled up at Ambrose. *And I can help Catherine too.*

*Catherine? How? What is this information?*

*I've felt your love for your princess, your queen—and she is in great danger.*

Ambrose shook his head. *What are you talking about?*

*Your love will die if you don't act to help her. Isn't your duty to protect her? Isn't that what you've vowed to do?*

*And if you've truly seen my memories, then you'll know Catherine has freed me from that vow.*

Frost shook her head. *But you aren't free, are you? You're tied to her through that vow forever. Well, she'll die soon unless you listen to me.*

*And why should I believe you?*

*Believe your own eyes, Sir Ambrose. Look around. This demon world is changing, isn't it? Changing faster and faster.*

It was true. The enormous column of smoke, the core, was rising higher with every moment and the whole cavern was getting hotter.

*And what's that got to do with Catherine?*

*This world is ending. I know how it will happen. I've seen into the demons' thoughts. I know how their world is built—and how it will die and be reborn.*

The demon world was changing, but could he trust a word this girl said? How could a world die and be reborn?

*Tell me, then.*

Frost shook her head. *I'll tell you everything if you take me back to the human world.*

*It seems to me more like you'll tell me* anything *if I take you back to the human world.*

*That's for you to judge. But you'll be glad to be there when I tell you. You'll want to be near your queen.*

Ambrose chewed his lip and looked at the situation around him. His mission had succeeded. They'd destroyed the smoke store and captured or killed all the Brigantines. Catherine had asked him to hold the cavern as long as possible, but Geratan could do that. Something was happening here and he needed to know what it was. Ambrose gestured to Anlax to summon the Demon Troop.

*Fine. I'll take you to the surface. But if this is a lie . . .*

*It's not a lie. It's the most frightening truth you'll ever know.*

# EDYON

## THE PITORIAN SEA

EDYON STOOD on the deck of the *Pilar*, squinting at the distant coastline of Calidor. Distant, but not distant enough. The *Pilar* was a small ship with great speed; however, that speed was dependent on wind. The wind had been light and steady at first, carrying them swiftly away until Calidor was a faint smudge on the horizon behind them. But as evening came, the breeze died completely and they'd sat, drifting in the darkness and the current, and at dawn they were horrified to see Calidor clearly in sight. And, worse, the current was carrying them slowly but surely back to land and to the dreaded boy army.

Edyon looked upward. The *Pilar*'s huge white sail was hanging like a saggy, heavy curtain—and also like a huge flag that could be seen from a great distance. They were sitting ducks, except that ducks had the option to fly, or even paddle.

"Can't we row?" Edyon asked.

"Apparently not in this type of boat," Byron replied. "We just have to wait for the wind."

"I feel like we're waiting for the Brigantines to spot us."

"Well, I suppose they won't have any wind either."

"Perhaps not, but they may have oars." Edyon looked back to Calidor. "I can see the castle," he said, noticing the smoke rising from the city.

Edyon turned to look the other way, toward Pitoria, but of course he couldn't see it. It was three days away with a good wind.

The sea was flat—so calm that the surface was glassy smooth. The *Pilar* sat in the water, the sun shone brightly on the blue sea; a flying fish whizzed up and away as if to show off its speed and freedom. But, looking down into the water, Edyon saw a large disk of creamy white substance floating past, then he spotted another and another, until it seemed like the sea was white beneath them.

"Jellyfish," Byron said.

Edyon shuddered. "Horrible. And so many of them."

"They sting, but they do no real harm."

Edyon didn't want to look at jellyfish or the coastline, so he sank to the deck and closed his eyes. He felt that he was being carried back to face his fate and there was nothing he could do about it. Perhaps too he was being drawn back to March. He closed his eyes, absorbed the heat of the sun, and listened to the slow creak of wood. He'd not slept all night and now, despite his nerves, he smiled at the thought of March coming to find him and dozed off.

He woke what felt like only a few moments later to a cool feel and the sound of a sharp slap. He looked up to see the wind filling the sail.

*At last! Wind!* Edyon smiled and stood up.

But his delight turned to horror as he saw how much closer the *Pilar* was to shore, and that a rowboat was leaving Calia harbor, heading directly for his ship. One of his guards spotted it too, and shouted, "Boats out the harbor!"

But were they refugees fleeing the Brigantines, or Brigantines coming after the *Pilar*?

Whoever they were, they were distant now that the *Pilar* was finally moving.

Edyon looked ahead. "We'll make it. We'll get away." He focused forward, feeling the wind on his face.

"Boats gaining on us!" came another shout.

Edyon looked behind. The boats that had come out of the harbor were already much nearer. There were three rowboats, and they were moving so fast that there could be no doubt that they were being powered by boys on smoke.

"The breeze is still light, but we're making better speed now. And those rowers can't keep that pace up," the captain said.

"Yes, they can," Edyon replied. "We need to prepare for them."

But the guards were on the alert already; they'd seen boys take Calia Castle.

The one thing Edyon had grabbed when he'd fled the castle was the bottle of demon smoke, and he held it out to Byron. "I think you should take some."

Byron nodded, took the bottle, and inhaled a wisp.

The distance between the *Pilar* and the rowboats was closing fast. The ship's captain shouted instructions: "Prevent them from boarding! Keep them away with fire, harpoons, arrows. As long as they can't get on board we'll be able to defend ourselves."

Byron added, "If any boys do get on board, they'll have considerable strength and speed. I'll go at them. Only if I'm down, or if there's more than one, must you attack them." He turned to Edyon, adding, "And you must go below, Your Highness. Wait down there. We'll call when it's safe."

"I'll go if they get close. We might get away yet." Edyon stared up at the sail, willing the wind to pick up some more. The breeze felt stronger on his cheek. He looked to the ship's wake, trying to assess if they were moving faster, and then to the land, which was definitely more distant.

*We are moving. The* Pilar *can do it.*

But the Brigantine boys could do it too. They were paddling fast and relentlessly. The rowboats were catching up, and soon the individual boys could be seen—and of course they were just that, boys. They shouted threats while Edyon's guards shot arrows at them, but they raised their shields and still powered the boats forward. One boy even let an arrow go through his hand. Laughing, he pulled it out and shouted, "Your arrows don't hurt us!"

"Get below, Edyon!" Byron shouted.

But Edyon didn't want to hide. He had to do something. "I'll take some smoke, Byron. At least it'll give me strength to fight them off."

Before Byron could object, Edyon inhaled the last of the purple smoke. He felt giddy and clumsy but also much stronger.

The three rowboats were closing in, but they were so low in the water compared to the *Pilar* that it seemed it would be impossible for them to board. But Edyon had no sooner thought that than he was proved wrong. One boy was launched into the air by two others. It was the sort of acrobatics seen at a circus, but here the boys went higher and farther. Except this boy had not gone quite far enough and landed with a splash, to much jeering from his fellow boys. Their leader was furiously barking instructions. "I told you to wait for the order. The rest of you get ready to boost your partners! If the prince is on board, I want him alive. Kill the rest."

The rowboats drew closer still, and the boy leader shouted: "Now!" Six boys were launched high in the air. But at that moment there was a gust of wind. The captain of the *Pilar* swung the wheel and the ship turned sharply. The sudden wind meant that three more boys landed in the sea. But three landed on the deck of the *Pilar*. The wind was increasing and the captain pulled the wheel back as more boys were launched into the air and the ship turned sharply again. The three boys on deck slid across it and Byron sliced into the first boy, then quickly turned to the next. The sail was full of wind now, and the *Pilar* was moving away from the Brigantine boats, as there were fewer of the boys left to row.

*We can do it. We can get away.*

But three more boys had landed on deck and one bowled the captain over, taking the wheel with a whoop, sending Edyon off-balance and careering to the side of the ship. The *Pilar* was heading back to the rowers.

Byron had three boys against him. As a noble with a lifetime of training, he was better than them with a sword. But he couldn't hold them all off, and one ran at him and stabbed him in the back. Byron fell to his knees, turning to look at Edyon. Edyon shouted as Byron slumped to the deck. Edyon ran forward, but more boys landed on the *Pilar* and something hit him hard in the face. He staggered back and fell to the deck, but the smoke healed him almost instantly. So he tried to get up, but there were boys all around him, holding his arms.

"Tie him down. Tie him down. Don't kill him. Harold'll give us a bonus for this one."

Edyon struggled to get free, but even with the strength of the smoke he was outmatched, and the boys knocked him back. He screamed in fury. Ropes were brought, his arms were bound to his sides. And all he could do was stand there and let them laugh. Byron's bloody body was motionless at his feet, his face still toward Edyon, his eyes open and empty. The other guards were all dead, Talin's body was sprawled out, and there were bodies in the water, floating among the white jellyfish.

"Does anyone know how to sail this heap of shit or do we paddle back?" the leader shouted.

It turned out that no one knew, and Edyon was tossed over the side of the ship into a rowboat, and they left the *Pilar*, Byron, Talin, and the others drifting and lifeless.

# MARCH
## CALIA, CALIDOR

HAROLD WAS gathering the brigades together in preparation for leaving Calia Castle. March needed smoke if he was to keep up with the boys, but he couldn't see Rashford and ended up having to ask Sam for some of his.

"I suppose so, but Harold won't like that you've used yours up. He hates boys wasting it. We don't have an endless supply, you know."

"I didn't waste it. The bottle top came off in the fight."

"I'll have to tell him what's happened," Sam warned as March inhaled.

March rolled his eyes. "Course you will, Sam. Make sure he knows you graciously shared your smoke too."

And Sam did go straight to Harold.

When March joined them, Harold eyed March, saying, "You lost your smoke, March? That's uncharacteristically careless of you. You're one of my golden boys. You should be shining. You should be radiant. You should not be careless."

"I'll be more careful in future, Your Highness. It's an honor to be one of your elite, and I do my best to be a good example for the other boys. Sam was generous enough to share some of his smoke with me." March was used to hiding his feelings, but with Harold he needed to grovel enthusiastically. He was determined to arouse no suspicion of being anything other than devoted to his prince. It was a horrible game, but he'd do his best to play it for a bit longer. And then, knowing that Edyon had safely escaped across the sea, he would find a way to kill Harold.

The boy army left Calia at a run, heading back to the border wall, leaving smoldering wreckage, debris, and bodies in their wake. They ran through the day faster than ever, using the coast road, but not stopping to destroy anything as they passed. And so, at the end of the day, as the sun was setting, they approached the Brigantine border and the point in the wall where they'd crossed a few days earlier.

Harold stopped the boy army on the top of a hill with a view of the wall. Smoke still rose from the ditch on its far side. The wall itself had been damaged and broken through to make a narrow gap. Thornlees must have done that. And then it appeared that he'd advanced, but no more than a few hundred paces, where a battle had clearly been fought. The ground was littered with bodies and weapons. Horses too lay on the ground; one was still whinnying, trying to get up but failing. A dog tentatively stepped over the bodies, sniffing at one, then pulling at it with his teeth.

Harold shook his head in disgust. "Thornlees couldn't even do this one simple task. Couldn't even hold the wall. That man is useless."

March had a feeling Thornlees was useless no more, but he said nothing.

Harold strode down the slope to the battlefield, and the boys slowly followed as their leader walked through the bodies, slashing randomly with his sword, killing the horse and kicking at the dog, which whimpered and skulked off.

A wounded Brigantine soldier was found and dragged to Harold. Rashford knelt by him and asked, "What happened here, soldier?"

The soldier replied, "We lost."

Harold's anger instantly left him and he laughed. "Well, I can't find fault with this man's analysis." He bent over the soldier. "Can you tell me why you lost?"

"There were too many of them."

"Too many for old fools like Thornlees."

"They came from the higher ground as soon as we'd come through the gap in the wall. The Calidorians outnumbered us three to one and forced us back, but the gap was too narrow to retreat quickly. Their bowmen took many. Lord Thornlees was shot in the neck early on."

"Thornlees is dead?"

"Yes, Your Highness."

"He deserved to die for this failure. He was supposed to hold the wall, not advance."

*So were you*, March thought. *If you'd stayed, this wouldn't have happened.*

"Where are my Bears?" Harold demanded. "I left them here to help you old men defend the wall."

"The Calidorian archers took most of them. The Bears

had no shields. The arrows were falling so thick there was no hiding from them, but they did have speed, so many of them fled."

Harold seemed to ignore this accusation of desertion by his precious boys. He stood upright and looked around, muttering, "They'll try the arrows again." In a louder voice he added, "Where are the Calidorians now? I can't see them on the wall."

The leader of the Foxes replied, "My scouts say they've moved into the hills around us."

Harold smirked. "They think to set a trap for us."

The Fox leader nodded. "And we've walked into it."

Harold shrugged as if it was what he expected. "It's a simple plan. Textbook stuff. A little unimaginative, but that's how old men fight. We'll win anyway. We can have Thelonius strung up by lunch tomorrow." Harold turned to March to add, "The final battle will be here on Abask land. Will you enjoy that, March? Will you deign to join in?"

"I will be with you all the way, Your Highness."

"You will indeed," Harold replied, and then he looked at the hills around them. "They have drawn us into their trap but they won't fight us in the dark. Their mistake was to wait. They should have attacked as soon as we arrived."

"So what do we do?" March dared to ask.

"We use the night, and we use our strength. They'll be feeling confident because they've just won a great battle, but they'll be tired too. They've lost men." He addressed the boys around him now. "Fox leader, take the best scouts. I want to know the enemy locations and numbers." Turning to

Rashford, he said, "Take Sam and the best assassins from the other brigades. I want you to pick off the Calidorian guards. Make them nervous. Slice their throats, spill their guts— make a mess of them. Can you do that, Bull leader? Have you got your nerve back?"

"I have my nerve," Rashford replied. "Should we attack silently?"

"Silently or noisily. Whatever is most terrifying. Stick the heads onto spears, throw them into the bushes, chop hands off, feet off. Tongues out. When dawn comes, I want these men to see their future."

Rashford nodded and glanced at March, saying, "Perhaps the Abask here can help us with the territory."

Harold frowned. "It's not hard. It's hills and streams with some soldiers hiding. Just get on with it and leave my servant be."

Rashford bowed and backed away, calling on others to join him, and soon they were running off into the hills.

Harold turned to the rest of the boys. "I want you to go over this battlefield and find all the Calidorian bodies. Cut off their heads. Put them on spikes."

The boys lit torches and set to their task. At first some were reluctant, but Harold shouted, "Anyone not doing their part will be punished! Anyone not following my orders is a traitor!" And suddenly the boys were hacking away at bodies with grim enthusiasm, trying to make jokes about the body parts and the blood.

Harold stood with March and surveyed the scene. "The

Calidorians will be watching. What will they think of this, March?"

In the flickering light the sight was ghoulish. Heads were set on spears, arms and hands too. The boys were competing at who could display the bodies in the worst way. March knew the Calidorians would think Harold was a Brigantine monster, uncivilized and barbaric. He said, "They'll find it terrifying. They'll dread you, Your Highness. As they should."

"Yes, as they should," Harold muttered.

Before dawn, the Fox leader returned with his report. "The Calidorian forces are split into three. The biggest force to the south is about two thousand men, two hundred on horseback. To the west and east, another thousand per side and the archers are with them—a hundred on each side."

"And any on the wall?" Harold asked.

The boy shook his head. "Only at the forts, which are farther along; none close in."

"Ha! That's why they didn't spring their trap as soon as we arrived. They're hoping we'll just go back to Brigant. They're leaving the door open for us to depart." Harold smiled.

*Just as some of the Bears must have done.*

"Well, we'll go to the gap, but we won't go through it. I want lookouts on the wall. The archers will be the first challenge. All boys must have shields. They can get them from the battlefield. After the arrows, it'll be the horses. The Calidorians know that's where they are stronger. It's hand-to-hand combat where we will win." Harold suddenly had a look of glee on his face as he had an idea. "We'll play dead. *Then* they'll come in close. And we rise up." He smiled and tapped his lips. "But Thelonius isn't a complete fool. He'll be cautious. I think this is where my little Wasps will come in handy again."

Harold summoned Tiff, the Wasp leader. "Your objective is to capture Thelonius. Nothing more or less. When we are playing dead, they'll send men forward to check. Thelonius, I hope, will be with these men, but if he's not, if he hangs back, then you come in from behind." Harold smiled. "You're so small and fast that these old men won't know if you're soldiers or children. Shout and scream too. Confuse them. Shout for help. As if they should be helping you, as if you're running from something. They'll hesitate. They won't want to kill children."

Rashford, Sam, and the other assassins returned at that moment, their hands and clothes splattered with blood.

Sam was beaming. "It was like slaughtering cattle. They're so slow. We could rush them, slice their throats, and be gone before anyone could move. It was like a game."

"And they lost every time," Rashford said, though he sounded less than happy. "We've removed a few guards, but there are a lot of Calidorians still up there."

The sun rose over the hillside now, revealing the horror of the battlefield, with corpses dismembered and hung up. Rashford didn't say anything but stared out across the field, and then he turned away with a small shudder.

March, however, had his own work to do. Harold, as always, was concerned about his appearance, especially on the day when he'd have a famous victory, so March had to clean his armor. Once March had polished it to a gleaming brilliance, Harold said, "You put it on."

It was so bright the enemy could not miss it. With a sinking feeling in his stomach, March understood the plan. The Calidorians would expect the boy wearing this armor to be Harold. When March was dressed, Harold grinned. "You almost look like a soldier now, March. But you'll never look like a prince."

"Perhaps if I had a sword," March suggested.

"Well, pick one up—there's a thousand lying around here," Harold said. Clearly he wasn't going to give March his own silver and gold weapon.

"Archers to the west!" The shout was from the lookout on the wall. "Archers to the east. Take cover. Take cover."

A swooshing sound came from the west, quickly followed by another from the east. The boys looked up as one, their eyes following the arrows high into the sky and raising the shields they'd picked up from the fallen soldiers on the battlefield. "Yes, use your shields. Protect yourselves. But I want some of you to fall," Harold said. "And scream. And some can try to run to the wall. Look like we're panicking. But try not to laugh, boys."

Harold held his shield up and walked confidently through the field of mutilated bodies. A few of the boys around him screamed and fell to the ground, pretending to be dead. "Keep your shield up, March. You're not dead yet. Prince Harold wouldn't fall so easily."

Harold walked to the center of the field. They were surrounded by bodies, dead and alive. Arrows rained down. One nicked March's thigh but he felt the smoke heal the wound. Another swarm of arrows came their way, and more of the boys fell with them. March didn't know how many were faking and how many—if any—had actually been wounded. There were only twenty or thirty boys standing, and Harold said, "Sam, March. Stay with me. We go for Thelonius. I want him alive. My prisoner. But first, it's time for some acting." With that, he grabbed at his chest, as if hit by an arrow, and made a dying noise as he dropped dramatically to the ground.

Rashford was standing close, and he looked at March with raised eyebrows before clutching at his chest and grunting and groaning as he fell. March dropped to his knees too as he saw movement to the north. The arrows had stopped falling. "Riders are coming," he said.

"I can hear their pounding," Harold replied. "Keep visible, March. And keep watch. Tell us how close your old master is."

March stayed on his knees. The riders were coming his way. They must have seen Harold's armor—who could miss it, after all?

"Can you see Thelonius?" Harold asked.

"Yes, but he's far back, on the edge of the field."

The Calidorian horsemen made their way to March. But the battlefield was a sea of bodies. It was impossible to determine which, if any, were alive, almost impossible to determine who was Brigantine and who Calidorian. The horses didn't like walking among the bodies, and some riders were having to urge and kick them forward. Most dismounted, swords held out, stabbing at bodies on the ground. The stench of blood and flesh had intensified overnight, and the flies had begun to swarm in the warmth of the morning sun. The Calidorians were cursing, disgusted by what they saw and smelled. March's knees were wet from kneeling on the bloody ground. His stomach was churning. He wanted a piss and a shit and to be sick at the same time.

The Wasps should be running in now, but they were nowhere to be seen.

Slowly the Calidorians approached, two men still on horseback in the lead. March lowered his head, his heart pounding. A black horse stopped in front of him and the rider spoke. "Raise your head, Brigant. Let's see your face."

March didn't move, but replied in Calidorian, "Fuck you."

"I said, raise your face."

"And I said, fuck you."

The man dismounted. As did another near him. They came toward March.

But at that moment, he heard a distant cry. The soldiers turned to look, and March raised his head to see the Wasps running as a group to the main Calidorian force that was massed on the edge of the battlefield. The Wasps were screeching and yelping for all they were worth.

"What the—" the Calidorian soldier began, but he never finished his question. Harold rose up and struck him, cutting through his neck. His head and body toppled in different directions as Harold shouted, "Attack!" But the boys were already rising up, leaping and screaming, moving so fast that the Calidorians, by comparison, seemed as if their feet were stuck in clay.

The soldier in front of March swung his sword, but March met the blow, and Rashford took the soldier out from behind. The Calidorian soldiers on the battlefield were already over-run, the ones on horseback being pulled from their mounts. It took only moments. Harold ran forward shouting, "To Thelonius! And to victory!"

The boys surged, heading toward the main Calidorian army. They leaped high over the outer rows of men to land farther inside the throng, cutting into heads, necks, and shoulders as they landed. It was chaos. Horses reared, men screamed, and, in the center of it all, the Wasps swarmed around Thelonius. Already a boy had leaped onto his horse, and another was clinging to his sword while Thelonius swung at boys below him. Then Thelonius disappeared from view, pulled down from his horse and lost in the melee.

March followed Harold as he slashed through the Cali-dorians.

Tiff shouted, "We have Thelonius! He's ours."

Harold hacked and whirled his way to the center of the mass of men, his sword fast and precise, until there were only boys ahead. The Wasps had Thelonius on his knees. Around them the fighting was petering out. Calidorians on horse-back were still trying to break through, but the boys were protecting this circle.

Harold shouted, "Calidorians, I have your leader! I have

Thelonius." Then he put the tip of his sword to Thelonius's neck and demanded, "Yield."

Thelonius looked up at Harold and shook his head. "Never."

"I thought you'd say that. But look around, Uncle. You've lost. My boys will kill all your men. You'll all die for your country, and then it'll be my country." Harold lowered his sword and crouched down so he could see Thelonius's face, or perhaps so Thelonius could see his. "I'll let you have a way out, though. A noble way out. A way that gives you a chance. A slim one, but a chance. We settle this one-on-one. You against me. If you win, we'll leave."

Thelonius was obviously tempted.

"You'll have to decide soon," Harold said.

"Your word on it."

Harold smiled. "My word of honor. My boys will leave if you kill me."

March was sure that Thelonius didn't believe Harold's word and certainly didn't trust that Aloysius would honor it, but, really, he didn't have a choice.

Harold shouted, "Stop fighting, boys! We have a truce."

The shout was taken up around them, and the last of the fighting abated.

Harold told the Wasps to release Thelonius and hand him a sword. "And give me my armor back, March. This will go down in history as a glorious fight, man versus boy."

March helped Harold back into his armor as the Calidorians and Brigantines gathered around, each grouping to one side or the other.

Thelonius noticed March and stiffened. He called out, "So you're here. Is this the side you've chosen, March? I was wrong ever to think well of you."

"Was I right ever to think well of you?" March replied.

Thelonius didn't reply but turned away. And March felt heavy in his heart. He knew Thelonius would die. It would be good to give him some words of comfort, at least to tell him that Edyon had escaped. But that was a luxury that March couldn't afford to give; Thelonius would have to bear his own burden.

Thelonius and Harold walked to the center of the open circle: the man and the boy, surrounded by men and boys. The two princes held their swords up, walking round, each assessing his opponent. Thelonius struck first and Harold defended. The first few clashes were conventional enough. Thelonius was an expert swordsman, but Harold was well-tutored too. Thelonius was bigger, more muscled, and far more experienced, but Harold had smoke.

The fight seemed almost mundane. The swords clashed; the fighters moved back. They met again, moved back again. But at the next meeting, Thelonius lunged. Harold turned quickly to avoid the blade and then whipped round, making a counterattack that cut low to Thelonius's leg before stepping back out of his reach. Thelonius staggered but raised his sword.

Harold said, "Well, this is all very well as a warm-up, but it's not a historic battle. It's far too dull. No one wants to see a fight like this. They want to see this." Then he ran and leaped up and over Thelonius, turning in the air and swiping at his opponent's left shoulder. Thelonius was knocked forward, but he managed to stay on his feet, blood pouring from a deep wound.

Harold paced around. "Your right leg is the weaker. Almost useless. You'd be better off without it." Then he shouted: "Would he be better off without his useless leg, boys?"

There was a huge cheer in reply. The boys thrilled at their power. And Harold ran at Thelonius, knocking his sword out of the way and turning, slicing at his leg, and then using the momentum of his own sword to lift him high in the air and somersault, landing firmly on two feet. The boys around him were cheering. March forced himself to cheer with them.

Thelonius was still standing. He roared in anger and tried to move forward, but his right leg fell away, cut clean through at the thigh. He stood a moment, blood pouring from his wound, before he toppled to the ground.

Harold stood over him. "Do you yield?"

"You're mad and evil and I curse the—"

But March never learned what he cursed, as Harold sliced Thelonius's head off with a loud scream of fury. "Don't you dare curse me, you pathetic old man!"

Harold stood triumphant over the body and ordered, "Put his head, body, and leg on display. Let everyone see him. All three bits." Then he looked up and around, as if trying to decide what to do with the huge Calidorian force. He shouted, "Lay down your weapons. Surrender."

Some of the soldiers threw their weapons down and dropped to their knees, but many ran for the woods. A group of boys chased after them, but Harold had lost interest already. He was too busy parading around victoriously and congratulating the boys. "We have taken Calidor. I have defeated Thelonius. Calidor is ours. We have taken it *all*."

March was sickened. Harold would do the same to Edyon if he ever caught him. The boys were mad too. Everything was mad and bloody and awful. He wanted to get out, but more than that he wanted to be rid of Harold. March could end this with a single stone. He plucked one from his bag, pulled his arm back—but then a Fox ran forward, blocking the shot and shouting, "Your Highness, I've news. We've captured Thelonius's son. He's our prisoner in Calia."

"Edyon?" March said.

And again March had lost his chance, but perhaps it had never been a chance at all.

# CATHERINE
## ARMY CAMP, NORTHERN PITORIA

*If you suspect something is wrong, you're probably right.*

Pitorian saying

CATHERINE HALF wished she could have stayed in camp with Tzsayn but knew she needed to be with her men. Without the king, the army was lacking a figurehead. She might not be able to fight, but she could lead. The route they took was through farmland and green hills, and Catherine marked their progress by the Northern Plateau, which was a constant presence, looming closer and higher all the time. And somewhere there, inside all that stone, was Ambrose. She remembered standing on the edge of the plateau with him, and how different things had looked from there and how far they could see. Anyone up there now would see her army for certain, and they'd see she was at its head.

Catherine suddenly felt very small. It was a sensation she'd had before—like being a tiny red ant walking across a paving slab, watched by her father, only now she was a shining white ant. And she knew she was being watched—the Brigantines would surely have lookouts on the plateau.

She felt a flicker of fear, but then she looked at the men around her and reminded herself, *I'm not an ant, and I'm not alone. I have hundreds of men with me. And we're not trying to hide. The Brigantines should see us, should see me, and* they *should be afraid.*

They advanced to the River Ross, then headed west all afternoon, seeing no sign of the enemy. After a bend in the river they climbed a small hill, which gave an excellent view of all sides. Catherine halted to take it in. Far in the distance was the dark blur of Rossarb, with the ruin of the castle spiking up from it. And on the plain before it was a mass of horses and men. The Brigantine army.

It was vast.

Once more Catherine felt fear threaten to overtake her, but she cast her eyes over her own troops and it was a reassuring sight. The white-hairs behind her were numerous enough, but away to her left she could see Davyon's blue-hairs moving in from the coast. From this distance they also looked like ants—but thousands of them.

"I'll advance the white-hairs farther, Your Majesty," said General Ffyn. "This is a good position for you to remain in—you'll be visible to our men but protected from the enemy."

Catherine agreed, and her bodyguard set up a small camp on the hill as Ffyn led the main force of white-hairs farther forward. By early evening, the Pitorian army was ranged across from the coast to the river. At dawn the scullers would land on the north shore. The Brigantines would be surrounded and forced to give battle.

By the light of a flickering candle, Catherine wrote and dispatched two messages—one to Tzsayn and one to Davyon. "Don't mix them up, please," she instructed as she handed them over, imagining Tzsayn receiving the formal notification that her forces were in position while Davyon opened the more intimate message meant for her husband.

And then . . . nothing. Catherine remembered this from the battle of Rossarb, how the waiting was the worst of it. She paced around her small camp, talking to her men, trying to look relaxed, trying to think positively, but desperately wanting to get on with it.

# EDYON
## CALIA, CALIDOR

**ANOTHER DAY,** *another dungeon.* Edyon would have laughed, except he felt that he would never laugh again. Not after seeing Byron and everyone else killed on the *Pilar*, and not after being dragged through the castle, seeing the bodies of nobles and servants lying in blood. Death literally was all around him. He couldn't escape it.

*Is it me? Is it my fault?*

*Maybe if I wasn't here, death wouldn't be either.*

Edyon sat in the dungeon of Calia Castle. It was dark, damp, and smelly. Not so bad as Lord Farrow's hut, but worse than Tzsayn's cells in Rossarb.

At least this will be the last one I see.

Edyon was sure of that.

*Just don't let me die slowly and painfully. Make it quick.*

The boy who had locked Edyon in the cell had told him, "Harold will want a big audience for your execution. You might be on the cart."

"Cart?"

"A cart pulled by donkeys, with a big blade on it for cutting people in two."

"Ah. Useful to have it mobile, I'm sure."

"He likes his contraptions."

"Shame that he doesn't like peace, order, fairness, civilization, serving his people, a quiet glass of wine, and a good view, or just being nice."

"Who wants to be nice when you've got his power?" And the boy slammed the door on Edyon.

I *want to be nice. I want Byron alive and all the people of Calia alive and . . .*

Tears fell from Edyon's eyes. There was nothing nice left at all, and the sooner he got away from it, the better.

As it happened, Edyon wasn't kept in the dungeon long, as the boys hated coming down to feed him. He'd not eaten a thing for a day when someone must have remembered him, and he was taken up to the Throne Room. Only a few weeks earlier he'd been crowned here. Now he was chained to the wall like a dog, with a bowl of water and some stale bread, and he was given a special guard—Broderick.

Broderick, however, was less interested in Edyon and more interested in watching the other boys play dice. They were betting with boots, daggers, and coins—all plentiful and all of which, Edyon assumed, had been pillaged from the bodies of those in the castle. But what was not plentiful was food, which was becoming increasingly valuable. Edyon watched from the side. The boys were disorganized, aggressive, rude, and lazy, and they'd soon starve.

*And good riddance to the lot of them.*

Someone brought in a sack of apples that ended up being aggressively haggled over. Broderick, who had only two coins, managed to get a bruised apple.

Edyon said, "I haven't eaten anything but a crust of bread all day."

Broderick stood over him, eating his apple. "So?"

"I thought I was going to be executed in a dramatic show, not starved to death in the corner of this room."

"You're not starving; you're just hungry. We've all been there. Get used to it," Broderick said.

"I'd love a slice of fresh bread, a cooked chicken—even a bowl of porridge would do. I don't suppose the kitchen staff are still alive, are they?" Edyon asked, knowing the answer full well.

"Even if they were, you wouldn't get any food," Broderick replied.

"How much did you pay for that apple?"

"None of your business," Broderick replied, and began to walk away.

"I have money. I could buy my own food."

Broderick stopped, turned, and came back. "Money?"

"Not on me—that's already been stolen—but in my strongbox. I can tell you where it is. It has more than enough to pay for food for both of us."

"Where is it?"

"You'd better share the food you buy, Broderick."

"Tell me where it is, and then I'll buy you some."

Edyon wasn't sure Broderick could be trusted, but he was hungry, and he didn't care about the things in the strongbox. He told Broderick, "There's a secret cupboard behind the panel to the left of the desk in my room. Press the right-hand side and the panel opens. The key's in the desk drawer."

A short while later Broderick returned, his pockets clinking and a smile on his face.

"Can I have a pie and a chicken?" Edyon said. "And an apple, for starters."

Broderick replied, "Soon enough." Then he went to sit in the corner counting coins.

"I'm hungry," Edyon shouted.

Broderick returned to him and said, "And I'm tired of your whining." And he kicked Edyon, saying, "You'll get food when I say so."

The kicks hurt, but so did everything. Edyon thought of Byron lying in a pool of blood and wept for him. His only hope was that March was alive and would somehow get away from this mad mob and live a long life somewhere free of pain and cruelty, and that Thelonius's army would crush Harold.

His hope didn't last more than two days, in which time he'd had a sliver of a rancid pie, two apples, and a chicken leg with more bone and gristle than meat. On the second day he was given a gentle kick by Broderick and told with a smile, "Harold's here. News is, he killed your father himself."

Edyon wasn't sure what to believe or even what to feel. Thelonius was his father, but Edyon couldn't say that he loved him. He hardly knew him. But he had hoped to get to know him in time. Ever since childhood he had imagined someday meeting his father, and once he'd learned who his father was, he'd imagined so much more—becoming close to him, learning from him, making him proud. And he had started to. He thought about how Thelonius had supported him even when Edyon had accused Regan of plotting his murder. Nothing in their relationship had been straightforward, but they had been getting to know each other; they had been father and son. He remembered Thelonius had said, *I couldn't hope for a better son, and Calidor couldn't wish for a better future than with him.*

He looked at Broderick. "You're sure of this? My father is dead?"

"They fought one-on-one to decide the winner of the battle and Harold won easy. Chopped Thelonius's leg off, then his head."

Edyon sat and stared and remembered his first dinner with Thelonius and how happy they had both been. That had been just a few weeks ago.

A kick and Broderick's boot in Edyon's thigh jolted him back to the present. "I said, I don't think Harold'll want to fight you, though. You won't be much of a challenge at all."

"For once we agree, Broderick."

"I reckon you'll be chopped in two."

"So you've said," Edyon remarked.

"It might be a better way to go. Messy, I guess, but it'll be quick."

"Thanks for your words of comfort, Broderick."

"Plenty of poor kids get strung up all the time in Brigant and no one minds."

"I imagine *they* mind. As will I."

"Well, you shouldn't have been a prince then, should you?"

"Indeed. I could be a poor student back in Pitoria. But I'm here and so are you, Broderick. We've been thrown together by fate, and why should I fight against that? We are together for my last few days, and there must be a reason for it, don't you think?"

"Well, I've been told to guard you. That's the reason."

"You have guarded me and you have stolen from me. You have failed to feed me as you said you would. We've been put together and that is why I will stay with you. Even when I'm dead, chopped in two, I'll stay with you, Broderick. I'm going to haunt you for all your days. You won't get away from me."

Broderick frowned. "You will not haunt me. You will not."

"Only on the darkest of nights. But I will come. You're helping to kill me, so I can only return the favor. I will come back and scream my deathly screams in your head." Edyon waved his hands and widened his eyes as he said this.

Broderick looked genuinely fearful and dealt with it by kicking Edyon again. But he'd only landed his boot once when he was distracted by shouts from other boys entering the room.

Edyon, curled up on the floor, lifted his head when he saw the boy in the center of the group. Dressed in armor, his hair plaited and tied with bows, small and delicate of body with a sweet-looking young face—it could only be Harold.

And, behind him, another, much sweeter face. March—his eyes staring at Edyon. Sorrow and fear in them.

*And bravery and love and—at least I've seen him again before I die.*

Tears filled Edyon's eyes for a moment, but he blinked them away as Harold came to stand over him.

"So, this is the bastard who thinks he's a prince?"

Edyon got to his feet, a little unsteady, and said, "I'm never sure about this bowing business, who's more senior and all that. But as you have me in chains and I've never really taken to the prince thing . . ." He bowed a deep bow. "Good afternoon, Your Highness."

Harold's face changed. "You speak well for a bastard."

"Thank you, cousin. Alas, conversation has been a little limited of late. My guard communicates mostly through his boot. I was wondering if this was, perhaps, a typical way Brigantine boys conversed?"

"We kick dogs that don't behave."

"I can assure you, Your Highness, that I have behaved like the perfect prisoner. A role I'm more familiar with than you might expect. In fact, it was your sister who last rescued me from a prison cell, releasing me to freedom. I hardly dare hope that you might be so generous."

"You can hope what you like, but you will be executed." Harold smiled. "But you were with my sister? Tell me about Catherine. How was she?"

"She was busy. Always busy. She led us across the Northern Plateau. We fled Rossarb together and she went into the demon world." He looked at March as he added, "Alas, I couldn't get into the world to see its wonders—I escaped south with another—a brave man I came to love and trust deeply." Edyon noticed a slight softening of March's mouth.

"Catherine went into the demon world?"

"And came out alive. Leading her men."

Harold scowled. "I've not been in it myself. I will go soon. It's not right that she does things I don't."

"She takes smoke too, I believe. When necessary. I assume that's what gave her the strength to kill your brother, Prince Boris."

Harold leaned closer to Edyon and whispered, "For which I'm extremely grateful." He straightened up, adding, "But still, it's not womanly at all. She's escaped our father's bonds and does as she will."

"Indeed. And she acted as judge when I was accused of a murder. She saw justice done."

"A judge? A woman as a judge! What's going on in Pitoria?"

"The world has indeed gone mad," Edyon agreed.

Harold paced away from Edyon and then back. "You're not what I expected."

Edyon smiled. "I think I can say the same." *You're smaller and even more of a shit.*

"You're very much like your father in your face, though."

Edyon glanced at March, whose eyes told him that the news was bad.

"Bring his father's face in here."

And, to Edyon's horror, a stake was brought in, Thelonius's head on it.

He turned away in disgust.

"The question is what to do with you, the bastard son from Pitoria. Your father is dead, so you know what that makes you."

Edyon swallowed hard. "It's true. I am Thelonius's son. I am a prince and I am thus . . . now the ruler of Calidor."

Harold smiled. "Except now *I* am. And I wish to make a display of those I've defeated. It's good that you look like your father. Your execution will go ahead after you've told me more about my sister's exploits. But first I want a bath." And, with that, Harold walked out, shouting, "March, don't hang back. Get me a bath. Now."

March hesitated, gazing at Edyon, before following Harold out.

Edyon looked at Broderick and said, "My head will be chopped off, my undernourished body put on display, but I'll still come to you in your dreams and scream at you."

Broderick put his fingers in his ears and muttered, "Shut up. Shut up. Shut up," as he kicked Edyon.

Much later that day, when the sky was darkening to night, Harold returned to sit on the throne and hear from his boys. Edyon listened to the reports and proceedings from his corner. There were a lot of complaints, as there was little food and no one to cook it. The castle stank, and flies swarmed in the kitchens.

Harold dismissed the complaints with an irritated wave of his hand. "I'm a prince. I'm not interested in this talk. What, do you expect me to clean up your mess?" He was cheered up when someone brought news that the strong room had been forced open and Thelonius's treasure found.

Harold disappeared for a time to look at his new wealth, then returned carrying a golden goblet and giving instructions about guarding the strong room. "A boy from each brigade to guard it, two from my Gold Brigade as well," he said. He clearly trusted no one. But still, he was in a better mood than earlier. As March filled Harold's goblet with wine, Edyon was finally dragged forward and made to kneel at Harold's feet.

"Prince Edyon, tell me more of what goes on in Pitoria with my sister."

"Well, Your Highness, let me think where to begin. So much has happened." Edyon wondered if he could talk forever and thus delay his execution. "When I was in Pitoria just weeks ago, Princess Catherine had been made Queen Apparent. She had married Tzsayn in Rossarb, before the castle fell. That's where I first met her. I'd been arrested and was in a cell. It's a complex story. But anyway, Tzsayn and Catherine were there. A happy couple, I believe."

"I met Tzsayn. He's handsome on one side, ugly as sin on the other. Interesting man, though. I met him when my father was keeping him in chains." Harold looked closer at Edyon as if assessing something. "You're very different and yet . . . you're like Tzsayn in one way."

"A good way, I hope."

"You're . . . civilized." Harold frowned as if not sure that was right. "No, perhaps not that . . ."

"Perhaps it's just that we both expect to die."

"Perhaps it's because there's a part of you that expects to live." Harold laughed. "But you won't."

"Though Tzsayn did."

At this, Harold frowned, but then he shrugged. "His days are numbered. Pitoria will fall soon enough." And Harold couldn't resist preening. "I have conquered Calia. I'm the youngest warrior to take this country or any other. I succeeded in a few days with what my father couldn't do in years. Pitoria will be next, and then Savaant and Illast. The world lies open before me; all I have to do it take it."

"And what will happen here in Calia while you are conquering the world?"

"I imagine my father will rule it—with an iron fist. And I will rule after him."

Edyon nodded. The world would be Harold's in a short time. It would not be Edyon's for much longer.

But what of March? He was standing to Harold's side, though Edyon could see he hated being there. Edyon knew that March would not leave him. He'd stayed with Edyon through all his trials, and, for good or ill, would be near him for this final one. And this gave him courage, made him want to do something rather than just give up.

He almost felt sorry for Broderick as he said, "And will you take all these boys with you on your conquests? Even those who would steal from you?"

"No one steals from me."

"Ah, so the boys have been looting the castle with your permission, I assume? Broderick sits on that very throne when you're not here, wearing one of my shirts, playing with a coin he's bragged about taking from Thelonius's strongbox."

Broderick was standing to the side, and his mouth opened and shut in shock as Harold turned to him and demanded, "You have a strongbox belonging to Thelonius?"

Broderick shook his head. "No."

"And where did you get that ring you're wearing?"

"Um. Well, that was from another strongbox."

Edyon knew he would die no matter what, but still, he allowed himself a very small smile.

# MARCH

## CALIA, CALIDOR

CURTIS, THE leader of the Hawk Brigade, came to Harold to beg for Broderick. He also came to blame others, including Thomas, a Bull, who was dragged before Harold and had his jerkin ripped open to reveal a very nice shirt with a gold trim at the neck, and three necklaces with pendants of diamonds and pearls.

"One of Thelonius's best shirts," March said. "And several of his less valuable necklaces."

"You see?" Curtis said. "It's not just Broderick."

This was the truth, but even so, March felt bad about accusing a Bull, one of Rashford's boys, and indeed one of his own for a time. Still, March could see that Edyon was trying to sow dissent in the boys' brigades, and he wanted to add to it. His own plan was to be seen as ultraloyal to Harold, and confirming the theft would do no harm to his own position. Thomas would undoubtedly get a severe beating, but he'd survive.

"But I thought . . . I thought I could have the shirt, and I sold some food in exchange for the pendants," Thomas pleaded.

"Everything here is mine! It's mine to gift, not yours to take or barter." Harold looked furious. "Whoever stole it should be reported. You are not here to trade like a stall holder. Have him punished, Bull leader."

Rashford stepped forward. "Yes, Your Highness." And he began to lead Thomas away.

"Wait a moment," Harold said. "I want to see his punishment. I want us all to see his punishment. Take his hand off, Bull leader."

Rashford stood gaping at Harold. "His hand? Please, Your Highness. He's one of my boys and a good soldier. He won't do it again."

"No, he won't do it again. Nor will any of them. He's one of yours, and you're one of mine, Rashford. And I'll have you cut in two if you fail to obey my order."

Rashford looked dismayed. Thomas made a dash for the door, but Sam and another of the Gold Brigade brought him back.

"Do it now, Bull leader," Harold ordered. "Take his hand off. And let this be a lesson to all the boys. You do not steal from me. The boy is not fit to serve in the boys' brigades, but he clearly has a future as a merchant. However, his future is with one hand, or else he has no future at all, and neither do you."

"But I didn't know," Thomas pleaded. "I won't do it again." He struggled against the boys who were holding him.

Rashford drew his sword. "Hold his hand out."

Thomas screamed, and Rashford turned and slashed down, cutting Thomas's left hand off at the wrist. Thomas's screams stopped abruptly. Rashford gave him an inhalation from his own smoke and bent close, talking to him.

March turned away. Even if he hadn't said anything, Thomas would have probably lost a hand, but it didn't feel good to be part of it. He went to leave the room, but Sam blocked his path. "Got a problem, March? Don't you approve of justice being done?"

March replied in Abask, cursing Harold and Sam and the lack of justice.

"What's that you said?"

March managed to bring himself under control and replied, "I said that of course the prince can administer justice however he likes. But Thomas was a Bull, and so were you, for a time."

"So your loyalties are to the Bulls, not to the Gold Brigade? Not to Harold?"

"I didn't say that, and you know it, Sam." March pushed past Sam and walked down the long corridor, away from the hall.

The castle was a mess, stinking of blood and bodies, swarming with flies. Harold had ordered it cleaned up, but the boys weren't as enthusiastic about cleaning as they were about killing. March needed to think. He needed to plan. He had to get rid of Harold and somehow save Edyon too. His mind could hardly focus, though, as he kept seeing Thomas's hand lying on the floor. He went back to his room and shortly after, Rashford joined him, shutting the door and then punching it with his fist.

"How's it going, Bull leader?" March asked.

Rashford didn't reply, but leaned his forehead against the door.

"How's Thomas?"

Rashford still didn't reply.

"Well, I'm sure he'll be fine. He'll heal quickly enough, and Harold says that he'll soon have a booming market stall. He's got a great future ahead of him."

"Shut up." Rashford banged his head against the door, then hit it with his fist again.

March wasn't sure what Rashford wanted, but he obviously had reached his limit.

Rashford finally turned round, and, with his back against the door, he let himself slide down so he was sitting on the floor. "I'm not sure how much more I can take. I was just going to leave, but I don't know where I'd go."

March nodded. "I'd had enough on the battlefield. Seeing the bodies cut up. I don't want to be a part of that."

Rashford leaned back, his eyes filling with tears. "I don't want to be part of chopping people's hands off. I mean, maybe the enemy's hand, but not my own boys."

"The longer we stay here, the more like them we are. And we've brought it on our own heads. Anyone working for Harold has only themselves to blame. That includes you, and me too."

Rashford's head was slumped down. He muttered, "I hate him. Thomas and Broderick can't be blamed for stealing from this place. They've never set foot in a palace before, never even seen this wealth. They want some of it. Why shouldn't they take some of it? There's still loads for Harold."

"But Harold's a prince. Nasty, cruel, and quite possibly mad, but still a prince. So he will punish any who disobey, and you will do his bidding, Rashford."

"What else can I do?"

March hesitated. This was risky, but Rashford had seen him on the beach and had said nothing. "Well . . . you can bow and scrape and do as you're told. You can chop off the hands of boys in your own brigade. Or . . . you can end it."

Rashford raised his head, his eyes meeting March's. "There's no end to it, though. They're all as bad as each other. If it's not Aloysius, it's Harold. If it wasn't Harold, it'd be someone else."

"No, that's not true. Edyon would be prince. Look at him—you can tell he'd not hurt a fly. He'd reward those who helped him. This country's still in the balance. Aloysius's reinforcements haven't arrived from the north, and who knows when they'll get here."

"But Edyon's going to be executed." Rashford frowned and lowered his voice. "Or are you planning on something else happening?"

"What can I plan, Rashford? I can't stop the execution. Unless . . . Harold was dead. Somehow."

"Somehow?"

"A sharp dagger to the neck. You could do it, Rashford."

"I don't think so. You've seen him—no one gets close.

He's on smoke all the time. The only person who can get close is you. If Harold was to die in his sleep, no one would give two fucks except Sam and a few others of the Gold Brigade," Rashford said. "You could do it."

"And the brigades would look to a new leader—one of them. Someone like you," March added. "Someone who everyone respects."

Rashford bit his lip but nodded.

"There'll be more boys being punished like Thomas if we don't act. Everyone must see that. There must be some others who'll join us. They look to you, Rashford. They respect you more than Harold."

Rashford shook his head. "Not all of them."

"But you know the ones you can trust."

"I'll speak to a few, only the ones I'm certain of—Kellen, Fitz, and a few more. There might be trouble afterward, but the Bulls won't hurt us. And if I get Curtis on board, then the Hawks will help us too. How soon?"

"It's got to be as soon as possible. Tonight."

Rashford nodded. "Agreed."

"I can get into his bedchamber, but he has four guards around him at all times. We have to overpower them. And Harold himself is strong; he never lets the power of the smoke leave him. But if I can make an excuse to clean his sword and keep it away from him . . ."

March knew this was a weak idea, but they'd have to try it.

In the meantime, March had to somehow continue with

his day and make an effort to appear as normal as possible. He went with Harold to view the metal construction on which Edyon would be executed. "The execution will happen tomorrow," said Harold. "I want Edyon's head on a spike before his father's face rots past all recognition."

After that, March saw Rashford once more, late in the afternoon. "We're on," Rashford reported quietly. "I'll bring everyone up late tonight."

March nodded. This was it. He had to do it for Edyon, for everyone.

That night, as Harold prepared for bed, March took his armor and sword.

"What're you up to, March?"

"They've lost their shine, Your Highness. I was going to clean them before tomorrow's execution." March's voice seemed strained; his heart was beating too fast. And Harold seemed to be assessing him. It looked like he didn't believe a word of it, so March added, "But if you'd rather I didn't . . ." And he made to put the armor back.

"No. I want them sparkling. Get on with it."

March took the sword to his own bedchamber and waited. He felt sick with nerves. He heard the guard change in Harold's room—four guards, as always, would be round Harold.

When it was dark and silent, he put his knife in his boot and went out to the corridor. Rashford was there with Kellen, Fitz, and Curtis. They would deal with the guards, but March had to deal with Harold. He took a small inhalation of Rashford's smoke and felt the strength of it fill him.

*I'm Abask. This is right. This is what needs to be done. For me, for Edyon. For all.*

March drew his knife and put it inside the fold of a towel and picked up a jug of water. He was just going to take these things to his prince in preparation for his morning ritual. Nothing unusual about this at all.

He made his way to Harold's room and walked in, past the guards, slowly moving forward to the bed. It was what he had done many times but never at this time of night. He put the jug on the side table. Behind him, he heard a struggle as Rashford and the others took the guards. Harold was covered in a sheet, his hair the only thing visible. March gripped the knife and pulled the sheet down to stab the prince's neck.

But . . . looking up at him was Sam, not Harold.

"Traitor!" Sam shouted, leaping up, pushing March back and knocking the knife from his hand, as March was grabbed from behind. Rashford was being held by the biggest of the Gold Brigade. The others were held too.

Sam shouted, "We have them all, Your Highness! March and the Bulls were here to betray you, just as I thought."

Harold stepped from the bathing room and looked at each of his captives. "Well, well, well. It seems that Sam has outsmarted you villains."

Sam grinned. "I knew you were up to something, Rashford. I've been watching you for days."

Harold came to stand in front of March. "It's such a shame that you Abasks are treacherous to your core. I won't find anyone with eyes like yours easily, March. But you can comfort yourself that I'll have them put on display near me."

March spat at Harold, and Harold slapped him so hard across his face that, even with the healing power of the smoke, March thought his head might come loose. "Take these traitors away. They will die tomorrow with the bastard prince. I look forward to watching."

# AMBROSE
## DEMON TUNNELS

EVEN IN Ambrose's head, there was something about Frost's voice that irritated him, and the way she could see into his mind, review his whole life, was horribly unsettling. But he couldn't risk ignoring her warning. He pulled Geratan aside and touched his friend on the arm.

*I need to go with Frost. She claims to have information about a threat to the queen, but she'll only tell me on the surface. I need you to stay here and guard the tunnels. The Brigantines are likely to counterattack. Keep your wits about you—there's something I don't like about all this.*

*Are you sure you can trust her?*

*Not as far as I can throw her. But she knows something, I believe that.*

Next, Ambrose went to Tash and took her hand.

*Thanks for your help, Tash. But I've more to ask of you. I need another tunnel.*

*No rest for the wicked, eh?*

*Can you make one that comes out in the south of the plateau? I need to be as close to the Pitorian camp as possible.*

*Are we leaving, then?*

*Just you, me, and Frost.*

*Her?!*

*I don't like the idea any more than you, but I need her information.*

Ambrose turned back to Frost and beckoned her forward. She sauntered past his guards and pressed her finger on his arm.

*I take it we're heading out on a mission to save the queen?*

*Your information'd better be correct.*

*Oh, it is. But do you really think that if you save her, your precious queen will realize that your love is the one she needs?*

*Just get moving.* Ambrose pushed Frost forward. *Tash is going to make us a new tunnel.*

*We could use a tunnel I know that comes out in the south. That's where you want to be, isn't it?*

*I do. But no doubt your tunnel will come out among a lot of Brigantines.*

Frost smiled wickedly. *Just a small post. Ten guards.*

Ambrose was tempted. It would be faster—if it was true. *We'll go along it most of the way. Then Tash can take us up to the surface nearby.*

Frost's smile wavered. *Oh, how lucky we are to have her.*

She led the way up several ramps, ducked into a low tunnel, and immediately sped up. Ambrose grabbed her and held her back. *You're not running off.*

*I was only stretching my legs. I won't run away and leave you. This is far, far more interesting. I really want to see your face when I tell you what's going to happen.*

*Just get behind me and stay there.*

Ambrose pushed Frost back between him and Tash and set off. The tunnel was narrow but straight, and he ran at a gentle pace. They might have to do this all day. Eventually Ambrose had to slow to a walk, though Tash looked like she could run forever.

*How much farther?* he asked Frost.

*Not far now.*

At last the tunnel began to head upward, sloping so steeply that Ambrose's boots began to slip. The tunnel walls were too smooth to offer any handholds, so he braced his arms against them while forcing his way up the incline. A screeching howl came from up ahead.

*A demon?* he asked.

*Yes, it's in a cage at the end of the tunnel. Nice and safe.* Frost's voice was matter-of-fact.

Tash's eyes flashed angrily, and she pushed Frost into the tunnel wall. *You're the demons, not them.*

Ambrose separated the two girls. *Calm down. We need to be quiet and get on with our task. Don't let her get you angry, Tash.*

*I wasn't.*

*Ha! Pea-Brain just loves her demon friends.*

*Ignore her, Tash. I need you to tunnel us to the surface from here. We need to come up far enough away from the entrance to this tunnel so the guards can't see or hear us. Can you do that?*

Tash leaned forward into Frost's face and said, *Easy.*

Ambrose sighed with relief when Tash took her hands from Frost and put them on the tunnel wall. Instantly the stone began to move back. Tash stepped forward, and a new tunnel formed in front of her.

Slowly but surely, they moved along, climbing upward until they broke out of the demon world and into the human one.

Ambrose held Frost back. *Stay close to me. I don't want you running off without completing your part of the bargain.*

He kept a tight hold on Frost's wrist as he climbed up the slope. The glare of bright sunlight blinded him for a moment as the cold air of the human world hit him. Frost twisted her hand, and Ambrose pulled her close and put his hand over her mouth. He hissed at her, "Scream and I'll break your neck."

Frost looked up with her huge silver eyes and blinked as innocently as a child.

Tash came over and spoke quietly: "We should be safe here. The Brigantines shouldn't be able to hear us."

"Perhaps not, but I'd rather not risk it."

As Ambrose took his hand from Frost's mouth, he drew his dagger, which he held to her throat, saying, "Now tell me what you know."

Frost began to speak, her voice as sickly sweet as it had been in Ambrose's head.

"You've noticed, I'm sure, that the demon world is sealing up. The tunnels to the surface are closing, and the central cavern itself is shrinking. And yet the core of smoke is getting bigger—a lot bigger since you released the smoke from the cage. And it's hotter too. More smoke, more heat, and less space. The demons are making it happen."

Ambrose nodded. "Tash told me they were returning to the core. But why?"

"It's as if they've given up fighting and are killing themselves," Tash said miserably.

Frost scoffed. "They don't see it as killing themselves—they see it as fueling the change. They don't consider themselves individuals. Not like you and I would. They see themselves as part of the one spirit—the one smoke. They are smoke people, made of smoke that can re-form, move, create new smoke people—and new worlds."

"New demon worlds?" Tash asked.

"Yes, Pea-Brain, new demon worlds. This isn't the first, and it won't be the last. Every time humans find their world, the smoke people end up being exploited and hunted. When that happens, they just . . . move somewhere else."

"How do you know this?" Ambrose asked.

"I've seen into the demons' thoughts. In the demon world, I see into everyone's thoughts quickly. Instantly. You know that, Sir Ambrose. I saw your whole life in moments. It's just something I can do." She smiled briefly, a genuine smile for once. "Something I seem to be uniquely good at. And I've seen into the demons' thoughts, their knowledge of the world. Knowledge they don't normally share with anyone, not even Little Miss Pea-Brain, but *I* saw it. It's like having a key to a door; once you have it and open the door, the information is all there, and you just have to walk through and see inside their collective memory."

It was certainly true that Frost had seen Ambrose's whole life in an instant. "So you've seen in the demons' thoughts that their world closes up, and the smoke moves away to form another?" he said.

"Yes, I have. That's exactly what I've seen. The tunnels close down, the cavern gets smaller, the old world dies as the smoke builds up. Haven't you noticed that the smoke is changing too? Getting paler and hotter. Eventually it'll go white and be so hot that nothing'll keep it in. It'll move up into a cloud of burning heat. A cloud of death."

"Death of the demons?" Ambrose asked.

Frost rolled her eyes. "Death of anything that's close to the smoke when it turns white." She kept her gaze on Ambrose as she added, "Not just the smoke in the demon world. All the smoke everywhere. It's all connected. It'll all burn and destroy anything near it. The smoke in the bottles carried by the boys' brigades. The smoke in the boys' lungs. And the smoke in that small bottle Queen Catherine carries close to her ever-so-fragile heart. It's all connected; it all belongs to the cloud. It will find a way to get free, and it will kill anything it touches." She blinked innocently up at Ambrose.

Ambrose felt his stomach clench. He turned to Tash. "Do you believe this?"

"I don't know." She shook her head. "But all the smoke *is* connected. And it is changing."

"How soon will it happen?" Ambrose asked.

Frost shrugged. "That I don't know, but I'm not going back in there to find out. Today or tomorrow or the next day . . . I'm not sure which, but I'm certain that if you come back here next week, there won't be a demon world to see. It'll have moved to a new place to start again." Frost blinked and smiled at Ambrose. "Anyway, lesson time's over. Aren't you off to save your lady love?"

Ambrose hesitated. "My men are in there. They'll die."

Frost frowned theatrically. "Oh, yes. I quite forgot about that. Well, you have a choice to make, don't you? Save them or save your queen. Or . . ." She turned to Tash. "You could always send *her* back."

Ambrose cursed.

Tash put her hand on his arm. "You warn Catherine. I'll go back. I'll get them out. It won't take more than half a day, if I'm quick. I can do it."

"But it could turn white at any moment."

"I have to try. But what are you going to do about her?" Tash asked, nodding at Frost.

"I'll think of something."

"Something painful, I hope." Tash gave a quick smile. "I need to go. Not a moment to spare, I guess." She made a fist and knocked it against Ambrose's. "Good luck—and don't fuck up."

"Um, same to you, Tash."

And then she turned and ran into her tunnel. Ambrose felt guilty about letting her put herself in danger, but he couldn't stop her, and he had to warn Catherine. But what to do with Frost? He couldn't kill her, but he couldn't release her either in case she raised the alarm. All he could do was take her with him until he came up with a better idea.

"Come on," he said, dragging Frost with him. He set off, keeping a tight hold of her wrist and was surprised to find her going with him, neither resisting nor slowing him.

Still she said, "You'd be faster if you left me."

"Yes, until you send the Brigantines after me, and then I'd be dead."

"I won't go back to them. Don't you get it? I was their slave! I didn't lie about that. They never let me out of those tunnels. They'd take me back in, and probably make me help fight you lot, even when everyone in there is going to die anyway."

"Very convincing. There's just one problem."

"What's that?"

"I don't trust a word you say."

Frost cursed and twisted her hand, but Ambrose kept a tight grip.

"Actually, I have a hankering to travel. South, I think. To Savaant. Maybe farther."

"Well, we're heading in that direction, so let's keep moving."

Frost sneered. "You love Catherine a lot, don't you? But you know she'll never be yours again, even if you save her life?"

"I know."

"And there's a good chance you'll never reach her in time—or die trying. Love seems to cause a lot of pain and suffering."

"And sometimes it's beautiful too."

"Hope I never suffer from it."

Ambrose laughed. "I don't think there's much danger of that."

They were walking fast along the side of a stream.

"I could do with a drink and a pee," Frost said.

"You can have both, but I'm not letting go of your wrist."

Frost looked at him. "I've been living as a slave with soldiers for years; you think that bothers me?"

But before Ambrose could reply, she had twisted free and jumped down the slope into the water. Ambrose raced after her, trying to grab her, but fell as she rolled away and splashed through the stream to the other side.

Ambrose got to his feet and stared across at her.

"You could waste your time chasing after me, or you could run to Catherine," said Frost. "I know what I'd do if I was you."

Ambrose watched her turn and run—away from him, away from the Brigantines, and, who knew, perhaps eventually to Illast or Savaant.

He headed south as fast as he could, trekking through the night, drinking from streams and following their flow southward. The sun had climbed a little above the horizon when he reached the plateau's edge. He could see the land below: the river and the road that ran along the far side of it.

He'd made it.

He shielded his eyes to see better. It almost looked like the model in the war room. Rossarb was to the right, and around the town were Aloysius's forces, and ringed around them were more forces—the Pitorian army.

*They're attacking.*

He could see that the Pitorians closer to him were white-hairs, and, on a small hill not far from the River Ross, was a small, tented area. It was a command post. Would Catherine be there?

But then he spotted something else—soldiers running through the trees along the north side of the Ross. They had to be Brigantines, and, if so, they were positioning themselves around the white-hairs' camp. Farther away, he could see more men running fast through the trees, but some leaped and somersaulted.

*They're not men; they're the boys.*

There were at least a hundred of them, possibly more. And then, down in the camp far below, he saw a small figure dressed in white.

*Catherine!*

Ambrose leaped down the steep side of the plateau. He had to get to her before the boys.

# CATHERINE
## ALSOP HILL, NORTHERN PITORIA

Fight to the death and then keep on fighting.
*Brigantine saying*

CATHERINE WALKED through her camp as the clear sky began to lighten with the new day. The imposing wall of the Northern Plateau was already touched by the sun, and the stone shone like silver. It was strangely calm. There was no wind. The river could be heard, but not seen.

To the west, the silhouette of Rossarb was just visible and, before it, the two armies ranged. Farther beyond them, Catherine thought she could see a faint shimmer of the Pitorian Sea. It was impossible to see ships from this distance, and certainly not the small scullers, but if the plan had gone well, they should have landed on the northern shore in the night and seized the forts there.

The battle had already begun, and yet here it felt calm. Catherine looked around at her personal guard, and beyond to the huge number of white-hairs before her, and felt pride that these men had chosen to fight for her against a common enemy—a man who had always been her enemy, her own father.

Horses were moving behind the Pitorian lines among herself, Ffyn, and Davyon, and even back to Tzsayn, and a rider arrived with a message.

>*The scullers have landed successfully and taken the forts despite stiff defense. Davyon and the blue-hairs are in position and ready to attack.*
>
>*I wish him well, and you too, my love. This is our moment. Today we will lay the first stone of our future together in a free Pitoria.*
>
>>*Your loving husband,*
>>*Tzsayn*

Catherine stroked her finger across Tzsayn's signature. *Husband.*

A shout roused her, her men pointing to the distance. The blue-hairs, led by Davyon, were advancing. The next stage of the attack was beginning. Knowing Tzsayn would be worried about her, Catherine went into her tent to write a short note to reassure him she was safe. She'd just picked up the quill when there was a different cry from outside. An alarm.

"Attackers! Attackers! Look to the queen!"

Catherine dropped her quill and dashed outside as one of her guard raced up to her.

"Boys, Your Majesty. They're coming across the river. Heading this way. They're *fast* . . ."

Catherine's blood turned icy. They were coming for her. Her father's spies had seen her from the Northern Plateau, and he'd sent the boys to ambush her. Why hadn't she foreseen this?

She turned to the guard. "Find General Ffyn. Tell him that the boys' brigades are attacking us. We need support. Go!"

The man leaped onto his horse, but the first boys were already running into the camp, heading straight for her tent, cutting down her white-hairs without seeming to break stride. One of her guards scooped Catherine up in his arms and half threw her onto her horse. "We must leave now, Your Majesty."

Catherine snatched up the reins, but where should she turn? She wanted to go to Ffyn and the main force of white-hairs, but the boys had already cut off that route.

"Follow the River Road. Head east." It was away from Ffyn, but it was the quickest route and Catherine knew she had to be fast. She kicked her horse, galloping hard, five guards close to her, ten or twelve boys in pursuit.

"We'll soon be away from them," one guard shouted.

"No. They can keep up this pace all day. Don't let up!"

But now some more boys appeared ahead. The river was to her left, and to her right she saw even more boys converging on the road.

A spear took out one of her guards.

Catherine kicked her horse on.

But the boys were getting closer. One appeared, running alongside her nearest guard's galloping horse, shouting and whooping as if it was a game. The guard struck at the boy with his sword, but then he was gone, pulled from his horse.

Another guard replaced his position, spurring his horse hard.

"Keep on, Your Majesty!" Then he too was gone. Catherine wanted to scream with anger and frustration. But the shouting came from the boys who surrounded her. All she could do was urge her horse forward.

And then a boy was somehow up in the air beside her, making an impossible leap, slamming into her shoulder, and sending her off the horse so she was flying through the air.

No. She was on the ground. And it was hard and the world was spinning, then black. Shouting continued around her.

Catherine forced her eyes open.

There were about twenty boys standing round her. She was dragged to her feet, and their leader looked her up and down. He had spots on his chin, and his teeth were almost green. He wore a leather jerkin with a badge in the shape of an eagle's head sewn roughly over his heart. He was perhaps sixteen years old.

"Queen Catherine." The boy sketched a mocking bow. "Nice to meet you this fine morning. Consider yourself a prisoner of the Eagles."

"I'll consider you a fool and a villain. You don't know what you're doing," Catherine said.

"Did I ask for your opinion?" The boy slapped Catherine hard across the face, and she fell to the ground, blood pouring from her nose. "Now stop yapping and start walking. We're taking you to the king."

As Catherine was pulled to her feet, a Brigantine soldier on horseback rode up at a gallop. Even in her dazed state, there was something familiar in his posture, but her scrambled brain couldn't quite place it until he was nearer, and then there was no doubting the handsome face.

*Ambrose!*

# AMBROSE
## NORTHERN PITORIA

AMBROSE HAD hurtled down the slope to reach the bottom of the plateau and stumbled across the bridge, grabbed a horse from the destroyed white-hair camp, and galloped in the direction he'd seen Catherine flee. He was beyond exhausted, and beyond desperate, and then ahead he saw what he dreaded most. Boys on their feet, and Catherine falling to the ground.

*No.*

But, as he rode on, Catherine was pulled upright.

*She's still alive.*

Ambrose raced to them, uncertain what to do. He couldn't fight all these boys—he probably couldn't fight just one of them—but he had to do something. He pulled his horse up and called out, "Well done, boys! You've captured the queen of Pitoria!"

"And who might you be, pink-hair?" one of the boys said.

"I work for Noyes."

Ambrose needed an excuse for his sudden appearance, and spying seemed the only vaguely plausible one. "I have information about the queen. Don't be fooled—she's still a danger. She uses smoke too, to give her strength."

"Well, she ain't got any strength now. She's as weak as a kitten."

Ambrose looked at Catherine. There was blood around her nose, and her right eye was blackened and swelling. Normally the sight would have filled him with rage, but Ambrose felt only relief. She wasn't healing, which meant she hadn't taken any smoke. Catherine stared back at him in disbelief, and Ambrose had to break his gaze in case he gave himself away. He said, "Has she any smoke with her, though? If so, she could still be a danger. I believe she keeps a bottle of it within her armor."

"How do you know that?" The boy speaking was older and was now pointing his spear at Ambrose's chest. "And what did you say your name was again?"

"Daniels. I work for Noyes. And I'd be glad if you pointed that somewhere else, boy."

"I'm Gaskett, leader of the Stags," replied the youth, lowering his spear a fraction. "And what are you doing here, Daniels?"

"I've been sent to protect the queen. Aloysius wants her alive."

"Indeed he does. I'm not stupid. But I still don't understand what you're doing here, or why you've got pink hair."

Ambrose sighed. "I told you, I work for Noyes. I've been undercover in the Pitorian camp."

"Well, as it happens, Noyes got back to our camp last night. I'm taking Her Majesty there, and you're coming with us too."

# TASH
## DEMON TUNNELS

TASH RAN on, the smoke giving her speed beyond anything she'd experienced before. It was wonderful to move at such a pace, even though her speed was driven by fear for herself and the Demon Troop. As she approached the cavern, a cacophony of clanging warned her that something was wrong, and she emerged from her tunnel into the middle of another battle. Geratan and his men were fighting Brigantines on the lower terraces, and more enemy soldiers were storming out of tunnels on the far side of the cavern. Clearly the Brigantines were trying to retake control of their precious smoke farm, and although Geratan and his men were fighting back fiercely, they were outnumbered and giving ground. The cavern itself seemed smaller still, and the billowing funnel of smoke in the central core was a pale lilac color rather than purple.

*But it's not white yet. We've got time.*

Tash headed toward Geratan, leaping down a terrace, but a huge Brigantine soldier blocked her way. He advanced slowly, his sword by his side, grinning at her. *Urgh, it's a game to him, is it? Well, let's see if he likes how I play it.* She grinned back and beckoned him forward before running directly at him. Full of strength and speed from the smoke, she barged his chest with her shoulder, sending him toppling off the terrace, arms and legs flailing.

But behind him was another soldier, and behind *him* more were coming.

Geratan's men were retreating up the terraces now, falling back toward the lopsided tunnel that Tash had marked as the way out. Tash had to head there too, but the Brigantines were coming from all directions. She was trapped. But then another figure leaped down to her.

*Twist!*

Grabbing the head of the nearest soldier, Twist yanked it round, breaking the man's neck, then lifted the soldier's body and used it as both shield and weapon to force three other Brigantines off the terrace. Twist took Tash's arm and ran. His thoughts flashed like images in her head, so she knew immediately what he wanted to do as he bent and held out his hand. She stepped on it, and he boosted her into the air with such force that she landed three terraces up, close to her lopsided tunnel. Twist then leaped down to help the crimson-hairs, bowling through Brigantines from behind and clearing the path for the Demon Troop to retreat upward toward Tash.

Tash grabbed Geratan's arm as quickly as she could.

*Listen, this whole place is going to close in and burn. We've got to get out of here.*

*I don't think we could stay if we wanted to!* Geratan glanced back to the Brigantines. *We need to get into your tunnel, Tash.*

Tash wanted Twist to come with her, and to her relief, he was suddenly beside her. He grabbed her hands and pointed upward. A vision filled her head—all the tunnels were closing in, closing in faster and faster. But one of the tunnels on the level above was a shorter route to the surface. It was the last way out.

Tash grabbed Geratan.

*Change of plan. We've got to use a different tunnel. Twist will show us.*

*You're sure?*

*I'm sure.*

She grabbed Twist's hand, and he set off running up the terraces, leading the Demon Troop to the higher tunnel. At the entrance, he pulled Tash to the side as Anlax began to lead the men in. Twist held Tash's hand, and she had a new vision. In it, the smoke in the core was getting more and more turbulent and turning white. The demons were in the small chamber she'd seen way down in the lower levels of the world, still walking into the core. There were only five left. Twist was one of the last. Horrible realization filled her.

*He's saying good-bye—forever.*

He couldn't come with her. He didn't want to. But he was her friend; she knew it—felt it.

*Good-bye. Thank you for being my friend. Thank you for helping us, even though you owe us nothing.*

She knew he couldn't understand her words, but hoped he understood her feelings, her gratitude. But now she saw a different vision. One of herself with a small flame of red smoke inside her.

Twist looked into her eyes and pointed to her chest.

In all the chaos, Tash had forgotten that she had smoke inside her. She'd inhaled the purple smoke when she'd broken the bottles *and* she had that element of red smoke deep inside her. That smoke had saved her, but now it would kill her. When the smoke turned white and the demon world ended, she would end too.

*I don't want it*, Tash thought to Twist desperately. *It doesn't belong to me. But how do I get rid of it?*

In answer Twist leaned forward as if he was going to kiss her. And then his mouth was on hers, but not in a kiss like she'd seen young lovers doing. Twist was sucking—sucking her breath out, then somehow sucking more until her lungs were empty and screaming.

*Stop! No!*

There was a searing heat in her chest and throat, and, as her head fell back, she caught sight of a small stream of lilac and red smoke coming out of her mouth, emptying her of strength. And only when the last wisp had gone could she breathe again.

*Well, that was shitting horrible.*

The smoke wafted round her neck and away, through the cavern and down to join the rest of the pale smoke that was swirling out of the core.

Tash felt weak and sick, but she tried to smile.

*Thank you, Twist. Thank you for everything.*

Tears filled her eyes, and she leaned up and kissed his cheek. *Good-bye. I'll miss you.*

They slid their hands apart.

Twist turned and raced off, disappearing into another tunnel, and Tash knew he was going back to the core, to become smoke again and help remake the world of smoke somewhere else.

Tash took one last look at the cavern. It seemed to be shrinking before her eyes: the terraces were narrowing, the tunnels closing in, the roof dropping toward her. And yet the smoke was brighter, almost dazzling.

Geratan's hand was on her arm. *We've got to hurry, Tash. Go to the front. Lead the way.*

She slipped past the Demon Troop and kept running as fast as she could.

*Twist showed us this tunnel. He'd know we'd have a chance. But please don't close. Please don't close . . .*

The tunnel spiraled up steeply. Her legs felt heavy, like she'd been running for days. Which, when she thought about it, she had.

*Just keep going. Keep going . . .*

And then she saw it.

Sky. Real sky. And the silhouette of treetops.

Her heart pounding, Tash forced herself up the last few paces and out into the coolness of the human world. She fell to her knees on the grass, gasping for air. She'd never pushed herself so hard in her life. She turned to look behind her and willed the others to arrive.

Anlax was next. Then more of them. All were breathing

hard, flopping on the ground. There was no sign of Geratan, and Tash knew he would be doing what he always did: bringing up the rear, making sure everyone got out.

"Please hurry, Geratan."

But he didn't come.

"They were fighting behind," gasped one soldier as he staggered out of the hollow. "The Brigantines attacked again as we were leaving."

Anlax swore. Tash turned away and stared at the trees as tears rolled down her cheeks. She couldn't bear it.

But then she heard a shout and turned to see a bloodied crimson head come out of the ground. Geratan, gasping and panting. His eyes met hers, and she ran to him and hugged him. There were no words. Tash cried and shook with shock and fear and relief. When she eventually loosened her grip, she saw the other men were watching them quietly, tears in their eyes too.

Tash looked at the ground beneath her feet. The hollow was the palest of pale reds, and then the glow faded, and in moments had gone completely.

# EDYON

## CALIA, CALIDOR

THE PRISONERS were sitting on the stone floor, their backs against the wall. Edyon was next to March, which was the one good thing about all this. Rashford and Broderick were in chains too, along with the six other Bulls who had been part of the assassination plot. It was cold and damp, and Edyon was hungry and thirsty.

Fitz said, "I'm not sure if we'll starve to death before we're executed."

Edyon nodded. "A thought I've had often recently."

Rashford let his head roll to the side to look at Edyon. "Harold wants a spectacle—I don't think starvation is on his mind."

Kellen said, "That doesn't mean we *won't* starve, though. This group can't organize shit."

"Actually, it's a long way down here, and there's not much food left," Broderick said. The others looked at him, and Fitz cursed him. Broderick replied, "Well, it's true!"

"Poor Broderick had to find food for me, didn't you?" Edyon said. "How you suffered."

"It's your fault I'm here," he said sullenly.

"Broderick, I know you don't have much longer to do this, but for fuck's sake, grow up," Rashford said.

"We shouldn't have long to wait. Harold's execution machines are ready," March said. "I saw them yesterday."

"I wonder how he'll do it," Kellen said. "One at a time, but with the others watching? Or all together? Not sure if I want to go first or last."

"Can you shut up about it?" Broderick complained, his voice breaking and a tear running down his cheek.

Edyon said, "Perhaps it'll be you and me together, Brod. Together until the last. Our bodies on display next to each other. Perhaps just our heads. Me looking at you."

"Shut up."

"You should be pleased. Despite the kickings you gave me, despite your theft and your treachery, I've decided I won't be haunting you." He squeezed March's hand and said quietly, "If there is an afterlife of any kind, I like to think I'll be with those I love."

March smiled and squeezed his hand back. "Me too."

Kellen looked to the door. "Someone's coming. It might be food."

It was Sam and some of the Lion Brigade, but they weren't bringing dinner. "Get up, you lot—you're going out," Sam said.

"What—we're being released?" Broderick asked, getting to his feet.

Sam laughed. "Harold isn't going to release anyone."

"So this is it?" Broderick said.

Rashford stood up. "This is fucking it. Let's get it over with."

But no one else moved. Edyon gripped March's hand, somehow hoping to hold on to the moment.

Then the Lions were moving into the cell. They lifted Kellen to his feet, and Kellen kicked and hit in return, but Sam darted forward and punched his stomach. And, of course, Sam and the Lions had smoke, while the prisoners had nothing.

There was no point in fighting. The end had come, and Edyon would face it as well as he could. He stood with March close to him, still holding his hand. Leaning close to Edyon's ear, March whispered, "I'm sorry. I can't say it enough, but I'm glad to have known you. Even now, even in this dire place, I give thanks to have known you."

Edyon squeezed March's hand again and said, "Death is all around me, but you always brought me happiness. You more than anyone believed in me, trusted me. Thank you, March."

Then Edyon was pushed out and led up the stone steps to a courtyard. A clear blue sky was above, and Edyon tried to take it in. Tried to enjoy it even—they were his precious last few moments on earth. He wanted to see the beauty. He turned to March and said, "It is beautiful. All of it. And I want to haunt the world. Will you wander it with me?"

March nodded. "Gladly. Forever."

"We'll live in Abask. In the hills, by a river. You and I, at peace at last."

"At peace at last," March echoed. "I love you now and always will, Edyon."

Edyon embraced March and kissed his cheek, but they were pulled apart. The Lions around him jeered, but Edyon hardly noticed. He focused on March, looking at him for the last time.

They were taken up to the large castle terrace, where the strange metal contraptions were lined up in a symmetrical fashion. There seemed to be a choice of execution methods— both slow and fast—though Edyon did not expect that he would be the one to make the choice. From the outside of the line, moving in, there were two methods of crucifixion, one on a T-shaped cross and one X-shaped, then a human-shaped cage hanging from a chain, then the two huge black, metal contraptions, and, in front of them, two boxes for beheadings, then farther along, another human-shaped cage, and X- and T-shaped crosses.

Edyon was taken to one of the large metal contraptions and tied to it, his arms outspread. March was taken to the block in front of him to be beheaded. Rashford was taken to the machine next to Edyon, and, in front of him at the other beheading block, was Broderick. The others were taken to the other crosses and cages.

Edyon, however, was wrong about being center stage. Harold, of course, wanted that position, and he now came forward and stood before them to address the crowd below. The people were mostly townsfolk, and none looked too jubilant to be there. Indeed, they looked miserable and were mostly silent. Edyon noticed that the gateways to the square were guarded by boys.

"People of Calia. Loyal boys of the boys' brigades. This afternoon we have a spectacle for you." Harold spread his arms out as if displaying his wares. "These are our enemies. They are traitors and villains. They have betrayed me. They will pay with their lives, and give us some entertainment as small recompense in the process. Their bodies will be displayed as a warning to anyone who thinks of opposing me. I am here as your future king. I am here to show you my power and my strength. Enjoy your entertainment."

There were cheers from a few boys and one or two townsfolk, but mostly there was stillness and silence.

And so the work began on Harold's display, starting from the outside in. The two farthest prisoners, Kellen and Fitz, were pushed into position, each held by two Lion boys and nailed by a third to their crosses. The prisoners screamed and Kellen kicked out, but it didn't take long for them both to go quiet.

Edyon tried not to think of the nails going through their flesh. At least his death would be faster than theirs—though, as he looked at the contraption to which he was attached, he wasn't sure how he was going to die. He couldn't move, but at least he was chained, not nailed, into position.

The next boys were nailed to their crosses, and then the boys were put in the man-shaped cages. All of them had metal helmets put on them that inserted something into their mouths. And as they breathed and panted, the noises were turned into whistles of different pitches.

Edyon tried to block it out. He looked at the blue sky and thought of his mother, and then he looked at March. But now they were coming to March and Broderick, who were forced into position. Broderick had gone limp and had wet himself, and the executioners kicked him and cursed him.

A metal helmet was put on Edyon's head, his mouth forced open, and a round metal tube forced in. As he breathed out, the high-pitched whistle hurt his ears.

Harold walked along the terrace and swayed to the whistles coming from the boys' mouths as if to music, though in truth it was just an awful noise that not even the strangest, saddest birds would ever make.

Edyon looked at March's back as he bent forward, his head on the block.

*I love you. I love you always and always will.*

Tears ran down Edyon's cheek as he closed his eyes.

*At least March will die quickly.*

There was a scream. And another.

Edyon didn't know what was happening. He didn't want to know. He kept his eyes closed.

*It'll be over soon.*

The whistling around him grew more frantic. He heard a thud, as if the ax had fallen, and then a scream—a scream that wouldn't end. And more screaming.

*Please. Just end this. Just end it.*

But nothing happened, except for more screaming and someone shouting for help. Edyon forced his eyes open but couldn't understand at all.

It was Broderick's executioner shouting for help—he

was on fire and grabbing at his clothes, trying to rip them off. White smoke was around his waist, curling round his chest.

The other executioner held his ax aloft over March and seemed undecided whether to continue with his job or help his friend, but before he could make his mind up, flames burst out of his mouth as if in a huge belch. His hair caught fire. The bottle of smoke at his waist cracked open, and a plume of thick white smoke puffed out around him, enveloping him completely so that all Edyon could see was the ax, which fell down toward March's neck, and Edyon screamed into his whistle as the ax blade landed—

Where March's head had just been. But March had moved back and was staring in shock at his executioner, whose body was now licked by flames.

All around was chaos. Shouts and screams, smoke and flames, had burst out from all the boys. Harold remained center stage, standing still, a curl of white smoke round his waist. He pulled the bottles of smoke from his belt and threw them at the crowd. Then he said, "Boys, throw the smoke away." He thought that would save him, but as he repeated his order, white smoke came out of his mouth. "I order this to stop!" he cried, but now fire as well as smoke was pouring out of his mouth.

"I will not have this!" he shouted, and he turned round, burning Sam with the flames from his mouth. Harold's eyes met Edyon's, and he ran toward him, shouting, though his words were more like flaming screams. March picked up the ax and swung it round, hard and fast, into Harold's chest.

The prince fell to the ground, his twitching body engulfed in white smoke.

Harold was dead. Sam was on his knees, consumed by flames. All around, the brigade boys were burning, and the white smoke clung to them. Edyon had no idea what was happening, but the purple smoke seemed to have changed to white, and any boy who'd taken the smoke or had it in a bottle was now being attacked by it.

March had pulled Broderick to his feet, saying, "Get Rashford out of that contraption, and be careful about it. Then help the others." Next, March was with Edyon, pulling the helmet off and asking, "Are you hurt?"

"I'm fine. But what's happening? What's going on?"

"I don't know. The bottles of smoke are exploding and burning. The boys who have smoke inside them—even their bodies are catching fire."

March freed Edyon's hands, and Broderick released Rashford. March and Edyon helped free the remaining boy in the cage, and then they had the grim task of getting the boys off the crosses, pulling the nails out. Rashford, all the while, was talking to the boys, saying, "You're so brave, Fitz. So brave. We're going to live through this. And you, Kellen, and you. You'll have some nice scars to prove all your stories are true, 'cause otherwise, who would believe it?"

The white smoke was rising up from the burning bodies of the boys and gathering in a low cloud, swirling in the courtyard. The crowd of people below were screaming and panicking. Some fled out the gates, which were no longer guarded. The white cloud of smoke hung ominously low over them, and a wisp of it dipped down and wrapped round a Calidorian man, who screamed as his clothes burst into flame.

It seemed the smoke would kill anyone it touched. Edyon shouted, "The smoke burns! Get away from the cloud. Run to the sea. Get in the water. Don't let the smoke touch you."

The crowd fled and March, Edyon, Rashford, and the other prisoners joined the throng, running down from the castle through the streets of Calia to the quay. The cloud seemed to follow them as if circling and looking for prey, swooping down and encircling another few men, whose hair and clothes caught fire.

"There's nothing we can do for them," March said. "Just run."

They raced through the city, out of the narrow streets and to the harbor. Edyon kept hold of March's hand as they both leaped off the quayside into the cool water, which was crowded with people. Children and old people were there, even babies. Mothers were crying. People were searching for their families. And, above them all, the white smoke hung, moving after them, but it couldn't get the people in the water. Licks of smoke came down, but people splashed the water and the cloud moved up higher.

"Stand on the bottom! Here, where it's not so deep!" Rashford shouted. "And keep splashing!"

Everyone joined him. Thousands splashing and shouting together, and the cloud of smoke rose higher. The crowd shouted and cheered. Someone threw a wet shirt into the cloud, and it fizzed and hissed before falling back into the sea, and the cloud rose higher still, as if it had given up on them. It rose higher and higher, and then it drifted over the hills and was lost in the brightness of the sun.

Edyon and March waded onto the beach, which was packed with people. Many wouldn't stray far from the water's edge, saying they'd stay there all day and all night, until they were sure the smoke wasn't going to return.

Edyon embraced March, and March put his head on Edyon's shoulder. "Are we safe, do you think?" Edyon asked.

"I've no idea. I think all the smoke has burned off. The entire boy army had it in them or in the bottles. They're gone—or powerless. Just ordinary boys now."

"So . . . am I in charge?"

March laughed a little against Edyon's shoulder. "Quite possibly."

# CATHERINE
## NORTHERN PITORIA

*Never surrender, at least never in your heart.*
*Queen Valeria of Illast*

CATHERINE AND Ambrose were taken on horseback to Aloysius. The boys didn't bother restraining them. They knew their prisoners could never outrun or outfight them. Catherine was stunned, partly from the blow she'd received and her bloody and broken nose, but also because of Ambrose.

How was he here? He was meant to be in the demon world. He must be here to help her, but why was he talking to the boys about smoke?

"Listen to me—you need to take the smoke from her. She may try to attack the king." Nobody responded. "Noyes will burn with fury when he hears about my treatment," Ambrose continued. "You'd better pray he's in a forgiving mood."

"Shut it," Gaskett replied.

"I know you're keen to show loyalty, boy. But I've just come from the demon world. My men have had great success. But something's happening there—something big. It's urgent."

"And you can tell Noyes soon enough. But for now will you just *shut up*?" Gaskett replied.

Catherine's mind was fuzzy. Why was Ambrose staring at her so meaningfully? He was trying to send her a message, that much seemed clear, but what?

*I've just come from the demon world . . . My men have had great success . . .*

Did that mean they had destroyed the supply of smoke? Surely not. These boys were proof that Aloysius had plenty of smoke for his boy army.

*Something's happening there—something big . . .*

It was impossible to tell what he meant. She could see his fingers twitching, as if he wanted to sign her a message, but they were being too closely watched.

They rode back through Catherine's destroyed camp, the ground littered with dead white-hairs. She had a vague hope that her message to Ffyn had somehow got through, and he might come to her rescue, but from the top of the hill she saw that the main battle was raging far to the west. Ahead, the plain was clear all the way to the Brigantine army. Had Ffyn's forces been overcome too?

They rode on, joined by more and more boys, all heading toward Aloysius's pennant, which was flying above a huge unit of armored horses. Catherine was relieved to see a cluster of white-haired prisoners on their knees; not all her men had been slaughtered.

Then she saw him. Her father. And that old, cold fear swept through her.

Aloysius was dressed in red and black with a black breastplate. Beside him was another figure she recognized: Noyes.

The boys pulled Catherine from her horse and took hold

of her arms, as if to ensure the king saw that it was them who had caught her. As she was brought forward, her father actually smiled and Noyes clapped slowly.

Noyes spoke first. "Boys, boys, boys. You have exceeded my expectations. Two for the price of one." He came closer, as if to check it was really them. "Sir Ambrose Norwend. And Princess Catherine."

"*Queen* Catherine."

Noyes chuckled. "Not for much longer." He ran his finger from her shoulder to her wrist. "And is this the arm that killed your brother? Are you planning more mischief? Have you taken more smoke?"

"No. But this one," Gaskett replied, nodding at Ambrose, "says she's got some under her armor."

Noyes smirked. "Indeed? Excuse me, *Your Majesty*." He slipped his thin fingers beneath her breastplate and deftly slid out the small bottle of smoke. "You can release them now. She is a *queen*, after all."

Gaskett did so. "He also said he worked for you."

Noyes smiled again. "Yes, well, Sir Ambrose is a liar to his bones, as well as a traitor."

Through all this, Aloysius had stood silent; his eyes, though, hadn't left Catherine, and she knew that she had to address him directly. She stepped past Noyes. "King Aloysius, Father, I demand that you release me and Sir Ambrose. He is my subject and this is my land. Mine and my husband's."

Aloysius's lip curled. "It may be your husband's land now, but not for much longer. The tide of the battle is turning in our favor, and I've not yet unleashed my boys. But once

I've finished with you, they'll rip the blue-hairs apart. By this time tomorrow you won't be my only prisoners. Tzsayn will be in chains too."

"I had such fun with Tzsayn last time we met," said Noyes slyly. "I can't wait to see him again. Has he missed me?"

Catherine couldn't stop herself from shouting, "You're a fiend, Noyes. I don't know how you've become so perverted to take pleasure in other people's pain. But you will get your punishment one day."

"No, it's *you* who will be punished," Aloysius boomed, "you treacherous whore."

Catherine raised her chin. "Father, whatever you accuse me of, I am still your daughter. You sent me to this country as a decoy for your true purpose—to invade Pitoria and farm the demon smoke. I say 'true purpose,' but nothing about you is true. You were never a true father to me any more than you are a true king to your people. But I learned truth from good people around me—my mother, Sir Ambrose, Tzsayn, my maid Tanya, and my many good soldiers.

"I learned, too, that truth has no limits. You murdered Sir Tarquin Norwend and Lady Anne Norwend to conceal your own lies. The truth about you and your cruelty is known across the world, but the truth about their honor will ring even louder. Your actions have consequences, Father, and you will pay one day."

Her father snorted. "A pretty speech from someone who killed her own brother."

"As you have been trying—and failing—to do for the last ten years?"

Aloysius's jaw tightened, and Ambrose cut in. "You've failed in that, and you'll fail again in this war. The smoke is gone. It's over. You've lost."

Catherine stared at him. What did he mean?

"Have you heard from your forces in the demon world recently?" Ambrose continued. "Oh, wait, no—my men have killed them and taken the cavern. And the girl in there, what's she called? Frost? The one helping you to farm the smoke? She sends her regards, Noyes. She's off to live the good life in Illast."

Noyes's face fell for a moment.

"And she told me something else too—the smoke is changing."

"Changing how?" Noyes sneered.

"I'll show you," Ambrose said, jumping forward and ripping the cork from the tiny bottle of smoke in Noyes's hands.

But nothing happened. Not even a wisp of purple smoke appeared.

Noyes snorted. "The bottle's empty."

However, as he spoke, white smoke began to curl out of the bottle. This smoke was so thick it was almost like a liquid, and it coiled down like a snake round Noyes's hand. He poked at it, but then shouted in pain and dropped the bottle, brushing desperately at his hand. "What is this? It's burning!"

But his sleeve was already on fire, his arm in flames. Aloysius shouted, "Just put it out, Noyes!"

While all eyes were on Noyes, Catherine grabbed the bottle of smoke from Gaskett's hip, clawed out the stopper, and threw the bottle at her father's chest. It smashed against the dark breastplate, and white smoke curled and billowed round the king's body. Aloysius stepped back, cursing. "Get it off me!"

But no one ran forward to help. Around Catherine, the boys were shouting, cursing, and running; all their bottles of smoke were heating up and bursting with loud cracks. Gaskett opened his mouth, but only flames and white smoke came out. Ambrose snatched the dagger from his waist and stabbed him, drawing his sword and moving to Noyes, who was still trying to remove his burning jacket.

"You want help, Noyes?" Ambrose cried. "Here you are. You're lucky to die so swiftly." And he swung his sword and sliced across Noyes's neck, severing his head. Noyes's burning body fell. His head rolled to Ambrose's feet.

The white-haired prisoners had seen their opportunity and were grappling with their captors. Some, already free, were racing to Catherine's side, snatching up weapons from the boys who were now all in flames. The boys were no longer able to fight, but the white-hairs were hugely outnumbered by the Brigantine army.

There was only one way to win and Ambrose knew it too. He picked up a fallen spear and turned to Aloysius, who was still flailing at the flames that licked at his chest.

"For my sister, my brother, and all those you have killed and ruined!" Ambrose shouted, thrusting at the king. But, even burning, Aloysius fought back, using his sword to deflect the attack. Ambrose struck the spear hard and fast at the king's chest again. The point hit the breastplate and this time Ambrose drove it upward, with all his force, into the king's neck.

Aloysius staggered back, staring up at the sky, blood coursing from his throat. Then he collapsed, stiff and flaming, to the ground.

Catherine stared. Her father, the king, who had seemed eternal and immovable, was lying at her feet. Part of her wanted to grab a sword and stab and cut his body, but Ambrose caught her wrist and gently pulled her back.

"Stay away from the smoke. Don't let it touch you."

"He's really dead?"

"He's dead, Catherine."

She looked up to see that the Brigantine army was in chaos. Boys were running among the soldiers in panic, sending flames from their mouths and bodies. Some soldiers were attacking the boys, others were themselves on fire. And hanging above them all was a low white cloud that seemed to be sending down long thin wisps of smoke that set fire to anything, or anyone, it touched.

Ambrose drew Catherine farther back and the white-hairs retreated from the Brigantines and the white cloud. Catherine stood at the head of her soldiers and watched the Brigantine army burn. The white cloud of smoke rose from the smoldering bodies, high into the sky, and drifted to the north. And there, above the Northern Plateau, was a larger cloud of white smoke. The two clouds seemed to join and then moved higher and farther north and out of sight.

Standing with Catherine, Ambrose said, "The demon world has closed. The smoke has gone. No more demon smoke and no more boy army. And no more Aloysius. I think it's over."

Catherine agreed. "The war's over. My father's days are over. But for us, it's just the beginning."

# Epilogue

# MARCH AND EDYON
## CALIA, CALIDOR

THE EVENING sun was warm on March's face as he walked along the terrace of Edyon's private rooms in Calia Castle. The sky was turning red in the west and the sea was the darkest of blues. A few sails were still to be seen, but most boats had come into the safety of the harbor. The warmth of the autumn day was still with them, and wind chimes sounded in the gentle sea breeze.

It was a month since the boy army had attacked the city, and, on the surface, most areas outside the castle appeared to have returned to normalcy—the city of Calia was bustling and clean, trade had resumed, and the market and quaysides were busy. But inside the castle, things had changed. The building itself was burned and broken in places, but the hole in government was even more obvious. Prince Thelonius had been killed, as had the chancellor and many lords. Regan, too, had of course been killed, though Edyon told March that his death had occurred not on the field of battle, but because of his own treachery. It gave March some comfort to know that even though his plan to kidnap Edyon with

Holywell had been wrong, it had actually, in the long run, saved Edyon's life.

And Edyon himself had changed and blossomed. He was a leader to whom the Calidorians looked, a surprisingly stable pillar of the system—one of the few pillars left. But the other parts of the system were being replaced: most of the lords who had been killed had sons who would fill their shoes, and a new chancellor had been appointed. Rashford and Kellen had also been given jobs.

The main problem for March was knowing where he fitted in this society. What was he? A servant? A friend? An adviser? He was definitely a lover. He was also a man. And, more than anything, March was aware that Edyon too was a man. And Edyon's role as prince was to rule but also to provide heirs.

"You look serious," Edyon said, putting a hand on his shoulder.

"Just a little tired."

"Tired, but happy?"

March nodded. *Mostly*.

Edyon frowned. "I thought we'd been through this, March. We had a discussion just yesterday, and at least two nights a week for the last few weeks, about how you need to talk to me and tell me what's on your mind."

March nodded again. That was true. He continually promised to do that, but old habits were hard to shake off.

"Well?" Edyon insisted.

"I was thinking how good this all is."

"And yet you manage to say that as if you're bored with it already."

March frowned. "I'm not bored. Never bored with you."

"There's a 'but' coming soon, isn't there? I can hear it on its way, looming ever nearer. So what is it?"

"*But* I still have concerns about the future. For you. And for me."

"You mean for us?"

March nodded. "I mean . . . they'll expect you to marry and have children. And I don't want to stand in your way if that's what you want and—"

"Stop it. Will you please stop it? I've told you that's not what I want."

"No. But it's expected."

"I don't care what's expected. No one expected me to be ruler of this country. But I'll do it as best I can for the time being. And I want you by my side all the time." He leaned forward to March and said softly, "Only you. And no one else. I can't do this job without you. And, what's more, I don't want to. I was wrong to allow you to be banished."

"The alternative was death, so all in all . . ."

"I should have fought harder for you."

"And then I'd have been on your side in the castle. I'd have been killed there or on the ship."

"I was still wrong not to listen to you."

"I was wrong not to tell you my secret earlier."

"So it appears that neither of us is perfect. But together we're . . . well, a lot better people. I'm not sure what the future holds, but I'm going to discuss it with my cousin, Queen Catherine."

"Discuss *us?*" March was horrified. *What would Edyon say?*

"Discuss my role. *Our* roles. Discuss who rules after I'm gone, should I not have an heir, should I not marry. Calidor always used to be part of Brigant."

March was even more horrified. "The Calidorians would hate to go back to that. Don't even think it. Remember what your father told you about how they value their autonomy? The lords' desperate fear is that to partner with any other country would lead to their loss of independence. They fought and died to keep the Brigantines out."

"To keep Aloysius out."

"And, much as Catherine is different from him, she is his daughter."

"I'm his nephew. Much as it repulses me to think of that."

March sniggered. "I'm sure Aloysius wouldn't have enjoyed the thought either."

Edyon smiled and nodded. "Anyway, as I was saying, I have an idea for a way forward that I want to discuss with Catherine and Tzsayn. They are the rulers of Pitoria and Brigant, and wish to move to a system more like that of Illast, which has a government of elected officials. Tzsayn has written to me about it. He's very supportive of new ideas. It seems to work in Illast in a manner no worse than ours. But the point is that change is possible. Change can work for us."

Edyon reached over the table, picked up the jug of elderflower water, and poured March a glass. "See, I am your prince and your servant too. Your partner and your lover. Your friend, who was once your enemy."

"And I'm changed too. Thanks to you. In . . ." And March wanted to say it but still struggled. "In my heart."

"Your heart?"

"Yes, I have one. And it's changed. It's yours." March blushed and looked at Edyon, then away.

Edyon leaned forward and kissed his cheek. "That's very good, March. Much more open and sharing. I like this new you immensely. And, as your heart is mine, there is something of yours that I'm definitely going to give up."

"Something of mine?"

"My title as Prince of Abask." Edyon eyed March. "It shouldn't be mine. I'd like you to have it. If you'd accept it. If you thought it appropriate."

March's eyes filled with tears. "I'm not sure."

"Think about it. I haven't rewarded you yet for all you have done for me. The least I can do is give you your country back, as you have helped give me and all the people of Calidor theirs."

# CATHERINE
## BRIGANE, BRIGANT

Don't bring kindness, don't bring anger—
bring justice.

*Illast saying*

HOW VERY easy it all seemed after the fact, mused Catherine.

After Aloysius's death, the Brigantine army had crumbled, the surviving lords scrambling to surrender to her and Tzsayn. Victory had been declared, and with victory came the spoils—a whole new nation.

With Aloysius and both his sons dead, Catherine rode through Brigant to claim the empty throne within weeks of her triumph at Rossarb, spreading goodwill as she went. Even so, it was clear that most of the population didn't trust her.

"I wouldn't take it personally," said Tanya. "They don't trust anyone. Not after Aloysius."

Catherine rode at the head of the procession with Tzsayn. He was, as ever, dressed entirely in blue, she in white. His leg had healed well, and, with the aid of a specially designed saddle, he was able to ride short distances, much to his delight. The procession moved slowly through the country day by day. Musicians and dancers as well as soldiers followed. The crowds who came to see them pass were a mixture of glum and cheerful faces, but all looked hungry.

"If we give them food and peace, they should be happy enough," Tzsayn said.

"I thought you were aiming for more than that, with your new ideas of government?"

Tzsayn chuckled. "I get the feeling Brigantines don't embrace change eagerly, but perhaps in time that too will happen."

"At the moment, I think the idea of a woman ruling them is more than most can cope with. They expect me to have children, keep house, and keep quiet, not run the country."

"They'll soon learn how a woman can do it better than a man," Tzsayn said, smiling.

When they arrived in Brigane, the crowds were not exactly welcoming. There was some jeering and many angry faces— this was Aloysius's capital, after all. The guard around the royal couple was increased, and Tzsayn said, "We must still smile and wave. They think of us now as the evil conquerors; in time they will think of us—of you—as their leader."

Catherine wasn't so sure; she dreaded to think that some people had the same attitudes toward women as Aloysius and Boris had held.

But the weight of these thoughts lifted when she caught sight of her mother, Queen Isabella. She raced to her and embraced her stiff frame.

"I thought I'd never see you again." Catherine looked up at her mother's face, which was still reserved, still cautious. There had been too many years of hiding her feelings, so she wasn't going to change overnight. Catherine guided her mother to a private alcove and kissed her cheek. "I've missed you more than you can know. I've so much to tell you. But I'm happy. And married."

Catherine's mother smiled. "And chatty and bold."

"And victorious and back. But still your daughter, and . . . have I said happy? So happy to see my mother?"

Queen Isabella nodded. "You have used the word 'happy' more than I've ever heard it said before."

"Are those tears in your eyes?" Catherine asked.

"Indeed. Happy tears."

"Then you'll hear the word 'happy' again and again."

Over the next few days, mother and daughter spent much time together walking in the rose garden and sitting in the library, but also going farther, Catherine encouraging her mother to step out of the confines of her small world.

Isabella said, "You're not my little girl anymore. You're my guide, but I don't want you to think you need to stay with me. I'm not weak—"

"I know that!" Catherine interrupted. "You're one of the strongest people I know."

"And I'll find my place in the world. A new place, perhaps, for a new world. What will you do next?"

"We'll be crowned here in Brigane in a month. Dignitaries from far and wide will be invited. We want to use it as an opportunity to bring more trade to Brigant, to open the country to the world after my father cut us off from it for so long." Catherine looked at her mother. "Much like he cut you off. Locking you up in the castle."

"Enough about me. I asked about your plans."

"After the coronation, we'll return to Tornia. Perhaps you'll come there to visit. It's only three days by boat. It's not a world away. And now that I'm an expert on shipping matters, I believe the Pitorian fleet will be constantly traveling back and forth across the sea."

"But your heart lies with Pitoria now?"

"It lies with Tzsayn and you, and Brigant and Pitoria. Not just one person or one place. They are all important to me, and I love them all in different ways."

"And your role as queen."

Catherine nodded. "I love that too. I have you to thank for that. You showed me how to use my mind and my spirit, how to fight with what's in here." She tapped the side of her head. "That book you gave me written by Queen Valeria was an inspiration too."

"Perhaps you'll write your own book one day."

Catherine laughed. "Perhaps."

That night in their bedchamber, Tzsayn asked, "How are you feeling about being back here?"

"Good. Though I feel I should be doing more."

He kissed her neck. "No. You need rest. And we agreed that once that door was shut, we would not talk of work."

"True." Catherine backed away and looked him up and down. "Shall we then talk about your jacket or your shirt?"

Tzsayn quirked an eyebrow. "Why would we discuss either?"

"Well, it occurred to me that they might be the cause of the jeers and boos we heard on our way here."

"Really? How easy it is to offend the Brigantine man. With a shirt!"

"Hmm, perhaps it wasn't so much the shirt as the blue body paint underneath. And, by underneath, I mean exposed by the slashes in the fabric."

Tzsayn lifted his shirt over his head and threw it on the bed.

"This body paint, you mean?"

# AMBROSE

## BRIGANE, BRIGANT

AMBROSE STOOD opposite Catherine. Tanya had finally left her hair alone and retreated to a distance. The coronation ceremony was about to begin, but Tzsayn hadn't yet appeared, so Ambrose still had a few moments.

Catherine smoothed her skirt—a habit he'd long recognized she had when she was nervous.

"May I offer advice?" he said.

"Of course. I always look to my nobles for their wise counsel."

Ambrose grinned, leaned close, and whispered, "Don't do anything wild today. But sometimes, perhaps once a year, get on your horse and ride along the beach and leap into the water."

She smiled at him. "I wish I could do that now."

Ambrose shook his head. "I don't think you do, really. You'd much rather be here, waiting to be crowned."

"Well, I'm glad you're here with me," she said, and she took his hand. "I wouldn't have made it without you."

"I am your personal guard, Your Majesty."

Catherine shook her head. "No, you're so much more than that, Ambrose. You're one of my threads—a vital one. One that held me when I could have fallen, not just in Pitoria, but before that, here in Brigant, when you gave me hope that people—men—could be good and kind. I can't tell you how grateful I am to still have your friendship and your support. I know it's hard for you."

"It's not hard to see you happy," Ambrose replied, though he was lying just a little. It was more painful than he could say to see her with Tzsayn. "You're where you belong."

"In an ugly, damp castle?"

Ambrose smiled and shook his head. "In the place you deserve. Queen. Ruler. And, I think, a fair and just ruler of Brigant and Pitoria."

"And you are also in the position where you belong, Marquess of Norwend, Duke of Northern Brigant."

Ambrose bowed. He'd discovered after the battle that his father had been executed by Aloysius, and the Norwend lands stolen from him. But they had now been returned to him by Catherine and Tzsayn, along with further lands in the north of Brigant.

"I need to get back up there soon. There's much to do. There's barely enough crops to last the winter," he said.

"I can't quite see you as a farmer."

"I would never have thought it either, but it feels good to have a home again." He looked down, then back into her eyes. "It has so many happy memories as well as the painful ones. But it is a special place."

"And will I get an invitation to visit at some stage?"

"You'll be most welcome anytime."

For a moment, Ambrose wondered what Tzsayn would think of that, but then realized he'd probably be unbearably supportive of it. He raised Catherine's hand and kissed it. "It's been an honor."

The following day, it was Ambrose's turn to be nervous. Catherine and Tzsayn were giving rewards to those who had supported them. His position as Marquess of Norwend was to be confirmed, as was his position as Duke of Northern Brigant. The ceremony also honored those who could not receive the king's and queen's thanks because they'd given their lives, including Sir Rowland Hooper, the ambassador to Pitoria; Rafyon; and Catherine's maids Jane and Sarah.

As the names were read out slowly and solemnly, Ambrose remembered each of them: Sir Rowland's sense of humor, his charm and wit, lost to the world. Rafyon, loyal and brave and stalwart, killed by a lunatic. Kind and gentle Jane, shot by arrows in the race to Rossarb. Sensible and practical Sarah, cut down by an assassin. Each death a waste. Each a person who should be with them. And then Tarquin's name was read, as was Anne's. And as tears filled his eyes, Ambrose chose to think of how brave they were in life, and how they were killed because they were true and honest and wouldn't bend to another's lies. He missed his brother and sister desperately and wished they'd known that the future wasn't as bleak as the world they'd experienced. That was another pain, the thought that they'd not know that things could be better.

Eventually the formalities were over, and music and talk and relaxed chatter filled the hall. Edyon joined Ambrose and raised his glass. "Congratulations, Lord Ambrose, Duke of Northern Brigant."

"Thank you, Prince Edyon. You still outrank me, though."

"Everyone does these days," March said, flicking the gold medal on his sash. He'd been made Prince of Abask at the ceremony.

"Well, I won't for much longer," Edyon said.

"You're really going to give up your position?" Ambrose asked. Catherine had told him some of this plan.

"Yes, in time. I like Tzsayn's ideas for a government of administrators. I'll have to keep an honorary title, though, just for fun. Something absurd."

"Duke of the Demon World?" Tash suggested as she joined them from the buffet table. She herself had been given an award and was now Lady Tash of the Northern Plateau.

"Not sure. Doesn't sound quite me."

Tash nodded. "How about the Knight of the Burning Smoke?"

"Oh, I like that." He smiled at March. "What do you think?"

"I have a bad feeling you're serious."

Tzsayn and Catherine joined them, and Catherine proposed a toast.

"To Lady Anne. The woman who started me on this journey. I wouldn't be here if it wasn't for her bravery." Ambrose raised his glass and drank the toast to his sister. Perhaps he too would not be the man he was without her.

"Well, I wouldn't be here if you hadn't stolen our smoke," Tash said, giving Edyon a gentle kick on the shin.

"And that's why I'm the Knight of the Burning Smoke," Edyon said.

"Yes and no," said March. "We're all here because of our own actions. Good and bad. Others influenced us, but we made our own choices."

Ambrose nodded, though he wasn't sure he agreed. He had chosen Catherine, but she had chosen Tzsayn. He stayed for the festivities that evening, then rode north in the morning as the sun was coming up.

It was a glorious day, and he'd be home soon.

# TASH

## NORTHERN PLATEAU, PITORIA

AT THE invitation of Edyon and March, Tash traveled to Calidor after a short stay in Brigant, but returned north before winter set in. She was Lady Tash of the Northern Plateau, after all, and she wanted to go back to her lands. She wasn't alone, though. Geratan went with her.

Now he sat gazing across the stillness of the lake.

"Anything?" Tash asked, looking at the fishing rod, which was propped by Geratan's feet.

"Not since the last time you asked."

"It's a bit boring this, isn't it? Can't we go hunting?"

"We agreed to fish. It's quiet. Relaxing. A pleasant change from fighting Brigantines and fleeing from demons."

"Actually, we didn't have to flee from demons much; it was mainly fleeing from Brigantines."

Tash briefly thought of Gravell, who hadn't been able to flee them.

"Do you think of him much?"

She knew Geratan didn't mean Gravell.

"Twist?" She looked across the Northern Plateau. The

demon world had gone. There were no demon hollows at all left on the plateau. "Yes, I do think of him. I'm sure the smoke will return—maybe not here, but somewhere. It'll seek out an undisturbed spot and make a new world."

"But that's just the smoke. The smoke needs a body to make a demon."

"I prefer to call them smoke people."

"Well, it needs a body to make one."

"Yes, and it may take a year, or hundreds of years, or even thousands, but eventually, somebody will fall into the smoke and the world will begin again." She looked at the lake. "Probably happen sooner than you catch a fish."

At that moment, the float bobbed down and Geratan struck. Tash yelped with excitement and ran to get the net.

That night they cooked fish over the fire and slept beneath the stars. They'd have a few weeks living up here before winter hit, then move south. Tash wanted to travel to Illast and Savaant, perhaps even farther. The smoke had moved to find a new home, and perhaps she would too. But the Northern Plateau would always be here, and she could come back whenever she needed.

# PLACES AND CHARACTERS

❧

## BRIGANT

*A war-hawkish country.*

BRIGANE: the capital

FIELDING: a small village on the northwest coast, where Ambrose found the boy army training

NORWEND: a region in the north of Brigant

*Aloysius:* king of Brigant.

*Isabella:* queen of Brigant.

*Boris:* Aloysius's first-born son. Killed by his sister, Princess Catherine.

*Harold:* Aloysius's second-born son and, with Boris's death, heir to the crown of Brigant. Fourteen years old.

*The Marquess of Norwend:* a nobleman, father to Sir Ambrose Norwend.

*Tarquin:* the Marquess of Norwend's first-born son, tortured and killed as a traitor.

*Lady Anne:* the Marquess of Norwend's daughter; executed as a traitor

*Noyes:* spymaster for Aloysius.

*Holywell:* now deceased, worked for Aloysius as a fixer, spy, killer; Abask by birth.

*Thornlees:* a lord and leader of one section of the Brigantine army.

*Pullman:* a commander reporting to Lord Thornlees.

*March:* an Abask. Once servant to Thelonius, and lover to Edyon. Exiled to Brigant.

*Sam:* homeless Brigantine boy who joins the boy army.

*Rashford:* leader of the Bull Brigade of the boy army.

*Killen:* second in command of the Bull Brigade.

*Frank, Fitz:* Bulls.

*Broderick:* a Hawk.

*Gaskett:* leader of the Stags.

*Tiff:* leader of the Wasps.

*Curtis:* leader of the Hawks.

# CALIDOR

*A small country to the south of Brigant.*

CALIA: the capital.

ABASK: a small mountainous region, laid waste during the war between Calidor and Brigant, where the people were known for their ice-blue eyes.

*Thelonius:* Prince of Calidor, younger brother of King Aloysius of Brigant.

*Castor, Argentus:* deceased, legitimate sons of Thelonius.

*Edyon:* illegitimate son of Thelonius, seventeen years old.

*Regan:* a powerful lord of Calidor and close friend to Thelonius.

*Byron:* a young nobleman, friend to Edyon.

*Ellis:* a young nobleman of Calidor.

*Talin:* personal servant to Edyon.

*Bruntwood:* a senior lord and chancellor of Calidor.

*Hunt, Birtwistle, Grantham, Haydeen, Brook:* lords of Calidor.

# PITORIA

*A large, wealthy country known for its dancing, where men dye their hair to show their allegiances. The wissun is a white flower that grows wild throughout Pitoria.*

TORNIA: the capital.

THE NORTHERN PLATEAU: a cold, forbidden region.

ROSSARB: a northern port with a small castle.

*Tzsayn:* following his father's death he is now king of Pitoria. Betrothed to Catherine. Twenty-three years old.

*Catherine:* Aloysius's daughter, Queen of Pitoria, and believed by most to be married to Tzsayn. Seventeen years old.

*Sir Ambrose:* son of a Brigantine lord, personal guard to Catherine.

*Arell:* Tzsayn's father, now dead.

*Tanya:* Catherine's maid, promoted to the role of dresser.

*General Davyon:* dresser and most trusted aide to Tzsayn.

*Geratan*: a white-hair loyal to Catherine.

*Rafyon:* a white-hair, killed protecting Catherine.

*Savage:* personal doctor to Tzsayn.

*Ffyn:* general, head of the Pitorian army

*Hanov:* senior general, head of spies in Pitorian forces.

*Farrow:* a powerful lord, who betrayed Catherine to her father.

*Anlax, Harrison:* soldiers, members of the Demon Troop.

*Lord Darby:* Calidorian lord heading the delegation to Pitoria.

*Albert Aves:* assistant to Lord Darby.

# THE DEMON WORLD

*An area below the Northern Plateau of stone and tunnels, where the air is hot and red and communication is by thought.*

*Tash:* a demon hunter. Thirteen or fourteen years old.

*Gravell:* Tash's demon hunter friend, killed in the battle of Rossarb.

*Twist:* a demon, whom Tash and Geratan saved.

*Frost:* an Abask slave girl familiar with the demon world, working for the Brigantines.

*Fallon*: Brigantine army commander, working with Frost.

# ILLAST

*A neighboring country to Pitoria, where women have more equality, being able to own property and businesses.*

*Valeria:* Queen of Illast.

# ACKNOWLEDGMENTS

I was listening to an ultra-running podcast the other day and one of the subjects being discussed was adventure racing. This is where a team has to navigate an unmarked course across challenging terrain, requiring the use of different sporting disciplines such as running, cycling, climbing, and swimming, and possibly much more obscure skills like roller-blading, rafting, rappelling, and riding (horses or camels!). The races can last hours, days, or even weeks. It sounds difficult, fun, and slightly bonkers. Which brings me to writing books. Writing a book is a marathon, not a sprint, and writing a trilogy is, perhaps, closer to an adventure race requiring a multidisciplinary team navigating across an unchartered wilderness. I'm not a planner of my writing, and my other team members, particularly my editors, Ben Horslen and Leila Sales, need to have huge trust in my ability to find my way to the finish line. Actually, my writing is less like a wilderness and more like a jungle of ideas, and I cannot thank them enough for their advice and support in helping me to find a way through the tangle—they are expert navigators, showing true professionalism, advising where I need to cut through and where I can afford a little detour. And most importantly they are always calm, supportive, and considered, even on the rare occasions I don't go the way they advise and hack off in my own direction.

My heartfelt thanks to all the other members of the team throughout this adventure, in particular to my agent, Claire Wilson of RCW Literary Agents (she'd also be a great asset if the course required skating, and I suspect she has other secret skills and wouldn't be surprised if she was a dab hand at camel riding). My thanks also to my wonderful copyeditor Wendy Shakespeare and her team of proofreaders, Ben Hughes and his team in design, Roy McMillan in audio production, and all the Penguin Random House staff in sales, rights, marketing, and PR. I would also like to express my gratitude to all the fantastic publishers of the Smoke Thieves trilogy around the world, to their enthusiastic staff and to the incredibly talented translators who work with them.

I'm also grateful to my family, friends, and fans, who have supported me in so many ways along my writing journey, keeping me going during the dark nights and helping me celebrate when things were going well.

As I write this in March 2020, I am working from home, like many members of the team, because of restrictions due to COVID-19. I hope that we can celebrate the publication of *The Burning Kingdoms* together at some future date, and I wish them and my supporters, readers, booksellers, fans, and friends all around the world the best in these uncertain times.

Thanks and love to you all.